Maya Blake's hopes of becoming a writer were born when she picked up her first romance at thirteen. Little did she know her dream would come true! Does she still pinch herself every now and then to make sure it's not a dream? Yes, she does! Feel free to pinch her, too, via X, Facebook or Goodreads! Happy reading!

Millie Adams is the very dramatic pseudonym of *New York Times* bestselling author Maisey Yates. Happiest surrounded by yarn, her family and the small woodland creatures she calls pets, she lives in a small house on the edge of the woods, which allows her to escape in the way she loves best—in the pages of a book. She loves intense alpha heroes and the women who dare to go toe-to-toe with them.

Also by Maya Blake

Snowbound with the Irresistible Sicilian

Diamonds of the Rich and Famous collection

Accidentally Wearing the Argentinian's Ring

A Diamond in the Rough collection

Greek Pregnancy Clause

Also by Millie Adams

The Forbidden Bride He Stole
Her Impossible Boss's Baby
Italian's Christmas Acquisition

The Diamond Club collection

Greek's Forbidden Temptation

FOR PASSION OR PAYBACK?

MAYA BLAKE

MILLIE ADAMS

MILLS & BOON

First published in Great Britain 2025
by Mills & Boon, an imprint of HarperCollins*Publishers* Ltd,
1 London Bridge Street, London, SE1 9GF

www.harpercollins.co.uk

HarperCollins*Publishers*, Macken House, 39/40 Mayor Street Upper,
Dublin 1, D01 C9W8, Ireland

ISBN: 978-0-263-34448-6

01/25

This book contains FSC™ certified paper
and other controlled sources to ensure responsible forest management.

For more information visit www.harpercollins.co.uk/green.

Printed and Bound in the UK using 100% Renewable Electricity
at CPI Group (UK) Ltd, Croydon, CR0 4YY

ENEMY'S GAME OF REVENGE

MAYA BLAKE

MILLS & BOON

CHAPTER ONE

WILLOW CHATTERTON REACHED for her coffee cup, projecting calm she didn't feel and composure that was fast dwindling. Any second now she expected the staid woman sitting opposite her to look up from her tablet, spear her with suspicious eyes and call her out for the less than straightforward means she'd used to land herself this interview.

This exercise had been a Hail Mary at best, one last-ditch effort to get the answers she needed before, if necessary, she took the final undesired but decisive step of cutting her losses with her father.

The squeeze in her chest returned stronger, but she pushed it aside.

Maybe it didn't have to come to that. Maybe there was something worth salvaging. But with the strain between them now at a breaking point with deepening indifference, and he having lost all interest in providing the vital information needed to save his own company and the many people who depended on them, she'd had no choice but to take this route.

Deep down, though, she hadn't imagined she'd need to push things this far. That her ultimatums to dig out the truth for herself would pierce through his inertia.

It hadn't. So here she was.

Asking her hacker buddy to get her on a shortlist of a job agency catering to billionaires had been tricky at best. Actually landing an interview had been an unbelievable probability until she got the call that had made her drive through the night across the border from California into Mexico.

She couldn't blow this.

Not when it directly affected the other important decision she needed to make about her future. Whether it was worth setting aside her seemingly unattainable desire for family and connection with the secret dream she'd kept close. The dream that had seen her through the previous fractured relationships—

No, she wasn't going to dwell on her mother. Or her ex, David. Her emotional bandwidth could only accommodate what remained of her relationship with her father. And if that ran out…

She held her breath as Rebecca Devlin, chief purser on the biggest yacht in the Los Cabos marina, looked up.

'It all looks great, and it helps that you know your way around boats.' The smallest smile cracked her no-nonsense demeanour, entirely unaware of the shocked relief pouring through Willow. 'Not that this particular one is your run-of-the-mill vessel.'

Compelled, Willow's gaze swung to the super-yacht, her ultimate destination.

La Venganza.

Its name was as spine tingling and ominous as the vessel was eerily beautiful.

Easily the most eye-catching with its unique matte grey-and-black hull, it was so large it had been given a special berth within the Marina Puerto Los Cabos.

A born-and-raised Southern Californian, she was used to ostentation on a decadent, eye-watering level that beggared belief sometimes. But the *La Venganza* was on a whole new stratosphere.

There were seven decks—that she could count. A sleek, top-of-the-line helicopter in the same matte grey-and-black theme sat on one of the higher decks. Since her arrival, she'd seen batches of the crew dressed in sharp, pristinely tailored uniforms, transporting deliveries from vendors that made her eyes goggle—Ossetra caviar, Norwegian salmon, boxes upon boxes of vintage champagne, lobster by the crate load. Hell, she'd overheard that there were ten barrels of water transported from a special mountain lake in the Himalayas.

That was before the steady stream of beautiful people—mostly women—arriving in sports cars, limos and luxury SUVs, tittering with barely suppressed excitement, were escorted by sleek tenders to the yacht.

The volume of activity and number of deliveries pointed to an extended trip. She couldn't let the yacht sail away without achieving her goal.

Which was to confront Jario Tagarro, famed recluse and owner of *La Venganza*.

The rumour that the thirty-two-year-old billionaire hadn't set foot on land in *years* had held up under her research, but Willow accepted that, even with the abundance of information on the internet, there was so much more she didn't know about the half-American, half-Colombian financial genius.

Chiefly, she remained in the dark as to why her father visibly quailed at the mention of Tagarro's name but kept an alarming amount of newspaper clippings and magazine articles of the younger man with the face of a fallen angel and the piercing blue eyes of a ruthless predator.

Her suspicions that her father was lying at worst, or severely underplaying Jario's role, had deepened when he'd insisted the billionaire had nothing to do with the troubles of Chatterton Financial after she'd brought his name up, then watched him dive straight into his favourite bourbon bottle for the better part of a week.

Knowing it wasn't the first or the last time her father would lie through his teeth hadn't been a palatable pill to swallow then or any of the times before.

It'd taken weeks of contemplation and heartache before

accepting that *she* was at a crossroads with only one final choice to make—to seek out the billionaire and find out the truth for herself.

Plus, her emotional baggage with her father aside, there were several families who depended on Chatterton Financial who didn't deserve her father's apathy and obfuscation.

She felt another stab of guilt for connecting the dots far too late. As her father's assistant, she should've acted sooner. It'd taken repeatedly seeing Tagarro's name among her father's things in the past few months to remember that the sea change in her parent had arrived after his return from Colombia over a decade and a half ago.

The Paul Chatterton who'd left for that trip had merely been prone to exaggerating his status among his country club peers, and ambitious to a fault. The one who'd returned had become near-obsessed with promoting a lofty image that didn't exist, drafting his wife and bewildered pre-teenage daughter into his schemes, commencing a fracturing that had only widened over the years, leading to a shattering of their family.

Rebelling against the forced subterfuge had driven a wedge between her and her parents. But it was their actual fall from wealth and prestige, and her mother's walking out and marrying a far wealthier man within months of Willow's sixteenth birthday and cutting both her and her father off, that had caused the seismic shock waves that changed the landscape of her family.

Willow pushed away those disturbing thoughts now and concentrated on her present goal. Despite the improvisations in her hastily cobbled-together résumé, her work ethic would remain unquestionable no matter her true reason for boarding the super-yacht.

All she needed was one audience with the billionaire.

And as she'd discovered via her research, there was always someone eager to fill her shoes once she got the answers she needed and left—

'So you'll be assisting Ripley, Mr Tagarro's personal valet until a permanent replacement is found,' Rebecca said, and Willow's heart jumped into her throat.

She hadn't deluded herself that it would be easy, but bluffing her way onto the billionaire's vessel was one thing. Being thrown into such close proximity was quite another. She nodded nevertheless, knowing to do anything else would raise suspicions she couldn't afford.

And surely once she got over the nerves eating her alive, she'd see the positive side to this. Like that proximity aiding her in getting her answers quicker so she could deal with this emotional purgatory.

Straightening her posture, she offered a cool smile. 'So I've got the job?'

Rebecca nodded, then glanced at the small travel case at Willow's feet. 'If you can start right away, barring final checks and your agreement to a little…sprucing up, yes.'

About to perform an internal fist pump, Willow paused. 'Sprucing up?'

Rebecca eyed the simple vest top and jeans Willow wore. 'Mr Tagarro expects a high level of professional decorum from his employees.'

Her five-mile daily running routine kept her in decent shape. But she hadn't worn make-up besides lip gloss or been to a hairdresser for the better part of a year while juggling her assistant job to a failing company and the gruelling violin practice that had become the one shining, soul-sustaining balm in a desolate landscape.

It was almost surreal that it'd landed her on a shortlist for a job on her dream symphony.

'We have a professional stylist on board. I hope you won't be offended if I ask you to swing by for an hour or two to get you properly outfitted?'

Willow shook her head, relieved that the purser didn't expect her to stump up precious cash to make herself over before hiring her. 'Not at all.'

'In that case, welcome aboard. There'll be the usual probationary period, et cetera.' She handed a document over, then rose. 'Read the contract and report to the vessel at two p.m. and I'll have someone show you the ropes.'

Willow was still in the café, after reading and signing the very detailed contract, when another group of the yacht's crew trailed in.

'I can't wait to get going tomorrow,' a young, too-tanned crew member, who looked barely out of his teens, gushed. 'I love Cabo, but I've been here, done this, you know? Bali, on the other hand, is going to be epic!'

Trepidation whistled through Willow as the information sank in.

Jario Tagarro was leaving for Indonesia tomorrow. While it'd hopefully be enough time to find out what she needed, did she really want to be stuck on his super-yacht on the open ocean? What if…?

No. There was no room for doubt. Not when her father's cold indifference to her trip had only convinced her she was on the right track.

Waste your time if you wish. Don't come crying to me when you find nothing there.

Those words had reverberated all the way from Orange County to Mexico, but so, too, had the naked dread overlaying his tone.

That dread had knotted fear in her gut. Hinted that she was potentially on her way to discovering something that would irretrievably shatter her relationship with her father.

Still. She needed to know.

So at five to two, she presented herself at the gangway leading to the super-yacht and the man who held possibly unpalatable answers.

The two guards on duty eyed her, the shorter one raising an eyebrow. 'You're the new hire?'

Her fingers tightened on her case, glancing over his shoulder at the large vessel that looked even more awe-inspiring and completely intimidating, its bold, commanding and utterly magnificent presence dwarfing everything in sight.

With every bone in her body she wanted to say *no, my mistake*. Turn and walk away. But she held fast.

And nodded.

Ten minutes later she was ensconced in a leather chair in a posh little salon, an immaculately dressed woman who introduced herself as Greta, the head stylist, reeling off a list of the staff's dress code requirements. Willow had barely nodded her agreement to have her hair washed and trimmed before a hairdresser was snipping away.

A little stunned at the brusque efficiency but secretly thankful she would at least look the part, she was released ninety minutes later, armed with a small silver case of make-up and a hanger holding two new uniforms complete with name tag and sensible heels.

'Ah, here's Ripley now. See you around, Willow.'

Greta walked away and Willow turned to see a tall, thin man in a three-piece suit. His expression wasn't unkind but Willow was thankful for the mini-makeover at his piercing, assessing gaze. Scrutiny over, he nodded, satisfied. She stifled the urge to roll her eyes as he stepped forward.

'Welcome to *La Venganza*. Come with me. I'll show you to your quarters. Get you settled in.'

The realisation that she wouldn't be meeting Jario Tagarro immediately struck a discordant note within her.

As if reading her mind, he added, 'Mr Tagarro is entertaining his guests on the upper deck. You'll meet him later.'

She nodded, then asked the question that had loomed in her mind since she'd overheard the conversation in the café.

'I understand we're sailing for Bali tomorrow. How long will the journey take?'

'Without unscheduled stops, about a week. Nine days to be flexible.'

A maximum of nine days to find the answers she desperately needed. Of course, there was the stark unknown of how Jario Tagarro would react when she revealed her purpose on board his yacht, but she'd cross that bridge when she came to it.

Alone in the room she was to share with another female crew member, currently on duty on one of the decks, Willow stood stock-still, heart thumping. She was no stranger to the wild turns of fate.

She'd watched her mother pack her bags and leave with head-spinning efficiency ten years ago, leaving a shocked, distraught daughter and a husband deeply mired in a depressed fog.

She vividly recalled her mother's pitying gaze skidding over a trembling Willow, sobbing in the doorway of their home as her mother walked to the limo holding the new, richer man she was leaving her husband for. 'Don't cry, sweetheart. You can come visit me soon. I promise.'

More lies. More promises broken.

Bitterness surged like bile as she recalled the number of times she'd called her mother. The transition from broken promises to frosty rebukes to stop being so needy, and then to total estrangement.

Yes, Willow knew how quickly one's life could turn. Knew the damage lies and indifference could cause.

And as she swallowed the building dread, she could only hope that whatever secrets her father had kept from her didn't completely destroy her.

Some nights Jario Tagarro wondered why he even bothered going to bed at all when the effort was so laughably futile.

He was averaging forty-five minutes at best. Fifteen minutes of tossing and turning, despairing or staring at the ceiling, quietly fuming when the demons were being especially prolific.

Tonight he was thoroughly bored with both. He'd dive face first into a liquor bottle if he didn't despise not having complete clarity at all times. Yes, he drank the odd cognac or glass of vintage champagne when the urge took him, but drinking to drown out the hell that unfolded in his sleep was a thing of the past. These days, he preferred to face his demons head-on.

Rising, he planted his feet on the hardwood floors in his stateroom. He'd forbidden the interior decorator from putting carpet in his rooms, preferring to feel the very subtle motions of his vessel beneath his bare feet.

He curled his toes now as the vibrations travelled up through his ankles, calves and thighs. Quivered through his midsection and into his chest, where it danced with his heartbeat, searching for an elusive rhythm. Attempting to ground him.

It wasn't enough. No matter *what* he tried, it was never enough.

He always remained in arrhythmia. Out of sync. *Abnormal.*

Those weeks in that South American jungle had changed him forever. He'd long accepted that. The only problem was while his brain coped during daylight hours, functioning echelons above most ordinary men, the nights *always* got to him.

The demons always came within a hairsbreadth of winning.

Elbows propped on knees, he absorbed the deeper vibrations as he bunched his fists, squeezing satisfaction and joy out of that minuscule hairsbreadth. As long as he kept winning, he was content, he told himself.

Because he had work to do, a way to go in this journey of exacting the sweetest of retribution. Until he was done, he would hang on.

And then...what?

He snarled under his breath, the taunting whisper firing up his fury.

And then...he would live the life he'd been destined to live before traitors had thrown vicious roadblocks in his way. Revenge wasn't a destination but a pit stop on the road to his greater self, he assured himself. And while the former may consume him for now, the latter would honour his father's memory.

His *sole* reason for all this.

Promise reaffirmed, Jario rose, glad he slept naked because it shortened the time needed to throw on the joggers and leave his suite.

Five minutes later he pushed open the door to the extensive gym and entertainment area that took up most of the lower deck. He bypassed the compact basketball court, virtual golf and bowling alley, and stepped into the enclosed area of his favourite stress reliever. Sucking in a breath, he wrapped his fingers around the hilt of the first axe and lifted it.

Reassuringly heavy, the black steel with the deadly blood-red blade glinted in the low lights.

Jario ran his finger along the side of the blade, a roar filling his ears. Three steps brought him to the centre of the mat, the ten-foot-high slab of wood twenty feet away. First, he tightened his grip on the wooden hilt, then deliberately slackened it.

With a bloodthirsty snarl dragged from his soul, Jario hurled the axe, watched it arc through the air before embedding itself with a satisfying *thunk* into the thick wood. He revelled in the slight burn in his arms and shoulders, the hum still vibrating through him as he approached the slab and yanked the axe free.

All sense of time and space faded as he threw axe after axe, sweat slicking his hair and skin, dripping into his waistband. He ignored the forming blisters, the sweat stinging his eyes, the weariness sapping at his muscles.

All he cared about was that the voices had stopped, the demons conceding this fight. He knew they would return in full force tomorrow night. And the night after.

For tonight, he'd won.

Arms raised for the next throw, a triumphant grin curved his lips, only to freeze at the shocked gasp behind him.

Whipping his head around, he was confronted with a pair of wide eyes, housed in the body of a tall, statuesque woman wearing a sleep shirt and shorts that ended midthigh and left the remaining mile-long legs on display. The shirt was buttoned up primly but still gave a punchy hint at the luscious breasts it covered. Low lights and protective netting made it difficult to ascertain the true colour of her hair, but the long tresses almost touched her waist, sparking a curious need to sink his fingers into them.

She wasn't one of his guests.

He'd dispatched them all back in Cabo yesterday. After a week of endless business meetings couched as entertainment with distant acquaintances and hangers-on, he'd been more than ready for solitude.

Which meant she was crew. Which also meant she knew better than to disturb him.

Infierno, he didn't have a stowaway, did he? Annoyed *and* acutely aware that she was damned stunning—breathtaking, in fact—he faced her fully.

Watched her eyes widen as her gaze dropped to his perspiring chest and torso. Her breaths quickened as she lingered on the V at his waist, then over his joggers before her eyes flicked upward.

The keen stirring of his manhood once their eyes reconnected was a surprising detail. While he thoroughly enjoyed sex and was enthusiastic in his liaisons, Jario hadn't reacted this strongly to a woman in a long time. He suspected it had something to do with the diminished thrill of the chase but he hadn't even bothered to test that theory. Why would he, when every woman he desired happily presented herself on a platter at the merest flicker of interest?

Her eyes lowered, veiling her expression, and he stifled a growl of disappointment. He only growled at his demons and his enemies. Never a beautiful woman. Unless during sexual games.

But he undeniably wanted her complete focus on him, so he could absorb her every reaction. Which was absurd. Impatience bristling his skin, he exhaled.

'Are you—'

'I'm sorry—'

His brows rose as they both stopped speaking.

Lowering his arms, he kept a loose grasp on the axe. 'Go on. I hope that's the start of an apology for disturbing me?'

He caught the smallest spark of irritation before she glanced at the axe. Interesting.

'I'm still getting used to being on a boat.' She shrugged. 'The constant humming, the motion and other noises makes it hard for me to sleep.'

'The yacht is fitted with stupidly expensive stabilising equipment to ensure it doesn't rock noticeably. As for the humming, some find it…reassuring.'

A small nod. 'I probably will, too, once I get used to being on board.' She glanced around, giving him a brief glimpse of her breathtaking profile. 'I was going for a walk… I didn't think anyone would be up at this time.'

His gaze travelled over her once more, a compulsion he couldn't quite curb. 'You're new to the crew?'

Did she just stiffen? After an infinitesimal hesitation, she nodded.

Irritation mixed with peculiar arousal stirred through him. His personal rules forbade him from interacting in any way but professionally with her, but…wasn't forbidden fruit the sweetest? 'Then you would've been told that wandering at night was strictly prohibited. So either you're flouting the rules or someone dropped the ball.'

Apprehension flashed through her eyes but although she'd just confirmed she was his employee, she didn't fall over herself to make excuses like most would.

His intrigued thoughts scattered as she stepped closer, dragging his gaze once more to her spectacular legs. *Dios mio*, they should be taboo they were so sexy.

Jario had learned early that he was a legs man. Watching her draw closer, noting her half-foot shorter but still impressive height, his fingers curled tighter around the axe as he entertained the idea that he was a face man as well.

Truly breathtaking, she possessed the kind of unadorned beauty that revealed itself gradually, like a veiled lover shedding her layers.

For instance, at first glance, her upper lip looked a little too thin, until they parted, showing it was perfectly proportioned to the lower, fuller one.

Cheeks that appeared plump but highlighted exquisite cheekbones when she stepped beneath the light. Limpid brown eyes once she was close enough showed flecks hiding subtle colours. Colours he itched to discover but cautioned himself against.

Because he wanted to stretch out the unveiling…?

As for her jaw and the elegant line of her neck…that pulse throbbing at her throat…they didn't need a second look.

'I didn't mean to disturb you.' Her voice was low, husky, hiding mysteries Jario wanted to discover. He wasn't so far gone that he didn't recognise that this might be his psyche's way of distracting him from his demons. That he was snatching this unexpected interruption to delay returning to his bed.

He was also aware that she hadn't owned up to her transgressions. Something he was inclined to let pass. Just this once.

Because… 'You want to try?' He held out the axe, hilt first, before he'd fully clocked his words.

Alarm gut-punched him.

What was he doing? He didn't fraternise with his crew. They were a bunch of skilled, carefully vetted individuals he paid handsomely to keep his home—and yes, *La Venganza* *was* his home—running smoothly. People who ensured his *vital* need to remain mobile was achieved without question or deviation.

Yet, even as fine tremors moved down his arm and into the fist clutching the deadly tool, he didn't withdraw his invitation.

She started to shake her head, triggering both relief and pique he didn't understand, then at the last moment, it turned into a wary nod. Other opaque sentiments flitted over her face. Sentiments he couldn't immediately decipher because his attention was shifting, confounded by the way she moved... *glided*...towards him like a siren straight from the ocean beneath him.

His gaze dropped to her *bare* feet, and the stirring notched up a thousandfold.

Perhaps he shouldn't have been in a hurry to leave Mexico... should've allowed one of the many women eager to share his bed to remain behind. Because the way his libido was revving...

Her gaze left his long enough to examine the protective netting that separated them. Reaching out, Jario detached the fastening and held it open in silent invitation.

She stepped inside, her nostrils fluttering delicately as she *scented* him. He bit back a growl, the very experience of her inhaling his sweat-coated skin driving astonishingly primal need through his body.

He wanted to attribute these insane sensations to the activity, the time of night or, hell, the movements of the planetary systems. But he knew they made little to no impact on the situation. His visitor possessed her own brand of mystery he was weirdly enraptured by.

Jario watched her examine the collection of axes, then the slab of wood, before glancing at him. 'I've never done this before.'

He wondered if she always sounded this raspy, whether it was from sleep...or the lack of it. Feeling his body heat rising higher, he stifled a curse. He *should* end this interaction now.

Send her packing below deck where she belonged. Return to his suite now he was worn out and try for another forty-five minutes of sleep.

Instead, he stepped closer, extending his axe, satisfaction swelling when she took it. He didn't release it immediately. 'Careful. It's heavy. Hold it away from you so if you drop it, it doesn't injure you.'

Her eyes met his briefly and she nodded. 'What do I do next?'

Jario stepped behind her, attempting to ignore how perfectly her frame complemented his. 'Widen your stance so your feet are just beyond shoulder width. Now wrap both hands one inch from the bottom. Hold it firmly. Good girl,' he murmured, then inhaled sharply as a little shiver went through her.

Gritting his jaw against sensations he shouldn't feel, he stepped to the side. 'First, you visualise where you want it to land and aim towards it. Then raise it above your head, swing hard and release when your arms are just above eye level. Understood?'

Her nod was confident, her eyes glinting with excitement.

Her arms rose above her head, displaying hard nipples pressing against her shirt and a delectable few inches of light golden skin above her sleep shorts that slashed his breathing.

Santo cielo, he was moments away from getting an erection in the presence of an intruder he should've sent away.

The absurdity of the situation wasn't lost on him. And yet…

'Take a breath and throw,' he said, a hoarseness to his voice revealing everything he was feeling.

She threw.

The axe arced through the air, silent and deadly, and imbedded itself at the lower centre of the slab.

She gasped, eyes wide as she swivelled to face him. 'Wow. That was exhilarating!'

'Indeed. Again?' He ignored the warning in his head.

A smile curved her luscious pink lips and Jario's insides twisted with lust. 'May I?'

In answer, he strolled to the board, yanked the axe free. Turning, he caught her gaze trailing his bare skin. The air, already charged with sensations, grew thicker. It would've been no difficult task to toss the tool aside, invite her to participate in a more…*involved* activity to quiet his demons. Thankfully, sense prevailed.

He held out the hilt. 'One more, then you'll have to leave.'

The flare in her eyes said his impending dismissal had surprised her. Good. Much better for her to know he wasn't to be trifled with, even if she was the most stunning woman he'd seen in a long time.

Taking the axe from him, she positioned herself and raised her arms.

'Higher. Right there.'

Her teeth sank into her bottom lip. His fists clenched, stemming the fevered need to touch her. To wrestle that bottom lip free with his own teeth, then bite it. 'Throw.'

It flew out of her hand, landing with a satisfying *thunk* just a little off centre, next to the cluster of his own truer aims.

Slowly, she lowered her arms, her eyes shining with pleasure and accomplishment. Then burgeoning awareness, probably at the heavy reaction he couldn't hide. Those maddening lips parted once more, her breaths shallow with muted pants as her gaze stayed glued to his face.

Right then, Jario could've sworn he'd never been more attracted to a woman. And it was *that* forceful reaction that made him turn his back on her, stride to the board to retrieve his axe, then remain there as he grappled with his self-control.

'Leave. Now,' he said without turning around.

Several seconds passed while she rebelled, inciting further excitement in his blood. It was almost a shame to hear her receding footsteps.

A full minute passed before his fingers wrapped around the axe and he returned to his task.

This time, however, the urgent need to hurl the sharp axe at the unyielding wood was more to drive away the fiery lust blazing through his needy body than the urge to silence his demons.

The moment he was showered and dressed the next morning, Jario activated the yacht's surveillance system via his tablet. He sipped his espresso while commending himself for waiting until the less ungodly hour of 6 a.m. to give in to temptation that hadn't abated one iota since she walked away from him last night.

A few swipes through the frames and he found her in the galley with Ripley.

Her long hair was tied back in a neat ponytail that made his fingers twitch with the need to see it wrapped around his wrist. She was dressed in the crew-assigned all-white uniform, with his yacht's logo displayed discreetly on her attire. But not even the modest buttoned-up shirt or the pleated skirt and apron could disguise her striking, coltish beauty.

Eyes followed her when she moved. Lingered when she smiled or laughed.

And when his assistant snagged her attention, Jario found himself in the startling position of experiencing stomach-churning irritation bordering on...*jealousy*?

Ridiculous.

But Ripley's appearance had reminded him of a failing that needed fixing. Setting the tablet down, he accessed the Bluetooth intercom that connected him to his assistant.

'Yes, sir?'

'Come to my office right away.'

'Of course, sir.'

Jario's fingers drummed impatiently on his desk, counting down the interminable three minutes till the knock on his door.

With one last look at the screen, he shut off the surveillance. 'Come.'

Ripley approached his desk, his easy stride broadcasting his self-assurance in his efficiency at his chosen profession. Usually, Jario appreciated his assistant's demeanour. He'd never had much patience for wallflowers or lazy scroungers, choosing to surround himself with hard workers like Ripley. But this morning he found himself *chafed* by the other man.

Because of the breach last night. Nothing more.

'How may I help you, sir?'

Not even the courteous respect twinned with his eagerness to serve mollified Jario. He'd slept like crap. Fighting demons *and* sexual frustration wreaked havoc on a man's disposition. He needed to ensure at least *one* of those didn't happen again.

'It's your job to ensure that all crew obey my code of conduct while on board my yacht, is it not?' he enquired evenly.

Ripley's laissez-faire evaporated. 'Of course, sir. And you have my assurance that they all know to follow your rules.'

'Do I? Then why did I find your newest recruit wandering the decks in the middle of the night?'

The flicker of surprise preceded the tiniest flash of quickly disguised ire that made Jario curb a smile. More than most, Ripley hated being called out for a flaw, and to his credit they rarely happened. It was why he was as close to being his right-hand man as Jario would permit.

'My apologies, sir. Clearly, Willow needs reminding of the rules. She was hired to assist me so she's directly under my supervision. Leave it with me. I'll make sure…'

Ripley's words receded as her name echoed seductively in Jario's head.

Willow.

Dios mio, it suited her down to a delectable T.

He shifted in his seat as fresh heat pounded through his bloodstream. Beyond Ripley's shoulder was the screen counting down the time until their next destination. Seven days till

Bali. Till he could do something about this savage need in his groin.

Until then, he had deals to close. One nemesis to take down another satisfying notch. And yet, he refocused on Ripley as he rose and poured another espresso before returning to his desk, the words leaving his lips as surprising as they were unsettling. 'If it's all the same to you, I'd like to witness it, make sure we're all on the same page?'

If he was surprised by the request, Ripley disguised it with a brisk nod. 'Of course. I'll get Miss Chatterton right away.'

Jario's vision hazed red, his pulse leaping from ten to a million in a nanosecond. For a ridiculous moment, he thought he would pass out from the shock filling his veins. He barely heard the espresso cup clatter onto the saucer, barely felt the hot liquid singe his skin.

'*Perdoname?* What did you say her name was?' The savage whisper blistered his throat.

Ripley's eyes widened as he lost several shades of colour. 'Willow Cha-Chatterton, sir. Is there something…?'

His hand slamming his desk made the other man jump. 'Bring her to me. *Now.*'

Ripley looked poleaxed for another half second, then he was nodding and striding from the room.

Alone, Jario surged from his desk, his hands tingling as disbelief filled him at her audacity.

She'd known who he was all along. Played him like a fiddle.

The wide-eyed expression. Those pseudo-innocent nightclothes hinting at false modesty. Her feigned breathlessness designed to trigger the right response in a red-blooded male. All an elaborate ruse he'd fallen for like a chump.

She'd wagered on his potent reaction to her beauty. And she'd *almost* succeeded.

Only Willow Chatterton had no idea what she'd awakened.

Mildly unnerving anticipation rushed through him like hot lava prior to a volcanic explosion.

They returned in double quick time. From their exerted breathing he knew Ripley had instilled the need for haste.

Jario's gaze fixed on her the second she stepped into the room, hating himself for noting *everything* about her. The light sheen of sweat dotting her upper lip, the rapid rise and fall of her chest as she tried to catch her breath.

Wide, *duplicitous* liquid brown eyes, blinking at him.

Ripley hovered in the doorway, his own gaze repeatedly sliding to her. Jario's blood boiled faster. 'I'll deal with you later. Leave us. Now.'

His assistant hurried away, shutting the door behind him.

In the thick silence that followed, he watched her dance between outright defiance and wariness, her mouth pursing twice before she exhaled whatever emotions were eating her alive. 'I can explain.'

'Can you? I'm dying to hear how you believe anything you say would mitigate your true intention for boarding my yacht.'

A flash of fire. 'I've been trying to get in touch with you. I had no choice,' she stated firmly.

There went the haze again. For a wild second, he couldn't quite catch his breath. 'Choice?' His ravaged voice grated his own ears, the word triggering a deep-seated repulsion that seared acid into his throat. Made his fists bunch at his sides as he battled to regain control.

Choice was the reason he was riddled with demons.

Choice was why he was without a father.

Choice was what had driven him from his home, the need to sail the seas, the need to keep moving, *always moving*, his only option.

'You have no idea what you've just walked yourself into, Miss Chatterton. But believe me, I'll take great pleasure in showing you.'

CHAPTER TWO

'YOU LIED YOUR way onto my boat. True or false?'

The accusation rankled, especially considering her own emotive feelings about lies. Willow's insides shook but her lips stayed shut, knowing any response would show weakness.

She'd thought she had time, that like all pampered rich people, Jario Tagarro would sleep until midday. It didn't help that she wasn't a morning person. That being summoned at 4 a.m. just to start preparing the mountain of chores involved in catering to one man's needs had rubbed her circadian rhythm the wrong way.

She fought to stand her ground now as he ventured closer.

'Answer me.' His body pulsed with the force of his turbulent emotions as arctic-cold eyes froze the marrow in her bones.

'No, I didn't lie. I was always going to introduce myself to you properly and tell you how and why I was here. And to be fair, I did try to get in touch with you, but none of your people would even agree to get a message to you.'

'Because believe it or not, they're trained not to allow random strangers to gain access to me.'

She exhaled long and slow to ease the building tension. And failed. 'Well, I didn't board your boat without permission. I was interviewed and offered a job and I took it.'

'With ulterior motives in mind. Or are you going to split hairs by suggesting withholding your true purpose didn't count as deception?'

She returned his stare. 'No, I'm not going to split hairs. I do have ulterior motives.' It felt good to unburden herself of that heavy truth.

Then remembering what Jario had said to the assistant, Willow's heart sank. 'What did you mean, you're going to deal with Ripley later?'

His eyes narrowed. 'You're concerned about him? Shouldn't you save that worry for yourself?'

'I can multitask,' she quipped and forced a shrug, despite the vortex of emotions swirling through her belly as her gaze moved over him.

Last night she'd thought the circumstances of their meeting had been, rightly, supercharged and intense enough for her to exaggerate the sheer raw, primal beauty of the man.

Dear God, had she been wrong.

Half-naked and covered in slick sweat with his long hair loose and swinging an axe, he'd been intensely masculine, animalistic and primal.

Clad in designer black from head to toe this morning, his jet-black hair neatly styled back and stubble trimmed to perfection, he was magnificently entrancing in a way that completely, terrifyingly commanded her attention.

'Believe me, even an endless supply of dexterity won't be enough to deal with what you're facing,' he answered silkily, white-hot fury, the kind that was almost invisible to the naked eye, vibrating from him. 'Tell me how you managed to get yourself an interview,' he demanded.

It was the absolute wrong time to dwell on other vibrations, especially the ones his voice and his proximity had evoked last night.

The way he'd guided her in throwing that axe. The rough seduction of his voice.

If Willow had been warned she'd respond so earthily to such simple praise this time yesterday, she would've scoffed, then laughed hysterically.

Even now, she couldn't entirely fathom why, last night, her

body had heated up, then tingled with disarming intensity between her legs, making her clit throb and her core dampen so brazenly, she'd moaned into her pillow.

She locked her knees tighter as he prowled towards her, the memory of him doing just that last night washing over her with renewed ferocity.

Enough! She had no time for that now. She'd wanted an audience with Jario Tagarro for the sake of uncovering the truth.

Her wish, however precarious, had been granted.

'I had a friend get me on the shortlist of the agency you use. And yes, I'll take full responsibility for that if you want. But Mr Tagarro—'

'You will remain silent, and you will listen. Interrupt me, and the authorities will be summoned, and you'll be arrested for trespassing. Is that understood?'

Defiance whistled through her at his domineering tone. 'Trespassing? Hardly,' she snapped, then bit her lip. The last thing she could afford to do was compound her situation with attitude. At the very least, she needed to comply until she got Jario to define his relationship with her father.

'What lies did you tell to weasel your way onto my yacht?'

Willow's teeth gritted. 'Everything I told Rebecca during the interview was true. But I do also want to talk to you, Mr Tagarro. About—'

The harsh slash of his hand through the air froze her speech. 'As Ripley's assistant you'll be assigned to my private and working suites, correct?' he enquired in a deceptively soft tone.

Her eyes darted to the file on his desk, wondering why he was questioning her when he probably had the information at his fingertips. Was he trying to catch her in a lie? 'I haven't yet discussed my full responsibilities with Rebecca or Ripley.'

'I see.'

The borderline pleasant response sent eerie shivers down her nape as Jario sauntered back to his desk and pressed a button. The purser answered immediately.

'Rebecca, bring up today's task sheet for Miss Chatterton, please.'

'Right away, Mr Tagarro.'

Lifting his finger off the intercom, he perched on the corner of his desk, arms folded. He stared at her, not a sliver of warmth from last night visible in his blue gaze.

Willow considered speaking a handful of times in the frosty silence, but the animosity bristling from him stayed her tongue. When the knock came, he barked an order to enter.

Rebecca barely glanced at her, her brisk strides crossing the room to hand her boss a sheet of paper.

'Will there be anything else, sir?'

Jario didn't answer for several seconds. Lifting his head after perusing the sheet, he said, 'Yes. I'd like you to give the deckhands the day off. Miss Chatterton will be scrubbing decks two and three by herself today. You'll let me know when she's done and I'll personally inspect it. Are we clear?'

'What? Are you serious?' Willow's vexed demand was ignored by Jario.

For her part, Rebecca quickly masked her surprise. 'Yes, sir.'

'Oh, and have security watch her at all times. If she attempts anything…untoward, inform me immediately.'

This time Rebecca's puzzled gaze slid to her, but it didn't stop her from nodding. 'Of course, sir.'

Jario rose. 'That will be all. You're dismissed, too, Miss Chatterton.'

She stayed put, fighting the volley of protests she wanted to launch at him. Because with a click of his fingers, this man could have her tossed off his yacht. So she took a deep breath. 'Mr Tagarro, I really need to talk to—'

'No. Your task awaits. Or would you like to resolve this another way?'

Navigating the twin paths of a relationship with her father and pursuing her love of playing the violin had taught her the arduous tasks of dealing with overblown but fragile egos while suppressing her own emotions for the greater good. And yes, while she'd lately realised that that particular bough was in serious risk of breaking, she'd saved herself a lot of heartache in the past by simply letting time cool hot temperaments.

She was thankful for that discipline now when she accepted that reasoning with Jario in his current state was futile. Her only option was to let time lessen the impact of his mood.

Except time *wasn't* on her side. The crossroads were drawing ever closer. But he was watching her with focus as deadly as the axe he'd taught her to throw last night, daring her to defy him. To give him the excuse he needed.

She sucked in a breath and accepted that she couldn't risk it. Not until she got the answers she'd come for.

Turning from his icy contempt, she walked on shaky legs to the door where Rebecca waited. She hesitated there for a moment, a compulsion she couldn't fight making her glance over her shoulder. His rigid expression was marred by a streak of bleakness that slashed through her. Before she could decipher it, Rebecca was shutting the door, her own gaze snapping with questions.

'You've been here barely twenty-four hours. What did you do?'

Willow shook her head. 'It's a long story I'd prefer not to share. This is between me and Mr Tagarro.'

Rebecca's lips thinned. 'That may be your view but whatever you've done doesn't impact just you. I've been summoned by the captain.'

Willow's belly clenched with regret. 'I'm sorry. I'll make this right.'

The other woman stared her down. 'How?'

Willow shrugged. 'Guess I'll start by scrubbing that deck?' Her attempt at levity fell flatter than a pancake.

'This may be a joke to you, but it's our livelihood you're messing with.'

Willow's forced humour dried up. 'It's not a joke. Trust me

on that.' She waved the irate woman on. 'Now, if you don't mind, I'd rather get started sooner than later.'

She wasn't helping her cause by not divulging her motives but in her short time on board, she'd noticed how fast gossip travelled. The last thing she wanted was to become ship gossip. Especially when she feared the bombshell she suspected Jario would reveal might annihilate her anyway.

The memory of Jario's anger echoing unpleasantly, she arrived on the designated deck to find three deckhands waiting. Their blatant surprise at being informed they had the day off turned to wild speculation when Rebecca asked them to show her where the cleaning supplies were kept.

Five minutes later, with a burly guard standing watch, Willow was elbow deep in cleaning solution.

The blazing sun beat down on her back as she swiped the soft brush over the expensive polished white oak. Curiously, while she'd had every intention of despising the grunt work, especially its effect on the hands she needed to safeguard for her violin and piano playing, her resentment lessened beneath the repetitiveness of cleaning the polished wood, her rioting mind calming as she settled into her task.

She could do this. For the sake of rescuing whatever remained of her relationship with her father, she couldn't fail.

Good news was, Jario Tagarro hadn't thrown her off his yacht. *Yet.* As long as that didn't change, she had a shot.

What if he's merely toying with you before he turns you over to the cops? Or worse?

She'd deal with that if and when it arose. For now…her gaze flicked across the very wide deck, satisfaction spiking through her.

She'd lost all sense of time and her knees were killing her, but she'd done one hell of a job, even if she said so herself. She dared the mighty Jario to find fault with—

A shadow fell over her. Shading her eyes, she looked up. 'Umm, can I help you?' she asked the stern-faced guard.

He held out a bottle of water and a tube of the eye-wateringly expensive sunscreen she'd only seen in the guests' suites. *Reserved for guests only.*

'No, thanks. I'm not thirsty.' She winced inwardly at the blatant cutting-off-your-nose-to-spite-your-face reply. 'And I've already used some…' Her voice trailed off as her skin tingled and she raised her gaze.

One deck above her, Jario leaned against the railing, a crystal tumbler in his hand.

'Orders of the boss,' the guard said belatedly.

Stopping herself from rolling her eyes, Willow stared at Jario. He returned her gaze with all the time in the world. Slowly raising his glass to his sensual lips, he took a healthy sip, content to watch her from on high as she sat back on her knees.

Willow absently accepted the items from the guard, barely registering his retreat as she and Jario locked gazes in silent battle. Her neck grew uncomfortable but she refused to look away. To back down.

Almost inexorably, sensations from last night began to seep in.

First, the thickness in the air that made it hard for her to draw breath.

Then the tight furling of her nipples. The dampness at her core.

The blaze and tingling of her skin that had nothing to do with heat from the sun.

It should've been maddening the sensations he drew from her, but Willow was too busy being disarmed by them to be livid. She'd never experienced anything like it and…hell, it was entirely too fascinating to wish it away just yet.

So she risked a crick in her neck as he held her gaze captive. He lowered his glass and his voice rasped, 'Drink. Now.'

The order was gruff, barely audible, but she heard every syllable as if he'd shouted it. 'You can't order me around,' she snapped to counteract the mystifying melting occurring inside her. 'Like I told your minder, I'm not—'

'You haven't hydrated in two hours. Inviting heat stroke or passing out won't get you out of this. Drink.'

Her parched throat screamed at her not to be stubborn. Hell, she suspected he would revive her just so she could keep scrubbing his precious deck. Ensuring her defiance was patently visible, she snatched the top off the glass bottle and tilted it to her lips, fighting a relieved moan as the cold water slipped down her throat.

Maddeningly, watching him take another drink as she swallowed hers sparked another volley of intense awareness that drew goose bumps all over her body. Her senses were going haywire when she lowered the empty bottle and raised an eyebrow in a challenge she couldn't seem to suppress.

'There you go. Any more orders you'd like to throw my way?'

He drained his glass, the ice clinking as he lowered it, then pointed a slim finger behind her. 'Yes. You missed a spot. Start again.'

She was Paul Chatterton's daughter.

Hours later fury still simmered in his veins at the knowledge.

Jario knew the unsettling feeling stemmed from the not so brief lusty thoughts he'd had this morning. The ones that arrived during his shower.

He'd been caught off guard by the very carnal near-eagerness to see her again. Enough to consider throwing caution to the wind.

Discovering her identity had dredged up a ton more emotions, none of them of the soft, fluffy variety. And yes, he felt a fool. Because for a sliver of time, when he'd demanded to know the reason for her presence, a part of him had *hoped* it was pure, eerie coincidence. Something he could excuse because deep down he didn't truly believe in visiting the sins of the father on the daughter?

Perhaps.

But no. Her motives were as he'd suspected.

And therefore, Jario had zero regret for the punishment he'd dished out.

Dios mio, the Chattertons deserved infinitely worse.

Rage galloped through him as he drew his hands down his face, the stress he'd marginally worked off last night back in full force, along with mild self-disgust for what he'd almost done. The *pleasure* he'd almost taken from the woman bearing the name of the man who'd decimated his family.

His father would be rolling in his grave!

Sorrow arrived hard on the heels of that thought, tightening his chest.

His father wouldn't *be* in a grave in the first place if not for Paul Chatterton.

Shaking his head to dispel the searing grief, Jario activated the cameras, sat back and watched.

The sun had long set, but she was still at work. She'd finished the first two decks with surprising efficiency, her work annoyingly productive.

Now she was performing her initially assigned duties in Jario's private deck. She'd cleaned his room and changed his sheets—three times under Ripley's exacting standards until she got it right. As he watched, she wiped her hand on the apron and tucked a loose curl behind her ear. Then leaning forward onto her hands and knees once more, she went to work.

Jario's gut tightened as his gaze dropped to her luscious behind, watched it sway back and forth with her exertions. When his mouth literally watered, he cursed and shoved back from his desk, his fingers spearing his hair as unwanted lust curled hot and hard through him.

Diavolo, was he so far gone that he was ogling the last woman he should be tempted by like some online creep?

No, he wasn't.

Then end it now.

He growled under his breath, the urge to know *why* she'd gone to the lengths she had, digging like a burr beneath his skin.

Not yet.

Breathing deep, he clicked onto another screen, his gaze tracking the satisfying downward trajectory of his prey.

It had taken years to successfully put the pieces in place after vital years of ensuring he'd become powerful enough to exact the purest form of revenge. Years during which he'd lived every day with harrowing loss. Of his father's last moments. Of his mother's deteriorating mental state.

But the tormenting existence had fuelled his purpose.

Now he'd almost completed the circle. He was weeks, months at most, from delivering the final, *deadly* blow.

He didn't need to hear Willow Chatterton out because her reasons weren't necessary.

Nothing would sway him from his goals.

Purpose restored, Jario's fingers flew over the keyboard, not resting until he'd dismantled yet another rung. An hour later he rose, ignoring his stirring senses as he made his way to his suite, then out onto the wide private deck.

Only to stop in his tracks.

She was fast asleep on his lounger, her knees drawn up halfway to her chest with her arms wrapped around them. The errant curl had escaped again, caressing her cheek and ruffling slightly with her breaths. It enraged him that even in sleep, this woman continued to be stunningly beautiful. That his fingers itched to tuck that curl back, trace her silky-smooth cheek.

Wake her in the most delightfully erotic way possible.

The diabolical thought jerked him forward to reach for her shoulder, shaking her awake.

Lush lashes fluttered then opened. Liquid brown eyes locked with his one moment before she hissed in surprised irritation like a scalded cat, surging up and away from him with innate grace that vexed and fascinated.

Unfortunately, the act sent her dangerously close to the railing.

He lunged for her, his heart leaping into his throat as he grabbed her waist and drew her against him.

'What are you doing?' she shrieked, outrage heating her cheeks.

His grip tightened as she struggled. 'What do you think? And stop acting like you're under attack.'

'I don't know that I'm not. I woke up to find you looming over me, startling the hell out of me! It's a natural reaction.'

'And sleeping on the job? Is that a natural reaction for you, too?'

Her nostrils fluttered with her aggrieved breathing. 'I've been scrubbing your damn boat all damn day. So I took a break for five minutes. Big deal.'

'It was more like thirty minutes. And scrubbing my boat is one of your assignments. If you don't like it, I'm happy to fire you.'

'There are labour laws against what you're doing, you know.'

'Feel free to call the authorities, then,' he taunted. 'Oh, wait, we're on international waters so I guess you're out of options, Miss Chatterton. Whereas I'm not.'

Her eyes sparked in anger, then chanced a glance behind her into the inky waters of the Pacific. 'What are you going to do? Are you going to save yourself the trouble of dealing with me by throwing me overboard?'

'Don't tempt me,' he rasped.

Willow inhaled sharply. Then she corralled every ounce of her composure. 'Look, Mr Tagarró, I know the circumstances of my presence on board don't thrill you. Trust me, this is the last place I want to be myself. But surely we can get this over with if you'll only hear me out?'

'No.'

She clenched her jaw to stifle a frustrated scream before she loosened it. 'For God's sake, just—'

'You can keep doing the job you signed up to do, plus whatever else I deem necessary, or you get fired, in which case Rebecca and Ripley get fired along with you for allowing you on board my yacht. That'll be a shame and put me in a worse mood because until very recently, I appreciated their work ethic. But you should know they'll probably sue the pants off you the moment you set foot on dry land.' He shrugged lazily and the movement reminded her that he still held her captive. That she could feel the imprint of his hands on her waist. 'I might even pay for their legal representation.'

Her jaw sagged at the cool, indolent way he outlined her less than ideal fate. She managed to hang on to her dwindling composure by the skin of her teeth, her heart pounding harder at the thought of any of what he'd threatened reaching the outside world.

While most things in her life had become tainted by indifference, lies and broken promises, the piano and violin had been her true, unwavering sustenance. Her way of bolstering herself and experiencing beauty when shades of grey closed in on her. She'd entered the competition to join the elusive, once-in-a-lifetime Mondia Symphony Orchestra on a whim, scarcely believing she would place.

Now she had a potentially life-defining acceptance email sitting in her inbox. An email she was avoiding because what would realising one dream mean if she walked away from her reality without a fight? If she cut ties with her father without discovering the root of their discord no matter how dire?

'Tell me why you despise Paul Chatterton so much.' She blurted the words out before she could stop herself, her belly twisting as his face instantly hardened.

'You will not say his name in my presence.' The words were guttural, wrenched from a dark, ominous place.

Earning both confirmation and denial in one breath zipped

another bolt of frustration through her. 'So I'm right? You know my father? Are you the reason behind Chatterton Financial's recent troubles?'

Jario's jaw clenched tight, then he released her abruptly, putting the distance of his deck between them, before spinning to face her. His fierce features made her take a step back. 'Whatever this act you're putting on is, I recommend you drop it while my last nerve is still intact.'

The unexpected response made her frown. 'An act? I don't have time for games, Mr Tagarro. As I'm sure you don't. I want to know what's going on. Now we've established you know my father, if you'd tell me why you're so upset—'

'Upset?' he echoed gratingly, both eyebrows risen in incredulity. The air crackled with his seething emotions as he slowly approached, intense, *livid* disbelief etched deep into the chiselled perfection of his face. 'Are you for real right now?' The question was softly voiced but infinitely more deadly.

Willow glanced away from the mesmeric eyes but almost immediately she was compelled back. 'Of course, I'm serious,' she murmured, slicking her tongue over dry lips. Then, because she needed to be certain, she kept pushing. 'So you admit you are behind this?'

His gaze openly derided her. 'Your tone suggests you think I was trying to hide something. I was not. In fact, I was hoping your father would come out of hiding and openly face me.' His eyes scoured her from head to toe, a sneer tainting his lips. 'Instead, he's proved he's not just a coward but one who has no shame hiding behind his own child.'

She gasped at the excoriating tone, even as her belly hollowed out at the confirmation that she'd at least uncovered this truth—something desperately alarming had happened between these two men. 'God, why do you hate him so much? What did he ever do to you?'

Eyes flaring in genuine shock, he let out a vicious laugh.

'You're serious, aren't you? You really came here clueless as to why he sent you?'

Heat rushed into her face at his mockery. It took monumental effort to fold her arms and hold in her temper. Not to...*dear God*, slap his handsome face. That would *most definitely* get her thrown overboard!

And while she would probably welcome the oblivion for a nanosecond, the knot of determination that had grown and hardened to become unshakeable these past few months, insisted there was no other course but this.

She was tired of being lied to, taken advantage of, so no, she most definitely would not be going out like that!

With each second that passed, she knew this was the right stance. That digging for the truth to find whatever Jario was withholding from her would determine whether it was worth cutting her losses or staying and demanding better than the crumbs of care and devotion she'd been tossed thus far. Would determine how she lived the rest of her life.

'For the record, he didn't send me. I came here on my own. And you can insult me all you want. I still need to know why you're coming after him.'

For an age he stared at her, eyes gleaming with emotions she couldn't entirely decipher, although disbelief and suspicion remained while her heart sprinted around her chest like it'd been supercharged with the purest adrenaline.

Eventually, he shoved his hands into his pockets and rocked back on his heels, the move so suave he could've been at a cocktail party exchanging pleasantries with friends. If not for the volcano rumbling from his very essence.

'No,' he said eventually, a mirthless smile twisting his lips before it was snuffed out. 'I don't think I'll give you the satisfaction. You can suffer along with your cowardly father or you can tell him to act like a man for once and admit his despicable past. Your choice.'

It was her turn to be stunned at his unexpected answer. 'Really? I'm surprised. Ordinarily, villains froth at the mouth to boast about their conquests. I was fully prepared to endure a smug diatribe in return for information,' she murmured, then tensed as she realised she'd said that aloud. But again, he surprised her by barely reacting.

'Then you'll find it refreshing that I'm no ordinary villain.'

Evidently done with her, he started to turn away.

'Dammit, just tell me! Then maybe I can convince you—'

'You can't. In fact, you've arrived in time to have a ringside seat to things kicking up a notch. Now that I know he intends to keep hiding like a coward, perhaps I need to finish this once and for all.'

She rushed forward, alarm quickening her feet. 'Wait! Can we not talk about this?' Her plea was husky, the weight of her own destiny pressing down on her. She licked her lower lip as she struggled for something…anything to slip beneath his armour. Even if it meant she was hastening her own heartache.

At this point, anything was better than enduring the despair she'd felt for years now.

She was so caught up in her scrambling that it took a moment to realise his gaze had fallen to her mouth, a darker gleam meandering through his stare that triggered a different seismic sensation within her.

For several charged seconds they shifted into a different space, existed in a fraught little bubble outside the circumstances that had brought her here. In those moments, Willow became viscerally aware that she was a flesh-and-blood woman squaring off with a rampantly virile male. One whose pheromones were triggering an unmistakable reaction that drove her a panicked step back. But it was too late.

The predator before her had latched on to the scent. On to the weakness she'd just revealed. Jario's nostrils flared in blatant victory even as his disdain grew.

'Is this why he sent you here?' His voice was a deadly, hypnotising rasp, flaring delicious electricity all over her body.

'I don't know what you're talking about,' she tossed back, despite the far too pleasurable sensation bombarding her.

His face hardened. 'Your mother is still alive, is she not?' At her puzzled nod, he continued. 'As are a few uncles and a smattering of the senior staff who haven't yet abandoned his rapidly sinking ship. And yet, here you are, his only offspring, served up like a sacrificial lamb. Or did you concoct this scheme together?'

She fought to shake off the sorcery of his proximity. 'What scheme? Seriously, you're not making any sense. My father knows I'm here but it was my idea to come talk to you, not…' She trailed off as his meaning belatedly registered. She snorted, then stunned laughter tinged with bitter memories burst past her guard, tumbling free and weirdly lightening the knots of tension within her. 'You think he sent me here to *seduce* you? Me?' Her hand went to her chest, shocked beyond belief.

This couldn't be happening again. She pushed David and his gaslighting and traitorous accusations aside as Jario's eyes narrowed.

And just like that, the atmosphere was snapping with live electric currents once more. 'You're either very clever or absurdly naive.'

He could've held one of those electric conductors to her chest and she wouldn't have jolted as hard as she did at his guttural observation. Her body was aflame in a way she'd never experienced before.

Fatal attraction.

She'd thought it was the stuff of fiction or OTT Hollywood movies. Somewhere in the middle of the North Pacific Ocean, Willow Chatterton discovered that it was a real and visceral thing, currently tearing mercilessly into her as Jario leaned in closer, his gaze pinning her in place.

'Which is it, Willow?'

Hell, no. She wasn't doing this.

'Neither. And I'm sick of men with overblown opinions of

their hotness accusing me of throwing rampant temptation around like candy at a kid's birthday party, okay?'

She froze the second the words tumbled out, then squeezed her eyes shut and silently cursed the ex whose rampant jealousy, gaslighting and ultimate betrayal had made their six-month relationship a living hell she'd thankfully escaped, even though it'd shattered even more of her heart and trust.

Swallowing the bitter memories, she raised her hand to a suddenly throbbing head, the corners of her vision blurring slightly as she stumbled forward. 'Look, all I want are answers to a few questions, then…' She sucked in a sharp breath as she grew dizzier.

'What's wrong with you?' he demanded sharply.

'Nothing. Well, nothing some food won't resolve. I get a little hypoglycaemic when I—'

'I know what hypoglycaemia is,' he interrupted sharply. 'When was the last time you ate?'

'You mean in between scrubbing three hundred miles of decking? I don't know, I can't remember.' Unfortunately, her smart retort came with another wave of dizziness.

Her hand shot out, hoping for something solid to steady herself. It connected with a hard-packed torso. Warm muscles jumped beneath her touch as her fingers reflexively dug in.

With a sharp inhale, Willow went to snatch her hand away.

But Jario, cursing under his breath, locked his fingers around her wrist, yanked her close once more, then swept her up into his arms.

If she'd hoped her diminished position would've softened him one iota as he marched towards his stateroom, she was wrong.

He stared down at her, a mountain of affront and testosterone and chiselled masculine perfection sending indecent and confusing fireworks shooting through her system.

'You think you're going to get out of this that easily? Think again, *querida*.'

CHAPTER THREE

AT SOME POINT during his militant march through his private quarters, Willow squeezed her eyes shut.

She told herself it was so she could regain her composure, but she silently conceded she needed to block out how infuriatingly captivating she found him. How watching those sensual lips, the vibrant skin of his throat where a pulse steadily throbbed, the way his silky hair caressed his nape as he walked, all colluded to drive further heat between her legs.

An unacceptable, inappropriate condition to be suffering right now so soon after reminding herself of what David had done to her. How his lies and her needy emotions had betrayed her into thinking *that* relationship, too, was worth salvaging until she'd learned how wrong she was.

She cringed as Jario's steps slowed, then resolutely opened her eyes.

He'd brought her to his private kitchen.

From her long to-do list today, she knew the double-wide fridge, freezer, cupboards and bespoke wine cellar were stuffed full of every incredible food and drink item a pampered billionaire could crave.

Not that this man looked in any way pampered. Feeling his tensile strength, she cursed the heat rising into her cheeks. Luckily, he set her down at the ten-seater dining table and walked away before she grew fully flushed. It didn't stop her traitorous eyes from dropping to his taut backside. To imagining—

Dear God, stop!

She wrenched her gaze away from his body, refocusing on her surroundings.

At this time of night, the sleek shutters usually parted to let in sunlight were drawn, inviting intimacy to the otherwise large space. Gleaming furniture and impeccable silverware created another masterpiece on a yacht that had repeatedly made her jaw drop at every turn.

Settled in one stylish chair she was sure cost more than a month's pay, she watched Jario briskly set platters on the centre island in preparation of a meal.

Decadent, delicious smells attacked her neglected senses, and she cringed harder when her stomach let out an almighty growl. His gaze flicked to her but she busied herself straightening a piece of perfectly placed flatware.

Had she not feared another bout of dizziness striking, she would've gotten up and left. The plate he slid in front of her, piled high with an assortment of hand-rolled sushi, tomato and mozzarella tacos, slices of ham on focaccia bread drizzled with oil, and a tiny platter of golden Ossetra caviar with crackers, defused any attempted mutiny.

As hodgepodge gourmet food went, it was the most incredible and delicious combination she'd ever sampled, and heaven help her, she couldn't stop her soft moans of appreciation as she devoured the food.

Only to feel an ominous tingling in her throat five minutes later.

Oh, God…oh, God…*oh, no!*

Her alarmed gaze flew over the food, attempting to identify the culprit for the oncoming reaction. Grabbing a napkin to spit out the mouthful before she worsened her situation, she shoved back from the table.

Jario jerked upright from where he'd been leaning against the island, hawklike eyes narrowing. 'What's wrong?' He closed the gap between them in one second flat. When she didn't respond fast enough, he gripped her arms, his face looming closer as the vise closed around her throat.

Oh, God...no.

'Willow.' The growled bite of her name forced words from her.

'Mmm…a-aller-gic…sh-shomething…' She waved a hand at the platter. 'N-need ep-EpiPen.'

'Que? Hijo de—' He cut himself off, released her and sprinted for the phone. 'Send the doctor up here, right now! Tell him to bring something for anaphylaxis.'

Three seconds later he was sweeping her off her feet, laying her on a nearby sofa.

'Mmm…fine—'

'Stop talking and breathe,' he grated, his hand on her cheek, eyes boring into her, his own breathing long and deep, as if directing her to follow.

She managed to squeeze one long, slow inhale, her lungs protesting at the time it took to replenish it. Willow knew from past, thankfully rare, episodes that as long as she didn't panic, she'd be okay.

And weirdly, watching the rise and fall of his chest focused her.

When footsteps pounded into the room, Jario let out a quick exhale. 'She's having an allergic reaction. Hurry the hell up!' he barked without taking his eyes off her.

Mere seconds passed before a sharp jab stung her thigh, efficient fingers testing her pulse.

'It should start working soon, sir.'

Jario didn't acknowledge the doctor. He seemed unable to take his eyes off her, his piercing gaze darting all over her face. The ferocity of it sent new needles stinging all over her body that had nothing to do with oxygen deprivation. The moment her breathing eased, she struggled up and tried to speak again.

'Mmm…fine.'

He ignored her, rising to his full height before scooping her up into his arms. Another minute and they were in his stateroom. He laid her down, stopped long enough to tug off her flats before drawing back the covers.

Something wild lurched inside her. 'Wha-ath are y-you doing?'

He pinned her with a vicious look. 'I'm not in the mood right now, Miss Chatterton. For both our sakes, don't test me.'

Dragging the covers over her body, he stared down at her for a taut second, then to her stunned surprise, he turned and walked out.

The doctor entered a minute later, asked a few probing questions.

There was no point telling him she was usually meticulous but she'd been severely distracted by her boss and hadn't thought to do more than a visual inspection of her food before she consumed it.

That boss strode in a minute later after she'd thanked the doctor and he'd left. Jario still seemed on the very edge of his patience. Arms folded, he stared down at her again, a tinge of bafflement in his eyes.

'You didn't think to tell me you had food allergies?'

She shrugged. 'I'm normally diligent…but I guess nothing about tonight has been…' She stopped, realising she was about to admit that he'd upset her equilibrium. She was unwilling to hand him that power. He had far too much of it already.

He shoved his fingers in his hair, Spanish epithets erupting from him as he jerked into agitated pacing. 'Are you blaming me?'

'No. Yes. Maybe.' Willow sighed. 'Look, it happened, but it's over now. I'm fine,' she repeated for the umpteenth time, wondering if she was attempting to appease him because, examining him closer, she spotted grooves bracketing his mouth. Something kicked inside her at the thought that the almighty Jario may have had a moment or two of worry.

Over her.

It'd been a while since anyone had shown her that kind of concern. Her relationship with her parents had saddled her with emotional baggage she knew had altered her. She'd compounded that by making the mistake of looking for emotional support and connection from David.

But...was it wrong to want a selfish minute of connection with someone?

Even if it felt entirely inappropriate that that care should come from this man, who so effortlessly dripped warm feeling into her veins?

Yes!

She tried to push the feelings away before they found further vulnerable spots inside her.

'The attacks are most often mild,' she said, trying to play it down. 'I can usually get to my pen before it gets serious—'

'The crew cabin is almost five minutes away. A lot can happen in that time. What the hell were you thinking?'

As he paced closer, she saw his jaw was set, his skin a couple of shades paler. And his eyes…they held a haunted look that made her stomach and heart lurch.

This wasn't the run-of-the-mill reaction she usually received. Hell, one time, her ex had implied she'd willed on an attack just for the attention!

Every instinct screamed that this was more. That her reaction had triggered something in Jario. Something unwelcome and unsettling.

'You don't need to worry,' she murmured, that warm place heating further.

His mouth twisted. 'If those words meant anything you would've taken better care to not let it happen in the first place.'

Her fingers tightened on the sheets, his agitation and irritation sparking bittersweet relief as that warm place cooled. She didn't want to have anything in common with this man who'd tauntingly admitted he was responsible for her family's excruciating slide into ruin. 'Yeah, I get that my episode inconvenienced you but—'

'But you're the victim here and I'm being unreasonable?' His sensual lips curled in derision.

'If there's one thing I hate more than anything, Mr Tagarro, it's having words put in my mouth,' she ground out. He froze, his incisive gaze fixing on her. After a moment's silence, she continued. 'I was about to say it was just an unfortunate accident and I'll make sure it doesn't happen again. I don't even know what it was that triggered it.'

Fierce blue eyes flared for a second, then he strode to his bedside table. 'Send up the chef and two crew members to my suite, please.'

Damn it.

Willow squeezed her eyes shut, abstractedly registering the lingering pain in her throat and eyes, the mild throbbing in her head. 'Seriously, what are you doing? You're overreacting.'

'Are you allergic to sesame seeds?' he clipped out.

She nodded.

His jaw clenched. 'You reacted to the sesame oil in the salad.'

Her breath whizzed past an aching throat as she exhaled. His eyes darkened as the sound echoed in the silence. Feeling her body surge with those volatile sensations, she lifted the covers. 'Thanks for letting me know, and for helping. Good night—'

'Stay where you are. I think you've caused enough upheaval for one day.'

She frowned. 'It's not my fault I was too tired from being overworked.'

'So you are saying this is my fault.'

'I'm saying you're overreacting. Which is weird since you clearly don't like me.'

He froze, his nostrils the only movement as he sucked in air. 'We're in the middle of the damn ocean. Do you know what could've happened if you couldn't have accessed help in time?'

The shards of anguish in his voice stopped her midrise, his expression charged with so many more issues than the subject of her allergic reaction. Willow opened her mouth, but before she could demand to know what was really going on, a knock announced the arrival of his chef.

His eyes still firing enigmatic currents at her, he barked, 'Come.' Then as before, he turned and walked out.

Her first attempt to follow him resulted in her sagging back on the bed, her not fully recovered body resisting her will.

Willow gave herself a few minutes to recover—while listening to the brisk exchange between boss and chef and cringing at being the cause of it.

Attempting again and succeeding to hold herself upright, she slowly approached the kitchen. Her stomach sank at the scene before her.

The contents of the fridge and freezer were being examined by three galley staff.

'This really isn't necessary, you know,' she said.

Jario approached, still in thundercloud mode. 'You should be in bed.' When she mutinously held his stare, he sighed. 'They're removing everything you told the doctor you're allergic to.'

Surprise jolted her. 'Why? I won't be eating my meals in here.'

'You're part of my personal crew. You may need to assist Ripley in here from time to time.' He closed the distance between them until he was blocking the doorway to the kitchen and its occupants. 'Or don't you care about suffering another episode?'

'Of course I care,' she replied tartly, a little bubble bursting at the query that sounded like the kind of accusation her ex would throw at her. And also because Jario wasn't doing this entirely out of concern for her but because he didn't want to be inconvenienced.

Enough already. 'I could've done the sorting, you know, as part of my job?'

The chef flashed her a mildly amused look, clearly detecting her snark.

Jario's jaw rippled. 'It's not your call. And as you've reminded me, you're exhausted. I'd have to be a special kind of monster to watch you choke to death one minute then put you to work the next, no?' The haunted expression lingering on his face stemmed any trite response. 'And you should be in bed. If you wish to help, return there now, if you please.'

His imperious demeanour said he wasn't joking, nor was he going to be baited by the challenging eyebrow she raised at that command.

But when her insides started to warm again at this latest skirmish and his flashes of concern, she took one bewildered step back. And another.

Yes, she hadn't felt a caring warmth for a while but, come on, she couldn't really be reacting like this to his high and mightiness?

Also, she was feeling better, so she should go to her own bed, not linger on why sliding back into Jario Tagarro's bed elicited sensations beyond a recovery from her attack. For the first time, it struck her that she'd slid between sheets *he* slept in, and heat immediately pummelled her.

It didn't help to recall that he'd suggested earlier that she was trying to *seduce* him. Her not so steady breathing juddered in her chest as they exchanged another charged look. Then, after just managing to drag her gaze free when she tried to peer past his mile-wide shoulders, he blatantly blocked her view. She pursed her lips, turned on her heel and marched away.

She was back in his room before she noticed he'd followed her. That he was poised in the doorway, watching as she slid back into his bed.

Willow pulled up the sheets to hide his effect on her body, her senses heightening when he made no effort to speak, only observing her with those ferocious eyes. As a final act of defiance—because apparently, she couldn't help herself—in what had been a monumentally challenging day, she turned her back to him, and when she was immediately attacked by his uniquely masculine scent, gritted her teeth and took smaller breaths. Promised herself she'd rest just until she felt a little stronger. Then they would get to the bottom of why he was fixated on her father.

She'd lost track of time, but she guessed it was sometime before midnight. If she got this resolved by morning, she could make plans to leave this yacht and its overwhelming, dangerously gorgeous owner as soon as possible.

Until then, she would ignore him and close her eyes.

Just for a minute…

Willow understood the true meaning of cringing in horror when she woke up and, even with her eyes shut, sensed the streaming sunlight.

Oh, God, no.

It didn't help that the sumptuous bed and soft-as-butter Egyptian cotton sheets were the best she'd ever slept in. Or that his scent still lingered, wrapping around her, forcing her to inhale deeply, chase after the baffling intoxication of it.

The shameful fact was that she'd fallen asleep *for hours* in his bed. Had wrapped her arms around one pillow and somehow positioned another between her legs as was her sleeping habit. Cataloguing her list of sins, Willow also clocked that her skirt had ridden up and said pillow was firmly wedged against her—

'You're awake. Open your eyes.'

She flinched, not because of his rasped command tinged with mocking amusement, but because she wasn't in the mood to see her embarrassment reflected in his eyes.

But short of stumbling out of here without opening her eyes, Willow had no choice but to blink them open. To the sight of Jario Tagarro reclined next to her, his eyes—dear God, did his eyes ever look anything but intensely predatory?—fixed squarely on her face. As she looked into them, she noticed that the blue was sparked through with midnight stripes. And slowly those stripes took over, darkening the depths as his bare chest rose and fell in a steady cadence.

'You've stopped breathing, Willow. Do I need to call the doctor again?'

Willow jerked away, aware she was in full retreat mode and not caring one iota. 'I didn't mean to fall asleep. I'll just—ah!' One leg tangled within the sheet, and she tumbled backwards out of bed, landing hard on her backside.

Out of sight, she heard him curse under his breath, and her face flamed. Two seconds later he'd rounded the bed, hands on lean hips as he stared down at her.

She sighed in frustration. 'Look, I know I sound like a broken record, but I just want some answers. Then we can be shot of each other. Surely you want that?'

One corner of his mouth twitched. 'Do I?'

He was mocking her. But despite it being at her expense, she wanted to see a fuller smile. Willow shook her head and scrambled to her feet. 'This might be amusing to you but I'm deadly serious.'

His face clenched tight, his humour evaporating in a flash. 'I assure you, the last thing I am is amused. And you've no idea what *deadly* means.'

She mirrored his stance, hands on hips despite the swell of anxiety at his bleak tone. 'Then enlighten me. Tell me what my father means to you.'

'Less than nothing,' he returned, his voice a lethal blade, warning her to tread very carefully.

Her disbelieving snort shot out before she could stop it. 'Obviously that's not true since you look incandescent every time I mention his name.'

The tautness in his body said he'd do anything *but* oblige her with an answer. That seeing how tortured she was by his withholding information was perhaps the response he was looking for.

But she couldn't remain here. Couldn't endure another day like yesterday. And now that she'd met him, felt the raw power and purpose steaming off him, she partly understood why her father winced every time she'd mentioned his name. 'Please.' The reluctant plea was part frustration, part exasperation.

A gleam passed through his eyes and the ferocity throttled back the tiniest fraction. 'It's a new day, Willow. Perhaps the sound of you begging might sway me. Let's have more of it.'

Her heart lurched, a different sensation stealing through her body as she stepped towards him. 'You think it debases me to beg? Good people are having to be let go because we can't afford to keep them employed. But if it strokes that monumental ego of yours, then sure. Please. If you told me why I can…'

His eyes hardened. 'You can what?'

She shrugged. 'Give them a solution or even rehire them when things get better. Most of them didn't want to leave, but we had no choice.'

He laughed. The damned infernal devil *laughed.* 'Did you bother to find out why they were leaving in droves?'

She frowned. 'What?'

'Tell me how many you've checked up on since you *had no choice* but to let them go.' His chest rippled with the mocking air quotes of her words.

She dragged her gaze from the distracting play of muscles to focus on his response.

'Why does that matter? The bottom line is that we couldn't keep them on.' To battle the shame for letting the employees down and anger at her father for blatantly lying that their problems weren't as devastating as everyone feared, she'd buried her hurt and despair in her music.

Should she have been doing something else?

'You seem concerned with the people you haven't bothered to check up on. Not so selfless as you like to project, are you?'

'I'm not sure…' Her eyes widened as the penny dropped. 'You're the one who's been luring them away?'

A hard smile twitched his lips. 'It takes very little effort when your leader doesn't give a single damn about you.'

'Because you're destroying him! Tell me why!'

He didn't answer. Instead, his gaze dragged leisurely over her, making her acutely aware of her dishevelled state. That she'd wandered far too close to him in her agitation. She caught his delicious scent once more and her belly clenched in visceral reaction. Heat arrowed through her, concentrating between her thighs as her face flamed at her body's shameless response.

And somehow he knew. With another maddening twitch of his lips, he breached the gap between them. 'That's enough for today, I think. Let's pick it up again tomorrow.'

Frustration bunched her fists. 'For God's sake! What's it going to take?'

He didn't speak for the longest time. Then, 'You look better. Breakfast is ready for you in the dining room. Then I believe you have a work schedule to be getting on with.'

'I'm not scrubbing any more decks if that's what you've got in mind for me. I'd rather—' She bit her tongue to stop the inflamed words she sensed she might regret.

'You'd rather what? Quit?' he taunted.

For the first time in her life Willow contemplated bodily harm. Such was the intense, unrefined emotions he triggered in her. Shocked by it, she stumbled back one step. Then another.

Through it all, he watched with single-minded focus. Cataloguing everything for his sadistic pleasure?

'I'd rather do the job I signed up for,' she amended tartly, then gestured out the nearest window. 'Like you said, we're in the middle of the ocean. Quitting or you firing me isn't really efficient when I can be working. Besides, I don't think you'd prefer to waste resources on feeding and housing me while I do nothing below decks?'

She was counting on his astute business sense although she accepted a billionaire probably would barely feel the impact of supporting one unimportant crew member.

Besides, she sensed that while he was revelling in withholding the information she needed from him, Jario Tagarro got a kick out of having her at his mercy.

Enough to keep her around...

After an age of narrow-eyed scrutiny, he caught her elbow in his loose grip and led her onto the sun-dappled deck she'd scrubbed only last night. There, on the pristine table that must've been set while she slept, laid a resplendent breakfast fit for the king of the vessel.

Fluffy, mouth-watering croissants she knew were made fresh because she'd watched the chef make a batch—God, was it only yesterday?—sat on an immaculate platter, next to a shallow tureen of golden scrambled eggs. Next to that a silver boat of black Ossetra caviar with a tiny spoon ready to sample. Rich smoked salmon sprinkled with shaved truffles were curled next to good old-fashioned plain bagels with not a sesame one in sight.

'Sit down and eat something.'

She tugged her arm from him, at once affected and mildly disturbed that he was eating breakfast with her. She was swimming in agitation when he leaned close, his breath washing over her ear. 'Get through one half-hour block without fainting, choking, or risking dehydration and you won't be fired. How's that?'

Pointing out he'd been directly or indirectly responsible for each of those incidents felt churlish, especially when in every single one he'd *saved* her.

The thought was bracing enough to silence her, to take the chair he held out for her, to ignore his piercing stare as she accepted the pile of food he placed before her one minute later.

Half an hour.

She could do it.

Then all she had to do was get through the next half hour.

Then the next.

Sweet heaven…

'Are you kidding me?'

It was both irritatingly reassuring and unsettling to hear her husky voice had returned to normal after listening to her fight to catch her breath last night.

Was that the reason he'd sat in the chair next to his bed until sunrise, then, feeling that taunting compulsion, had allowed himself to be pulled to his own bed to sleep that puzzling but satisfying half hour before the demons had roused him?

Jario ignored the questions, his gaze riveted to her sparkling eyes as she glared at him one moment longer before redirecting her affront to the floor of his dressing room.

'This is what you want me to do? Colour-code and pair up your socks? There must be over two hundred pairs here. Who even needs that many socks?' Did she know her sexy mouth pouted just a tiny bit when she was riled?

He turned away as his body jolted to life. 'Me. And that's your first task. Your second is to pack away the left side of my closet. You'll be informed of what comes next when you're done.'

She glared harder. 'Where's Ripley? Shouldn't I be doing something to assist him?'

Good question.

He was fast approaching chagrined levels for the way he couldn't seem to distance himself from this woman. 'He's busy with other duties. Are you objecting to yours, Willow?' Chalk up another objection to how much he liked her name on his tongue.

She spiked another glare at the socks, sparking unwanted amusement at her naked loathing of the task. 'Guess it's better than scrubbing,' she begrudgingly offered. Then she slowly, defiantly, sank to her knees.

He didn't want to consider why the thought of her in his bedroom made his blood sing faster through his veins.

Hell, he wasn't going to think about Willow Chatterton or what the sight of her on her knees did to him. *Not at all* for the next several hours. Not when he had two urgent deals to close.

Yet, a ludicrously wasted half hour later, Jario tossed his stylus on the table. His concentration was shot to hell.

He was going insane. He was sure of it.

He should've sent her off to the opposite side of his yacht. Where he couldn't see her. Smell her. Be reminded of that pulse of horror when he'd seen her choking, panic building in her eyes.

'Hijo de—' He bit off the curse as his gaze wandered back to the screen showing his dressing room.

He should head to the lower deck to his wave-powered swimming pool, where the only views were of the endless ocean, work out until he was too exhausted to think. But even as the thought teased him, his eyes remained on the screen.

She'd dealt with his socks in record time and was almost halfway through rearranging a closet that didn't need it. Watching her touch his things, sometimes bringing his suits close to her body as she moved them, Jario shifted in his seat, the heat she'd ignited in him that first night when he hadn't known her true identity, mocking his every effort to douse it.

It felt like some cruel cosmic joke for him to be *this* attracted to his enemy's daughter, but he wasn't laughing. There would be no amusement while the man responsible for his father's not being here—*and the stunning daughter whose motives remained unclear*—remained unpunished.

And yes, it stuck in his craw that she was hard-working and diligent.

But watching her standing on his bed, her arm risen high above her head to reach the light fixture with her feather duster, the movement showing a few inches of golden skin, was the last straw.

With a growl drawn deep from a place he didn't want to examine too closely, he launched from his desk, flames he told himself were born of irritation heating his blood as he headed for the last place he needed to go.

'Enough of that. Time for a break.'

She whirled, her bare feet dancing on the covers, her mouth agape at his unannounced entrance. 'It's only eleven-thirty in the morning,' she stated suspiciously.

'And you've proved that you're too frail for long stretches

of hard work.' Not entirely true but… 'I won't have you near collapse. Break. Now.'

'Sugar versus vinegar. You've heard which one gains you better results, right?' She walked on the balls of her feet to the edge of the bed.

Jario barely registered that he'd moved and was holding out his hand to help her down. A gesture she refused, one leg sliding down the side of his bed with absorbing poise, then the other, all as she glared warily at him.

'One rots your teeth and lulls you into a false, temporary sense of pleasure. The other leaves no doubt as to your intentions. But if you insist, you can keep working.'

Liquid brown eyes examined him and he sensed what was coming before she spoke. 'Trust me, I'm far from frail. But fine, I'll take a break. On condition that you answer one question.'

His heart thumped hard as he turned away from the sight of her maddeningly alluring body and walked to the door.

'No. You're in no position to request conditions.'

He wasn't entirely sure why he was withholding the information. Because he wanted her to experience a fraction of the suffering he'd endured all these years? Or was it something else?

A visceral reluctance to catch even a sliver of pity in her eyes? Because wouldn't he be opening his deepest wound? Laying it bloody and vulnerable to her judgement? Enduring the same pity he'd had no choice but to face when he'd first lost his father? When he'd been carted off to foster care because his mother had been too broken to care for him for months at a time? Jario didn't want to recall the taunts from false friends who'd suddenly realised they had something to laud over him and viciously wielded it, nor did he want to relive the pity from their parents he'd received in those harrowing years.

Of course, none of them had lifted a finger to help the boy whose family had been shattered by one selfish man's decision.

His stomach clenched hard in rejection at the thought at the same time as he was devising ways to make Willow pay if she so much as looked at him with any of those much-loathed emotions. Because Jario knew he would tell her sooner rather than later. Paul Chatterton had hidden in the dark long enough. His deplorable actions needed to be laid bare.

For now…he intended to enjoy this little game he was playing with his daughter.

'Are you coming?'

Her elevated chin gave him a glimpse of her smooth skin, her delicate jaw. The pulse that continued to leap so frantically at her throat.

The throat that had attempted to close last night, spiking terror he hadn't felt since—

Enough.

It wasn't his fault that she'd failed to mention she had allergies.

'You can stop with all the glaring. I'm very aware you hold the power. For now.'

Her taunt almost plucked a grin. He managed to kill it just in time. 'For now? You expect the balance of power to change?'

She shrugged, approached him slowly, the roll of her hips far too entrancing as her fingers flicked between them. 'I'm not going to do this with you forever. Besides, I've only been here a little over a day and you've confirmed there's a connection between you and my father. If you don't answer my questions, I'll find out some other way. And this will end one way or another.'

Surprise—and a touch of unwanted disquiet—punched him hard in the gut, both at her continued defiance and the fact that for the first time since her arrival, his reaction didn't come tinged with anger.

Instead, he was…intrigued. By her confidence and daring.

By how far he could push this woman.

By what it'd take to test her. To see if underneath all the bluster, she wasn't as fickle and lily-livered as her father.

Is that all?

He ignored the snide query as he led them down one level, then another to the sea-level deck where some of his favourite toys were laid out, awaiting his pleasure. He considered then discarded the most obvious toys like his super jet ski and water skis.

Then he turned to her. 'First things first. Can you swim?'

She frowned. 'I thought I was taking a break?'

He let loose a smile he was sure didn't look at all amiable. 'From your duties, not from me. Answer the question.'

She eyed the equipment. 'I grew up in Southern California. It's a cardinal sin not to be able to handle yourself in water.'

'Good. Pick one.'

Her eyes narrowed. 'Why?'

Jario didn't respond. He was well aware that his charged silences prodded most people into speech, were they minions or heads of states. And he wasn't surprised when she held out long enough to make him wonder if he'd met the first person to challenge that gauntlet.

But eventually she wandered closer, that hip-skimming skirt and tiny waist spiking his temperature once more.

'That one.' She pointed to the e-Foil surfboard.

She hadn't gone for his absolute favourite and he grittily dismissed the surge of disappointment. This game was just to prove his point. To keep his goal straight and true.

Nothing else.

'We'll race. If you win, I'll allow you one question. If you fail—'

'I won't,' she interjected, that defiant nose up in the air again.

'*If* you fail,' he stressed the word, ignoring the sparks of excitement igniting in his belly at the thought of engaging with this woman, 'you'll forfeit all your questions. You will leave my yacht at the next port and we will never speak again.'

He said that with enough conviction to believe it.

Almost.

CHAPTER FOUR

EVERYTHING HAPPENS FOR a reason.

Willow wasn't one for ascribing such meanings to her life, but as she kicked her feet in the crystal-clear blue waters of the Pacific, ready to board the e-Foil, she couldn't help but wonder if Addie, the sweet, grandmotherly, Tarot-loving former Chatterton housekeeper they'd sadly had to let go due to lack of funds, had a point with that saying.

Because wasn't it only three months ago that she'd taken a rare break from both work and violin practice to try out the e-Foil at her local beach and discovered she loved it so much she'd started using it for much-needed stress relief when she got the chance?

Jittery excitement licked through her veins as she watched Jario stride to the edge of the swim deck. Like her, he'd changed into swimming gear.

Unlike him, she didn't feel so at home in the minuscule borrowed designer white bikini clinging to her skin, a world removed from her usual all-in-one or better yet, the wetsuit she favoured but had foolishly omitted to pack in her hurry to get on the road. She tried not to openly stare at the chiselled body on display, especially those powerful thighs that flexed and gleamed bronze in the sunlight.

She heard him drop into the water with barely a splash, swim over to take control of his own e-Foil. The board was black like hers, but with red, meaner-looking stripes. Admonishing herself for allowing a simple water sport toy to intimidate her, she sternly reminded herself why she was doing this.

He'd finally given her the smallest green light, to get the answers she wanted. Yes, she'd jumped through hoops to get here but so what?

'Ready?'

Her head jerked up to the speaking glance that said he'd seen her ogling him. Face flaming, she shifted her gaze to his muscled shoulder and nodded briskly. 'Bring it.'

A lip twitch compelled her eyes to his well-defined mouth, and her stomach clenched as lust unfurled low in her belly. God, what was wrong with her? How could she find him—yet another man bent on playing mind and *literal* games with her, and the one attempting to destroy what was left of her family—so compellingly attractive?

Everything happens for a reason?

Hell, no, Addie! Not this.

Gritting her teeth, Willow secured her helmet and adjusted the remote securely strapped to her wrist before launching herself onto the board. She ignored how smoothly Jario did the same, not even bothering to rest on his knees before he started his motor. As much as she wanted to prove she was just as adept, the last thing she wanted was to be rash and blow her chance.

'We start and end there.' He indicated the positions. 'Two turns around those buoys. First one to the finish line wins.'

She started the propellor, her stomach dipping a little when the board shot forward at the second setting. The e-Foil's max speed was a whopping fifty kilometres. If Jario went anywhere near that, she was toast.

The fastest she'd ever gone—on a particularly trying day, when her father's mood swings and heavy drinking had driven her from the house—was thirty-three.

She pushed thoughts of failure from her mind as she approached the starting point, which just happened to be one of the junior crew, poised on a jet ski half a kilometre from the yacht.

After her charged exchange with Rebecca yesterday, Willow had expected the crew to treat her with hostility. She'd been quietly stunned when they'd remained entirely professional, albeit with a touch of inevitable frost. While she was sure the speculation was rife, short of blurting out the private and personal reasons she was on board the *La Venganza*, she had no choice but to keep her eyes on her ultimate goal.

She sucked in a steadying breath as she drew level with Jario.

Without glancing her way, he rose lithely on his board, the movement so effortless it was mesmeric to watch. Praying for a fraction of that agility she followed suit, her breath catching when she wobbled, earning herself a raised eyebrow from him.

Unfortunately for him, it had the effect of lighting a fire in her belly.

'Still want to go?' he drawled.

She responded by flicking up her speed to bring her alongside him, then dashing past him at the starting point.

He toyed with her for the first few minutes, matching her speed and accelerating when she did. Far too soon, she crested thirty kilometres. Heart climbing into her mouth, she pressed the remote to take her faster at the first buoy.

The wind whipped by, snatching at her breaths as the e-Foil rose higher in the water. Zings of excitement whistled through her, the sensation of the superior machine cutting through the water, almost addictive.

Only to be dashed when Jario easily zipped past her, fearless and supremely confident, his loose-limbed grace as he taunted her with weaving instead of straight lines making her teeth grit.

Willow increased her speed, her heart hammering when she closed the gap between them, reminding herself why she was doing this.

A make or break with the only parent whose indifference, lies and apathy might hurt but whom her heart insisted might be worth saving.

She willed the nerves away and concentrated on keeping herself stable as she went up another notch, secretly thrilled when the machine responded with barely a ripple. Confidence growing, she dared to add another kilometre, smiling wide when Jario glanced over his shoulder and scowled to find her so close.

Whether it was her smile or the open challenge within it that caused it, his momentary distraction turned out to be her ultimate advantage.

Willow spotted the incoming rogue wave before he did and flicked up her speed so the lip of her board rose higher in the water, easily cresting over the strong current when it hit a few seconds later.

Jario didn't have time to adjust.

The wave slammed underneath his board. He wobbled. By the time he deftly adjusted his stance, Willow had shot past him. His tight, frustrated growl made her smile wider, and despite the force of his will pressing down on her as the buoys marking the finish line beckoned, she held her nerve.

She won by half the length of her board, the pump of adrenaline dragging a whoop of relief from her. The young crew member she recognised from the café smiled and winked as she passed him.

She lowered her speed to a more comfortable level and redirected the board towards the yacht, intensely aware of Jario's gaze.

'Pleased with yourself?' he asked silkily, his voice so deceptively soft a shiver raced over her exposed skin.

With any other competitor, she'd have laughed outright and cracked a joke. But the man who raked his sodden hair back and speared her with a narrow-eyed mixture of irritation and disbelief wasn't the kind to respond well to jokes, especially on a game he'd arrogantly assumed he'd win.

Still, she would not be cowed. 'A win is a win. So yes, I'm pleased.'

With a rough grunt, he headed for the swim deck.

She followed at a slower pace, her skin tingling when, after grabbing a towel, Jario turned to her. And as much as she hated herself for it, Willow couldn't stop her gaze flicking over his deliciously masculine form, to the wet trunks moulding his trim hips and strong thighs.

Cursing her body's reaction, but knowing she couldn't stay in the water forever, she climbed the steps to join him on the deck, quickly snatching up a towel to cover the tell-tale peaks of her nipples.

'I hope you're going to honour our agreement.' She said it mostly to keep herself grounded, to remind herself why ogling him should be low on, or hell, *shouldn't* feature on, her to-do list at all.

For an eternity, he didn't answer, his movements brusque as he towelled his torso and fine-haired legs. Tossing the towel aside, he rasped, 'Let's go inside. I'm not doing this here.'

After towelling off, Willow followed him into one of the many private lounges. Plush camelhair sofas, cashmere throws, breathtaking rugs and three entertainment and liquor stations coaxed rest and relaxation. But neither of them felt any inclination to take advantage of the comforts.

Jario marched to the nearest drinks cabinet and poured himself a stiff drink. Just seeing the tension gripping him fuelled her own tension.

Okay, enough of this.

'Are you annoyed with me because you lost or because you bet something you obviously value on a stupid game?'

He slammed the glass down and spun to face her. Willow sensed she'd shocked him with her blatant observation. That not many people dared speak this way to Jario Tagarro.

'Watch it, *querida.*' He confirmed her theory.

Perhaps she should've heeded the warning, but flushed with

scooping triumph from the jaws of defeat, she couldn't curb her response. 'Why should I when you obviously don't?'

His nostrils flared wide, his eyebrows clamping into a thunderous frown. 'If you think baiting me is a good way to get what you want, you're ridiculously mistaken.'

'So far, nothing indicates I'll get what I want. You keep slithering away from telling me what I want to know. I did some research on you, you know. Everyone thinks you're some honourable man.' She laughed. 'I guess you should be commended for pulling the wool over their eyes, right? Because so far, I've seen nothing but a man who likes to throw his weight around just as fast as he throws axes in the middle of the night. And when that doesn't intimidate enough, he growls and plays games just for kicks. You're no better than my—' Her vocal cords seized when she realised she'd been about to compare him to her father. To David, even?

But that same instinct that shrieked at her when it came to the other two men who'd hurt and betrayed her wasn't sounding now.

So she swallowed it down as he stepped up to her, his eyes ablaze. 'You really enjoy playing with fire, don't you?'

'No, I don't!' She punctuated her words by poking a finger at his hard chest, then immediately regretted her action when electricity zapped down her palm and spread through her body. 'You think I want to be here? I have a life waiting for me, you know. Responsibilities that don't include scrubbing your decks or folding your stupid socks. Answering my calls or emails would've saved us both this…this circus. Instead, this is what you've driven me to, you bastard!'

'Oh, yes? Like you've driven me to this?' The incensed query arrived right before demanding fingers spiked into her damp hair, clamping down hard to drive her head up to meet his.

Jario's lips seared hers in a kiss so fiery, Willow's breath punched clean out of her lungs. The sizzling kinetic force made her surge up onto her toes, a long moan leaving her throat as sweet, decadent sensation pummelled her.

The *yes, yes, yes* trilling at the back of her mind laid bare the naked truth that she—*they'd*—been moving inexorably towards this. That the first night in the axe den had ignited the spark for this explosion. But never in her wildest dreams had she expected the spectacle of it would be this…*seismic*.

The lips moulding hers, the tongue coaxing entry, the hand clasping the back of her head, the other on her hip, holding her tight, all coalesced into a blinding, *thrilling* magic that inflamed every cell of her body.

Whether she took the step back or he stepped forward, Willow would never know. Yet, between one second and another, she was pressed against the wall, caught between one immovable object and a towering pillar of magnificent Latin male intent on delivering ferocious magic to her unsuspecting system. Magic she *yearned* for.

She shuddered as the skin on hot skin contact reminded her of their scantily clad bodies. How indecently delicious it felt to be pressed against him like this. She muted the cautionary voice and raised her arms, mirrored his movements by spearing fingers into his hair just as his tongue swept into her mouth.

The hand on her hip tightened, his thumb pressing into her bone, drawing another head-to-toe shiver. She hadn't even thought it possible to awaken an erogenous zone this way. Too quickly, the caress changed course to her bottom, squeezing her firm flesh as he groaned thickly.

'Santo infierno.'

He cursed against her mouth and bit her bottom lip right before he plunged back in, boldly inviting her tongue to play with his, his body pressing her harder into the wall until she couldn't mistake the untamed evidence of his arousal against her belly.

Dear God.

Had any previous kiss, including David's, felt like this?

No. *Absolutely not.*

Willow was at once chagrined that she hadn't known the true meaning of a good…hell, *great* kiss until now and exhilarated she was experiencing it. Even if it was delivered by the devil himself.

Even if…? Oh… *Oh, God.* What the hell was she doing?

With a strangled yelp she pushed against his shoulders.

He stepped back, his chest rising and falling in an elevated rhythm that was still maddeningly slow compared to her heaving one.

'This isn't… I'm not going to sleep with you if that's what…' She shook her head to clear her lust-addled thoughts.

One eyebrow cocked. 'You don't sound sure about that,' he said.

'I am. One hundred percent. Y-you're not even my type.'

He laughed. Deep and just the right amount of rough to evoke dangerous, erotic thoughts that reignited flames barely banked.

A shadow flitted across his features. His eyes hardened, before trailing down her body.

She didn't need to follow his gaze to know what he saw. Aching breasts with nipples standing to attention, making her wonder if she'd lost her mind by depriving them of the sweet torture they craved. A moan was furiously flattened in her throat as she prayed for the hard throbbing between her legs to cease.

'Tell that to your body, *mi precioso.*'

She pried herself from the wall she would forever associate with the most wanton act of her life to date, and crossed her arms over her chest. 'It's just a chemical reaction, which I stopped because I came to my senses. Let's not blow anything out of proportion. I'd rather crawl over hot lava than let you touch me again.'

He sucked in a slow breath and did the opposite of what

she'd expected. He smiled. Genuine mirth, dissolving the fearsome expression and causing her heart to lurch, her jaw to gape, before she rapidly resisted the betraying action. Because evidently, a smiling Jario was *transformative.*

He didn't quit being dark and formidable. But when brooding gave way to glinting eyes and heart-stopping, softer lips, he was lethally compelling…*addictive* to watch. With the very dangerous side effect of yearning to keep that experiencing it.

'Fighting words. I look forward to watching you take them back with the dirtiest apology I can conjure up.'

She groaned inwardly and shook herself free of this need to keep throwing gauntlets at him. She couldn't remain at this crossroads of her life forever, kissing, challenging and prevaricating with the very man who held the key to swinging it one way or the other. 'My question.' She blurted it out, the prompt far overdue.

His smile faded so swiftly that if her heart hadn't still been racing wildly, she would've doubted it'd ever happened.

But she didn't allow that to deflect her.

Not even when he visibly gritted his teeth and said, 'Ask it.'

'Why are you hell-bent on destroying my father?' she demanded in a heartbeat, her voice low but firm enough for him to hear it.

A single step brought him back to her, his marble-hard frame filling her vision as he leaned close, intent on her not missing a syllable of his answer. 'Because he was directly responsible for the death of mine.'

'You can't just walk away after that!'

Her father was deeply flawed, prone to exaggeration, outright lies and riddled with an overblown ego. But he wasn't a *murderer.*

Horror and disbelief speckled her frantic words. Admittedly, his answer had frozen her solid for several seconds until the knowledge that he didn't intend to elaborate—dear God, was he seriously not going to?—sent her after him. The buzzing in her head grew louder as Jario continued to ignore her.

She shot past him, then pivoted to stop directly in his path. 'I'm talking to you!'

He attempted to freeze her out with his clinically detached stare but Willow saw beneath it to the faded pallor and the shadows leaping in his eyes. It struck her that she'd forced his hand by insisting he reopen this particular can. But…hadn't he provoked this outcome by ignoring her initial attempts at contacting him?

'Jario—'

She gasped as he seized her waist, picked her up and set her aside and carried on walking.

'The agreement was one question. I've answered it.'

'You're kidding me, right?'

His ominous silence and rigid, unbroken stride said he was not. Whether by design or pure coincidence, one of his security guards strolled into the hall. A nod from Jario, and the burly guard was blocking her way.

Heart dropping, Willow forced herself to stop before she collided with the meat mountain. 'What are you doing? Wait! Jar—Mr Tagarro!'

'Miss, your break is over, I believe?'

The combination of the game, the kiss and the shocking revelation leached the fight from her. She sagged against the wall, battling frustrated tears.

She didn't allow them to fall.

The last thing she'd do was give that insufferable man the satisfaction. Even if his accusation triggered memories of her father's return from that business trip a changed man, with the rabid need to succeed and the demons that had chased him into the bottle.

Was he? Could…?

No!

The moment she finished her last task from Ripley—a surprisingly easy one of collating RSVPs for an upcoming dinner party on the yacht—she tracked Jario down to the topmost deck.

He was lounging on a sofa, a tablet balanced on one knee, the cognac he favoured in one hand.

'What you did before was cruel,' she shot out, the turbulent feelings she'd bottled up for hours spilling free.

She searched his face, desperate for a sign that it was all a terrible hoax. He stared back, his gaze flat and unresponsive.

'I'm certain you don't have the first clue what true cruelty looks like,' he drawled, before returning to his tablet.

Her insides shook at the absolute conviction in his voice but she pressed on. She couldn't afford not to. 'It's not true. It can't be,' she murmured.

'You think I would lie about something like that?' His accent had thickened, the soft, deadly reply almost melodic.

'I don't know! But I need more.'

A flash of bleakness was quickly replaced by implacable censure. 'You're under the misapprehension that I'm the one who owes you an explanation.'

'But I'm stuck here—'

'Through no one's fault but your own.'

'I'm aware. Trust me if I could get off this boat, I would.'

'Are things not going your way, then, Willow? Tell me, what would you do if you were at home right now? Confront the father who hasn't had the guts to own up to his actions in decades?'

Her belly flipped over. 'Is that how long you've planned this?' Her voice was a ravaged echo.

He stared back for an age, then his gaze swept away to the side. It was clear as day that he hadn't meant to reveal that.

'When?' she asked shakily.

The eyes that snapped to hers were even bleaker, cold and unfeeling, the silent confirmation sending chills through her.

'I'm not going to stop.' She felt like it needed stressing again, both for herself and for him.

In the time between his shocking announcement and now, she'd contemplated retreat, salvaging her sanity and heart because if what he'd said was true, then she feared for her already fragile relationship with her father.

But more and more, those instincts insisted there was another, less soul-destroying explanation. That the father he'd lost—and from everything she'd observed about Jario, from the very name of his yacht to the man plagued with demons, she knew at least that was true—had perished in some other way than the stark one he'd stated.

Please...let that be so.

Moments turned into minutes, each one constricting her chest until she couldn't breathe.

'It happened when I was fifteen years old. And before you think to assign some reasonable doubt explanation to ease your mind, know that I was present. That I saw the whole thing unfold before my eyes. And that I'm entirely justified in blaming your father for what he did.'

Dread surged through her. She yearned to label him a liar, but the raw, undisguised anguish—and the fact that she was sadly well versed in reading liars—knocked any intention sideways.

Which meant…

Her thought stalled, the alternative too awful to bear. 'There must be—'

Livid eyes dared her to speak her doubts aloud. She clamped her lips shut, letting the words shrivel and die.

Several heartbeats later, his gaze flicked past her. She turned to see the bodyguard mounting the steps, his eyes fixed on her. Her dismissal couldn't have been clearer.

'You seem to think you can have unfettered access to me whenever you please. You can leave of your own accord, or I can have you escorted to your quarters.'

'That won't be necessary.' She may not have the full picture still, but what she'd learned required desperate, much-needed regroup mode.

'Good,' he murmured, as if she'd finished discussing the wine list.

Then he calmly went back to his tablet.

'Can I get you anything else, sir?' Ripley asked.

Jario carefully set down his fork. He had a mile-long list he could recite to his hovering assistant of the many things he desired in life.

Three days had passed since that incident in his salon, yet his insides continued to churn. He'd been forced to relive memories buried just beneath the surface, where he wouldn't normally have to confront it every day. Only when he had to deal with destroying his enemy.

But a few hours with her and his hell had tripled. Even the scant sleep he'd resigned himself to was now a figment of his imagination.

Consciously relaxing his jaw, he shook his head. 'No, that will be all.'

He wanted to ask where she was, what she was doing, but he already knew. Another unwanted thing she'd cursed him with, besides that kiss he couldn't stop reliving, was a rabid need to know her whereabouts at all times. So he knew she'd retreated to her cabin half an hour ago after a solitary dinner in the crew kitchen.

He launched himself away from the table, his barely touched meal forgotten as he strode over to the liquor cabinet.

How long can you keep this up? Pretend you haven't... missed her presence these last three days?

The mocking voice in his head riled him further until he felt as if his skin was turning inside out.

Enough.

Setting down his untouched drink, he headed for the pool.

The temptation to go for a swim in the deep, dark ocean, let the obsidian waves wash his bitterness away, was strong, but the depths of the Pacific wasn't the place to test the elements while exhaustion and insomnia sapped his reserves.

So his pool it was.

Shoving off his jogging bottoms, he activated the artificial wave that powered the pool's current.

Turning up the setting for a more challenging workout, he walked to the edge of the fifty-foot pool, and dived in. Perhaps it was in the third minute or the thirtieth, but the image he'd been trying for three days to shut off rose in his mind again.

That dreaded flash of pity he'd seen on her face.

Shock and disbelief had followed but the pity was what tightened his chest. He didn't need it. So why couldn't he get it out of his damn mind? Why, additionally, did the softening in her features affect him so *intensely*?

Jario swam harder. Faster. Determined to drive the unnerving sensations away once and for all. And when he rose out of the pool much later, his muscles soaked in weariness, he was at least glad that he was on the point of exhaustion.

On feet that didn't feel quite steady, he entered his steam room.

Only for his every effort to shatter when the steam parted momentarily and he saw her perched in one corner, her knees drawn up to her chest.

Por el amor de Dios.

She didn't respond to his muttered curse, but he felt her eyes on him, watching. He prowled closer, every sense daring her to give him that look one more time. But the one she sent him was devoid of pity, instead brimming with awareness and defiance.

'Are you this insubordinate in your everyday job?'

Unbridled pride mingled with concern and regret flashed across her face, reluctantly reminding him of how distressed she'd been over losing Chatterton's employees.

'Actually, I excel at my job, and I plan to maintain my zero-complaints level for however long I have it,' she stated with a curiously solemn tone that spiked unease through him. 'Besides, I think one perk of this job allows me use of the gym and relaxation area, doesn't it?'

He'd wasted enough unnerving emotions on this woman. 'So this isn't just a fun exercise in pushing my buttons?'

For a stretch, she didn't answer. When she raked her fingers through her hair, he saw subdued weariness on her face. Did it make him feel better?

Infinitesimally.

'No.' Resignation tinged her tone. 'Believe me, that's the last thing I want.'

'And yet, here you are, disturbing my peace again.'

'Peace?' She scoffed lightly. 'Are you sure about that?

He gritted his teeth. 'What are you doing here, Willow?'

'You dropped a bombshell that's given me the same sleepless nights I'm sure you're experiencing. I thought you might be somewhere else, maybe throwing axes, so I came here.' She lowered her legs from where she tucked them against her body and rose.

'Where are you going?'

She raised an eyebrow. 'Leaving. Isn't that what you want?' The hint of challenge sparked to life. And yes, he much preferred that to her subjugation.

Turning away from her after one hunger-stoking glimpse of the white-bikini-clad body, Jario sat down on the bench. 'You're already here. It's a little too late to flounce off.'

She sighed, but sat back down, her long legs far too close for comfort. But he was damned if he'd show it. She'd upset his equilibrium enough. Ordering her out of his sight would only prove her power over him.

He sucked in a breath, his senses jolting at the pleasurable scent that teased his nostrils. '*Dios*, what's that smell?'

'Oh, it's lemongrass. It's meant to have relaxing properties.' A tiny green bottle appeared in front of his face. 'Would you like some?'

'No.' The word was a forced countermand to the *yes* his brain instantly leapt at.

Her hand remained extended for several seconds before she withdrew it. 'Look, I've got the message, okay? You don't want me here, I get it. I told you I won't do this forever. We arrive in Bali in a few days. Then I'm leaving. We don't have to see each other again.'

Something hard and entirely disagreeable lodged in his churning gut. She was granting his wish—her off his yacht and out of his sight. Yet, the reality of it made him angrier?

'Good,' he replied anyway. 'You're saving me the effort of firing you.'

The soft gasp melted into the steam, then silence wrapped around them.

'So you've decided to go and confront your father after all?' he asked after tense minutes.

Dread and anguish chased over her face. 'What does it matter to you?'

'It doesn't,' he said, ignoring the muscle ticking in his jaw.

Silence reigned for longer in the hazy little box, and he found himself staring, itching for insight into her feelings. When he couldn't, frustration bit through him.

'Yes, I'll ask my father when I get back.'

'And if he doesn't admit it?' he demanded, his voice gruff to his own ears.

She tensed and tried to hide the next flash of distress. 'My father isn't perfect by a long stretch. But… I need to hear what you say he did from him. It's too…dreadful for me to just…' She paused, shook her head.

The disconcerting sensation intensified. She was returning to a father who didn't deserve her devotion or naïve belief that he was a good man. The man who deserved nothing but the worst punishment.

But as much as he wanted to despise her for it, he couldn't quite bring himself to. She might be misguided in her loyalty but he couldn't lump her into her father's sins. Which left him where, exactly?

Let her off his boat in Bali and be done with it? Why did that idea dig spikes into his skin?

'Jario.' Her voice was soft, not pleading, but slightly questioning.

'What?' Had she moved closer?

'Whatever happened, I'm sorry.'

'No.'

'What do you mean, no?'

'I mean you don't get to have the upper hand.'

She gave a soft exhale that absolutely made him feel worse about this whole situation. 'I wasn't apologising for myself, or even my father.' The clench of anger when she mentioned her father curiously soothed him. 'I was expressing sympathy that such a horrific thing happened to you at all.'

A roaring started in his ears, filling him with emotion he didn't need or want.

Dear God. He needed to get some sleep desperately. Or barring that, some distance. Hell, if he could have, he would've left his home for the first time in six years.

But why did *he* have to?

Thoughts batting against his brain, he shoved his wrists into his gritty eyes, the beginnings of a growl working its way up from his throat. Lost in his head, he didn't realise he'd moved until his shoulder bumped hers. His muscles clenched, but for the life of him he couldn't move away.

After a tense moment, she started to rise again.

She reached for the door before a visceral reaction caused him to mutter, 'Stay.'

She paused. 'If I do, it'll be on condition that I'm officially off punch-bag duties.'

He shook his head, unsure why her defiance made him feel less tormented. 'You're infuriating. And you're also fired.'

Another soft scoff. 'That just saves me quitting. Also saves me from burning your stupid socks.'

A fizz of amusement threatened to lighten his mood. 'Then perhaps you should leave.'

'I'll be gone soon enough.'

The breath he took next was shaking, his muscles quivering under the weight bearing down on him. He rolled his shoulders, seeking elusive relief.

'What's wrong?' she muttered.

He laughed under his breath. 'Admitting flaws isn't in my nature, *querida*.'

'But saying that means you have them, so, you're admitting them anyway.'

Her hand rose, hovered in the air for a moment, then dropped.

His belly hollowed. 'You have something to offer?'

'Not without an explicit request,' she replied, that muted distress making another appearance. 'If you want my help, ask for it.'

'What makes you think I want—'

Her fingers dug into his muscles, prodding the hard knots beneath his skin. The growl died, then was reborn into a groan he bit back as his flesh loosened. But just as abruptly, she stopped and retreated.

'Ask for it, Jario. Clarity is important to me.'

He clenched his jaw, his senses jumping faster than he could contain them. Eventually, the words tore free from his essence. *'Por favor.'* He wasn't entirely sure why he said it in his father tongue. And no, he wasn't going to examine it right now.

Still, she hesitated, perhaps even regretting the offer.

But finally, she shifted closer, and with both hands, went to work on his muscles, the scent of lemongrass much stronger than before. It washed over him, and Jario's eyes drifted shut.

In silence, she worked her way down his back to his waist and then up again. When she stepped down and went to the door, he tensed, thoughts of her leaving sending disappointment and desolation ploughing through him. Before he could speak, she cleared her throat.

'This will work better if you're lying down.'

Again, her voice was soft, devoid of defiance or pity. He found himself glad for the absence of both. Found himself welcoming this small sliver of soothing versus strife.

Of soft hands versus the grind of demon's teeth.

It was ill advised in the extreme.

Yet, he rose off the bench when she opened the door to the steam room.

And followed her.

CHAPTER FIVE

IN PROPER LIGHTING Jario saw her bikini-clad body, full and ripe and weakening his already battered senses. It occurred to him that he was risking even more. That perhaps she'd seen a hint of weakness she intended to exploit. Yet, thoughts of self-preservation gave way to a rare benefit-of-the-doubt-giving as he trailed after her into the nearest living room.

That and her magic hands.

She turned towards him. 'Sit.'

He frowned at the order, and yet he moved to where she indicated, the lounge seat overlooking the night-shrouded view. 'This means nothing. You're still fired.'

The smallest smile curved her lips. 'I know. Take this as thanks for not throwing me overboard the first night.'

The last crumb of common sense remaining said this was a mistake, but he couldn't have stopped himself if he'd tried. Adjusting his towel around his waist, he stretched out on the lounger.

His pulse leapt as her hands glided over his back and neck once more, unravelling knots so effectively, another groan built up in his chest. Tensing, Jario forced it into a grunt.

'You've done this before.'

Her fingers paused for the tightest second before continuing. 'Yes, but not in a while.'

Unwelcome sensations blasted through him, surprising him when he recognised it as jealousy. 'Explain,' he said before he could stop himself.

A throb of silence passed before she expelled a soft breath. 'My mother taught me when I was a teenager. She was always hobby hopping. She got into Thai massage for a whole nine months before she jumped onto miniature pig breeding.'

Perhaps it was the exhaustion blocking the resentment from flowing through him, reminding him that his other parent was near enough as out of reach as his father. But he couldn't add his mother and her problems into the bonfire of his challenges right now.

Not when his enemy's daughter's hands were creating disarming magic, pushing back the teeming chaos with one stroke. Then another.

'She taught you well,' he admitted.

Again, the pause was small. But he felt it. Dragging open eyes gone drowsy, he sneaked a glance. Saw her face set in anguished lines, the corners of her sinfully tempting mouth turned down. She was fully concentrating on her task, not realising her expression was giving her away.

He should've shut his eyes then, blocked out whatever was going on with her and just allowed this curious scene to play out while he regained his weakening control.

'What is it?' Seriously. What was wrong with him?

Her head jerked up, her wide eyes catching his. Her lips firmed. Then with another wary glance, she dug her fingers into the small of his back.

His muted groan filled the room as she answered.

'It was one of the last things she taught me before she left.'

'Left?'

She half nodded. 'She packed her bags one afternoon and announced she was leaving my father for another man.'

One more thing Chatterton had destroyed? Jario should've found vindication in that knowledge. But all he could summon was a flare of bitterness before it dissipated, leaving behind a perplexing flash of sympathy. One he attempted to kill immediately and when it wouldn't die, he shoved it away to tackle later.

'Why?'

Pain darted across her face and again her mouth thinned as if she wanted to hold the words in. Her gaze fixed on her moving hands. 'There'd been a strain between them for years. Ever since…he returned from a business trip.'

Jario tensed at the sharp tug in his chest.

Dios, were his defences so weakened that he was concerned for her suffering? He closed his eyes to shut off the feeling. Only to open them three seconds later, in time to see a deeper pain etch into her features.

'It worsened. They started rowing. A lot. They were close before…whatever happened occurred. He started drinking heavily, keeping things from her…from us, and she…sought attention elsewhere.'

'And you? How did that affect you?' Somewhere deep inside him, that kernel of unwelcome concern grew larger.

She shrugged. 'I fell through the cracks caused by the fractures, I guess.' The flippant answer didn't ring true.

But he couldn't summon the energy to gloat. Not when his senses had gone hyper-alert. 'Did you ever wonder what had triggered the change?' he asked, even though he didn't need to. They both knew.

Paul Chatterton had returned home from cruelly betraying his partner and partner's child and hadn't quite been able to pick up the pieces of his life. Had the cosmos sought to right the wrong for him?

Not thoroughly enough. If life was fair, his father would still be here.

She exhaled. 'I assume that business trip was the one involving your father?'

'Sí.' The confirmation seared him to the soul.

And in that moment, he grudgingly accepted that while it'd appeased him for a while to visit her father's punishment on her, it now left him hollow and unsatisfied. *Because she'd suffered, too?*

'Do you want me to stop?'

Did he want her to leave? To dwell on this new detail, dissect it until he was brimming with more grief and bitterness? When he'd tasted the absence of it with her presence and her touch?

'No. Stay. Continue. If you want,' he added gruffly.

A minute passed. She resumed her massage. And something deeply soothing settled over his senses.

Dios.

'Anyway, I came home from violin lessons one day to find my mother on the driveway, about to leave with another man.'

Her fingers slowed halfway up his back and he wanted to command she keep going. But different words formed. 'She left without you?'

He caught her nod. 'She remarried and moved to New York. She promised I could visit her when she settled. She never called. And eventually, I realised she never would.' Her eyes drifted up to meet his. 'As for my father, his drinking got heavier.'

Jario held her gaze, waiting for the predictable plea on her father's behalf. Something hard jolted inside him when he realised it wasn't coming. That not once this evening had she demanded more answers. That conversely, he'd spotted flashes of anger mingled with her own pain.

Sí it would be a betrayal of his father's memory to offer solace to the daughter of his enemy, and yet cruelty just for cruelty's sake left a bitter taste in his mouth. So he didn't gloat. And he said nothing as her hands moved again, skirting his buttocks to dig into his traps and quads, offering a kindness that baffled and disarmed. That drew longer, deeper breaths from him, slowly slackening the tightness in his chest and leaving a curious swell of peace he hadn't felt in a long time.

Until hands shook his shoulders once. Then again.

Jario turned over, eyes snapping open. 'What are you doing?'

Her bikini was now partly covered by a monogrammed dressing gown but he still smelled the lemongrass on her skin as she bent over him. Still caught glimpses of her delectable body through the opening.

'You fell asleep. I think you were having a bad dream,' she murmured, traces of that kindness she'd shown him softening her eyes.

The chest tightening returned in full force.

He wanted to say her probing gaze would find nothing. But wouldn't that be shutting the barn door after the horse had bolted? He'd already shown her a physically weakened Jario Tagarro. Displayed the lake of desolation and grief rushing beneath the surface.

And she hadn't taken advantage of it. She'd offered a helping hand.

Pushing that voice away, he startlingly realised something else.

Although the room mostly remained in shadow because of the position of the yacht, the sun was streaming through the farthest window. He jerked upright, alarmed at how refreshed he felt, despite the nightmare that had eventually disturbed him. 'How long was I asleep?'

'Six, maybe seven hours?'

Six...seven hours?

He exhaled sharply in shock. 'That's not—' He caught himself before he added *possible*, reluctant to draw even more questions. But the truth that he hadn't slept for seven hours since before that fateful, deadly trip to Colombia was unavoidable as he glanced at his watch, his mind churning.

She did this. She's responsible...

Even as Jario pushed those whispered thoughts away, he was catching her hand before she turned away from him. 'You're not leaving.' He wasn't entirely sure if he meant out of his living room or out of his life. Perhaps sleep hadn't offered the clarity he sought after all.

That sexy, challenging eyebrow rose. 'Why the hell not?'

Yes, this should be interesting, Jario.

He ignored the taunting voice, pushed it away in favour of the gut instinct that had made him billions in a shockingly short space of time. Then hardened his resolve. 'Because I'm not quite done with you.'

She faced him fully, the defiance firmly back in place. 'If you think I'm going to stick around to be used as a punch bag just so you—'

'I'll tell you what happened with your father.' The offer grated in his throat and he wished he could snatch it right back. But that brief moment of peace last night had felt…good. He wanted it back, for however long he could have it. Because ultimately, it wasn't sustainable. *Right?*

She inhaled sharply, a mixture of pain, anger and hope in her searching eyes. 'You will?'

His nod felt jerky. '*Sí*. But in my own time and on my terms.'

'What does that mean?'

'How much time do you have? I assume you're on vacation, which is why you could board a yacht heading for Bali without a second thought?'

She scoffed. 'Trust me, I had second, third and fourth thoughts.'

He remained silent.

'I'm overdue vacation, yes. But…'

Her hesitation riled him. 'But what?'

'But I also play the piano and violin,' she said eventually, pride flaring in her eyes and squaring her shoulders. 'I've been offered a place on the Mondia Symphony Orchestra as a violinist in the fall.'

Surprise spiked through him. 'And you signed up to be a deckhand?'

'As Ripley's assistant. I think we both know how I felt about scrubbing your deck.'

His gaze dropped to the hand he was still holding, turning it over with a frown and a spike of guilt. They didn't look the worse for wear for what he'd made her do. Hell, they were still soft…silky and firm…

He sucked in a breath, dragged his mind back to the relevant topic. 'That makes you free for how long?'

She eyed him warily. 'Two weeks, give or take.'

Jario ignored the kick in his chest and the heat prowling through him when her hand jerked within his. 'Good.'

The faintest tremble went through the fingers he held. 'You couldn't wait to get rid of me a few hours ago, and now you want me to stay? I'm not fond of mind games, Jario,' she said, triggering that need to drill into her reticence. Dismantle her bewilderment.

Because by tackling hers, he might better understand and defeat his own?

'You didn't have the decency to stay out of my way. So now we bargain.' The heady smell of lemongrass from her skin—from both their skins—heated his blood and made his mouth positively water.

Her lips parted in surprise, but she didn't tug herself free when he pulled her close. As the silence thickened between them, as their bodies reacted as they had from the first, from the insane chemical reaction their proximity created, his gaze dropped to the tightening nipples so very tantalising close to his mouth.

Hunger stalked through his veins, savage, more potent than he'd ever felt in his life. Sharpened by long months of abstention? Perhaps. But more than that, it was a need to conquer the unfamiliar threat she posed, this indescribable fixation he'd developed for her.

Letting her leave as she'd threatened would be the best option, but that need to win, to dominate this problem, wouldn't free him from its claws.

'If I stay, I'm not sleeping with you to get you to tell me what happened with my father.' Again, there was something behind her tone that spoke of past, deeper subtexts.

Something kicked again, then half settled, partially mollified he was getting what he wanted. 'Good. You'll come to my bed because your every sense screams at you to take me because you want me. But whether you do or not, you'll also use the time to convince me why I shouldn't destroy your father. You won't succeed, but at the very least he'll have two weeks' grace from my plans for him.'

Her gaze remained on his. Bold. Defiant. 'And if I refuse this bargain?'

The vibration in his body announced his response to that even before he spoke. 'Then you can pretend you quit instead of being fired and leave my yacht when we get to Bali and I'll forget you exist.'

Her eyes shadowed a little but she didn't back down. 'You think you can forget me that easily?'

He resented the trace of derision in her voice. But Jario couldn't deny that the riling turned him on even harder. He would tolerate it. For now. He'd never prized overeager bed partners. There was a certain thrill in the chase that made eventual capitulation that much sweeter.

And while he didn't want her to leave for reasons that were still mystifying, he wasn't about to give up this new game he'd become curiously invested in.

Releasing her hand, he transferred his hands to her hips, groaning inwardly at how her soft, firm skin warmed beneath his fingers, almost smiling when she gave herself away by leaning just a fraction closer. Gliding upward, he tightened his hold on her waist, banding his hands until they touched, and his brain immediately threw up erotic images of just what he would do to her when she eventually capitulated.

Dios mio.

'The past three days have been evidence enough, no?' he taunted while skirting the glaring admission.

The unwelcome pang that invaded his chest when her eyes shadowed once more, he chose to ignore. He wasn't here to make Willow Chatterton feel better. Or comfortable.

She was here to extend this curious respite she induced—

He bit back a grunt as her fingers danced a little hesitantly over his shoulders, giving away that touch of inexperience. Then she surprised him by spearing those fingers into his hair, her touch a little tart as her fist clenched. His shaft thickened beneath the towel still tied around his waist.

'There's a world of difference between three days where I'm out of sight, and whatever you're planning for the next two weeks, Mr Tagarro. Anything can happen.'

Further images bombarded him and not just the carnal kind. He'd never tolerated guests on the *La Venganza* for more than a few days at a time. He preferred his own company. Craved the privacy and even after all these years, the distance from seeing happy families that reminded him of everything he'd lost.

The idea of having this woman on board the very vessel that proclaimed his intention to annihilate her father to the world should've been anathema to him as it'd been that first morning he'd learned her identity. And yet, the way she went toe to toe with him, those flashes of anguish and anger that had ignited a curious affinity…

Jario grudgingly admitted he was not ready to be done with it. *Yet.*

Because he was…lonely?

Diavolo, no.

He was merely taking a stimulating detour to his final destination.

Dragging her even closer, he trailed his nose over her midriff, circling her neat little navel. Smiling to himself when she gasped and her clenched fingers shook. Gratified when she *still* didn't pull away. He suspected the scent of lemongrass would haunt him after he'd finished dealing with her. Lemongrass and sexy woman. He inhaled her deep into his lungs and her belly muscles quivered delightfully. Sexy *responsive* woman.

It struck him abstractedly—because a wave of intoxication

was washing over him—that she could very well derail his goals. Far more than she already had.

Then send her away in Bali.

Reluctantly unclenching his fingers from her delicious skin, he set her aside and forced himself to rise, his painful erection demanding satisfaction he didn't intend to provide as he sauntered to the door. 'Indeed. Which is why you should think carefully before you give me your decision. Take the day off. Find me at seven p.m. tonight and give me your answer.'

Willow stepped beneath the shower despite a heavy reluctance to wash off the events of last night and this morning. It felt like she would lose something more vital than the scent of lemongrass.

Something had changed in the past twelve hours. Her burning need for answers had diminished, while in direct proportion her anguished fury had grown towards her father. Because deep down, she knew he bore the blame, if not for all, then for some of what had happened to Jario and his father.

She lowered her head as the shower jets pummelled her.

Had she crossed the Rubicon where her relationship with her father was concerned by accepting the Mondia violinist position ten minutes ago?

Or was it to do with Jario himself?

Learning that despite seeking his revenge, he hadn't callously walked away from the people who'd been within the direct fallout of his action had touched her. It'd been far more than her own father had done.

Or perhaps because he hadn't gloated when she'd told him about her broken family? Maybe it was something as simple as offering him a means of solace and seeing its effect on the formidable man most cowered before.

Whatever the true cause, she welcomed—temporarily, she knew—the muting of her rioting emotions where her father was concerned. She knew she'd have to deal with it later. Just as she welcomed the easing of the intense turbulence between her and Jario. Hell, she borderline understood him now, or as much as she could dare to grasp the grief and anguish driving him.

Although a different sort of intensity had taken the place of the old.

She would never make the mistake of calling him soft because that would be likening a jungle predator to a cuddly house pet.

And yet…she'd felt safe enough to tamp down her reservation and ease the weariness and the shadows in his eyes and body.

More, she'd stayed at his side while he slept—and no, the rabid need to see him rest wasn't something she intended to contemplate yet—and woke him when bad dreams had triggered those awful, anguished sounds.

She'd barely been able to stop herself from blurting 'yes' when he'd offered a new bargain, not because her first thought had been about her primary reason for being here but because agreeing meant remaining on board.

With him.

Willow squeezed her eyes shut, a ragged moan of confused excitement breaking free, thankfully washed away by the streaming water. But the sensations stalking through her wouldn't be rinsed free, bypassing every warning from her brain.

She was treading a dangerous path.

Willow recognised that. And yes, she would be tracking him down come 7 p.m. Because more than wanting to uncover the whole story—and most likely have her fears confirmed—she also wanted *more.*

She wanted Jario Tagarro.

Her breath shuddered out as the admission settled deep into her bones.

That thing he'd done with his nose over her belly still made her nipples hard and her core hot just thinking about it.

But she also wanted to explore the complex layers beneath his cool facade. Why? Was there a psychological explanation to this fascination?

Or was it something as simple as intense chemistry pulling her to the most intriguing man she'd ever met?

Gritting her teeth at the chaotic thoughts, she wrenched off the faucet and stepped out.

Molly, her cabin mate, was rarely around, which thankfully left Willow with the space to herself most times.

Dressed in jeans shorts and a white cotton top, she padded barefoot into the crew living area. After making herself a coffee and helping herself to a croissant, she was heading for the dining table when Rebecca walked in.

The few times they'd run into each other since the incident in Jario's office, Rebecca had been coolly neutral.

Clearing her throat, Willow took the bull by the horns. 'I owe you an apology.'

Rebecca searched Willow's gaze for a second, then shrugged. 'Whatever your reasons for wanting the job, you still worked harder than half of the guys on board.' She headed to the coffee machine. Once she'd filled her cup, she leaned against the counter. 'But I'm guessing I'll need to find your replacement?'

Willow grimaced. 'Yes. I'm sorry.'

After a moment's silence, Rebecca asked, 'Are you okay?'

Willow's fingers curled around her coffee cup, her muddled emotions swirling faster. 'Not entirely. But I hope it'll get better.'

Far too revealing words, plucked from the centre of the maelstrom within her, made her face heat up.

A flash of softness cut through her aloofness before Rebecca approached. 'Well, good luck. When you're ready to leave, come find me for your ticket home.'

When you're ready...

As the hours ticked by, Willow knew deep down that she wasn't ready yet. And that the decision she'd be making scared the hell out of her.

* * *

Her spaghetti-strap, thigh-length sundress was nowhere as stylish as the chicly dressed women she'd watched heading for his yacht back in Los Cabos… God, was it only a handful of days ago? But it was better than shorts and a tank top.

As her fingers lingered on her favourite lemongrass-based floral perfume, nerves attacked her before she pushed them away. Jario had the most beautiful, sophisticated women at his beck and call. Her choice of perfume wasn't going to turn his world upside down. Nor was he insecure in his manhood to accuse her of some sort of entrapment like David once had.

Hell, if anything, he was *too arrogant* in that department.

After spritzing the perfume at her pulse points, she applied a coat of lip gloss and left her cabin.

Climbing up from the lower decks, she realised she didn't know where to find Jario. On a yacht this size, she could easily waste fifteen minutes looking for him.

She was wondering the best way to find out when Dylan, the deckhand who'd refereed their e-Foil race, appeared.

'Good evening, Miss. Mr Tagarro will see you on the fifth deck.'

'Oh. Thanks. And it's Willow.'

He nodded politely. 'I can show you the quickest route if you want?'

At her nod, he led her to a sleek lift she hadn't spotted before. She knew why she'd needed the escort when he used a silver key card to activate it. When it slid open, he stepped back, ushered her in, then pressed the appropriate button. 'Enjoy your evening, Willow.'

He was gone before she could answer. And in the short ride up, all the nerves she'd tried desperately to suppress surged up with her.

Jario was standing tall and a solid six feet away when the doors slid open, giving her zero time to collect herself.

His gaze raked over her, as brooding and incisive as they'd

been the last time she saw him, when he'd held her captive between his thighs and awakened a hunger that hadn't abated despite her efforts to suppress it.

Don't think about that!

'What was that with Rebecca this afternoon?' he asked abruptly, but she caught a flash of something vaguely resembling concern in his eyes. 'Did something happen?'

Her eyebrows shot up. 'Something like what?'

His shrug was offhand. His fierce stare was anything but. 'Another allergic reaction?' He bit the words out like they offended him.

'No, but…how do you know? Are you watching me?'

His exhale was slow, heavy, like he was…relieved? The hard glance he slid her a moment later diluted the notion but didn't erode it altogether, making her heart race even faster.

'You're on my property, Willow. I'm well within my rights to do whatever I want.'

'Sure, but I thought you'd have better things to do than to watch me.' Why saying that sent hot tingles arrowing through her was a reaction she pushed to the back of her mind. Fairly unsuccessfully.

'I'm great at multitasking,' he said, his voice silky-smooth and devastating.

'One of those tasks isn't to fire her, I hope?'

His jaw gritted at her sharp tone. But he didn't answer immediately. He approached her, his loose-limbed strides belying the power and dynamism packed into his hard body.

The back of his knuckles drifted down one cheek, leaving a trail of delicious fire. 'Pretend all you want that outrage on Rebecca's behalf is the reason your cheeks are flushed and your body is reacting so…interestingly. We both know differently.'

'You can think what you want as long as you don't fire her. She's done nothing wrong.'

His gaze drilled into her for nerve-shredding seconds while they both acknowledged the subtext of their open conversation.

And when he answered, she knew better than to think she'd won some sort of battle, never mind the war. 'She's a valued member of my staff. She's not going anywhere.'

Relieved it was something she wouldn't have to add to her list of mounting problems, she murmured, 'Thank you.'

A glint lit his eyes then, but he turned away before she could deduce its meaning.

'Have you eaten dinner yet?' he asked, again taking her by surprise with his abrupt change of subject.

She wanted to rile him by asking if he didn't know the answer since he'd been watching her but she stopped herself, reminded of the less...aggrieved times they'd spent so far. Like when he'd taught her to throw the axe. Or in the moments before she'd won their race on the water three days ago. When she'd watched him sleep.

Glancing past him to the deck, she saw the dining table laid for two. 'No.' Her stomach had churned too hard all day to sustain an appetite.

Displeasure pursed his lips briefly before he threw over his shoulder, 'Then come.'

'I'd rather talk before we eat,' she said, knowing she couldn't stand another minute of the cyclone of baffling sensations inside her.

He paused next to an exquisitely carved dining chair. 'You find it a challenge to have a discussion at the dinner table? The chef has gone to a lot of trouble and apparently cooked some of your favourite dishes.'

Her eyes widened. 'He has?'

Another flicker of enigmatic expression. 'Indeed. You seem to create an impression wherever you go.'

He pulled out the chair, unwavering eyes drilling into hers.

Willow blew out an inner breath and joined him, his scent teasing her nostrils as he tucked her in. He leaned closc and she heard his slow inhale, but when she looked up he was straightening.

He sat perpendicular to her, the view of the setting sun streaked with oranges, pinks and mauves too spectacular not to take full advantage of. The climate had turned progressively sultry on their approach into Asia, and the breeze washing pleasantly over her bare skin eased one of the many knots inside her.

Caught between the dynamic man next to her and the magnificent view, she furiously attempted to focus on the latter.

'Wine?' He plucked a Chevalier-Montrachet Chardonnay from a Baccarat cut-glass ice bucket, and held it poised over her glass.

Her father's steep decline into alcohol dependence had made her wary of drinking around him. But he was a couple of thousand miles away.

And since she was taking a much-needed stance…

At her nod, he poured her a glass before his own. Then he reached over and lifted the silver cloche covering her dish. Willow's eyes widened, her mouth salivating instantly as the smells wafted over her.

'Oh, my God, that looks amazing.' The cheeseburger looked like no cheeseburger she'd ever seen. Yes, the prerequisite ingredients were there—meat, cheese, bun. But just by looking, she knew it was superior. For starters, the yacht only stocked prime Wagyu beef and she'd seen the chef mince it himself. Just as she knew the cheese and truffles were flown directly from superior vendors in Europe.

'I had the pickles placed on the side,' Jario stated, not bothering to hide his outraged disdain.

'Because you believe pickles don't belong on a burger?' she asked, fighting a smile as she tried not to reach too eagerly for the silver platter.

'Exactly so. Pickles shouldn't be allowed anywhere near prime beef, lobster and truffles.'

She'd resisted too hard, apparently, because with an air of impatience, he set the plate in front of her, then uncovered another bowl that held skinny golden fries, exactly the way she liked them. 'Eat.'

She ignored the disgruntled order, her revived appetite too keen to be offended. Reaching for the juicy stack, she took a bite and groaned as heavenly flavours exploded on her tongue. 'Oh…'

With her next mouthful, she snagged a slice of pickle with her fork and bit into it. The explosion of tartness combined with the richness of the burger and cheese was deeply delightful, dragging another groan. 'You don't know what you're missing.'

'*Gracias*, but I'll pass.' His bone-dry tone triggered amusement and she was smiling before remembering that this wasn't a social event. That she and this man weren't friends.

She froze when she saw his rapt, ferocious stare. 'Umm… something wrong?' she asked, after she swallowed.

His nostrils flared, his gaze remaining on her for several more seconds before he sat back and reached for his wineglass. 'Let's not invite indigestion by dwelling on things that are wrong.' He nudged his square chin at her plate. 'Continue.'

She was several more bites into her meal before he stopped staring and started his. Willow didn't want to notice his voracious appetite or the way his jaw moved as he ate. The way he cradled his wineglass, twirling it almost absentmindedly between his fingers before each sip.

But she did. And it affected her just as potently as everything else about this man. So it was almost a relief to be done eating. To drain her own glass and refuse a refill—because bold emotional stance was one thing, reckless tipsiness quite another—and rise from the table.

Her very skin on fire from the seismic sensations and wild anticipation unfurling through her veins, Willow headed for the railing overlooking the darkening waters.

The sea had almost swallowed the sun, leaving an awe-inspiring vista.

But it was nothing compared to the man watching her every move, whose fixation on her ignited wilder heat. She knew the moment he rose, his silent approach crackling the very air until she couldn't breathe without electricity vibrating along every stretch of her skin.

She'd expected him to join her, but he stopped just behind her. She didn't turn around. *Couldn't.* Her fingers curled around the railing, her breathing truncating as she heard him sip another mouthful of wine.

Just when she believed she'd expire from the insane rush of anticipation, one hand gripped the railing next to hers.

Close but not touching. A column of heat at her back.

'*Dios mio*, your scent is intoxicating,' he rumbled almost peevishly. As if admitting it annoyed the hell out of him. 'It drives me insane.'

Despite wanting to laugh, she bit her tongue, partly empathising. She wasn't so swept up in her stormy feelings about her father's lies and betrayal not to recognise that Jario was torn about any liaison with her.

The prospect of eventually ripping off the Band-Aid to examine her own feelings shook through her, congealing her insides.

Jario stepped closer, trailed his nose up her neck, lingering on the pulse at her throat. 'You're fired,' he murmured, almost conversationally.

Another bewildering mix of excitement and apprehension swelled within her. 'I'm aware.'

'Which means you're no longer allowed to stay in the crew quarters. I've had your things moved.'

Her eyes fixed on the churning water left in the wake of the powerful vessel, Willow tried not to react despite the stronger charge of emotion. 'Have you? And where am I going to sleep?'

He didn't answer immediately. She heard him take another sip of wine. 'All in good time. I believe you owe me an answer.'

The combination of light breeze from the front and heat

from his body made her light-headed. Or was it the power and effect of looming decision? 'And my answer determines where I sleep, does it?' Her voice was husky, heavy, pulsing emotion.

Several beats of silence passed. 'Perhaps. I haven't decided yet.'

The urge to face him, to gauge his emotions, pummelled her but some stronger instinct kept her from doing so. Because she needed to do this for herself, not be influenced by the hypnotic dynamism of the man standing behind her. Not to be swayed by the force of his willpower.

She'd already taken two life-changing steps today, accepted that there may be no salvaging the relationship with her father, and embraced her music. She could take a beat with the next one. Assess whether Jario wanted her for her instead of as a tool against her father.

Reassure herself that it would be worlds away from what she'd experienced with David.

Because it would be a simple, meaningless fling. Right?

'Answer me, Willow.' A bite of impatience in his voice accompanied the low rumble that echoed through her chest, then down through her body. 'Will you stay?'

'Yes. My answer is yes.'

CHAPTER SIX

THERE WAS A long inhalation, as if he was drawing her response directly into his soul. Then he leaned closer still. 'Again. And turn around and look at me this time, *querida*.'

The moment she did, he set his empty wineglass on the railing and braced his free hand on the other side of her, caging her in. Eyes the colour of the churning waters drilled into hers, then dropped to her mouth, willing her to repeat her words.

She licked her tingling lips, inhaling sharply when he groaned under his breath. The moment his eyes shot up to reconnect with hers, she repeated, 'Yes. I'll stay.'

'And?'

And as insane as this situation is... I want you. Badly.

She wisely kept those power-yielding words to herself. 'And whatever happens, happens. On terms we both agree. Including how long I stay.'

His eyes narrowed a fraction, digging behind those words for leverage, perhaps? She met his gaze boldly, even while her heart hammered.

'You will not rule me. Accept that.'

She snorted. 'As if.'

Faint amusement flashed in his eyes before gravity returned. 'But the same cannot be said for me. I crave control.'

His honesty snatched her breath. 'Thanks for telling me, but that doesn't mean I won't fight it when I need to. I'm no pushover.'

Another flash, this one of approval, lit up her insides. He relished that. Was perhaps even weighing how to test that control.

'Our time together will be interesting, if nothing else.' His gaze dropped to her mouth again, setting it tingling wildly all over again. He stepped back, gesturing towards the steps leading below deck. 'Come.' The command was thick and terse.

'Where are we going?'

'To show you your new sleeping quarters.'

'I can find it on my own, I'm sure.'

One eyebrow arched. 'Is that an objection or are you regretting that you may have bitten off more than you can chew?'

'It's neither.' Rather a stalling tactic because the need rampaging through her was frankly overwhelming. 'Just a fact,' she blurted out when he simply waited her out in silence.

A hint of amusement flashed again. 'Consider it a vested interest in ensuring you don't fall off a balcony or pass out somewhere until tomorrow at the very least.'

The urge to laugh with him, even at her own expense, struck again. And again, he seemed to remember himself, to kill his amusement a second later. Even look a touch bewildered by the display of humour.

That small defusing of tension drew her away from the railing. She joined him as he strode across the deck to the lift. He gestured her in, then followed. The space built for small groups immediately felt even smaller, Jario's masculine scent overwhelming her.

He in turn took another long breath, and recalling what he'd said about her scent, Willow angled her head to meet his blazing gaze.

Neither of them said a word as the lift reached the designated floor—*his*.

He caught her elbow to steer her right, towards his private suite. The roar in her ears almost drowned out the swarming butterflies in her belly.

She believed she'd settled her decision in her own mind but now the reality was rushing at her, she desperately needed a minute. To remind herself that Jario wasn't David. That—

She froze when Jario stopped halfway down the long hallway and nudged open a guest suite door.

Confusion battered her as she looked into the exquisitely decorated room. Unlike Jario's, it was softer, blending pastels with modern luxurious wood furniture, paintings and exquisite mouldings that wouldn't have been amiss in any bricks-and-mortar mega-mansion.

Through an open doorway across the room, she saw her meagre belongings, neatly folded on backlit shelves. She glanced back at him. His heated gaze swung from her face to the bed behind her.

His nostrils flared as he took a breath. 'Is it satisfactory?'

'More than,' she muttered, still battling confused disappointment. 'Thanks.'

He didn't respond.

Feeling supremely self-conscious, wanting more than anything to fling herself at him, Willow forced herself back one step. Then another.

Jario slowly raised his hands to the top of the door and braced his hands right there, sculpted biceps tensing as he gripped the solid wood. Fascinated, she stared at the riveting image he made, the stunning realisation that he was fighting the urge to step inside her room.

Because he wanted an explicit invitation?

Because unlike her father, his integrity and principles were unshakeable? It would've been easy for a man like him to take the seduction route, to use her clear attraction to him to his advantage, like David had, and especially considering who and what she represented.

The fact that he wasn't sent waves of respect and, yes, *gratitude*, sweeping through her. Making her attraction surge several notches higher. Making her stop, stare at him, words crowding her tongue.

Jario's fierce stare almost dared her to.

Only by sheer willpower and the last residues of common sense did she resist. 'Good night, then.'

She caught a flash of respect, jarring with his quickly curbed disappointment. After an age, his hands released the jamb, his exhale long and slow. He nodded curtly, turned on his heel and left.

Deflating, she shut the door and leaned back against it.

Faintly resenting him for mastering his control, she looked around.

Her beautiful bed looked lonely. And she cursed herself one more time as she undressed and crawled between the cold sheets.

She wanted to blame the motion of the vessel for her tossing and turning, but her inner voice mocked her excuse. The only reason for her restlessness was the absence of Jario Tagarro in her bed.

And as the seconds slowly ticked away, she admitted that the suffering she'd glimpsed on his face also unsettled her, that whatever was going on beneath his facade had somehow gained greater importance for her.

For now.

She gritted her teeth, wishing for one selfish moment she could push her emotions down deep where they wouldn't affect her. But for good or ill, they swelled, ever persistent.

And as ever, the image of her mother walking away, of staying away, because Willow hadn't quite been enough, replayed in her head.

With a frustrated grunt, Willow tossed back the sheets and slid out of bed. It was pitch-black outside her window, sunrise nowhere in sight. But she knew she wouldn't be able to sleep.

Almost on automatic, she padded to the door, a compulsion she couldn't deny pushing her forward. Just like it had last night when she'd ended up in the steam room, Willow wandered into the recreational area, her heart and breath and skin rousing with an innate awareness that she wasn't the only one awake and restless.

She found him in the axe room, just like on her first night here.

Clearly, he'd been at it for a while because his back glistened with sweat and his damp hair clung to his neck.

'Are you coming in or leaving?' He didn't turn around.

'That depends.'

'On?'

'Is what you're doing helping with whatever's bothering you?'

He stiffened, then shot her a warning look over his shoulder. 'You've picked the wrong time to amateur psychoanalyse me.'

'Is there a right time?'

His eyes flared with surprise at her snapback.

Then he sauntered towards her, axe in hand. Something about watching him wielding such a dangerous tool sent primal heat swirling through her. Willow was nowhere near willing to examine why the man staring at her with hooded eyes crackling with coiled energy excited her *this* much.

They surged towards one another a second after he tossed the tool aside, diving into a fevered feast of kissing that seared her soul.

'I want you in my bed,' he muttered against her mouth after ending the kiss. 'Against my every better judgement, I want to possess you, to be inside you so badly I can't think straight.'

Against...better judgement.

The words, far too reminiscent of David's, stopped her cold. Raising her hand, she pushed back from him, breaking the kiss with a decadent noise that further compounded her confusing feelings. 'Then you should stop. After all, only one of us deserves to burn in hell, right?'

His control gathering was mesmeric to watch. For long

moments he stared at her, then he shook his head, a touch of self-deprecation in the motion. 'Indeed.' One hand rose, traced down her flushed cheek. 'If only you didn't look like a damned delicious angel while doing so.'

Spikes of distress and unease stopped her insides from melting this time. Propelled her to take several steps back.

Made her turn and walk away.

But not before she saw surprise flare in his eyes at her retreat.

'Where are you going, *tesoro*?' he called after her. Faint amusement laced his tone but there was something else. *Hunger.*

Looking over her shoulder, she saw blazing eyes rushing over her body, unwavering in its intensity, making her acutely aware of every exposed inch, and even those parts that were covered but wanting.

It stirred up her roiling feelings, making her swallow before she could speak. 'Anywhere but here. You can return to your axe throwing.'

One corner of his mouth kicked up in fleeting amusement, which thrilled her far more than it should've. 'Are you sure?'

'Positive,' she snapped.

She shouldn't...*couldn't* care about the shadows lurking in his eyes. The fissures of pain, bitterness and torment fighting for supremacy that made her heart lurch, made her want to reach out, soothe him until they dissipated.

She *shouldn't* want to pour herself into the cracks of his pain, hold him together if even for a short time.

Make him hurt...less.

She had her own emotional baggage to be dealing with.

She was thankful for the strength in her legs as she hurried away, for the willpower to keep walking away as she wandered through the semi-dark stateroom. Her destination wasn't exactly clear but, in this moment, anything was better than remaining in Jario's unnerving presence.

Really? Anything?

The softly voiced challenge drew a shiver, a tiny self-preserving voice demanding to know why she wasn't retreating to the safety of the bedroom he'd visibly restrained himself from entering.

Was it because there was something decadent and deliciously illicit about their small-hours meetings? Something she would miss when she left?

She lost half a breath when a hollow opened up inside her at the thought. Yet another thing she pushed away.

On bare feet, she headed for the large salon she'd seen but not yet visited.

As with most areas on the yacht, automatic lights came on when she entered, but special spotlights were trained on the Wilh. Steinberg concert grand piano with gold-plated casters, hinges and feet, set on its own platform at the far right corner of the room. It was stunning and imposing enough to forget her roiling emotions for a moment.

Approaching, she perched on the dark purple velvet-covered bench, stingingly aware of the soft material brushing her bare thighs. Despite the mildly intimidating awareness that the superior piano she was about to play cost more than she'd earn in three years, the ivory and ebony keys gleaming invitingly settled her nerves. She'd been playing the same set of keys since she was seven years old.

And right now, she yearned for the soul soothing that music always provided.

Without conscious thought, she struck the first key, then smiled.

Chopin's Nocturnes was a little predictable perhaps, but she'd played it enough times that it came to her fingers easily enough. She fell into the soft notes with shuddering, almost tear-jerking relief, then transitioned into Giazotto's 'Adagio in G Minor,' followed by a few more of her favourites.

It was as she was ending Peter J. Malmsjö's 'Soft Caress' that she realised Jario was leaning in the doorway.

'You're very talented,' he observed softly.

She shrugged, furiously fighting against warmth pushing at her emotional firewalls.

'May I come in?'

'It's your yacht. Stay. Go. Wouldn't want you to do anything against your better judgement.' She grimaced at the bitterness she couldn't quite hide.

'Ave Maria.' That always lifted her spirits.

She launched into it as he made his decision, crossing the room to the liquor cabinet. His favourite cognac in hand, he reclined on the sofa, his stare even more brooding.

When the last haunting strains echoed, he rose again. She didn't see what he'd done until he walked over and held out the spritzer. 'Nightcap?'

She took shallow, careful breaths so she wouldn't greedily inhale his intoxicating scent. 'Peace offering or trying to get me drunk?'

A glint lit his eyes. 'I struck a nerve before.'

Her heart lurched. 'You think?' she replied, playing for time, searching his gaze to see if he knew the true depths of her unsettled emotions.

He raised the glass higher. She took it, her belly flip-flopping when his warm fingers brushed hers.

'Tell me.' His voice rumbled over her, and maybe it was because the music had done its job? She sipped her drink, set it down.

Returning her gaze to the piano, she found herself speaking.

'There's no subterfuge in music. It doesn't pretend to be one thing and deliver another. I'm not afraid to let it in because I know it won't hurt me. Not like…'

'Your father?'

She nodded. 'As you've probably guessed, he hasn't been

prolific with the truth. Just like with my mother.' She pursed her lips. 'And my ex.'

'I know what your mother did. But what did he do, this ex?' he asked, an edge in his voice.

Her shrug weighed heavily with bitter recollection. 'He worked at the company for a while as some hotshot marketing guru. He had big plans. Was forever trying to get my father to take bold risks. And… I know I should've trusted my instincts when I suspected he was using me to further his career, but I didn't. Not for six months while he told me my suspicions were all in my head.'

Jario's eyes narrowed lethally. 'I trust that you didn't tolerate such a thing for long?'

Her short laughter scraped her throat. 'Well, I guess finding him in bed with his ex and being told that, too, was my fault finally did the trick.'

He cursed under his breath. 'Tell me his name.'

Willow started at the feral tinge to his tone. Cursed the curl of warmth at his rage on her behalf. She really needed to stop melting every time he displayed his unique brand of care. She was in danger of growing addicted to it. She forced herself to wave him away. 'It's fine. He was the one person I took pleasure in letting go on Dad's behalf when the company started failing…' Her words drifted away at the reminder of who was responsible for that failing.

'And what I said about better judgement rankled?'

She nodded. 'He used to say things like that to me all the time. Like he was trying to find his better human self and I was holding him back from it.'

'You're aware that's the knee-jerk position of a loser, *sí*?'

His vehemence flared heat to her cheeks that she prayed he wouldn't notice as she shrugged and tucked a strand of hair behind her ear.

After a beat he continued. 'So you sought solace in music?'

She inhaled a calming breath. 'Yes, music has always been special to me.'

'You mentioned you also play the violin. How long have you been playing both?'

She glanced up and was relieved to see the shadows recede a fraction, intrigue replacing them.

He sauntered over and sprawled his towering frame on the sofa again, one hand cradling his cognac on his knee while his other arm lay along the back of the seat. Lights gleamed lovingly over his naked torso, sending further shafts of heated desire between her legs.

She dragged her gaze from the sexy sight he made and approached the piano, half wishing it was positioned so she wouldn't have to see him from the corner of her eye.

'Since I was seven. My goal was to join a symphony.'

'A dream you're on the cusp of achieving.'

She nodded, the pangs of her decision pricking her. 'Yes.'

'But?' She felt his gaze intensify on her.

She shrugged. 'It didn't come without its challenges.' In the form of her walking away from her father.

Jario's expression dimmed, but not out of anger. It was more of a sombre reflection of her words. Or perhaps how his own life had changed because of the past directly involving their fathers?

He watched her with hooded eyes, slowly lifting his glass to take a sip. Then he lowered it to rest on top of his six-pack and nodded at the piano. 'I'd love some more,' he said, his voice a little gruff.

Foolish pleasure heating up her insides, she turned back to the keys. Played a little Elgar. Lyadov.

At the end of another arrangement, she glanced over, her breath catching when she saw his eyes were shut, his glass set down next to him.

Jario was asleep.

She didn't stop playing, smiling to herself a little when she played Puccini's 'O Mio Bambino Caro.' Jario's response to the childish lullaby probably would've been acerbic, but Willow, her heart tugging with emotion she didn't want to examine, hoped the boy inside the grown man would find a little elusive peace in sleep.

You're aware that's the knee-jerk position of a loser, sí?

Those words reverberated through her, soothing her right along with the music until, her fingers starting to cramp, she played the last tune.

Then tiptoeing over to him, she plucked a cashmere throw from the stack nearby and draped it over him. He stirred, and she froze until he settled again, his head lolling to the side.

Releasing her breath, she contemplated her next move. Leave him to sleep or stay with this man who disrupted her emotions with one hand then soothed her with another? Who compelled her like no other.

She knew which was the saner, safer option, but her feet refused to move. Almost on automatic, she fetched another throw, chose the lounge seat farthest from him and stretched out.

His demons rose, jibing and howling, making him twitch in his sleep. Curiously, though, where previously they'd flooded every inch of his memory and churned fresh nightmares, this time they remained at a distance, as if caged in and staved off by the warmth surrounding him.

Warmth that filled his starving lungs with hints of lemongrass and his arms with a supple, welcome weight.

A soft sigh escaped the bundle in his arms.

Right before reality pierced through the warm fog.

Jario's eyes cracked open and immediately fell on the piano, minus its enthralling pianist. A glance down showed where she'd relocated, the encroaching dawn through the wide windows proving how long he'd been asleep.

Dios mio, she'd done it again.

He couldn't decide whether to be annoyed with her effortless power over his previously unbeatable insomnia or be grateful. As for how she'd curled so trustingly into his arms, his deep pleasure at having her there…

He tensed as she stirred, his arms tightening of their own volition.

Dios.

He should be doing the opposite, should be—

'Good morning.' Beautiful, sleep-sexy eyes drifted from his face to the view and back again. 'You slept.'

The pleased lilt in her voice, as if his peaceful sleep meant something to her, struck alien discord within him. When was the last time anyone had cared how he'd slept? Whether he was well or not? Not since before his father died, and his mother—

His teeth clenched against unearthing that memory. 'You believe you're the cure for my insomnia?'

She shrugged, and where others would've been wary at his gruff tone, she replied, 'That's twice now you've fallen asleep with me. So I'm either magic or I bore you so hard it puts you right to sleep.'

It was technically three, but he didn't feel like offering that risky admission. Just as he didn't feel like admitting that he'd found himself admiring her last night for finding a way through her own battles with her music.

While he threw ineffectual axes.

'What else can you cure?'

Another shrug bared a few more inches of her silky skin, and his groin stirred harder. 'Tell me what else ails you and we'll see.'

The need to expose his dark shadows struck for several heartbeats, eager to bask in her illusionary light, but he ruthlessly doused the urge. So she'd succeeded in somehow granting him more hours of sleep in the past few days than he'd known in years. She was just a novelty that would lose its sparkle soon enough.

He let his eyes rake her face, unable to throttle back the hunger clawing through him as they settled on her pink sensual lips, sending untamed need surging through him.

Jario saw the moment she recognised it, luxuriated in the reciprocal hunger of her sharply drawn breath, the budding of her nipples beneath the soft satin of her nightie. In the flush climbing into her cheeks, and the splayed hands slowly drifting up his chest.

When she licked her maddeningly beautiful mouth, gave a catchy little moan and restlessly undulated her hips, Jario cursed under his breath and gave up the fight.

Flipping their positions, he laid her flat on the sofa.

Gleaming brown eyes widened with that flash of innocence but she didn't protest when he nudged her slim thighs open and made space for himself exactly where his body yearned to be. One hand moved up to her caramel-blond hair that was spread out in luxurious temptation, raking his fingers through before clenching a handful, while the other grabbed her hip, then rolled his savage erection on that covered heaven between her thighs.

Her choppy moan was sweet music to his ears, almost matching the sublime pleasure…the peace she'd evoked on his piano last night.

Leaning over her, he brushed his mouth whisper-soft over hers, stretching out the moment when he tasted her while knowing nothing short of an apocalyptic event would move him.

'I'm sure you can feel for yourself exactly what ails me, *cara*.'

Her eyes fluttered before she forced them open, meeting his with a naked sultriness that made his heart gallop harder.

'So you need me? To make it better?' she teased, a satisfying fever raging in her eyes that tore through him.

The breathless baiting released another surge of sensation. Unnerving because it skated far too close to the truth. Albeit a *temporary* truth. Because Jario Tagarro didn't need anything or *anyone*. Right?

He'd learned through torment and hardship that the only person he could rely on, *could ever need*, was himself.

'Want, *hermosa*. Maddening.' Another brush of his mouth over hers. 'Unstoppable.' The faintest taste of her lower lip drew another moan. 'Beguiling.' He drifted over to the sensitive area beneath her ear, grazed his teeth over it and was rewarded with a delightful whimper before he caught her lobe between his teeth. 'But still only just…want.'

Fingers that had drifted to his shoulders dug in, dragging a hiss from his throat.

'Still against your better judgement?' The careful undercurrent warned him that his answer mattered. That however intoxicating the chemistry, she possessed the admirable willpower to deny him.

And…did it even matter anymore what his judgement dictated? He wanted her, badly. She wanted him almost as much. Perhaps it needed to be as simple as that. He'd proposed a ceasefire. The crucial mandate of vengeance could be delayed for a while…longer.

'My every instinct dictates that I possess you, *carina*. And that is what I intend to do.' He revisited that place beneath her ear, his hand moving up to cup one luscious breast as he rolled his steel erection between her thighs. 'Object. Or agree. Now.'

It was hell itself to pry himself away from her silken flesh. To exercise the last crumb of self-restraint and fast-dwindling patience.

She tortured him by dragging out her response. But Jario couldn't bring himself to fault her for it. He hadn't been this turned on in a long time. Hadn't felt this alarming tightening in his chest that mocked this mere *want* he'd professed. With every woman recently, his pursuit had ended with a heavy dose of ennui that'd made the process lukewarm at best.

This…*she* was different.

He couldn't entirely dismiss that there was an edge associated with who she was. But she was also her own woman, with her own fears and battles, enthralling and challenging, with talents that had repeatedly taken his breath away. So he could only watch, captivated beyond reason, as her shapely legs dragged up his thighs to wrap around his waist; as her eyes locked on his, her chest rising and falling in hypnotic rhythm that threatened to drive him insane.

As she whispered, 'Agree.'

He was devouring the consent from her lips before she'd finished saying the word, tasting the impending feast straight from the source.

Urgent fingers spiked into his hair, dragging against his scalp in pain-edged enthusiasm that made him grunt in satisfaction as his hands frantically freed one button, parting it so he could cup her firm, supple breasts.

'Oh.' Her breath gushed between their lips as he toyed with the stiff peaks, tortured and teased until her back arched into his grip. Blood roared through his veins as her legs wrapped tighter around him, her movements shoving him closer to the edge. Already?

He reared back, shook his head to clear the insanity ravaging him. 'How are you so intoxicating?' His voice was slurred and rough, drunk on a strain of lust he'd never felt before.

Lips swollen from their potent kiss parted and she licked her bottom lip, looking as hungry for him as he was for her. 'Don't stop,' she pleaded.

Jario grabbed the halves of her shirt and ripped them open, her shocked gasp turning him on harder. Then her top half was completely bared to him. *Then* a different madness took over.

A distant part of his brain was aware of the primal urgency of his caress, the drive of his claiming, but he couldn't have stopped himself if he tried. Swooping down, he closed his mouth over one rose-pink peak, a thick groan erupting from him at the sublime taste of her. Laving her until she was back to clawing at him, he feasted on one breast, then the other and back again, until the scent of her arousal bloomed with an insistence he couldn't ignore.

Her shorts and flimsy panties were just as easy to rip off, feral hunger roaring through him, driving him to take, devour what was offered.

'Destroying my clothes shouldn't be this hot,' she half moaned, half protested.

Slivers of amusement she seemed to frequently draw almost made him smile. That urge was smashed to smithereens when her breathtaking body was *finally* bared to him.

'Santo cielo,' he muttered under his breath. Hell, even her belly button was sexy, coaxing his fingers to drift over it, his erection jumping when a decadent shiver chased through her. 'You're so responsive.'

Her flush grew as she trailed her own fingers down his chest, her nails raking over his flat nipples and drawing an unguarded hiss. 'So are you.'

Only for you.

Jario was glad the words stayed locked in his throat. So many confounding things had happened with this woman. He wasn't about to admit more. Once this insane nee—*want* was out of the way, he'd find his way into essential clarity.

Batting her hand away—because, *maldita sea*, he was already teetering on the brink—he slid one finger into her wet heat, glorying in her cry of pleasure as he explored her silken flesh.

'You're so wet for me,' he rasped.

Her hips chased his caress, her nails digging into his arms. 'Jario…'

Another wave of satisfaction eased through him at hearing his name half sobbed from her lips. A mixture of pleading and anticipation. Wide-open and breathless with need. He had her where he wanted her. Under his control. A slave to his pleasure.

The man he'd been a mere fortnight ago would've been

pleased at this development. The man he was now was deeply unnerved.

'Jario?'

'If I haven't rendered you speechless yet, *tesoro*, I'm not doing an adequate job.'

Her eyes widened. Then she smiled. 'You're welcome to try.'

'First things first.'

The effort it took for him to drag his gaze up made her pelvis tighten, then throb with shameless need.

'Yes?' she prompted breathlessly.

'You're fired.'

Her smile widened, welcoming the momentary relief from turbulent sensations she'd never experienced before. 'Are you sure? You've repeated yourself a few times now.'

A glimmer of a smile ghosted over his lips. Then he sobered up as he picked up her hands. 'No more scrubbing for you. I'd prefer to see these hands make music.'

Words fled her thoughts as feeling bloomed and bloomed in her chest. She'd known he was formidable the moment she met him. She hadn't accounted for just how powerfully he could affect her emotions. How he could make her dizzy with profound yearning with a handful of words.

When her throat started to clog with feelings she didn't want to name, and the pressure behind her eyes warned that improper tears beckoned, she freed one hand, braced it against his taut cheek.

Hooded eyes pinned her as he inhaled sharply, as if her touch and the charged words affected him, too. 'Not that I didn't find your scrubbing sexy, of course,' he added, but Willow sensed he was just tossing words into the maelstrom.

And because she wasn't quite ready to deal with just how affected she was, she summoned another smile and trailed her hand down his chest.

'I knew there was a reason you were watching me.'

'Indeed.' His nostrils flared as she involuntarily squeezed her legs around him. Jario's gaze dropped to her thighs, watched for a few seconds before climbing back up. 'It was quite tormenting imagining you doing it naked,' he admitted gruffly.

Her unguarded gasp darkened his eyes until they were almost black. Then, struck by an uncharacteristic streak of wickedness, she pushed him away and stood.

'What are you doing?' His voice throbbed with hunger and frustration.

Without answering, she spun herself around and walked outside into the sun-splashed private deck.

Glancing over her shoulder, she slowly dropped to her knees.

'Dios mio,' he muttered under his breath. 'You're exquisite.' Every drag of his gaze over her body produced tiny explosions of fiery sensation, until her whole body was dipped in blazing liquid lust.

Caught in that weird vortex of wanting to grant his fantasy—bolstered by the comforting knowledge that she wouldn't be maliciously branded a temptress when this was over—and wanting him at her mercy, she made a show of widening her stance just a fraction, granting him a tiny glimpse of her womanhood before, sinking slowly onto her haunches, she dropped her arms in front of her.

'Is this how you imagined me?'

Jario's Adam's apple bobbed hard, and large masculine hands bunched convulsively on his thighs before he loosened them and croaked a response. 'Yes.'

His eyes remained glued to her swaying breasts, a rumble of sound he probably didn't know he was making, amplifying his need. Glorying in the altered balance of power in her favour, she paused, raised her hands to scrape back her hair, catching a traitorous moan when a breeze washed over her puckered nipples before it slipped free.

'Come here, Jario. I'm no longer your employee. If you want me, you'll have to come down here and get me.'

The words were barely out of her mouth before he was launching himself at her, dropping to his knees to wrap a demanding hand on her nape to direct her mouth to his. 'Is this what you want, you saucy little witch?' There was a bite to the question, even as he caught her lower lip between his teeth.

'Y-yes.'

Another edgy curse, and he was lowering her onto the warm deck, impatiently parting her legs with his stronger ones. He tugged a condom from his pocket, loosened the tie of his joggers, then drew out his impressive shaft and sheathed himself.

It was her turn to swallow and fight not to beg. Because he was breathtaking. 'Jario…'

Smug that the upper hand he rarely relinquished had been reclaimed, he breathed in deep, stroking himself as he watched her struggle. *'Sí?'*

Please.

She caught the word at the edge of her tongue but parted her thighs helplessly. When his chest rose and fell, when he continued to tortuously stroke himself but made no move towards her, Willow shoved at the lingering vestige of insecurity, danced her hands down over her belly, paused for one provocative second, then slid her finger into her wet folds.

Lightning fast, Jario's hand lashed out, seizing hers. 'No touching what's mine, *tesoro.* Or there will be consequences.'

Her breath shuddered out then as he raised her captured hand, drew her fingers into his mouth and sucked, his lust-hooded eyes darting between her face and core.

'Consequences?'

'Look at me.'

The moment she did, Jario thrust hard and true inside her, a deep groan surging up his throat at the sublime sensation.

'Oh, God…oh, God.'

He shook his head, cursing the near-mindless nirvana of being inside her. Then he was gritting his teeth, the need to retain control eroding fast.

Had he ever felt like this? Not in recent memory. Sweat beaded his temple, drifted down his face. 'You feel…' *Dios.* Why couldn't he speak the words? 'Incredible.' He ground the word out at last, his fingers tightening their grip on her as he searched her gaze.

A gaze that widened for a moment, before turning a little hazy with desire. 'You, too,' she whispered.

For a nanosecond, he wished there was nothing between them. As foolish as it was, he couldn't bat it away. It drilled deep too quickly, leaving him feeling jagged and incomplete. Like a breath that didn't quite catch properly. A slammed door that didn't quite shut.

'Please…don't stop.'

Her hitched breath, the tightening of her hot channel around his steel length, the glaze of lust in her eyes… It was too much for a man on the very edge of his endurance.

And, *sí*, it was simply easier to abandon thinking about it as he thrust home, bottomed out with a thick groan and heard her cry out in pleasure.

Spreading her wider, Jario struck a fast and blinding rhythm, bliss like he'd never felt before drowning him in under a minute. The very naked, conceited fear that this would be over before he'd given her the release she craved and deserved, made him finally slow down.

To suck one nipple into his mouth, savour it while he teased the other, then kiss his way back up her neck to the corner of her mouth, flicking his tongue there until she opened up for him. Then, their tongues duelling as he slid slowly in and out of her, he listened for the rapid change in her breathing, those nails digging deeper as her pleasure built. Until tearing her mouth from his, she screamed in magnificent climax.

Watching her unravel was Jario's most mind-altering experience to date. *Dios*, he never wanted it to end. Never wanted that biting urgency and the confusion already snapping at his heels to gain any more momentum.

So he redirected his hold, rested on his knees and swept her up to straddle him. Tugging her arms around his neck, he dragged his lips up her neck to her ear. 'Ride, *mi linda*. Ride.'

And then he exulted in watching a woman at the tail end of one climax tumble into another. Then another. Taking him along for the most intense carnal journey of his life while he barely hung on, groaning and grunting until a roar ripped his release from his soul. Until his vision turned black and senses detonated.

Leaving behind sublime pleasure that was far too soon flooded by an unnerving sensation that the want he'd brazenly sought to conquer was far from defeated.

That the cracks had only grown wider, turned into *need*, wrapped in despair.

Because far from detangling himself, all he was capable of doing was rising, with Willow held tight in his arms, and heading towards his suite.

Because he was nowhere near done with her.

CHAPTER SEVEN

WILLOW REGISTERED TWO things as she clung to Jario in the breathless aftermath of their lovemaking.

One, that she wasn't nearly sophisticated enough to attempt post-coital banter with the billionaire who'd propelled her to the very edge of ecstasy and then thrown her overboard.

Two, that the widening chasm in her heart might never be healed because what she'd experienced with Jario would never be repeated. Ever.

Touching heaven once was soul shaking enough. Twice? Multiple times...because surely the relentless string of climaxing was the very definition of multiple orgasms? Not likely.

Especially with the man whose future had been so indelibly altered by her father. And she would never see Jario again once she left this yacht. Because taking a stance in her relationship with her father was one thing, but what possible future was there for her with Jario when they were all so mired in betrayal?

None at all.

'Are you going to say something?' he murmured in her ear as he carried her into his luxury cabin. The same cabin she'd cleaned from corner to corner only a handful of days ago.

The reality of how much had changed since that morning settled heavier on her, her stomach tightening at the enormity of what she'd done.

'Is this where I laud your sexual prowess?' Attempted humour emerged breathless when she remembered he remained fully embedded inside her. That he was hardening again.

Inhaling sharply at the renewed hunger, she glanced at him to find him examining her with those intense eyes.

'No need. I'm aware of my magnificence.' His own attempt at levity fell equally flat, the undercurrents rising in the charged atmosphere.

'In that case, I'll exercise the right to remain silent so you can bask in your glory.'

Another twitch of his mouth shattered by the weight of the moment. As he rose with her and crossed the room, she fleetingly hoped he would take the responsibility out of her hands, toss her on the bed and strip her of the need to ponder what came next.

Instead, he headed for the bathroom and into the large walk-in shower.

If she'd expected him to put her down, to carve out a few moments to absorb the impact of the past few hours, she was sadly mistaken. Jario seemed reluctant to release her, even as his expression grew increasingly shuttered. And since she still couldn't find the right words to express her chaotic, shaken emotions of their coming together, she allowed him to pin her against the bathroom wall while he set the water to his desired temperature. Then as he washed her hair, back and parts of her body he could reach, he slowly rocked in and out of her, stealing her breath clean away in yet another climax that soared so high, she tasted heaven.

Small talk was completely nonexistent when they exited. Jario silently held open a luxurious robe, which she shrugged on, then, catching her elbow, he led her outside, where a sumptuous breakfast had been laid out. Seconds ticked away as they both sipped their coffees.

Until she couldn't stand it one more second. 'Are we going to talk about this?' she demanded as he poured her orange juice and slid it over to her.

He didn't answer immediately. His gaze was busy conducting a thorough scrutiny of every dish before he looked up. Knowing it was for her benefit, that her anaphylactic episode remained on his mind, shouldn't have softened something inside her.

Yet, it did.

She ate a few mouthfuls of heavenly croissant, ham and eggs. Then after passing her several segments of fruit, he spoke.

'What's the point in dissecting it? Did we not agree the sex had no bearing on the reason you're here?'

The words were clipped, further ratcheting up her tension. Her fingers shook a little as she set her glass down. 'That's what we told ourselves, yes, but…' She sucked in a breath. 'Are we honestly going to pretend it doesn't?'

His clenched jaw rippled, then he waved a hand at her. 'Let's hear it, then.'

His invitation was as surprising as it was unnerving. 'What?'

Glinting blue eyes challenged her. 'Tell me what has changed. How that affects either of us.'

The question ricocheted in her head, and with each second that passed, she realised there was no clear-cut answer. At least none that wouldn't reveal the utter turmoil churning inside her. She wasn't so fully at ease with her decision to wall herself off from her father's lies and indifference to blurt it out to his enemy.

'Exactly.' His voice was soft but an inferno raged in his eyes.

And the hell of it was she didn't think that inferno was aimed at her. He was battling seething emotions of his own.

'Your father connived, cajoled and convinced mine to go on a business trip to Colombia when I was fourteen years old,' he said in a voice so stark, shivers poured over her despite the sun's hot blaze. Tight, white-knuckled fingers clutched his knife. After a moment he tossed it on the table, his breath whistling as he inhaled sharply. 'My father didn't deserve what happened to him.'

'What happened?'

'Yours lied to him,' he seethed. 'They were relatively new business partners, both ambitious and keen to grow their new venture capitalist business.' His lips twisted. 'Your father was a little more reckless in his approach than mine. Before you refute that, I have the evidence.'

Willow nodded, recalling the fights that'd started the fractures that eventually broke her family. Her mother screaming that she felt neglected, that she came second to Paul Chatterton's love for his company.

Perhaps her agreement mollified Jario. After a beat, he continued. 'He told my father the business meeting he'd arranged was taking place in Bogotá.'

Willow frowned. 'What was wrong with Bogotá? Wasn't it safe there?'

Lines bracketed Jario's mouth, his eyes turning midnight blue. 'Compared to where we ended up, Bogotá was a theme park,' he said chillingly.

'Did your father know the risks? Why would he...?' She paused as he stiffened. Then a flash of bleakness shadowed his eyes.

'You think I haven't asked myself that over the years?'

'But it's easier to blame the living?' she murmured.

His eyes blazed. 'You dare to say that to me?'

'You said you've thought about it. So you've probably considered why he went along with my father when he knew it was risky.'

He appeared a touch nonplussed, a frown creasing his brows before he shook his head.

'With the right safety measures in place, Bogotá was safe enough. And he believed he had kidnap insurance should the worst happen.'

Willow stiffened. 'What do you mean, he believed? Didn't he know?'

A furious tremor ran through him. 'He trusted your father when he said he'd arranged it. But he lied. He took it out for himself alone while assuring my father that he and the son he'd brought along, because said son wanted to spend his fifteenth birthday in his father's country of birth, were covered.'

Cold horror washed over her, acid from the fruit rising until she feared she'd throw up. 'Where did you…? What happened?'

He named a place she'd never heard of. 'We were barely on the ground before we were taken.'

A vise squeezed her heart. 'Jario—'

'We were held for four months in a series of caves and basements, relocated often so we never knew where we were.' His voice was devoid of inflection. Almost. His stony face contorted with cold bitterness and icier fury. 'But your father was released after three weeks.' His gaze speared into hers from across the table. 'I bet you didn't even realise he was gone?'

Horror blended with sympathy for him. 'He was gone a lot on business when I was growing up. But I noticed a difference when he got back. That was when…'

'His own demons started haunting him?' he filled in bitterly. At her nod, a dull sheen swept over his eyes. 'At least he's alive.'

Her heart squeezed. 'And your father isn't. You must hate me.'

He dragged a hand down his face with an exhausted laugh. 'A week ago, I probably would've. But…' He stopped. Frowned.

'But?' Far too much rode on that single word.

Eyes weighted with bewilderment, pain and a resolution she couldn't quite fully determine regarded her steadily. 'But for reasons I can't quite work out, I find myself not at all consumed with destroying you and a little less consumed with destroying your father.'

Her mouth dropped open at the raw admission. But when she rose, intending to move towards him, he raised his hand. 'Jario—'

'Don't take that to mean I've gone soft, Willow,' he said forcefully. Perhaps a little *too* forcefully.

She dropped back into her chair, her insides still twisting over the admission.

'I don't intend to revisit this story again. Do you want to hear what happened to us after your selfish father left us behind?'

'Yes,' she whispered, shame and anger dredging through her because she recognised the selfishness Jario described. Her father had laughed off his naked ambition as single-minded dedication to growing a successful business, but she recalled the mood swings, the irrational lashing out and the icy indifference. He'd knowingly tainted her in his selfish guilt and haunted suffering.

But it was nothing compared to Jario's harrowing loss. She started as he rose from the table, dragged agitated fingers through his hair.

She watched him pace the deck, once, twice, before he paused to lean on his clenched fists, anguished eyes boring into her. The matching white linen pants and shirt highlighted his bronzed vitality and with his shirt unbuttoned, his stunning physique was unmissable. But it was his visibly haggard demeanour that commanded her attention.

'Here's the absolutely deplorable rub. He had a chance to redeem himself. He could've come up with the ransom.' His jaw clenched in recollection. 'It would've meant the business possibly going under and them having to start over. But it wasn't impossible. Yet, he refused.'

'No…' The word shivered from her lips.

Jario's smile was completely devoid of humour. 'Yes,' he hissed. 'My father begged him on his knees to sell the company. It would've been cents on the dollar, but it would've been enough to bargain with the kidnappers. When he wouldn't relent, he asked him to take just me. To return me to my mother. Your father claimed it would be quicker if he left first then arranged for us to be released. Even then, I knew they were empty promises. I spent my fifteenth birthday in chains in a cave, two weeks after your father left.'

Willow's hand flew to her lips, for the first time, feeling true disgust for the father she'd loved despite all his flaws. Despite the tainted legacy of his name and what he'd done, shame she now knew would remain forever.

She wanted to ask how he'd managed to get free but anger, sorrow and horror blocked her throat.

But Jario, now he'd opened the floodgates, couldn't stop telling his harrowing ordeal. 'Every day my father pleaded for my life, offered up whatever he could. My mother tried to sell our house but the economy was in the toilet and the pennies she was offered were laughed at by our kidnappers.' He swallowed thickly and somehow, she knew the worst was yet to come. 'In the end, my father decided we had to escape.'

Dread made her frame shudder. Their breakfast had long gone cold, the view blurring in the face of his heartrending recounting.

'He was shot trying to smuggle me onto a food truck in the kidnappers' compound.' The words were delivered in a ravaged croak, barely audible.

Willow couldn't remember rounding the table, ignoring his stiff form to throw her arms around him in inadequate commiseration. He didn't flinch away from her, because she strongly suspected he didn't register her insufficient gesture. But she held on, desperate to reassure him, and her, that he'd made it through. That he was alive. Because despite everything he'd been through, the idea that she would've never met him, that the profound impact of him was something she would've been denied, felt criminal.

'Do you know what it feels like to watch your parent die in

front of you?' His voice bled pure desolation, unfathomable anguish. Her heart bled right along with it. 'That kind of grief and rage, it swallows you whole, and it never lets go. Never.' His bunched fist slammed against his breastbone, his exhales rippling through the morning air. 'It changes you here.' He pressed harder. 'From one moment to the next, you see your life altered forever. And knowing it didn't have to happen…'

'Jario… I'm so sorry you had to go through that. God, I'm…' She shook her head, knowing her words were insufficient but trying anyway because the thought of him dwelling in that desolate landscape, the way he clearly had been for years, utterly demolished her. 'Tell me what I can do.'

He grasped her shoulders, shadows dancing in his eyes. 'You can start by refusing to fall on your sword for that coward.'

Her throat closed tighter as tears prickled her eyes, her heart clenching despite the wrenching decision she'd made for herself. 'You…don't need to worry about that. I'm at a crossroads where my father is concerned.'

Surprise jolted him, then his hard expression returned. 'The problem with crossroads is that you can turn back. I prefer burnt bridges.'

Willow wasn't sure which one cut deeper. She could only stand there, dragging tiny bursts of air into her stunned insides. 'That's a decision for me to make, Jario. Not you.'

Censure and disappointment etched deeper into his face. 'Then we have nothing more to say on the subject, do we?'

Anguish squeezed her chest as she watched him stride off the deck. The gentle breeze felt like ice pellets against her skin. She barely remembered drifting over to the railing, gripping it hard and staring at the water churning in the vessel's wake.

Several times she tried to swallow and make sense of everything Jario had said. How could her father have done that? When the pressure of it grew too much, she hurried to her cabin. She'd texted Addie and left a few voice mails for her father since she left home, but she hadn't spoken directly to him.

It felt imperative now that she did even if, as she suspected, he would still be in the same state she'd left him in. Or worse.

A minute into listening to the ringing, she knew he wasn't going to answer. Her fingers tightened on the phone as she waited for the voice mail.

'Hi…it's me…'

She stopped and shook her head. There was no easing into this. Nor did she truly want to. What he'd done, what he'd put Jario and his family through…

Willow squeezed her eyes as tears threatened to spill free. 'I know what happened in Colombia when you were kidnapped. What happened with Jario Tagarro and his father. How you… got yourself free and…' She swiped a shaky hand across her wet cheek. 'How could you do that?' she whispered. 'I can't… do this anymore. This is your last chance, Dad. If you want a relationship with me, then…'

Maybe it's not too late to fix this.

'Call me. We need to talk about this.

She hung up, the weight of her father's sins bearing down on her shoulders. Only to open her eyes moments later to a different landscape.

Red, white and green set against the backdrop of a green landscape and the large cruise ship and smaller boats that made up one side of Benoa Harbour.

They'd arrived in Bali.

An hour after most of the crew had disembarked for their much-needed day off, Willow was pacing her room. Since she was now a guest instead of crew, she was free to come and go as she pleased.

She'd declined the crew's half-hearted invitation to tour temples and rice paddies in Ubud. She wasn't in the mood to field curious questions about her connection to Jario. And deep down, she'd been reluctant to leave Jario.

Now she suspected why he'd chosen to make his home on

a floating vessel, albeit a breathtaking one, a greater weight of guilt wouldn't let her go and explore Bali with a carefree spirit as if the man whose blood ran in her veins wasn't the reason behind Jario's suffering.

Returning to the bedside table, she checked her phone, although she was close enough to have heard a ring or text.

It was early evening back in California. Yet, her father hadn't responded, and with every passing second, her pain-tinged anger grew, suspecting that like everything else in his life, he would ignore this, too.

Her mind kept replaying Jario's ordeal on a loop. Being kidnapped was bad enough. To be left with such harrowing scars from what came after was soul shredding. Conversely, she recognised now where his implacable will had been born.

What hadn't killed him had made him much, *much* stronger. Unfortunately, that strength had also calcified a large portion of his heart. She refused to believe it was all of it.

Because you hope to find a chink soft enough to reach him?

Why not? Surely that wasn't such a bad thing to—

Approaching footsteps paused her thoughts; Jario's appearance a second later stilling them both in their tracks.

'You're still on board?' Despite his faint surprise, his expression was shuttered.

She wished she could give a cool, offhand reason for remaining behind, but she couldn't bring herself to be flippant. 'I didn't feel like going out.'

His eyes narrowed. 'You think locking yourself up in your room instead of going out to explore with the others pleases me?'

'I'm not trying to please you!' She grimaced at her overheated response. 'I just…didn't feel right going out there to play tourist while…'

'While what? While poor old Jario is stuck on his boat feeling sorry for himself?'

'No! Don't put words in my mouth. I told you how much I hate that.'

He exhaled and she fooled herself into thinking she saw a flash of contrition on his face before he cupped her chin. 'Don't waste your pity on me. It's neither welcome nor will it be tolerated.'

'It's not pity. It's empathy. There's a difference.'

Predictably, his eyes narrowed. 'Another useless emotion designed to make the donor feel better and leave the recipient barely altered. Find a better emotion. I dare you.'

Desire and irritation zipped through her, burning away the edges of desolation and, sweet heaven, she was tempted to clutch the distraction with both hands.

'There we go,' he murmured. 'Much better.'

'You don't really want…you can't expect…'

'Why not? I recall you riding me like I was the last man on earth a few short hours ago. As performances go, it hit a few excellent spots I wouldn't mind—'

She wrenched herself from his grasp. 'That's not what I'm offering.'

Disappointment filmed his eyes before he veiled it. 'Too bad. What, then?'

Catching his restless tension, she cast around wildly, then settled on the familiar. 'Stress relief of a different kind. Come with me.'

As invitations went, it was near flippant enough to trigger his further annoyance. But it *was* an invitation couched in a challenge, one he couldn't resist, especially if he craved a distraction from newly uncovered old wounds. And for her, doing something other than waiting for a call from her father that she suspected wasn't coming felt imperative.

Delaying the inevitable much?

So what if she was? Who said she had to actively embrace heartbreak?

What about this new heartbreak you're risking? This fling that isn't quite as meaningless as you're fooling yourself into—

'I'm waiting with bated breath, Willow,' he mock-growled.

She started, realising some of her inner turmoil had spilled free when he arched an eyebrow.

'You'll need to change. Meet me at the swim deck in five,' she said briskly, not just to respond to Jario, but to quell the frantic internal debate.

She held her breath when his probing stare lingered. Then, eyes sparking with enigmatic thoughts, he nodded and left her room.

The bikini she'd worn previously had somehow found its way into her belongings, along with two more swimsuits and a few other items usually reserved for guests. Like the silk kimono that matched the suit, three pairs of sunglasses, soft suede slippers with the yacht's logo discreetly embroidered on them, and several luxury sun and skin creams.

Resisting them felt like a petty battle when she had bigger problems, so she slipped into a gold-and-white polka-dot set she'd never have chosen for herself in a store but was mildly agog at how well it suited her. Snapping her gaze away, she applied sunscreen, shoved her feet into the slippers and tossed one of her shirts over her shoulders.

Although she hurried, he beat her to the swim deck, his eyes tracking her.

The yacht had sailed on since dropping off the crew at the harbour, and they were now in a semi-secluded bay with no other vessels nearby.

'You wish to challenge me to another game?' he asked, eyeing her steadily.

Willow shook her head and made a beeline for the top-of-the-range flyboard while wondering if she'd gone mad. 'No, I want you to teach me how to ride this one.'

'Why would I want to do that?' he asked silkily.

She sucked in a breath and let it out slowly, even as her

heart banged against her ribs. 'Because I hate heights and the thought of getting on this terrifies me, but facing one's fears takes guts. I'm willing to face it. With your help.'

Emotion wild and blazing flared in his eyes. He fully understood the subtext and she knew she risked him reacting adversely.

For a while he didn't respond, his gaze fixed on her face. *Probing.*

She started the flyboard, stepped on it and struggled to keep her balance. Another minute passed before she held out her hand.

He didn't take it.

Her heart climbed into her throat, the notion that her gamble would fail smashing through her. His refusal would spell the end of their interaction.

Was that what he was hoping for, an excuse to shatter the truce they'd agreed to and end things once and for all?

Her shaking hand started to drop. He jerked forward, grabbed it and her heart lurched. Eagerly, her fingers curled around his.

The expression that had begun to harden morphed into faint surprise then eased into latent satisfaction, right before he stepped onto the flyboard, flipped their hands and meshed their fingers together.

His balance and control were formidable.

'Ready to take flight with me?' she whispered.

'I should be asking you that,' he drawled.

A dozen responses crowded her throat. In the end, her answer was easy. And terrifying. 'You won't let me fall. Because that's not who you are.'

Butterflies swarmed her belly as she accepted where the answer had come from. She knew in her bones that while he had every right to despise her, he wouldn't deliberately harm her. 'Or if we fall, we fall together.'

Another flare of his eyes as he lost a shade of colour. Then he wrested back his control. 'I haven't fallen yet. I don't intend to.'

Coarse knots tightened around her chest with his words but she pushed away the alarming distress of it. There would be time to dissect everything.

Later.

His eyes flicked to her mouth and she realised she was licking her lips, and cursed under her breath when heat rushed into her face.

'Hold on to me, Willow.'

In the end it was as easy as breathing. And letting down her guard and *trusting.*

His arms circled her waist, firm and tight, and he breathed steady instructions into her ear. At her nod, his feet flexed, manoeuvring the flyboard with the ease of a well-honed athlete.

The e-Foil had been exhilarating, but this was a delirious mind trip the likes of which she'd never known before.

She was experiencing something she'd hankered for from afar and hadn't had the courage to try out. Like watching bungee jump videos, wishing you had the courage but knowing you probably never would. Now…she shrieked and laughed in delight as Jario charted a lazy arc over the water, then executed a faster loop. She gripped his shoulders as her belly flipped and flopped with sensations of pure delight.

Delight trebled when he sent her a lazy, hooded-eyed smile, then slowly elevated them until they were easily thirty feet in the air, spinning in slow circles, dancing high above the ocean.

There, he stared at her for an age, his smile slowly disappearing and one expression after another chasing across his face. 'Why are you still here, Willow?' His low voice rumbled through her like a freight train through a mountain pass, their plastered-together bodies making her stingingly aware of the slow rise and fall of his breathing, the steady thump of his heart against her breast. The flexing power of his thighs as his feet manoeuvred to keep them aloft.

Because I can't turn my back on you...on this. Not yet.

She pressed her lips together against blurting out the exposing remark. 'Because those crossroads I mentioned? They're new to me. I'm taking a minute to take stock, make sure I'm doing the right thing.'

His mouth twisted but his expression stayed riveted on her face, those incisive eyes analysing her every word and expression as if it mattered to him. 'The right thing or the necessary thing?'

The hand on his bare shoulder trembled. Tightening her grip on him was just to steady herself, nothing else. 'I'm not perfect by any means, but I'm hoping if I'm successful, right and necessary will be halves of a whole.'

'And what do you think is *right and necessary* where I'm concerned?' His sibilant hiss would've made her shiver if his arms and his body hadn't kept her deliciously warm. Even in debate she felt perplexingly…cared for.

She glanced away from the hypnotic pressure of his gaze, the tiniest flare of hysteria questioning if this was the place to be doing this. 'Ultimately, that's up to you, but I'm here… if you need me.'

His exhale was audible and disbelieving. 'So you intend the impossible?'

Willow glanced over his shoulder at the distant majesty of the pura temples and the mountains, then beneath them, and her breath caught at the sight of a pod of dolphins streaming through the sapphire-blue waters.

'Half an hour ago I would've said it'd be impossible for anyone to convince me to step onto a flyboard and hover fifty feet in the air,' she whispered. 'Yet, here I am.'

His nostrils flared, bringing her attention to the sharp blade of his nose and the deeply sensual mouth beneath it. Heat unfurled in her belly.

A sound rumbled from deep within his chest. 'You're trying to change paths set in stone, Willow. I won't allow it. Do you hear me?'

His vehemence cut through her, but so did the sure-fire knowledge that she'd reached him on some level. A level he wasn't pleased with, sure, but the reality was stark and moving enough to make her look deeper into his eyes to catch the swirling bewilderment on the edge of deep determination. Eating away at it?

'Pressure and stone make diamonds, Jario. Ever heard of that?'

'Are you being clever with me, *querida*?'

'I'm just offering a different viewpoint,' she replied, returning his stare with a bold one. Then movement from the water behind him caught her eye. 'Like the one behind you right now,' she whispered, nudging her chin at the breathtaking display.

His gaze lingered on her face for several more seconds before he turned. The dolphins she'd seen earlier were circling again, growing in number. In seconds, there were dozens leaping, arching and flipping through the air in a spectacular, awe-inspiring show.

Jario slowly dropped their altitude by several feet for a better view. One particularly nimble dolphin jumped so high, it came eye to eye with them before the creature flipped, its iridescent grey skin catching the light as it nosedived back into the water.

'That's…amazing.'

'They're migrating pods,' he said, his breath brushing her ear. 'There are thousands of them in the water here at this time of year.'

'Are we disturbing…?'

Before she completed the question, Jario was already retreating, angling the flyboard towards the yacht, giving the beautiful creatures room for their aerial acrobatics.

When they reached the swim deck, she expected him to let

go of her, but he kept his arm around her when they stepped off. Her gaze flicked up to his, but he was still watching the water.

Then one arm lifted, pointed to the left. 'Over there. Watch.'

Seconds passed, and she wondered whether he was directing her to another dolphin display. But the water heaved mightily, and a giant fin the size of a tanker's propeller lifted out of the sea, and in majestic slow motion, a giant blue whale followed, conducting a perfect somersault before, with a humongous splash, it disappeared beneath the waves.

Her head snapped up to Jario, her gasp of delight ending in a smile she couldn't have stopped if her life depended on it. His breath hissed out as he stared down at her.

In the next heartbeat they were slamming into one another, lips fusing in a hot, hard kiss that knocked the breath from her lungs. His tongue swept into her mouth, devouring her delight, then flicked in erotic friction, igniting a firestorm of desire that tightened her nipples and dampened her core. Willow whimpered at the force of need that slammed into her. It battered her so hard she barely felt him lift and carry her off the deck. All she could do was hang on as he carried them deeper into his vessel.

'Where are we going?' she asked, despite suspecting his destination.

A light nip at her shoulder sent a decadent shiver through her. 'To see where else you can be necessary,' he replied.

A sting of hurt lanced through her, then it was swept beneath a heavier layer of desire as he nudged her closer in definitive demand. Willow leapt up and wrapped her legs around his waist. His eyes darkened.

'Is this necessary enough?'

His resolute look was weakened by a tiny wave of bewilderment. 'It's a start.' His lips trailed over to the erogenous zone beneath her ear, laved it with deliberately erotic strokes of his tongue.

Then he raised his head, turbulence swirling in his eyes. 'He doesn't deserve your consideration, you know.'

She swallowed. 'Most people don't deserve how life punishes them, especially when they're good people who're awfully wronged. I may not be fighting next to my father, but I'm not joining your war—'

He interrupted her with something pithy and Spanish under his breath, then sealed her mouth with his before she could speak. He was shutting her up. But her words had gotten through, even if he hated her for them.

But as they frantically divested each other of their damp suits, Willow hoped that she'd at least planted a seedling that might offer a path to lessening the burden he'd had to carry.

And also alter his path of total vengeance towards her family.

CHAPTER EIGHT

'HAVE YOU VISITED Bali before?'

She looked up, surprised by the question. They'd relocated to the third largest salon after making love, with Jario once again monosyllabic. But she'd been fiercely aware of his contemplative looks for the past hour in between the furious taps on his tablet.

She shook her head, the butterflies in her belly fluttering wildly as his gaze raked over her face to linger heatedly on her mouth. 'The extent of my international travels so far was Cancun for spring break when I was in college, and Los Cabos…last week.'

The tiniest flattening of his mouth greeted the reminder but a moment later he set down his tablet and rose. 'Let's change that.'

'We're leaving the yacht?' she asked, amazed.

He'd been reclusive on his yacht for years. Surely, it couldn't be as easy as stepping off when he chose? And why now? Her heart lurched then flew at the thought that it might have… something to do with—

His face tightened, killing that lofty notion that her presence had triggered some miracle. 'We're not going ashore if that's what you were hoping,' he said tightly.

Her heart plummeted but she held on tight to her composure. 'Then where are we going?'

'There are ways to tour a place without setting foot on it or shutting yourself off within four walls.' He rose. 'Come.'

She told herself it was curiosity that made her join him, not the deep compulsion to remain in his company.

He was dressed in another loose-fitting pair of white lounging bottoms and a white T-shirt and she couldn't take her eyes off his magnificent physique until she realised where he'd led her.

The gleaming top-of-the-line helicopter sat on the H of the helipad.

'You fly?'

'Are you surprised?'

A snort escaped before she could stem it. 'From what I've seen so far, there's not much you can't do. Except scrub floors. That, I think you'd be absolutely terrible at.'

His mouth twitched and she was slammed by the need to see it bloom into a full smile or laugh. Her stomach dipped at the very idea because she knew it would be amazing.

'Reverse psychology, especially a half-baked one, is a ploy I'll never fall for so save yourself the energy, hmm?'

Her own smile burst free. 'It was worth a try.'

The smallest flash of his teeth made her hold her breath in anticipation of the full works, but a nanosecond later he was turning, opening the door to the sleek cockpit of the chopper, hand out to assist her.

She took it and hopped up onto the seat, then exhaled sharply when he hung on to her, his thumb caressing back and forth, almost contemplatively over her knuckles. For another eternity, they remained caught in yet another charged bubble as the sun blazed down on them.

'Something on your mind?' she ventured when the silence stretched her nerves tight.

His free hand dropped to her exposed thigh, then slowly slid beneath the hem of her white-and-turquoise sundress. 'You have no right to be this stunning. To keep me this knotted over you.'

Her mouth gaped, her face flaming so bright she feared

she would catch fire. 'Am I supposed to apologise for the way you feel?'

Jaw clenching, he dropped a hard kiss on her knuckles before rounding the aircraft to take his seat beside her. With sleek headphones in his strong hands, he sent her another brooding look. 'For making me fight two battles instead of one? Shaking foundations you shouldn't? I'm minded to make you pay for it one way or another, *pequeña*.' He handed her the headphones.

Willow was still grappling with that unexpected exchange when he eased back the cyclic, and the chopper lifted into the air. Threat or promise? She couldn't tell, because a minute after they'd left the yacht behind, his voice flowed like warm honey over gravel into her ear as he pointed out the first landmark.

And for the next hour, he showed her a spectacular piece of the Island of the Gods, with its stunning Hindu temples, rice terraces and unique black sand beaches. She marvelled over the semiactive rumblings of the Gunung Agung volcano, then suffered stomach-churning anxiety when his gaze rested on her for long, nerve-shredding moments.

It was clear Jario, far from being able to compartmentalise what was happening between them, was perhaps attempting to wrestle with the not so tidy ramifications of their connection.

And yes, she was half-ashamed to admit she liked him as unnerved as she was. Because maybe, out of that confusion, they could chart a different course? That maybe she wouldn't have to step off her crossroads alone?

That notion stayed, steeped and grew stronger legs as the tour progressed, as he pointed out little-known places on the island and exposed for her a deep well of interest of his surroundings.

Grasping that she could listen to him forever wasn't akin to the wide-eyed yearning of a giggling teenager but an appreciation for the complex, compelling man his circumstances had moulded him to.

And if the way he did everything with intense passion deepened her appreciation? She fought the way her heart lurched at that thought.

Because all too soon they were landing and he was helping her out. His mouth pinched as he stared down at her for an age.

Then, sliding both hands into her hair, he took her mouth in a deep, erotic kiss, leaving her completely breathless before pulling back. 'I have guests coming tonight. Join me at seven?'

She'd barely nodded before he was gone.

Willow stepped onto the designated deck and stopped in her tracks.

So far, Jario had favoured casual wear, albeit all *GQ Magazine*–worthy.

Seeing him in a formal dinner jacket, his dark silk shirt open at the throat and matching trousers, the hem of which rested on highly polished shoes, was an unguarded punch to her solar plexus.

Dear God, but he was beautiful. And why did seeing him with a glass of cognac in his hand *always* do silly, feverish things to her? When had she developed this insane fetish?

He turned as he took a sip, then he froze, too, at seeing her.

Arrows of self-consciousness stabbed her as his gaze raked over her.

Besides the swimsuits and various accessories that had been appearing in her room steadily over the past couple of days, the dress she wore had been the most surprising.

It had been laid out on her bed when they'd returned from their helicopter ride. Her belly had flipped with a mixture of excitement and apprehension, but the overwhelming feeling that despite his gruff resistance, he wasn't ready to end this fling yet had made her heart pitch and race. Also, she'd already crossed several lines by sharing his bed. What was one more step?

The one-shoulder orange charmeuse gown had an exquisite ruffled, rose-petalled hem that ended just above her knee and billowed softly with her movements, showing off her tanned legs. The gold hoops in her ears, a thick gold bangle and matching gold-heeled pumps topped off her confidence, helped square her shoulders at the prospect of joining the twelve influential guests arriving shortly for Jario's business dinner.

'You wore the dress.' He handed her a glass of champagne.

'Yes.' God, could she sound any more breathless?

'You look magnificent.' The deep throb in his voice made her heart race even faster.

'Thank you,' she said, then on a silent prayer and remembering the battles he'd referred to earlier, she took a deep breath. 'We have time before your guests arrive. Tell me about your father.'

He stiffened. 'Willow.' A rumble of ominous thunder, his body vibrating with intense emotion.

She laid a hand on his arm. 'I know. I may be overstepping but just loosen the reins for a little bit. Tell me your happiest memory of him.'

His whole body was one giant mass of tension, ready to snap. She would be caught in that ballistic fallout but for the life of her, Willow couldn't remove herself. Safety was a weak position to take in the face of something so monumental. So vital.

So she waited.

Slowly, the tension seeped out like wisps of fog dissipating in strengthening sunlight, leaving behind a landscape bearing less desolation and more promises of new beginnings. *She hoped.*

Staring deep into his drink, his voice was a low rumble. 'He could make me believe anything. If I woke up one morning and he told me I could fly without wings, I'd have believed him. He had a powerful charisma.' A clench of anguish shredded her heart. 'Which was why I always believed we'd escape that hellhole alive.'

'He may not have, but you did. He made sure of that. So

maybe you should honour him with happy memories. A life lived to the fullest?'

He inhaled sharply, and his lips parted, but whatever response he'd intended to give was cut short by the whine of an approaching tender.

The sleek vessel passed by the bow of the yacht, a handful of elegantly dressed men and women gazing excitedly at the lit boat.

His guests had arrived.

For the first hour, Jario ignored her. Well…not entirely.

He escorted her from small group to group long enough to introduce her, then proceeded to conduct his conversation around her as if she didn't exist, while perversely caring for her by questioning every server who approached with appetisers, almost absent-mindedly offering her tiny platters and bowls of *perkadel kentang*, *lumpia* and spicy tom yum soup.

The chef was clearly outdoing himself at the rate of knots, and Jario's determination to feed her would've been touching and amusing if she didn't feel the undercurrent of his mood.

He was upset with her, she got it. She'd dared to suggest his father might not entirely be on board with his plans for retribution and she'd raked his wound raw. But wasn't that better than letting it fester the way it'd been? Wasn't that a way to make him confront it and heal faster?

Faster…because her time was running out?

Willow shook her head and contemplated leaving the deck. Her roiling emotions would probably be better examined in the solitude of her cabin.

As the thought solidified and she turned to put it into action, a man appeared next to her. Nick…something. A Bali-based British entrepreneur.

Around the same age as Jario, he wore a deep, slightly oily tan that suggested he'd been in this part of the world for a while. 'Not thinking of leaving us already, are you?' he said with a mini pout she suspected was meant to charm women.

He was handsome in a surface-only way, unlike the brooding man who stood a dozen feet away, staring into his drink while another guest gesticulated frantically to make a point. That man with unfathomable layers she feared she might never get the chance to explore.

'Only, I need someone to keep me sane until it's my turn to sing for my supper. Past experience and my place as a lowly millionaire mean that might take a while.'

Willow looked from him to where he nudged his chin at Jario and back again. 'You do this often?'

'Chase an eccentric billionaire around the world in hopes of capital funding? Yes, unfortunately,' he said, mouth quirking with amusement.

'No, I meant disparage your host to other guests?' she asked with saccharine sweetness, taking entirely too much pleasure in watching him turn puce and blink in alarm.

'Well, no, I didn't mean…' He gestured at the yacht, then back at her. 'Then what do you call this, then?'

'A unique life decision,' she said with conviction fuelled by burning loyalty. 'I'll leave you to train that singing voice.'

She walked away, aware that she'd drawn stares, including Jario's, which narrowed as she passed him.

Setting down her barely touched champagne, she took the steps farthest away from Jario off the deck. Minutes later she was in her cabin, her heart climbing into her throat when she spotted a missed call from her father.

Hitting redial, she listened to the call ring. And ring. Then click into voice mail.

An unladylike growl tore from her sternum as she tossed the phone away and dragged her fingers through her hair, dislodging a few pins holding up the swept-back style. Her pulse throbbed, the feeling that time was running out escalating. Her phone rang. She snatched it up, absently noting her hand was shaking.

'Dad?'

A beat of silence. Then, 'Willow.'

Her heart flipped in her chest, knowing the true test of her decision had arrived. 'How are you?' she asked cautiously.

'How am I?' He gave a bitter chuckle. 'I'm not sure. It's not every day you get a call from your daughter condemning you for something she really knows nothing about.'

Her fingers tightened on the phone. 'Then tell me. I've been asking you for months. Years. Maybe if you'd been forthcoming, I wouldn't have—'

'Rushed headlong into enemy camp?'

Her eyes squeezed shut, dread and hopelessness drenching her. 'It's true, then?' She realised then she'd held on to a kernel of hope that this was all a giant misunderstanding.

'Yes. No.' A heavy sigh. 'Willow, it was complicated, okay?'

'Did you take out insurance for just yourself before the trip to Colombia? And did Jario's father ask you to save his son?' It felt like everything in her life hinged on *that* burning question. 'And did you refuse?'

The pause was longer this time, his breathing heavier. 'You and your mother were depending on me. I had to make it home. And the insurance thing, they were Colombian… I thought they wouldn't need it.'

Knees weakened, she sagged onto the bed. 'Dad…no…'

'You can judge me if you want but I tried to get them released when I got back. I just didn't… Things didn't work out the way I'd hoped.' Indignation bristled in his tone, but it died down when he added, 'I never wanted you to fight my battles for me, but since you're there…' He cleared his throat. 'Is there a chance you can salvage this situation?'

Her heart squeezed tighter, the sliver of shame to be his daughter growing. To be faced with the stark truth of her father's character. It thickened the lump in her throat, forcing her to stay silent.

'Willow?'

'That's all you care about, isn't it? How you come out in all of this? Not that your actions shattered a family?' she muttered numbly.

He swallowed audibly. 'Look, I can't change what happened in the past…' *But.* 'Is there a chance he'll let things go?' he asked, a mix of hope and fear in his voice.

Willow wasn't sure why she wasn't ready to divulge that Jario had agreed to suspend his revenge plans. Because as much as it hurt, she didn't want her father to think he could get off the hook that easily? That Jario was entirely justified in seeking reparations for his suffering?

'I don't know. Maybe you should pick up the phone and ask him yourself. Or better yet, do it in person.'

He inhaled sharply. 'I see. Well… I'll think about it.' He hung up.

Exhaling shakily, she registered that he hadn't asked how she was, about the possible toll all of this was taking on her. When was the last time he'd simply asked whether she was tired, sad or happy?

Whether she was fed or rested the way Jario had done?

Anger stung her for the moment's wish that he would've done something…anything to change her mind about him. Maybe then she wouldn't know the acute wrench of realizing there was no hope for them?

'Did he admit it?'

She jumped and pivoted towards the voice.

Jario stood in the doorway, hands thrust into his pockets, a thick lock of hair falling over his forehead as his eyes burned into hers. God, had he heard her conversation? Her hand gripped the phone as she stood up. 'Jario. What are you…?'

'Did he?' he said through clenched teeth.

He knew she'd been speaking to her father. 'He said it was complicated. But that he tried…'

Censure blazed in his eyes, right along with a stomach-hollowing disappointment and resignation. 'And you gave him a free pass, *sí*?'

Her skin tightened with shame because she'd been doing that for years. The words to admit that stuck in her throat. 'I…'

His hand snapped up. 'No need to create excuses. Dinner is ready. Are you coming?'

She itched to ask whether he'd come down to deliberately catch her out. Examining his face didn't bring enlightenment. He was even more shuttered now than he'd been before dinner.

'We need to talk properly. Maybe after dinner?'

He shrugged. 'I'll think about it.'

That stung, as he'd probably intended. Still, pride kept her chin up as she returned to the deck with him, where a long table was immaculately laid with tall and short lit candles, silver tableware and crystal glassware.

He went to the top of the table, pulled out the seat at his right hand. Willow couldn't stop the disarming warmth that bloomed anew in her chest, even as she berated herself for not heeding the danger in swimming in these weighty feelings.

But it'll be only for a little while, because this thing we're doing isn't going to last much longer. Right?

'Oh…hey, I thought I was over there…'

The loud voice distracted her from her unsettling thoughts. Nick was frowning at his place setting halfway down the table, his slight swaying announcing that he'd imbibed a fair amount.

An annoyed rumble from Jario startled her but when she glanced at him, his expression had settled into suave neutrality.

Easy conversation flowed among the guests, the mouthwatering Balinese dishes, superb wine and the flickers of stars above their heads aiding easy conversation, regrettably interspersed with lewd jokes from Nick mostly aimed at the unfortunate woman next to him.

Jario's fingers drummed on the table just loud enough to get Nick's attention as the man leaned obnoxiously closer to the woman. 'Is there something wrong with your seat, Mr Matthews? You seem to be having problems staying in it. I can have it removed if you wish?' he drawled with steel in his voice.

The table fell silent, aware that Jario hadn't suggested *replacing* said chair.

Nick flushed tomato red, straightened, grabbed his wineglass and gulped down another mouthful. 'No, you're all right,' he mumbled.

'Muy bien.'

Conversation resumed a fraction stiltedly, but Jario appeared entirely unconcerned. His glance swung to her, catching the mouth twitch she tried to hide. He slanted her a droll glance as he refilled her wineglass.

'You were talking to him earlier. Do you find him amusing?' he murmured.

Bolstered by several sips of wine, she returned his stare. 'Not particularly. I prefer men with a little more…substance.'

'Glad to hear it.'

She raised a brow. 'Is this you metaphorically thumping your chest and pissing on your territory? A little primitive for me but by all means, you do you.'

His nostrils flared but her heart fluttered to see a different heat filling his eyes. She knew she was fooling herself by believing the episode in her cabin had been forgotten. 'I always do, *pequeña*.'

She hated that his response left her on a knife's edge for the rest of the evening. Hated that even though the atmosphere between them remained charged, his hand on her waist, her hip, in the small of her back, smoothing a strand of hair behind her ear before his fingers drifted briefly over the pulse racing at her throat, also kept her breathless and yearning.

That mood prevailed as he called an end to the dinner at midnight. The last guest was barely off the deck when he wrapped his hand around her wrist and tugged her firmly towards the steps.

'What are you doing?'

'Taking your advice. What was it you said—*you do you*?'

Heat arrowed between her legs, but she resisted his pull and disentangled herself from his hold, immediately missing his heat when he stepped back. 'You know what I meant. You're deliberately twisting it to suit your purposes.'

He shrugged. 'I'm still taking you to bed. Now.'

She glanced at his outreached hand. The resolution etched on his face. 'We need to talk about what you heard. And a hell of a lot more. You can't use sex to shut me up every time you don't like something I say.'

His hand remained extended, one eyebrow rising to join the sheer challenge brimming from him. 'Can't I?'

As she kicked herself for the deep yearning that racked her body, for the traitorous gasp that left her lips when he swung her into his arms, she vowed to wean herself off the insanity.

Please, God. *Soon.*

But, she amended as her arms curved around his neck and her fingers spiked into his hair, *not tonight.*

Three soul-shaking hours later, their bodies slicked with sweat, she gazed into his fierce blue eyes. He'd taken her with an edge that'd left her breathless, but she'd felt his bewilderment, as if he was stunned by what was unfolding between them. Perhaps his inability to resist it?

Her breath locked in her lungs now as he raised himself onto his elbows over her.

'I should take more victory in this beyond the sublime pleasure of being inside you. Instead, I crave your pleasure.' His jaw tightened. 'Even above mine.'

The gruff, stirring admission lassoed several strings around her heart. Even from the first, she'd known he wasn't a man who readily admitted to being bested, either by the demons that kept him awake in the night, or the fact that something had driven him from his stone-and-concrete home into a floating palace. Or something as base as carnal pleasure.

Knew that this declaration was just as important as an emotional one.

She framed his face in hands that trembled, daring to look into his pain. To attempt to absorb some of it into herself. 'Don't you see why you can't? Is accepting that you're a good man so hard?'

He sucked in a long breath. 'I'm not a good man. My ultimate goal hasn't altered. Don't be fooled into thinking otherwise.'

She wanted to believe strongly enough to tell him that it was only a matter of time before it did. But she knew his formidable willpower. Chemistry may have applied the brakes on his intentions but it was only temporary. She couldn't stay on his yacht, sharing his bed forever. Her hand drifted down his face and throat, over his clavicle to rest on the strong, steady, thumping heart. 'I wouldn't dare. That will have entirely come from here.'

She expected another scoffing remark or at the very least a brusque denial. Instead, a shaft of bleakness swept across his face. 'You put too much store in an organ that malfunctions, *tesoro*.'

'It sounds perfectly fine to me. All you have to do is listen to it.'

CHAPTER NINE

YOU CAN'T USE sex to shut me up every time you don't like something I say.

The indictment reverberated through his head long after another explosively sublime sex marathon had left them blissed out. The culprit of his restless mind was passed out beside him, her sex-tousled hair half obscuring her face. Even as he resented her pointed words, he was gently pushing back her hair so he could stare at her. To attempt to figure out how… why everything she did affected him so viscerally.

He'd stopped trying to convince himself it was because of her father.

Willow was very much her own person with a complex ability to delve into his psyche that left hollowed-out spaces within him he wasn't keen to peer into.

But she'd forced him to face a few. His own father's decisions, for instance. She'd dug up Jario's previously muted resentment for his father's naivety and blind trust in his business partner; made him accept that his father wasn't entirely blameless. That perhaps the anger Jario carried was partially misplaced.

That he'd been entirely too quick to pick up on her suggestion to suspend vengeance in order to get some peace?

Question was: How long was he prepared to tolerate this? Especially after overhearing enough of her phone call with her father and knowing, even now, she refused to take a stance against him. *That* continued to slash at a place deep inside he didn't want to examine. And even as another, far too reasonable, voice questioned why he, Jario, was owed her loyalty when he would've probably done the same in her shoes, and not turned on his own father, no matter what.

She arched into his touch in her sleep and his breath stalled, a flare of something he was loath to label *panic* wedging in his chest at the thought that she might never side with him. That he would lose…this.

He could deliver the *coup de grâce* he'd been savouring for years now to Chatterton Financial and be done with it. Watch it burn to useless ash as a final homage to his father so he could move on with his life.

But if he did, would he find peace then…or be left with a purposeless existence propped up with hollow billions? If… *when* she left, would his nightmares return? Join forces with the phobia that kept him wandering from sea to sea?

His brain rebelled at completing that desolate picture.

She'd flatly refused to burn the bridge between herself and her father. Any further push from him might trigger her immediate departure from his yacht and his bed.

But did he even deserve to have her stay?

Merciless rejection clenched his belly. He surged upright and planted his feet on the polished floor, eager for the calming hum to soothe him.

It was quite ridiculous how much he resented her leaving. But perhaps it was a good thing. Even before her arrival, hadn't there been times when he'd wondered if he'd dragged out this revenge for far too long?

Was it time to draw a line under this?

Digging deeper inside himself past the point of resistance, he reached beneath his pain and brought up the image of his father. The times they'd played catch in the front yard of his family home. The subtle ways his parent had approached a know-it-all teenager and attempted to guide him the best way a father could.

Be your own man, no matter what influence anyone tries to impose on you.

It doesn't matter how you succeed, but do it in a way you can be proud of.

Family is everything, mijo, but I'll be proud of you no matter what you do with your life.

That last one had often caught him on the raw. But more so now since Willow had shone a spotlight on him. Would his often even-tempered father be proud of him avenging their shattered family to the exclusion of all else barring his stratospherically successful company?

Would his father be disappointed that he'd never sustained a relationship past a few months? That he hadn't been able to set foot in their home in over a decade?

That the thought of becoming a father himself drew acid bile to his throat and doused him in horror? That the notion of experiencing even a fraction of what they'd endured but with him as the role of a father desperate to save his son, would've driven him to insanity so it was better not to go there at all?

Questions careened around his thoughts until he raked shaky fingers through his hair, gripping tight in the hopes of the pain shutting them off. And it disturbed him deeply that for once, perhaps when he needed it most, he couldn't hear his father's clear response in his head the way he had so many times.

All he heard was… *Honour your father with happy memories... All you have to do is listen to it...*

With a growl he wrapped his arms around her, squeezed his eyes shut, even though he knew sleep would fight him as hard tonight as every night. He didn't care. She was here, and until he was done with her, he would take the balm she offered—

'No. No. Dios mio. No!'

'Jario! Wake up. Jario, you're—'

The moment he realised what was going on, that he'd fallen asleep despite thinking he wouldn't, he jackknifed from bed, dislodging her head off his sweat-slicked shoulder. His frantic eyes searched his upturned hands for blood.

His father's blood. Flowing freely from his bullet wound as he died in his arms.

There was nothing to see, of course. It all remained locked in his head, ready to spring loose the moment he closed his eyes.

'Go back to sleep.' He cringed at the raw rasp in his voice, the result of tormented screams he didn't want to discuss.

'How can I? Jario, you sounded so…distressed.' Worry drenched her words, seeped into his tortured soul. A soft hand rested on his shoulder. 'Are you sure you're all ri—'

He twisted towards her, ready to shut her down. The bitter words dried in his throat. Sympathy blazed from her eyes, the same emotion he'd claimed he didn't need, and wrapped around him unbidden, warm and powerful enough to leach the resistance from his bones.

He wanted…he wanted…

He *needed*—

Jerking to his feet he stormed towards the bedroom door.

'Where are you going?'

He was deeply disconcerted by the thoughts and yearnings weighing him down, foiling his plans to escape his own bedroom, stopping him at the door. 'I think we both know by now how this works. Go back to sleep, Willow.'

He firmed his gut against the hurt that slashed across her face. She had no right to be hurt by anything he did. He was the wronged one here. He was the one who needed—

Dios mio, *enough!*

A few dozen rounds with his punch bag should wear the demons out. Or…as a last resort, another marathon bout of steamy sex. And the way she looked, sitting up in the middle of his sex-rumpled bed, with her sex-tousled hair and those rose-pink lips swollen from his kisses—

With a muffled growl he slammed the door, shutting off the thought.

If the demons and this new witch he'd willingly brought into his bed were going to plague him, they could do so while he made himself a few hundred million.

Half an hour at his desk was enough to prove his concentration was shot to pieces. Another ten minutes confirmed Chatterton Financial's decline had stagnated since he hadn't devoted energy to it recently. After confirming the affected staff had been secured jobs in his own organisation, Jario clicked on the next email.

The email from the director of the facility where his mother lived these days threatened to tip him over the edge. It reminded him that in some ways, he was also failing the much-loved remaining parent he only now saw twice a year. Guilt bit into him as he replied before leaving his desk to seek some semblance of peace from the calming blue ocean, his head buzzing with enough discordant thoughts to fell a lesser man.

But the paramount one he couldn't rid himself of was the one that clamoured for Willow Chatterton.

So he wasn't entirely surprised when she appeared in his doorway just after sunrise, conjured up by the force of his thoughts. Resigned to how the mere sight of her excited and rejuvenated him, he braced his shoulder against the glass window and simply stared at her.

She didn't rush to fill the silence, another annoyingly endearing trait most women of his acquaintance lacked. She copied his stance, tucking her hands behind her back and resting her shoulders against the doorjamb. But she went one better and drew up one foot, hardening his shaft just from one glimpse of her shapely leg. Heat pummelled him at seeing her in his T-shirt, the hem skimming the tops of her thighs.

Here he was caught in a riptide of *am I doing the right thing?* and a dangerous desire that would distress his remaining parent, yet he couldn't stop hungering for Willow.

She radiated power she either didn't know she possessed or was cleverly wielding, combined with wary attitude. It was intoxicating to watch the many facets of her character and he was caught in its spell.

'I'm tempted to take you to task for what you said before you left me alone in bed, but I'm unwilling to ruin that perfect sunrise with a fight.'

Jario was unprepared for another punch of sensation, this one skirting the rim of disquiet. 'You think me a monster?'

Wary eyes flitted to the stunning horizon before returning to his. 'I think you're a determined man who can't be easily swayed from the path he's set himself, even if that path leads to an abyss.'

Jario resented her for the verdict that struck a cold chill in his veins. Because hadn't he caught chilling glimpses of that very abyss as the years passed? He gritted his teeth as the inner *yes* grew louder.

Dios mio, what the hell was she doing to him? That she would so easily bat away the power that only moments ago sent a wave of unease through him further riled him. 'Unlike you to admit defeat so easily, no?'

Jario refused to admit he welcomed, no craved, the glare she sent him. Was he so far gone that he would pick a fight simply to step away from emotions he didn't want to confront? The repeated *yes* made his gut clench as her eyes sparked indignation at him.

'You want me to tell you what I truly think?'

'Can I stop you?' he replied, all the while thrilling to her fire. Letting it warm him in places that had long known only grief and cold desolation.

She dropped her foot and glided across the floor towards him, and he was at once enthralled and mildly terrified of her allure.

Because it was now beyond just allure?

'You've delayed seeking retribution because deep down, you're searching for another way.'

Forced laughter seared his throat with acid…and unwanted truth? He swatted the thought away. 'I'm beginning to think you're the sort who believe they can will a thought into being.'

'I think we're called optimists. And we're not as rare or as ridiculous a species as you'd like to think,' she replied.

'Maybe not, but against those who have their feet firmly planted in reality, you'll lose every time,' he said softly, almost pityingly.

She stopped in front of him, contemplating him with a far too probing stare 'Will I? I'm almost tempted to bet against that.'

One eyebrow arched. 'Almost?'

'Almost,' she echoed firmly. 'And I probably would if this were a game. But it isn't, and you…' She paused, took a breath. 'I can't help but wonder what your father would think—'

'Don't you dare.'

She shivered at the chilled warning. 'Why not? Because it's sacred? I know it is. But I also suspect that hasn't stopped you from wondering. Has it?' She dared to say it anyway.

He pushed away from the window and stalked back to his desk before he did something unthinkable and exposing, like pull her into his arms and bury his frustrations and unease within her welcoming flesh. Even as much as he wanted her, he knew that would be admitting his weakness to them both. 'I don't know whether to be stunned at your recklessness or commend you for the spine your father lacks.'

'Thank you, I think. And hate me if you want, but we both know all this is coming to a head. You're standing at your own crossroads, Jario. You need to decide which path you—'

'Enough.'

The word seethed between them with jagged warning and determination.

And one look at him confirmed this wasn't the right time. Between their unresolved situation from last night and waking up to the tortured sounds he made in his nightmares, his formidable defences were up.

She, too, needed several moments to work out why her heart continued to twist, bend and take flight with the ebb and flow of his emotions. She'd lain awake after he'd left the bedroom, anguished for him and terrified for herself at the depth of her feelings. At the suspicion that it was too late to step off the slippery slope of giving more than her body and empathy to the man who'd suffered so much.

That everything since that morning she'd stepped into his office had always been destined to end here, with her heart far more invested than she'd intended.

So she backed away from his desk, ignoring the deep clamour to do the opposite and step closer.

His head snapped her way as she took another step, and, right there, lurking within the sardonic gleam in his eyes, was a sliver of uncertainty. Perhaps even apprehension.

His lips parted. She expected another verbal tussle. Perhaps an order for her to stay put. It was breakfast time after all, and she doubted he'd lost the urge to feed her. But those control-wrecking lips that had explored her body so thoroughly last night thinned.

'I'll see you later…' She cringed at the hint of a question and plea trailing her statement.

He didn't respond, just stared hard.

Squaring her shoulders in false bravado, she left his office. Showered and dressed twenty minutes later in her denim shorts and the T-shirt she'd snagged from his room—because apparently, she was a glutton for punishment and couldn't resist having something of Jario's with her even when they were locked in battle. After another ten minutes online buying tickets to the first decent sightseeing tour she came across, she took her first step onto land since boarding the *La Venganza*.

She half wished his security guard would've stopped her. And how pathetic was that?

They'd returned to Benoa Harbour between last night and this morning, and the tuk-tuk she'd arranged awaited her on the pier. The chatty driver snagged her attention for all of five minutes before she was back to thinking about Jario.

A minute later her phone buzzed in her pocket. Her heart lurching when she realised it was a video call. She answered, suspecting the caller even though the number was unfamiliar.

Even on-screen Jario's gaze probed deep. Or maybe it was the ocean-blue T-shirt he wore. 'You left the yacht?'

Was that faint concern her imagination? 'I need to clear my head.'

His gaze searched every inch of her face. 'Because of me?'

She shrugged. 'What do you think?'

A handful of seconds ticked by. 'Where are you going?'

'On my way to tour Ubud. First stop, something artsy, I think.' Her attempt at cheeriness half succeeded.

His eyes narrowed and he leaned in closer. 'Who are you with? And what's that contraption you're in?'

She turned the camera. 'In a tuk-tuk with a very knowledgeable tour guide.' She summoned a smile for the driver, who flashed a white-toothed grin of appreciation. 'Now, if you're done with the third degree, I'd like to get back to my sightseeing.'

'When will you be back?'

'Why?'

His nostrils flared. 'We'll finish what you started.'

Her heart jumped. 'Now you want to talk?'

His blue eyes grew hooded. 'I'm willing to hear you out,' he compromised grudgingly.

As wins went it was more than she'd expected. But she wasn't going to gloat just yet. About to respond, a wide yawn took her by surprise.

Jario's eyes sharpened. 'I kept you awake for most of the night, Willow. You're operating on limited sleep.' His low, deep and sensual voice drew shivers over her body, and her face heated even as she searched his gaze to see if he was referring to the sex or the nightmares that had eventually woken him up. Wondered if he finally wanted to talk about it.

'I'll survive,' she murmured.

A moped horn blared as it zipped past, making her jump.

His jaw tightened. 'Going off gallivanting without adequate rest isn't wise, *cara*.'

'You operate on little sleep most of the time. Are you foolish?'

The smallest flash of vulnerability flitted across his face. Had she not witnessed his indomitability she wouldn't have noticed the fleeting absence of it. 'It's not entirely out of choice, as you well know.'

That brought a deeper pang that snatched at her breath. But there was also a sizeable chunk of peevishness she knew was entirely derived from his rejection. 'I'm not coming back,' she said. And then just because not defining that response left her insides hollow, she added, 'Just yet. But you can join me,' she offered before she could think better of it.

He looked surprised. After a moment, he nodded. 'I'd like that. *Gracias*.'

Willow smiled. 'Before you thank me, I have conditions.'

'More questions?'

'Volunteered information.'

Another stare-off occurred, during which her driver navigated bustling streets heaving with colourful stalls and fruit sellers with exotic fruit that probably would've made her mouth water had she not been caught in the more powerful vortex of Jario's stare.

'Very well.'

The low rumbled response, only registering because she'd been staring at his mouth, sent another shock wave through her.

Her knee-jerk inclination was to dig into the thorny subject of what he saw in his nightmares, but she suspected it would receive a frosty reception. So she chose a different one.

'Why the yacht? Why not a reclusive private island where no one will bother you if that's what you want?'

'Seventy percent of the planet's surface is covered by water. Some would argue I'm getting the better end of the deal by making the oceans and seas my playground.'

She would've laughed off his flippancy if she didn't believe there was deeper meaning behind him being out here, living on his floating palace and never going ashore. Something significant to his restlessness and his inability to sleep through the night.

She remained silent, watching a muscle ripple in his jaw.

'Also… I needed something else. The moment I stepped onto this boat it felt like home. As for security, it wasn't the problem. I'd made sure of that.' The dark promise in his voice left little doubt he meant that. 'And because I found solid ground beneath my feet…intolerable.'

Sorrow dredged through her belly. 'But don't you miss…' She trailed off when nothing came to mind. At least nothing this man couldn't attain for himself despite the unique way he'd chosen to live his life.

'Yes?' He eased back in his chair. 'What could I possibly miss that I can't have? You'd be surprised how eager people are to grant even the most outlandish requests when there's money involved.'

'So that's it? You throw money at people, they bring you things on your yacht and that's living for you?'

His amusement vanished, his features morphing into iron and ice. 'I live by no one's definition of what life should be. I've taken what was thrust on me and bent it to my power and will. That's more than most people will achieve, including your father.'

She hesitated a beat before exhaling. 'I don't disagree. As for my father, his sins are his. The next step is up to him. And I'm all for living your life how you want…if it makes you happy.'

Disappointment clouded his vision and Willow was shocked that it was the emotion that most seared her. 'This so-called happiness may be your gold standard. It's not mine.' He flatly dismissed her words. 'And your father well knows it's not just the mistakes you make that count but how you fix them.'

Since she didn't disagree, she kept silent. His nostrils flared once, then he looked beyond her shoulder to the art museum she'd entered. For the next ten minutes, they pretended to explore colourful Balinese art while they both gathered themselves.

'Why do you push so hard for this, Willow?' he muttered at length.

That emotion that lingered at the edges of her relationship with her father pushed harder at her. Maybe it was a good thing they weren't in the same room. It made her confession easier.

'There's another reason I came to find you.'

His gaze sharpened. *'Sí?'*

She found a quiet corner of the museum and leaned against a cool wall. 'I've accepted the violin position with Mondia. The symphony travels all over the world. I could've stayed with another orchestra in Los Angeles, but I wasn't sure whether I wanted to cut ties.'

He inhaled sharply. 'And now you know?'

Her heart screamed her answer. 'It's time to live my life on my terms.'

Piercing eyes narrowed. 'I hear traces of guilt. You feel guilty for wanting to live your life, for achieving the goal you've dreamed of since you were a child, the dream you found solace in while contending with a self-serving father?'

'Wow, don't hold back, please.' Her snark was demolished by her aching heart, despite her soul reassuring her she'd done the right thing. That perhaps even seeing Jario's battle with goodness versus vengeance had shown her which path to finally choose.

'Look at me, Willow.'

After a beat, she met his fiercely blazing gaze. It burned right through to her soul.

'Your talent is entirely your own. No one else's. This is who you were born to be. So ditch the guilt and own it completely.'

Her eyes searched his. Felt that aggressive bolstering she'd missed from her absentee mother and indifferent father. Support Jario had shown her in his own unique way since she'd stepped on board, even though it'd been mostly couched in gruffness or brusque impatience.

'Why do you try so hard to convince everyone you don't care?'

He stiffened. 'This isn't about me.'

'Sure, it is. There you are, convincing me to not lose sight of what makes me happy, while you're actively blocking your own. You realise you have no choice but to accept my advice now, right?'

One brow arched. 'How do you intend to enforce that?'

She shrugged. 'I'm not sure. All I know is it'll be tough as hell. So…finish telling me why you're on a yacht?' she urged softly.

He sat back, his deep voice tingling right down to her toes as he continued. 'It didn't happen immediately after I returned home, which felt even worse. For a while everything felt… numb but normal. Enclosed spaces triggering unwanted memories I could understand. At first, I didn't understand why the scent of trees and soil, exhaust smoke, riled me. But then, walking on solid ground, knowing my father was buried somewhere beneath my feet became…impossible. I thought it was just being in the house I grew up in. Knowing he would never walk through the doors again. I couldn't live there, not with my father not being there.' His mouth twisted. 'But I didn't need to worry about that for long. Foster care dealt with that problem.'

She inhaled sharply. 'You went into foster care?'

'Sí.' The word was hard-edged with rough memories.

She frowned, then realised she didn't have definitive knowledge about his mother. 'You mentioned your mother before. Is she…?'

'Alive? Yes.'

'Where is she?'

'Are you sure you want to know?'

Swallowing, she nodded, the hand gripping her phone shaking. With every sinew in her body, she wished she were back on the yacht, within touching distance while he relived these memories. But she also suspected that the distance helped this closed-off, tormented man, whom she suspected she had deep feelings for, in opening up. For that, she would endure the wrench of being separated from him.

'In the weeks of our captivity, she slowly lost her mind. She never fully recovered. Now she's in a full-time mental health facility that moonlights as a fancy resort. She takes six different medications just to keep her balanced. She's allowed to visit me occasionally under supervision.'

The words, chiselled from ice and mired in deep bitterness sent waves of desolation through her.

'The kidnappers…were they ever brought to justice?'

His eyes grew colder, bleaker. Until she felt as if she was looking into an unforgiving abyss. 'Trust me, those responsible have paid the price.'

'What does that mean?'

He tilted his head. 'What do you think it means?' he returned almost conversationally, except for the deadly blade of retribution very much present in his voice.

'That you have closure there, at least?'

The whites of his teeth flashed in a smile so devastatingly gorgeous and deadly, she didn't know which her body was reacting to as it swung from hot to cold and back again. But then the smile slowly disappeared, his eyes turning sombre and introspective. 'I've kept my word. I haven't instigated anything against your father in almost two weeks.'

'But let me guess, that all changes if I say something wrong, right?'

'You've said and done many wrong things, *cara*,' he rasped. 'You challenge and infuriate me more often than should be allowed.'

Her heart gave a wild leap. 'But you allow it because…?'

'My first full night of peaceful sleep was found with you,' he admitted gruffly. And while she was gasping at the raw admission, he added, 'I'm interested in testing a few more of your theories.'

She had drifted towards the entrance of the museum as they

spoke, a part of her mourning not giving the breathtaking art the attention they deserved. But this was more important. Far more profound. 'Jario…'

'When will you be back?' he asked gruffly. 'I'll have lunch waiting for you.'

'My driver assures me Ubud's street pancakes are an experience not to miss.'

His jaw clenched. 'You have no idea what's in them. Do not risk another allergic reaction. The chef will have pancakes ready for you if that's what you crave.'

What she craved was the impossible. What she craved was for his occasional droplets of possessive care and attention to turn into a torrent that drenched her. For his patent desire to turn into explosive need that would embrace every longing for fulfilment for both of them.

'Willow.' Her name was another rumble, a deeper one this time.

'Hmm?'

His lips pursed at her distracted response. 'You're testing me.'

'Am I?'

'Security can be there in twenty minutes,' he coaxed thickly.

She looked around her. 'Bali is beautiful. It'll be a shame to miss this opportunity.' She met his gaze. 'And you don't need me, do you?'

He opened his mouth, then hesitated. 'I need to feed you. Because you're hungry.'

It was nowhere near sufficient but still her belly flipped and her heart jolted with enough emotion to make her breath stall. Regardless, she forced herself to shake her head.

'I'll get my own lunch, thanks. See you in a few hours.'

She ended the call with shaking fingers.

And as she'd feared, after hours of exploring sights and sounds and food, as she made her way back to *La Venganza*, she remained terrified that she would find it near impossible to walk away from Jario when the time inevitably came.

CHAPTER TEN

TWO WEEKS FLEW by in a breathless kaleidoscopic blur of good food, exquisite lovemaking and a deep delve into everything that sparked pleasure.

Specifically, *her* pleasure.

It was almost as if Jario had made it his mission to discover every contentment point so he could explore and fulfil it. To drown her in pleasure to the exclusion of everything else.

Everything *important*.

Because blurred but not entirely suppressed was the premonition that things were coming to a head even though, by unspoken agreement, they didn't speak of her father or his parents.

The moment she'd stepped back on his yacht five hours after her Ubud tour she was directed to the topmost deck where he'd had a lavish breakfast-for-dinner feast of pancakes and waffles waiting for her. He'd insisted she sample each iteration of the yummy pastry, topped it with exquisite milkshake, then caught her in his arms and carted her off to his bed, where he'd tortured her until screaming his name was the only thing she'd been capable of.

They'd sailed into European waters two days ago and had explored Iceland and Denmark by helicopter. Willow had been stunned to discover his mother was Swedish-American and that he'd spent a few Christmases in Stockholm as a child. Those nuggets had been shared with her mostly after lovemaking, in those seemingly stolen minutes when she held her breath and prayed he would fall asleep and find nightmare-free rest.

More and more, her heart swelled with joy when that happened, often staying awake to watch over him.

It was in those cherished moments when she glimpsed the carefree boy he'd once been, the one who still cared enough to revisit his mother's homeland, albeit from a high distance, and to fight for his father's memory, that she finally admitted to herself that she'd fallen in love with Jario Tagarro.

She'd been thankful that he'd been asleep when emotive, panicked tears fell. Then she'd allowed herself to whisper it to him as he slept. And as his arm tightened around her in his sleep, she accepted that she had two choices open to her—leave or fight.

Jario raced across the water on his jet ski, another unfamiliar grin cracking his face—and his insides if the warmth easing through him was a testament—as he executed another arc around a frustrated Willow.

He should be ashamed that thoughts of retribution had receded like light mist in sunlight—not quite disappeared but not as urgent.

Just as he should be contrite for ignoring the facility director's emails for the past two weeks. Hell, he hadn't bothered to open the last three in his inbox. But he'd checked with security and they'd assured him his mother was safe and healthy.

Whatever the director wanted to discuss could wait…a while.

Willow Chatterton had challenged him to be happy. And he'd never backed down from a challenge.

He watched her slow to a stop, rise to straddle the seat as she dragged irritated hands through her wet hair, and his body stirred wildly.

Dios mio, she was stunning.

Both inside and out, he was discovering. Every time she smiled, he got hit by a wave of vertigo.

The tiny veering off track that had occurred when she'd left his yacht unannounced, triggering panic, had continued to widen a crack he couldn't quite close. One that impressed ever strenuously how essential the daughter of the man who'd wronged him was becoming.

They'd woken from a snooze half an hour ago—a staggering surprise in and of itself since he couldn't recall the last time he'd fallen asleep in the afternoon—to find her beautiful eyes on him, a faintly perturbed look lurking within the brown depths. She'd smiled brightly and attempted to compose herself.

But it'd ruffled his own emotions enough to make him drag her out onto the water. To jump into another activity to overrule the rising clamour.

It'd worked. Up to a point. Now, raking his gaze over her supple body, lingering in all the places that delighted and aroused him, he knew he was shutting off the subject they were both ignoring.

'Fine, I give up. You win.'

Words he was used to hearing. Only this time, victory felt hollow. And the ticking time bomb at the back of his head was growing louder.

He powered his ski closer until it bumped hers, then leaning over, he cupped her nape and brought her irresistible mouth to his. A long, belly-flipping kiss later, he watched more sombre shadows chase across her face.

She pre-empted his question with one of her own. 'What was that for?'

'Spoils of war?'

The spirited response he expected didn't arrive, a resigned look skittering over her face. 'Is everything a battle?' Before he could answer, she waved him away. 'Actually, don't answer that. I'm heading back in.'

She left him with the roaring in his head and a bigger hollow in his stomach.

Both of which remained immovable when he tracked her to his bathroom. She'd finished peeling the wet bikini off her body, a fact his own body fully approved of then mourned when she covered up with a robe while ignoring him.

'What's going on? Are you ill?'

An edgy bark of laughter spilled free, snagging at something inside him. 'Is that the only time I'm allowed to get away with disagreeing with you?'

'Ah, so we're in disagreement about something?'

Tiny embers of her usual fire stoked her glare, but her face remained carefully composed. 'No, we're not. At least nothing beyond the obvious.'

'Willow.' His warning tone heightened the charge between them and as much as he wanted to dial it back, a visceral urgency took hold of him. Enough to make him close the gap between them. And jolt to a halt as she stepped back. *Away from him*. Watch her hands shake as she secured the belt to the robe, then grimaced before consciously loosening it.

'What's wrong?'

For jarring seconds, she kept her mouth firmly pursed. Then she repeated that batting away thing she'd done on the water. 'It's probably nothing—'

'It's definitely something.' The hollow in his belly filled with cold unease. 'Tell me,' he insisted after another pulse of silence.

'It's…my period…it's late.'

She lost a layer of colour as the words tumbled free, a wave of dismay washing over her face.

He was abstractedly stunned that despite the shock barrelling through him, it was *her* reaction that stayed with him. That roared at him that she was perhaps horrified by the thought of being pregnant.

And then that shock grew because Jario discovered that he

absolutely despised that reaction. That he wanted to shelve his own confounding emotions and drill down on *hers*.

Which was absurd because…he needed to explore his own feelings on the matter. Not dwell on whether she hated the thought of carrying his child…

He spiked his fingers through his hair, pulling a handful taut in vain hope that the sting would centre his thoughts enough to formulate words.

Enough to work out why the thundering of his heart wasn't born of self-blame for not being careful enough with protection, but with what kind of father he'd be. Whether he had what it'd take to do right by his child.

If there was one.

The silent observation slammed even more confounding feelings into him. Because again, he wasn't filled with the aversion he'd expected.

'Are you going to say something?' she murmured, her eyes dancing over his face before meeting his eyes. The way he'd wanted her to a minute ago. The way that felt far too incisive now, because surely he wasn't skilled enough to conceal the shock waves pummelling him.

'What did you mean by *it's probably nothing*?' He barely recognised the charred roughness of his voice. All he cared about was her answer to this suddenly important question.

'Sometimes, I'm late by a day or two. But—'

'How late are you now?' The words were fired bullets. Urgent and unstoppable. Much like his runaway heartbeat.

'Three days. But like I said, it might be nothing.'

He reached for relief and found it absent. 'Except you're worried enough to mention it.'

Her flush made her paleness stand out even more. And wasn't it the wildest thing that he found her even more alluring in that moment?

'Because in the past I hadn't been sleeping with anyone,' she rasped.

He wanted to cockily remind her that their activities in bed involved much more than mundane sleep. But it wasn't true. He'd found his most restful nights in years with her.

An addictive peace. Warmth. A sense of homecoming after restlessly wandering the seas. The truth of it hammered harder at him.

He opened his mouth to say something…anything…to rationalise his way through the myriad weighty sensations pouring through him.

The distinctive sound of helicopter rotors was a minor distraction that soon turned into a major one as the sound grew.

No one would dare land on or approach his vessel without express permission.

No one except…

Dulce cielo.

The implication of his possible visitor's presence sent cold tremors through him. He wanted to curse the demons for this untimely interruption, but he knew he only had himself to blame as he forced himself to turn away from her, to ignore the flash of relief, then anguish across her face when he immediately turned back. Cupping her jaw, he locked gazes with her, ensuring she didn't miss the unequivocal response. 'If you're carrying my child, then I will claim it as is my right.'

Her eyes flared wide. 'What? You can't just—'

'We'll pick this up later. But you wanted my response. Now you have it. I respect your rights, but I also keep what's mine.' The pulse of deep possession that throbbed through him cemented his feelings about this bombshell. He would rise to this challenge, too, as with everything else in his life. And he would succeed.

Without her? Are you sure you don't need her?

The power of that inner voice terrified him into turning for the door.

'Where are you going? Who are you expecting?'

Quiet alarm stiffened his spine. 'Expecting? No one. Someone I can't turn away? Most likely.'

With every leaden step that took him to the second helipad reserved for guests, he swung between dread and elation.

But even as he watched his mother step down from the chopper and turn towards him, a blinding smile creasing her face and a large part of him thankful that she looked the best he'd seen her in years, he knew his past, present and possible future were on an unstoppable collision course.

Willow couldn't fight the compulsion to follow Jario minutes after he left the suite, even though she wished she could. Every moment since boarding his yacht in Los Cabos felt like a series of compulsive reactions drawing her deeper into a vortex of inescapable emotion.

Even discovering she'd missed her period felt almost…inevitable. Another domino falling as hard as she'd fallen for Jario, regardless of the mountain of turbulence awaiting her if it turned out to be true.

She'd barely stopped to throw on her shorts and tank top before she raced barefoot after him, dragging her fingers through her damp hair to control the dishevelled mass.

Now, in the salon closest to the visitors' helipad, she watched the someone he couldn't turn away enfold him in an embrace, the woman who bore a striking resemblance to the man she loved. Fierce premonition that the end she'd dreaded was in sight took hold of her.

When a mocking voice joined in the chorus of chaos, suggesting she only had herself to blame, one hand dropped to her belly, while the other tried to smother the hoarse sound that escaped her throat.

It was no use.

Jario and his mother turned towards her, his face a rigid mask that slashed at her heart, his mother's morphing into wary confusion at her son's expression.

The death knell arrived when the crew member who'd just served his mother's champagne approached Willow with a tray. 'What would you like to drink, Miss Chatterton?'

The sequence of clenching her fists in resignation, hearing Jario's muffled curse and seeing his mother's face whiten in horror would be etched in Willow's memory forever.

'Chatterton?' Jario heard his mother's ravaged echo before she swung towards him, her face crumbling as the champagne glass fell and shattered on the deck. '*Mee-jo*, what have you done?'

He winced, the crack in his chest widening at hearing the butchered endearment. Once upon a time it'd been a great source of teasing around the kitchen island, his father laughing as he painstakingly enunciated the word Ana Tagarro could never get right.

Now it was a reminder that his father had never been given the chance to finish teaching his beloved wife his native tongue. Because of…

His head swung to where Willow stood frozen a dozen feet away, her haunted eyes filled with pain, remorse and deep sympathy. Emotions his mother was clearly oblivious to when she stalked to where Willow stood.

'From my son's expression I can see this isn't some cruel coincidence. You're that vile man's daughter, aren't you? Are you the reason he hasn't been answering my emails?' Without giving Willow a chance to respond, she carried on. 'I don't know what you are to my son or why you're here but I suggest you absent yourself. Immediately.'

Anguish twisted Willow's face, but that fighting spirit rallied admirably. 'Mrs Tagarro, let me explain—'

'Mama, you will treat my guest with respect,' he interjected firmly.

The possible mother of his child. *Dios mio.*

Eyes the same colour as his flew to him. 'Your guest? No!'

His mother's shrill tone rang across the deck. The woman who'd complained for all of a minute before forgiving him for making her stage a surprise arrival instead of the planned one she'd asked the facility director to arrange, had disappeared. In her place was the mother who'd spent several months at the mercy of debilitating grief and anger until she couldn't function as a parent, forcing the authorities to place her son in foster care, a course he accepted now that neither of them had entirely recovered from, even though Jario had forgiven her for it a long time ago.

His chest squeezed at seeing her trembling with adverse emotion.

Because he'd taken his eye off the ball. Plunged himself neck-deep in shameful lust and desire, and…possible father-hood?

He pushed away the peculiar leaping in his chest as his mother continued.

'Did you not hear me? Leave!'

She raised her hand, galvanising him into movement.

'*Dios mio*, control yourself!' Jario wrapped his arms around her and drew her back before she could do the unthinkable and strike his…his…

He shook his head to clear the label threatening to burrow deep into his psyche. 'I love you, Mama, but I will not con-done violence.' Especially against the potential mother of his child. 'Is that understood?'

A sob ripped from his mother before she collapsed against him. 'Then tell me what she's doing here. Why, Jario?'

He gritted his jaw at the plaintive demand. 'We'll discuss it later. It's nothing for you to worry about.'

He didn't need to look to feel Willow's haunted eyes fixed on him. To feel her castigating disappointment, deadlier sliv-ers of shame slicing him.

'Come, Mama. I'll show you to your room.' He led his distraught mother off the deck, the vise lassoed around his chest growing tight.

Tighter.

Until he couldn't quite catch his breath.

A mere half hour ago, she'd imagined the toughest thing she would be doing was confessing her late period to Jario. Then mitigating the leap of joy when he'd said he'd claimed their child in case that claiming might not include her. The need for clarity had been partly why she'd raced after him.

She knew differently now.

Her very bones were weighted with lead as she shoved her meagre belongings into her small case. She wished her body would move faster but it seemed to be working on its own timetable, probably locked in shock at Jario's searing rejection.

It's nothing for you to worry about...

A definitive, damning evidence on her position in his life if ever there was one.

She stiffened at his approaching footsteps, her skin tingling wildly beneath his penetrative stare.

'What are you doing?' he demanded edgily.

Before his mother's arrival she would'vc put a different slant on that tone, fooled herself into believing he *dreaded* what her packing meant. She knew better.

'What does it look like? I'm leaving. That's what you want, isn't it?'

'Is it? That's curiously astute of you, considering I don't know what I'm feeling myself.'

Harsh laughter seared her throat. 'Well, that's just the problem, isn't it? You're happy to drift from wherever the wind takes you while pretending you're in control of your destination.'

He inhaled sharply. 'Excuse me?'

'You're not excused. Face your fears or throw down your sword, Jario. You can't have it both ways. You're still trapped in that cave but the only one keeping you there this time is you!'

Angry colour tinted his cheekbones as his eyes narrowed. 'I know you delight in pushing my buttons but even you can see you're seriously overstepping.'

True. But this was much more important. 'Am I? Why did you ignore your mother's emails? Because I was *nothing for you to worry about*?'

His nostrils flared and silence bubbled between them before he responded. 'Whether I do or not doesn't matter.'

The lacerations on her heart grew wider. Deeper. 'That's crap and we both know that.'

'Willow—'

'Here we go. You're about to issue some form of threat? A warning to watch my tongue? At the risk of sounding like a broken record, we've been there, done that. We both knew this was going to end one way or another.'

He sneered. 'With you running back to your father?'

Her heart twisted harder. 'Actually, no. If you want to know, being here with you has given me the clarity I need. I'm done with lies and indifference and accepting half-hearted crumbs of imitation love. I want the whole feast or nothing at all.'

His silence weighed heavy and as it lengthened, her despair grew. And grew.

Her fingers clenched around the flip-flops she'd just picked up. 'There's no need to watch me pack. I'll be out of your hair in ten minutes.'

He exhaled heavily.

Cursing against the infernal compulsion, she glanced his way. He looked fierce, predictably, but also…shaken. Determined but bewildered.

This is really happening.

She'd fallen in love with this man somewhere between dropping to her knees to scrub his pristine deck and listening to his mournful voice as he narrated what had happened to break up his happy family.

Her heart had urged her to find him over and over on the

nights when his demons had tormented him, to offer solace because it already knew it belonged to him.

That heart shrivelled now when unshakeable resolution settled onto his face. Unbending like the mountains soaring into the sky behind them. She knew as well as she knew her name that his resolve rested at the opposite end of what her heart yearned for.

Her heart may have chosen him, but Jario Tagarro was about to choose a path that didn't include her.

'Travel will be arranged for you. This thing was always on an extended pause.'

Her heart shrivelled even more and dropped to her toes. 'This *thing*? Tell me something. How do you feel about that?'

A tic throbbed at his temple. 'Excuse me?'

'You've been doing what you think your father wants. What you believe will make your mother happy. But what do you want, Jario? These last two weeks… I thought…' She shook her head. 'Why does one have to suffer for the other to be fulfilled?'

His expression wavered, rippling like a disturbed pond. Then it settled back to chilling stillness. 'Do you know what you're asking?'

The strings around her heart pulled with vicious yanks, until she feared they would be ripped to unsalvageable shreds. 'You want me. But more than that, you need me.' Her boldest declaration yet. The roaring echo in her ears said so.

The shocked flare of his eyes evidenced it further. But the power of his immutable will crushed it, as she'd feared he would. 'You put too high a premium on yourself, *pequeña*. You're hard to resist, I accept, but you're not entirely irresistible.' His lips twisted as his eyes turned flinty. 'Luckily, I'm used to doing hard things. Sometimes even the impossible.'

'Commendable. But why do that if it's unnecessary? Why deprive yourself of something that is…right here for you to take?' Her voice shook as she stepped closer, offering herself with her heart on a platter.

A platter he stared down the blade of his nose at. And for the tiniest moment, he wavered. His Adam's apple bobbed in a thick swallow.

Then his gaze flicked over her shoulder. There was nothing but the vast stretch of ocean behind her so she knew he was looking anywhere but at her. Avoiding her.

So she moved into his eyeline. 'Look me in the eye when you respond, Jario.'

He may have flinched. Or it may have been her longing imagination that this affected him as much as it did her. Because when he deigned to reconnect his gaze, there was nothing but implacable resolution. 'Whatever you thought you'd get at the end of this, I'm afraid I'll have to disappoint you. My mother's visit may have been unscheduled but it's also timely—'

'Why, because you can safely hide behind her pain instead of moving forward?'

His face shuttered with a finality that struck true terror into her heart.

He doesn't need you. He never did.

The searing realisation served an immediate purpose. It cauterised her bleeding heart, enough for her to lift her head and look him in the eye without crumbling. 'I guess we're done here.'

His gaze dropped to her belly, a flash of hunger and resolution etching into his face. 'For now, at least. But if you are pregnant, we'll see each other again.'

CHAPTER ELEVEN

THE FIRST-CLASS TICKET was woefully wasted on her because after two sodas and a mouthful of vichyssoise, she asked not to be disturbed, flattened her bed and pulled her blanket over her head. Then she spent the next fifteen hours swinging between silent tears, hopeless rage at herself for falling in love with the most incredible man on the face of the earth, and pulses of rage at Jario for being devastatingly irresistible. For leaving her with the lingering promise that she might see him again. But mostly for showing her far too many glimpses of what could've been between them if their circumstances hadn't been so impossible.

But…had they?

She pushed the misleading voice away. It had been why she'd been tempted down the wrong path. She vowed never to listen to it again.

Especially when it disregarded her deep focus over the next week on the final practice sessions on her violin and stayed with her, insisting her job wasn't quite done. That even if her love had been rejected, her one avenue of solace still remained to her.

It drove her to hunt down her father for the tough conversation they needed to have.

And for the first time in her life, perhaps coming too late, she saw naked emotion in her father's eyes when she said, 'I'm leaving, Dad.'

He swallowed, red-rimmed eyes filling with…fear. 'What?'

'I've tried, but I can't do this anymore. Maybe you love me in your own way. Maybe you don't. But…it's time for me to take care of myself.' At his heavy silence, she turned towards the door, then immediately turned back. 'You shattered his family. And you never owned up to it. I don't know that I can live with that. I don't know how *you* can.' Tough words that hurt her throat and made her heart bleed for Jario. For herself.

His demeanour crumpled almost immediately, his hand shaking as he dragged it down his face. 'I know.'

'You said you tried. If that's true, you need to tell him that.'

He nodded again, his expression downright miserable. 'You're right. I know I haven't been the best father.'

She couldn't refute it, so she pursed her lips, swallowed the lump wedged in her throat. After a moment, his rheumy eyes rose to hers and a sad smile curved his lips.

'I see you're not disagreeing.'

'If there's any hope for us, what matters is what you do from now on.'

Panic flared briefly in his eyes, then he gritted his jaw and nodded. 'One way or the other, it has to end, right?'

Words echoing far too closely to what Jario had said sent a shaft of trepidation through her, but she nodded anyway. 'Bye, Dad.'

The San Francisco Harmonic auditorium was packed.

The constant buzz of excited voices, which was nowhere as soothing as the vibrations of his yacht's engines, pressed in on him, attempting to dislodge his sanity. But Jario held on.

He'd stepped off his yacht and onto dry land for the first time in years three days ago. His first instinct had been to track Willow down, but he'd needed to do a few things first.

Now, as his fingers tapped nervously against the programme page where her stunning picture was displayed, he wished he could dislodge the other refrain in his head.

You're too late. You're too late.

By the time her piece came, he was almost crawling out of his skin.

Her violin solo wasn't long. But it was profound and haunting and magnificent enough to have the entire audience enthralled. To have them applauding louder and longer when it was over. To keep him on his feet and clapping longer still. Until heads turned his way, until eyes widened, speculation drifting through the crowd.

But Jario only had eyes for her.

As he'd had right from the beginning.

As he should've before committing the sin of allowing the past to dictate his future.

He'd have only himself to blame if he was too late. But she'd taught him to fight, to find a different path, and *santo diavolo*, he'd fight to the death for her, given half a chance.

That chance-seeking was interrupted when the event ended and he was making his way backstage, by a man he'd know anywhere on earth.

Since their last face-to-face meeting drink had taken its toll on Paul Chatterton. As Jario looked into his eyes, he saw another emotion that tormented him.

Guilt.

'Tagarro. Can I have a word, please?' the older man rasped.

Jario's nostrils flared. Meeting Chatterton had been on his list but here and now wasn't how he'd planned it. But perhaps it was right that he went to Willow with even less baggage.

'You have five minutes.'

'I know this means less than nothing in the grand scheme of things, but I tried to help when I got back. The banks refused to lend me money, and the company wasn't worth anywhere near what was needed. It was why we went to Colombia in the first place. If that deal had happened, we would've…'

Jario watched Paul Chatterton take a deep breath, his pallor ashen. 'Why did you lie about the insurance?'

Chatterton's face crumbled. 'I thought it was too expensive. And yes, I know it was stupid. And wrong.' Chatterton grimaced. 'But I honestly didn't think any of us would need it. I called the Colombian police every day. I even tried to get a charitable fund going but as you can guess, it didn't get far.'

Jario wished he'd shut up. Not because he didn't want the overdue show of remorse but because the alarming *compassion* building inside him overwhelmed him.

Because now, with Willow's father in front of him, he recognised that emotion as the one that'd delayed Chatterton's destruction. It'd been there all along, a seed that had flowered with his daughter's arrival.

He didn't want to deal with that on top of the wrenching anguish tearing up his insides. He'd suffered through the longest ten days of his life after dropping off his thankfully calmer mother at a wellness resort in the Maldives. Starting with the short, stark and stomach-hollowing text from Willow two days after her departure.

I'm not pregnant.

Three words that had shattered him far deeper than he'd anticipated, killing hope he'd secretly harboured. He'd wandered his yacht for two more sleepless nights before summoning the courage to call her. She'd declined to answer.

And why should she after the deplorable way he'd treated—

'I'm sorry.'

The thick remorseful voice cut through his wretched mood, forcing him to focus on Chatterton. To stare into his own misery to know he meant it.

'I was a coward. A terrified coward who didn't want to lose his company,' Chatterton said regretfully, his fingers twisting frantically before he shoved them into his pockets. Sweat beaded his upper lip.

Looking around, Jario saw a table holding bottled water.

Fetching one, he handed it over. Willow wouldn't forgive him if her father passed out at her opening night.

And he *needed* her forgiveness.

'As for the business, you probably know it never really took off.' Guilt lurched across Chatterton's face. 'Your father was the true visionary behind the company. I've been using his business model for the better part of a decade and a half. But times have evolved. I don't think I have what it takes to stay afloat even if…'

Even if I hadn't lent a dismantling hand...

There was no satisfaction in that admission. Not when Willow's voice flowed softly, firmly in his head.

What would your father think?

'I'm sorry,' Chatterton repeated.

Jario watched the husk of a man before him, and slowly felt the last embers of vengeance wither and die.

Enough was enough.

The peace that settled on him when he nodded acceptance was the kind he'd only felt with her. He opened his mouth to dismiss Chatterton. Instead… 'Is she well?' The words were ripped from a deep, desperate place inside him.

He knew what pain felt like, wouldn't diminish the agony of losing his father in light of this new brand of torture. But that had been a full-body, constant *shroud* of pain while with this one…every breath felt like an ice pick stabbing him in the chest, screaming at him to *do something.*

Her father's eyes dimmed further. 'I don't know. She's… left home. I have a lot to make up for with her, too, but I'm hoping it's not too late.'

Jario wanted to insist that her home was the one she'd created on his yacht with him. But again, what right did he have to that claim? When he'd championed and evangelised his pain against her every effort to help him through it? When he'd reduced her importance to wants instead of the well of fulfilling need she'd offered so freely.

Understanding lit the older man's eyes, so perceptive, Jario wanted to fold his arms, hide his flagrant, desperate yearning.

'You probably don't want my blessing but let me offer some advice when it comes to my daughter. She won't accept half measures. Without a full commitment, you'll never have her trust and love. I had that and I squandered it.'

The kick in Jario's chest felt awfully like…hope. He didn't offer Chatterton a handshake—he wasn't quite there yet—but a nod for the show of remorse, and the advice curiously eased his debilitating despair as he watched the other man walk away.

He inhaled sharply at the thrust of missing the woman he loved.

Do something.

He strode purposefully backstage, gratified when the security guard took one look at him and stepped aside.

Immersive therapy sucked, especially when it stopped working.

Willow hid in her dressing room, willing the all-encompassing pain of desperately missing Jario to pass.

She could take some consolation that tonight's performance had gone well. The audience had appreciated her small solo.

Especially that last one who'd clapped longest.

The dim lights had prevented her from seeing them but for a moment she'd hoped…*wished* it was Jario. Before harsh common sense mocked her.

He was on his yacht, probably throwing axes or wandering the decks.

The hollow in her heart made her regret her period's arrival that'd shattered her hope of being pregnant. Of retaining one final connection to the man she loved.

The force of her despair had made her reject his calls, terrified of his indifference or worse, relief that she wasn't pregnant after all. But in her weak moments, she kicked herself for not gifting herself the chance to hear his voice one last time.

A sob caught in her throat, and she was thankful she was alone in the dressing room she shared with three other performers. They were out there, mingling with VIP guests and receiving deserved accolades. She hadn't been in the mood, escaping into the dressing room now filled with two dozen vases of exquisite yellow roses. She didn't read the card, didn't want to deepen her heartache—

'Willow.'

She froze. Then her head snapped up, her gaze zeroing in on the man standing in the doorway, staring at her with his beautiful blue eyes.

Jario…was…here.

Her fractured heart leapt to her throat as she shook her head.

'Jario?' He'd left his yacht. To find her? 'Wh-why are you here?'

He took a hesitant step forward, his brows clamping as if he was concentrating on walking. On land. Which he'd done… why?

Shouts of laughter and a clink of glasses in the hallway made him flinch.

'May I come in?' A shudder raked through him. 'The sounds. The people. It feels… I feel…'

The enormity of what he'd done propelled her upright. She reached for his arm despite knowing that touching him would only make missing him worse when he left. But feeling the tremors running through him, her heart ached. 'Come in. It's fine.'

Jaw clenched, he stared bleakly at her. 'Is it?' He shook his head, glancing around. 'Can we sit, please?'

'Yes. Of course.'

He sat, his gaze never leaving hers.

While she tortured herself with his scent, noting he looked a little haggard. While she basked in him not taking his eyes off her.

'You play the violin even more beautifully than the piano.'

'Oh...thank—' She stopped. Her eyes widening. 'That was you applauding, wasn't it?'

'Sí.'

She spun around, taking in the flowers with fresh eyes. 'And these?'

'A fraction of what you deserve, *mi amor.*' Then, 'Have I lost you, Willow? Is it too late?'

Her throat clogged, thankfully stopping her eager answer. She needed to know what she was dealing with before her shattered heart disintegrated even further. 'That depends.'

'Tell me.'

'Can you ever forgive what happened in the past? Can you ever look at me and not see the daughter of the man who destroyed your family?'

'I never held what your father did against you. I never would.' His jaw tightened. 'He's here. He wants another chance with you. If it's not too late?'

Her breath caught. 'I'm willing to try if he is,' she murmured.

Jario swallowed. 'We've spoken. I haven't told him yet, but I'm buying his company. Everyone who wants their job back can have it. And... I've forgiven him, *tesoro.* You should take that win because you taught me that.'

'I did?' Elation surged with increments of hope.

He nodded. 'Your ability to see the good in everyone. To believe that everyone, no matter how flawed, is redeemable. I...want...no, I need that. You showed me there was light at the end of the tunnel. What the hell am I talking about? You're my light, Willow. It took watching you leave my yacht to realise that. But if you'll take me back, I promise I will never let you go. I love you.'

Her jaw dropped. 'You love me?'

'Probably since that night I turned around and saw you. It felt especially cruel that the fates would send me the woman of my dreams with the name Chatterton, but what I didn't know was that it was a blessing in disguise. You were exactly who I needed to knock me off my destructive path.' His eyes darkened. 'My only regret is that my father never met you.'

Tears prickled her eyes. 'Wherever he is, I'm sure he's looking down on you with pride and love, Jario. That if this is what you want, then he would want that for you, too.'

His breath shuddered out. 'There you go again. Being the blessing I don't deserve.'

'You more than deserve me. And… I love you, too, Jario. So much. But…your mother—'

'Will come around eventually. She'll see the beautiful, considerate person you are and know that I'm blessed to have you.'

The shattered pieces of her heart coalesced in a soaring rush that made her gasp. 'Oh, Jario.'

'Kiss me, *mi corazón*. Then let me fly us home.'

'To the yacht?'

Despite the pained look on his face, he shook his head. 'I left the yacht, and I've changed its name. To *Luz Guia*.'

She roughly translated it. 'Guiding light?'

He nodded. 'That's what you brought to me. But it was time to return home. To Los Angeles.'

'You've been busy. But I thought you said the yacht was home.'

'And it was a home of sorts before you arrived.' His hand drifted down her cheek and over her neck to gently cup her nape, his thumb tilting up her chin so she could look into his face. See the surfeit of emotion in his eyes. 'Now home is where you are. Home is in your arms and in your heart.' His hand dropped to her belly. 'In the family I hoped had started already but am committed to having with you if you want it, too.'

She blinked the tears back so she wouldn't miss a second of that loving smile. 'I do. So much. Oh, Jario. I promise to wrap those arms tight around you, always. Never let you go.'

His blinding smile caused a wild somersault in her chest. Then his own, more powerful and infinitely loving arms drew her close to his body. 'I'm going to hold you to that, *mi amor*. For several lifetimes.'

Standing on tiptoe, she brushed her nose over his, then a kiss over his mouth, her heart full to overflowing when she murmured, 'And a few more after that.'

* * * * *

Were you swept up in the drama of
Enemy's Game of Revenge*?*

Then why not try these other sensational stories by Maya Blake?

The Greek's Forgotten Marriage
Pregnant and Stolen by the Tycoon
Snowbound with the Irresistible Sicilian
Accidentally Wearing the Argentinian's Ring
Greek Pregnancy Clause

Available now!

BILLIONAIRE'S BRIDE BARGAIN

MILLIE ADAMS

MILLS & BOON

To Jackie, Lorraine and Caitlin—long may you roar.

CHAPTER ONE

The Pitbull is on board.

SHE SENT THE text off quickly.

Woof.

That was the response from Irinka, which was *liked* by the rest of the chat.

Auggie, short for Augusta, looked down at her phone and allowed her lips to twitch, just slightly. Then she looked up at her boss and his current companion of choice.

Auggie didn't judge women for associating with Matias.

A light shone upon him.

He was the single most beautiful man Auggie had ever seen. Tall and broad shouldered, with hair black as a raven's wing, and eyes like the night sky. They were different sorts of black, she had always thought.

The raven's wing spoke to the glossy, sleek nature of his hair.

The night sky spoke to the perils of space and the inevitable destruction a woman might face if she were to be pulled into his orbit.

Still, though, she couldn't blame the woman.

Matias was responsible for his own appalling behavior.

Though the media enabled him, in her humble opinion.

Glorious Golden Retriever Matias Balcazar Seen Out and About With New Woman!

Golden retriever, her well-rounded behind.

The man was a pitbull.

He would eat your children.

It was how he'd gotten his nickname in the group text, which was appropriately named Work Wives.

Because Irinka, Lynna and Maude were her work wives. And best friends. They'd started Your Girl Friday five years earlier with nothing but a dream, fantastic organizational skills and determination, and it was thriving now.

They were freelance assistants who operated with the utmost discretion. They assisted the richest of the rich with their lives, from managing their personal affairs—Irinka's specialty—to providing culinary brilliance—Lynna—to the rehabilitation and management of the elaborate grounds of ancient estates—Maude.

Auggie was not as specialized as her friends. She was a wrangler, of sorts. An assistant of all kinds. Currently, for Matias, she was his air stewardess. But he spent all his time jet setting around the world in a private plane, and that meant she functioned as a traveling secretary too.

And whether he knew it or not, she did her best to keep his secrets.

She was—happily—coming to the end of her contract with him. Your Girl Friday wasn't designed to ensnare them into full-time employment for one person. So when a job was all-encompassing it had a hard limit. Six months. But her contract with Matias was only for three.

Praise be.

She could tell the exact moment he perceived her. One of her greatest assets was her ability to function as wallpaper in whichever surroundings she currently occupied.

She was a chameleon.

One who had been spotted by the Pitbull.

She ignored the way that it affected her. The way that her stomach went tight when his dark eyes met hers. For heaven's sake, he had a *woman on his arm.* He was her boss—even if for a set period of time. And she… Well, she knew him. She might well be the only person on the planet who did. The image that they painted of him in the media was laughable.

Matias Javier Hernandez Balcazar, beloved by all, was the son of Javier Balcazar, the most ruthless Spanish billionaire in recent times. A man wholly uninterested in ethics, in kindness, in basic human decency. A conquistador of the modern era, and on and on.

There were really only a couple of things a person needed to know about Matias to know him.

The first was that he could not be told. He did whatever he wanted, whenever he wanted, as befitted his position as a billionaire. The second was that he hated his father. And from those two pieces of information flowed the truth.

The media spun a story of his life that just didn't make sense, not when you had met the real Matias.

Somehow, they saw his entry into his own father's industry as him taking what he had learned and building something with it. Not what it actually was. A cold-eyed attempt at taking over his family business and crushing it. She was certain that was what he was up to.

Of course, everyone imagined that he stood to inherit his father's wealth.

Auggie thought that the truth was perhaps slightly more complicated. Though she didn't have all the details, she knew that the truth of the matter was, Matias was anything but what he seemed.

"Augusta," he said, his accent rolling over the syllables of her name in a way that made her want to purr. "Could you get myself and Charmaine a drink?"

"Of course," she said, smiling like the decorative femme bot she was supposed to be and moving to the bar, anticipating exactly what he would have, and what the lady would be having. It was easy enough. She smiled as she poured his whiskey, and then mixed up an overly sweet drink with cherries in it for Charmaine.

Then she melted away into the background again, while standing quite in plain sight.

She picked up her phone again.

If I see another headline about what a glorious himbo this man is I will punch the next starry-eyed reporter I see.

Oh, come on, don't spoil the public's fascination with him.

This came from Lynna.

I won't, because I signed an NDA, as you know. But I'm just saying, I don't think I have ever met anyone whose public persona is as big of a lie as his.

Maude chimed in.

That can't be true. Billionaires are notorious liars. They're also usually okay with being the glorious bastards they are in full view of the public.

Is he awful?

That was Irinka asking.

No. But he's not what he seems.

At that point, Charmaine and Matias abandoned their drinks and disappeared into the bedroom at the back of the private plane. The really fun part was when Auggie had to accompany the women back to whatever city they had come from, if Matias had long-term work in the city they were landing in. That didn't happen every time, often transfer would be arranged in a different way, or the woman would stay over in the city, but never long-term with Matias. It really was an amazing trip. He managed to be a shameless womanizer who was loved by all. Even the women that he had finished with.

Nobody could hate him.

It made Auggie even more suspicious of him, frankly. Because that was some black magic. Different than the black of his hair. Different than his eyes. A kind of sorcery that she couldn't quite access.

That was the problem with him. He was *interesting.*

When she had taken the job with him she had been so certain that he would be dull. He was the world's favorite boyfriend, as Irinka had pointed out. He had a reputation for being polite, a generous employer, a man who gave extravagant tips to anyone who served him. He was quick with a smile.

But that smile never reached his eyes.

She put her headphones in because she didn't need to hear anything happening in the adjacent room. No, she did not.

She managed communications for Matias while they were in the air, and then did some finessing of his schedule. And once the time was appropriate, she put her ear to the bedroom door. And then she opened it slowly. They were both asleep, in bed. She had become very good at simply not looking at the man. Half-dressed, enjoying the aftermath of his liaison. It wasn't her business. He was allowed to conduct himself in whatever way he chose. But she had something she needed to do.

She snagged the woman's phone off of the nightstand and turned it so that it was held up to her face. Then she flinched, swiping up the screen on the unlocked phone, and going to the photos. There were none taken. Thank God. She had deleted pictures of Matias sleeping from multiple women's phones.

There were no photos, but she could see an email banner pop up with some text.

Once you finish with him, I need you to...

And then it cut off.

She sat there and looked at it. And she felt a vague sense of disquiet. Granted, Charmaine could be getting that email about anyone. In any context.

She might not have told anyone she was having a dirty weekend with a hot billionaire.

Auggie hovered her thumb over the email app. She had lines, and boundaries. She didn't invade people's privacy. She didn't go through texts, she didn't surf through all the photos, the only thing she tried to do—historically—was keep Matias's penis off the internet.

This went outside the boundaries of that.

Whatever it is, it isn't your business.

She let out a breath, and placed the phone back, gingerly. There were no pictures. That was all that mattered. The rest wasn't her problem and couldn't be.

She snuck back out of the room, and not for the first time, gave thanks that she was nearly at the end of all this.

Matias was so much more work than any man she'd ever contracted for. Usually she found her job a delightful challenge. She liked the freshness of having a new client every few months. Typically, what she was doing was giving extra and specialized help while someone increased workload for a new project, or needed help with some image maintenance during a challenging time.

She wasn't PR. But she often worked alongside a PR person to help with the flow of work, so that the subject of her help would look good, efficient, less stressed, etc.

Working with Matias just made her stressed half the time. And strung out on his beauty, which was a complication she'd never experienced before.

When the plane landed in Barcelona, both Matias

and Charmaine tumbled out of the bedroom. Looking disheveled, but lovely, both of them.

She wondered if Matias would ever settle down, or if he was destined to remain unattached. He seemed to exist in the eternal now, but she knew that wasn't true. Because a man didn't accidentally become as successful as he was. Not even if he came from a rich family. Because he had not used his father's money to get where he was.

There was just more to him. It constantly surprised her how the world was willing to take his enigmatic smile as the truth. To assume that he was simplistic, because he was happy to let them believe so. To trip through life as a man winning at the lowest difficulty setting. Which more than one person had said about him, and he seemed completely happy to take that on the chin. He was… Pleased to let people think he was a fool.

And that, to her, was the most suspicious thing of all.

"Charmaine will be staying in Barcelona for a couple of days, she wishes to see the offices."

"Oh," Auggie said. "So I won't be making a return trip, then."

That hit her strangely, and she knew it was because of the email.

When you're finished with him…

What had the email said? She was so mad she hadn't read it.

"Are you sure she wants to see your offices?" Auggie asked.

"Yes," he said, looking at her like she was a fool.

Charmaine's eyes clashed with Auggie's, and Auggie knew a moment of deep disquiet. She didn't like the look in the other woman's eyes.

Auggie was a girl's girl. Auggie was all about the freedom and power women had to shag Matias to their heart's content without judgment.

Being a girl's girl, though, meant when she didn't trust a woman, there was a reason.

This was nothing more than a gut feeling, but it was a strong one.

"Matias, can I speak to you for a moment?" she asked.

"No," he said smoothly. "Enjoy the city. I shouldn't need you for a couple of days."

She lifted her brows. "Really."

She didn't like this at all.

"Yes. You only worked for me for three months. I find that I can function just as well without you."

"Indeed." She hesitated. "Matias, I wonder if I should just go to the offices with you?"

"No, that won't be necessary."

Maybe he was a dumb, gorgeous idiot.

She swore Charmaine gave her a small smile before they turned away and began to get off the plane and Auggie was stewing.

She didn't know what Charmaine could do being at Matias's offices, but she just felt…she felt *something* about it.

And it had nothing to do with the fact that every day, every week, Matias got more and more attractive to her.

He was like a beautiful object in an art gallery.

Nice for some, but Auggie couldn't afford him. So she would look, but she would never touch.

She packed up her things and watched as Matias got

into a waiting limousine with Charmaine. Auggie was ushered into a town car. She was totally happy with that. Happy with the quiet, and the luxury that surrounded her. She was not happy to be told that she wasn't needed, mostly because she didn't believe it.

The Pitbull is disconcerting.

Why is that? Lynna asked.

Because he has brought a woman to the offices, and he said he doesn't need me.

Well, maybe he is a himbo. Only thinking with the Pitbull downstairs. Perhaps he wants to have her on his desk, Irinka said.

He is most assuredly only thinking with his downstairs brain, but he isn't stupid.

She got to the hotel room that had been reserved for her and set up her computer, and all her peripherals. She opened up Matias's schedule, and her calendar. Then she initiated a video call with the work wives.

"I'm in Barcelona."

"You look fantastic," said Irinka, who was always gorgeous in the most immaculate way.

"Glowing," Maude said. Maude, for her part, had mud on her cheek. She was wearing dungarees, and was standing out in a field.

"Irritated," said Lynna, who was standing in a large, commercial looking kitchen.

"I am irritated. Because he has deviated from the script, and I don't like it. I'm only glad that this is my last outing with him."

"Your next contract is at least for a shorter amount of time," Lynna said. "And with a slightly less infamous man."

“We need more female clients,” Auggie said, feeling full of woe.

“I would be happy to have more female clients,” Irinka said, “it’s only that men see our pictures and want to hire us. Also, women are happy to break up with their partners on their own. Men are the ones who typically need my services.”

Irinka was a dark horse. She always had been. She acted publicly as His Girl Friday’s secretary, and their avenue for connection to the rich and elite. But in reality she was a breakup artist for hire, and master of disguise. Her services required discretion, and backdoor connections, and she was an expert at both.

Auggie herself wasn’t built for subterfuge. She was too honest. Keeping her opinions to herself when her clients were being ridiculous was hard enough—and also why she spent so much time in their group text.

Lynna was the best chef in the world, in Auggie’s opinion. To taste her food was to taste magic. Some women could make a man long for them forever after a night. Lynna did it after a meal.

Maude was a fae thing, more at home in nature than in the city. She had once rescued a mouse from the science lab when they were at uni and had brought it to live in their dorms. Even now, her affinity for nature was her specialty.

Auggie, Lynna and Maude had all been friends since university, even though they were all from very different backgrounds.

Irinka was the illegitimate daughter of a duke, and a rumored Russian spy, and Irinka had inherited wealth, connections and a penchant for mystery. Maude had been an odd girl out, by virtue of her otherworldliness, and Auggie had related to her, because even though it was in a different fashion, Auggie felt like she was from a different world.

The American in the group.

Lynna was from Wales, but raised in Greece, with a wealthy family, who had lost everything while poor Lynna was at university. Her father had died during the horrific aftermath, and all the friends had rallied around Lynna to make sure she could still complete her studies. To make sure she could still have her life.

They'd stayed together after university too—starting His Girl Friday. With their powers combined, like they were Voltron, from the old cartoon. Individually, they were great. Together they were a powerful force. They'd overcome their past adversity and they'd turned it into something successful. Amazing.

Though she wasn't feeling all-powerful at the moment.

Worry nagged at the back of her brain.

"What?" Maude asked.

"I'm just… I don't trust this situation. And I am not his PR person, so this isn't my problem." She thought back to the number of times she had deleted pictures of his body off of women's phones. She had always squinted when she hadn't looked at those photos. Careful not to see more than she should. Also careful to make sure that he didn't end up plastered all over newspapers as naked as the day he was born.

So no, she wasn't his PR person, and he wasn't an *idiot*, but he did make questionable decisions where women were concerned.

“You don’t have to take care of him,” Lynna said. “It isn’t your job. You’re supposed to *assist* him. This isn’t… Caregiving.”

She said it kindly, but it lodged itself firmly in Auggie’s chest all the same.

“I know that.”

“You have that look about you. That paranoid look, that says you’re attaching life or death stakes to this situation, and he is not…”

“I know he isn’t my mother,” she said. “Also, he isn’t my problem after this. But you know, if he gets into a serious situation while I’m working for him, it is not going to help our business.”

“What do you think is going to happen?” Maude asked.

“I don’t know. I have a bad feeling about that woman. I have a bad feeling about this situation.” She just did. Even if she couldn’t say why. And Augusta Fremont had learned years ago to trust her intuition.

She was in Barcelona. And he wasn’t her responsibility, her friends were right. She wasn’t his babysitter. So she was going to go out, and she was going to have paella. She was going to let Matias sort out his own issues.

CHAPTER TWO

WHEN HER PHONE rang at five thirty the next morning she knew an instant shot of regret over taking the night off.

"Hello?"

"Is this Augusta Fremont?"

"Yes?" She rubbed her eyes and rolled over in her large, empty bed. If she was like Matias she would have gone out and found herself a bedmate. She would have batted her eyelashes and seduced a gorgeous Spaniard. But she was not, and she was alone. As per always. Her and her cell phone.

"Augusta Fremont of Your Girl Friday?"

"The very one," she said. She did not tell the woman on the other end of the line that everybody called her Auggie. She had hoped, when she was younger, that the nickname Gus might catch on. It was cuter, in her opinion. But no. She was Auggie forever. Now though, when she thought of the nickname, she heard it in her mother's voice, and it softened things inside of her.

"Do you have a comment to make on the news that Matias Balcazar is a fraud?"

"Excuse me?" she asked.

"Yes. Media outlets received reports this morning from an anonymous source alleging that he has engaged in a years-long corporate espionage campaign which has stolen information from his father, Javier Balcazar, and therefore he has built his image on lies."

"It isn't true," she said, sitting up and pushing her brown hair out of her face. "I know that for a fact. Matias is a self-made man whose reputation as such is very important to him. I've spent a great deal of time with him, and I can tell you, he never even mentions his father."

"Well, the evidence that was faxed to us this morning is quite compelling. It doesn't really matter whether you have a comment or not, the story is going to run everywhere."

"Expect a cease-and-desist," she said, hanging up the phone. She was panicking. Not so much because she cared about Matias, but because she was so connected with him.

She scrambled out of bed and put her clothes on. She was his keeper. For better or for worse. And Your Girl Friday was associated with him. His name was going to be strongly linked to them no matter what, and if this...

She was immediately spinning stories in her mind. Even as she was FaceTiming the work wives.

Irinka was lying in bed, glaring intently at the camera. Maude was out on a country road somewhere, she seemed to be walking a spaniel, but the camera was jiggling wildly, so it was hard to say.

Lynna was in a chicken coop. "Fresh eggs," she commented, lifting a shoulder.

"Well, here are some not fresh eggs. There's going to be a major scandal connected to the Pitbull."

"What, did he get caught with his hand in the honey jar, so to speak?" Irinka asked, rolling onto her back and bringing the phone with her. She sat up, revealing that she was wearing extremely luxe-looking pajamas.

"I wish. He got…" She covered her face with her free hand. "Somebody stole something from his office. It was Charmaine. I'm convinced. So that is some commitment to the bit, because she definitely slept with him."

"Auggie," Lynna said. "We've all seen him. It's not really hugely sacrificial for a woman to sleep with him."

"Like you would know," Auggie said.

If Lynna was put out by that shot about her nonexistent love life, she didn't let it show. Instead, she stroked a chicken's head, and stood, holding the phone up toward her face as she began to walk out of the chicken coop area.

Lynna was professionally unbothered.

"I have to fix this. What am I going to do?"

"You're not his publicist," Irinka pointed out. "She needs to get involved with this."

"But they called me. They called me in the morning, and they asked if I was Augusta Fremont of Your Girl Friday. And I am. We are all Your Girl Friday. If my most prominent client that I have ever had goes down in flames while I'm embedded in his life like this…"

"You need to be embedded in fixing it," Maude said, red-cheeked in the cold English air.

"Right. I do. You're right. I have to fix it. We built this business ourselves. And I can't count on anyone else to do this. Not a publicist, who thinks that the best way to shape his image is to paint him as an idiot. This just makes him look even more stupid."

"He's probably not *stupid*," Maude said thoughtfully. "It's just that he's egotistical. Overconfidence gets beagles into a lot of trouble also."

"He's not a beagle," she said.

"No, I know that," Maude said.

Auggie decided to let that go. "Remember in *Jaws*," Irinka said.

"I don't," Auggie said. "I don't share your affinity for shark movies."

"Well," Irinka said. "In *Jaws*, when they actually see the size of the shark, they realize they need a bigger boat. If you can't have a smaller shark, get a bigger boat."

"I'm not following," Auggie said.

"If there's a big headline, make a bigger one."

"Well, first I need to talk to him, I need to find out what's going on. I need to find out if there's any truth to this. Because we can always squash it with the truth."

Irinka laughed, the sound like a fork on crystal, and sat straight up in bed. "Are you that naïve, Auggie? You can't fix lies with the truth. Because there's a certain point where the truth doesn't matter. That's not what the public wants. They want a narrative. The idea that he might've done something underhanded to gain his success is a fantastic narrative, because you know he has secret haters."

"He doesn't. Everybody loves him. A light shines upon him. He is the most beautiful man in the world."

"He has slept with more women than most men have ever *met*," Irinka persisted. "He's rich, he's gorgeous, and people love to watch a guy like that fall. They really do."

"You think they're going to turn on him."

"I think that's what mobs do," Irinka said.

"Hedgehogs also do that," Maude said.

No one said anything in response.

"Okay," Auggie said. "I'll keep you posted. I have to go to… Wherever he's at."

"Good luck," Lynna said.

"We all need it," Auggie said, hanging up the phone. She took a couple of deep breaths and looked in the mirror. She was not quite as done up as she would like. But there were things she had to do. Very important things.

And then she was off like a hare, making a beeline straight for the residence that he kept in Barcelona. The address was in her files, and she had gotten a car before even finding it.

The whole drive she became more and more agitated. She was supposed to be finished with him soon and this was a logistical nightmare.

She had been nice, and she had been silent, and she had been the wallpaper, and look where it had gotten them both.

He was going to be reamed for this. She wasn't going to handle him gently here. She had tried to warn him when he'd gotten off the plane and he hadn't listened.

When she was dumped summarily out onto the sidewalk, she went to the wrought iron gates that led to a winding driveway, and pressed a button on the intercom. She was fueled by indignation and outrage. "Hello, Augusta Fremont is here to see Mr. Balcazar."

She did not expect Matias himself to respond to the intercom. "Of course you may enter, Augusta."

The gates swung open toward her, and she took two hopping steps backward, and then skittered inside, running up the steeply graded driveway toward the most opulent hacienda she had ever seen in her life. Tucked into the hills, with bright pink flowers spiraling all around, vines growing up a tall wall that encircled the outside of the stucco masterpiece. The red-tiled roof gleamed in the early morning sun, and Auggie had never been so full of hate. She leaned against the front door, trying to catch her breath. And then it opened, and she nearly tumbled inside, and right into the solid wall of Matias's body.

She gasped, and lunged backward. "You are in a crisis," she said.

His dark brows lifted, and he looked around. "Am I? I do not see a crisis anywhere in the vicinity."

"Of course you don't. Because it's not printed yet. You took Charmaine to the office, didn't you?"

"She wished to see the headquarters."

"She wished to do some digging. I'm convinced. I saw an email on her phone…"

"You were on her phone?"

"I always check their phones, Matias," she said, not breaking eye contact with him. "For photographs of your penis."

He looked shocked. Not by the word *penis*, she supposed. But by her pushing back against him. She didn't care. She had absolutely nothing to lose in this moment. She pinched the bridge of her nose and continued.

"I got a call from a media outlet this morning claiming that they received evidence that you engaged in corporate espionage."

And that was when the smile melted right off his face. "What?"

"They're claiming that you've been stealing from your father. *Everything.* Leads, information. I don't know what all. I'm not an expert in corporate espionage, I am an expert in… Knowing that this is a very bad thing."

"I have taken nothing from my father," he said, his voice suddenly hard.

"Well, they seem to think that you did. And supposedly there's evidence to that effect."

"Why do you think it was Charmaine?"

"I picked up her phone, and there was an email preview. It said, When you're done with him... I didn't read the rest because that isn't in my scope, but when you said you were taking her to the offices, it got my antennae up. I tried to get you stay back and talk to me, but you didn't."

"No," he said. "I didn't, but you didn't say you were worried she was going to do something nefarious."

"I didn't know what she was going to do, because I didn't know what she might find evidence of at your offices, Matias." That he might be guilty of corporate espionage was a problem, she supposed. It was just that she didn't care. Trying to apply ethics to billionaires was stupid, and in her opinion, based on everything she knew, his father was the worst, so what did it matter if he took some of the old man's trade secrets?

On moral grounds, she couldn't care less if she tried.

But if he was guilty, it was a complication in the practical sense.

He paused for a moment. "Why do you care?"

"What do you mean, *why do I care*?"

"Your contract with me ends next week."

"Exactly. And if I leave you in the rubble that is going to be... Smoldering when all of this comes out, it's going to reflect badly on me. On my company." And she was not a billionaire with generational wealth. She was worried about herself.

"And for a second I thought you cared."

Her phone buzzed and she pulled it out of her pocket.

Did you find the Pitbull?

His eyes glanced downward, and he caught the message on her lock screen. She put it away quickly.

"The Pitbull?" he asked.

"You have a code name, obviously, with my coworkers. Because we have to talk about logistics, but of course we're discreet." She gritted her teeth and did not say: unlike you.

"You call me a pitbull because you find me dangerous?"

Well, to his point, she had a week left on her contract with him. And no reason not to tell him exactly what she felt.

"I call you a pitbull, because pitbulls are *silly*, and *emotional*, and make very abrupt reactionary choices. That is what makes them dangerous, not their aggression. And apparently it's what makes you dangerous too."

"I am not *silly*," he said, the hardness in his eyes that she had never seen before.

"Well, you're going to have to do some work to prove that to me."

"I have nothing to prove to you Augusta. If you find me inconvenient, then leave."

"No. We have to fix this. We have to… We need a bigger boat."

"I don't know what that means."

"If you have a big shark, you need a bigger boat.

That's… That's what I know. This is going to hit the headlines, and it is going to create a sensation. You have to make a bigger sensation."

"I'm listening."

"What would be the biggest thing. The biggest thing…"

She turned to him suddenly. "You have to get married."

He stared at her for a moment, long and hard. "You're right, Augusta. I have to get married. And I think I should marry you."

CHAPTER THREE

FOR THE FIRST time Matias realized that he might have taken this too far.

He could have ruined his father in a variety of ways. He had decided to do it with a smile on his face. Because one thing Javier Balcazar had been very clear on when he was in the process of trying to bend his children to his will, was that you had to be ruthless to be successful.

You could not be kind. You could not give love. You could not receive love. You had to show no weakness, no happiness, no zeal for life.

So when Matias had made the decision that he was going to start a business competing with his own father and ultimately, absorb his father's company, he'd made the decision to cultivate a public persona that was opposite to Javier in every way.

To prove he was, and always had been, wrong in every way.

That he was cruel because he liked it, not because he had to be.

That he could have been a good father if he weren't a bad man.

Matias had thought that he was playing a game with his playboy persona. He had been certain of it, in fact.

Auggie might call him the Pitbull, but he felt more accurately, biblically, even, he was a wolf in sheep's clothing.

Innocent until proven otherwise.

But he had gotten to the point where he had let his guard down, where he had lost himself so much behind the polished veneer of playboy that he had made the sort of miscalculation that meant he had allowed someone to gain access to information about him, then he had retreated further beyond the veil than he had imagined.

The path was set. He had walked it for so long he didn't have to think about the destination.

Maybe that was the problem. This life, building wealth, acting like nothing mattered, taking a new woman to bed nearly every night, it was its own all-consuming endeavor. He never paused to think, because he never had to. He had, in the beginning. He had decided, after Seraphina's funeral that he would be everything his father had never been. That he would take his father's hallowed name and twist it into something different. That he would style himself as an entirely new man, and that he would exceed his father's success by more money, and more notoriety than the other man could ever fathom. He had never stolen from him. He had never needed to. Whatever Charmaine had found… It wasn't what she thought it was.

But he supposed that didn't matter. Public perception was what mattered.

His legacy was what mattered. Not in the way his father saw it, no, quite the opposite. What he wanted was to prove the old man useless, obsolete. His methods an exercise in pointless cruelty, and if he or anyone else believed that he had achieved his success by stealing from a man he despised he would feel like a victory had been handed to Javier.

He would not allow it.

"Me?"

He looked at Augusta. She had been his assistant, his flight attendant, for the past three months. She had practiced utmost discretion in all things. He practically lived on his jet, and the person who attended him there was the one that he saw most of anyone in his life.

She was beautiful, but in an almost nondescript way. Though, this morning, there was something different about her.

Perhaps it was the high color on her cheeks, the way that she was breathing hard. Perhaps it was that her long brown hair was loose around her shoulders, and wild from her running up the driveway.

Perhaps it was that she had no makeup on. Usually, she had a full face of it, very natural, but very polished.

There was something intimate about seeing her like this. He imagined not many did.

That was unimportant.

Her beauty was secondary to everything else. Though, he did feel that if he was going to show up with a random fiancée, she had to be believably beautiful.

Also, he had spent so much time with her over the last three months, and that was well documented.

There would of course, be women who tried to sell stories of him sleeping with them on the plane. There was nothing he could do about that. He didn't ask women to sign NDAs. Often, his treatment of them earned him respect even after they parted.

They didn't know him. Of course they didn't. But the performance he put on with them was a pleasant one.

If he could say one thing for the way he chose to live his life it was that he didn't cause harm without intending to.

And he would never hurt the innocent.

The guilty, on the other hand…

"We will have to come up with a convincing story, obviously," he said.

She blinked, her mouth dropping open. "About what exactly?"

"There have been witnesses," he said. "To my being in the same space as you while enjoying the company of another woman."

"Well, and maybe your plan is crazy," she said. "Did you ever stop to think of that?"

"No. Because it must be a woman that I have spent significant time with, and there is no one else."

"Well… Obviously we just got together then," she said. He could see the brightness in her eyes, a frantic thought process turning there. "It can work. So yes, there have been other women, but we were trying to keep things professional."

"Obviously. Because we have a contract."

"It's up next week," she said.

"Too long," he said. "We have to get the news out immediately. We almost have to make it look as if this is a backlash to our announcement. We have no time."

He picked up his phone and texted his PR firm. "There. I told them that they need to see the story that we are engaged. We will supply photographs within the next few hours, but we need the rumors to get out now."

"This is… Well, this is utterly unhinged," she said,

flexing her hands like little claws, looking extremely twitchy.

An odd thing, because Auggie had, in his view, always been polished and calm. But she'd shown up here in a rage he'd never seen before, and had not seemed to take a full breath since.

"Very few things matter to me, Augusta. But one is that I extricate myself from my father's legacy, and I will not have a narrative dominating the media that I have stolen my success from him. My father is a horrible man."

"I got the feeling that you didn't like him very much."

Few people spent large amounts of time in his presence. He was always on the move. But he wasn't shocked that Auggie had picked up on that after being around him so frequently these past months. Even with his most polished veneer on he never said a nice thing about Javier Balcazar.

She'd been present when his father had called on a couple of occasions. His father only ever called to remind Matias of the past. He only ever did it to drip poison into his ear, and he knew in those moments his veneer…slipped.

"An understatement," he said. "I hate my father. I hate him with every fiber of my being. I hope that he dies an old, lonely man. I wish him a long life only so that time can begin to twist everything that he is so proud of. That he might lose control of everything, including his body, so that he can know what it was like to grow up in his shadow. I despise my father," he said, all of the darkness in him rising up to the surface. "And this is the most appalling claim that could've ever been made against me."

"Do you think perhaps it's worth combating the rumors?"

"No," he said, his voice rough. "If we deny them, it cannot be right away. And it must be with the sort of attitude that suggests I find the rumors beneath me. I am living my life."

"They aren't true, though," she said.

"No," he said. "They're not true. I keep information on my father's company, but it isn't to steal from him. It's to keep tabs on him."

"You have stolen information," she said.

"No one will understand why except for me," he said.

"Well, all the world thinks that you're this… Dumb handsome log who sort of charmed his way into success."

"Because it doesn't benefit me to have them think of me otherwise. I like it that my enemies don't see me coming. You know I'm not dumb, Augusta."

"Yes," she said. "I do. Except the whole thing with Charmaine was dumb."

"It was… It was thoughtless. I… I have been playing this part long enough that sometimes I forget."

She shook her head. "I just… The problem is, if we pretend to get engaged, and then eventually we break up, how is that going to reflect on Your Girl Friday."

"We will part as I always do with my exes, Tesoro. Amicably. I remain friends with every woman who has ever graced my bed. I like women. I don't use them out of an abundance of disdain as many do."

"How nice of you," she said.

"Are you mocking me?"

"Yes," she said. "I am. Because you're trying to paint this… This confusing thing that you are, that you're doing, as something that is perfectly normal when it is absolutely not."

"I don't care what normal is," he said. "It has always been about revenge. Always. Do you know what my father wanted from his children? Compliance. He wanted us to be perfect mirrors of him. His daughter had to be angelic and feminine, pure in all ways. And I was to be his right hand. We were not raised with love, affection or care. We were raised under the iron fist of his authority and that does not make for a normal childhood. Therefore, it does not lead to a normal life."

Her eyes darted away from his. "I can understand that."

He very much doubted she could understand it. At least to the degree that she thought. She had no idea what it was like to grow up with a father like his.

Perhaps that wasn't fair. But he did not traffic in fairness.

Also, he trusted her. Even if it made no sense. But she'd seen him. In more unguarded moments—even if not many—than any other person had in years. She was here. She knew him. She knew this. It had to be her.

"We have to negotiate the terms of this," she said.

"You have already signed an NDA," he said.

"And you will have to sign one as well," she said, her dark eyes boring into his. She was a tiny little thing, but she was determined. He had always seen that quality in her. He had... Liked Auggie from the moment he had met her, though he refused to refer to her by the nickname he had heard the other women at the company call her.

It was a strange name for a small, cute woman. And yet,

in some way she exemplified it. But nicknames implied an intimacy that he did not experience with… Anyone.

"If you insist," he said.

"I do. Because if the truth of this came out, then it would be seen as entirely unethical. Already, we are walking a fine line. Because my clients will think that it's possible for me to become sexually involved with them. And…" Her cheeks went scarlet, and when she looked up at him then, he felt an answering tightness in his stomach.

Ridiculous. He'd had sex not twelve hours earlier. With a woman who had betrayed him, no less. Why should he get physically excited by the woman standing in front of him?

Because she interests you. Not the you that you pretend to be. The one that exists underneath.

He ignored that internal voice.

It was true, he was the living embodiment of the duality of man. But he didn't spend a lot of time thinking about that.

It was his ruthlessness that propelled him, it was his charisma that kept him afloat.

There was that very old concept. Being like a duck. Calm on the surface, paddling like hell underneath. He wouldn't compare himself to a duck. Perhaps a shark.

Though the media had chosen to compare him to a golden retriever.

"That's why you call me the Pitbull," he said, suddenly realizing. "Because you know that I'm not what they say."

She rolled her eyes. "Of course I know that. Do you really think you seem like a golden retriever? Like a happy, biddable, people-pleasing family pet?"

"The press seems to think so."

"You're a handsome man. And people love to apply positive qualities to men, particularly when they're handsome. But I've never thought the description of you seemed at all legitimate. Not even close."

"What is it you see?"

She drew back, just slightly. "I think you're dangerous. I haven't decided quite in what way."

"You think that I might've committed corporate espionage," he said.

"I actually don't. Mostly because you don't seem like a man who is angry that he got caught. I believe you. You're angry because you think stealing from your father is beneath you."

"Yes. But more than that, it defies the very point of… All of this."

"You have to tell me the truth."

"I don't talk about the past."

She sighed heavily, pinching the bridge of her nose. "Let's go into the dining room."

"Why?"

"I need coffee. I got woken up by a reporter demanding to know if I wanted to spill secrets about you. And I ran straight over here to try and fix it. When did Charmaine leave, by the way?"

"She didn't stay the whole night. Women never do."

"Well, undoubtedly not women on your father's payroll."

He growled. "Unconscionable…"

"Why did you let her in?"

"Because I…" He did not like this. Being centered by a tiny little creature. This was how he had lived his life for years. And of course, this was where his father saw weakness. He hadn't believed that it really was a weakness of his. He had thought it was part of the show. And yet, the show and the man had become one and the same. He engaged in the behavior, so what did it matter?—Was it part of a put-on or not? The truth was, he was indiscriminate when it came to taking lovers. His father knew that. And so of course that was the avenue that he took to come at him.

The mistake he had made was that in his disdain he had begun to minimize who his father was. He had shrunk him down to being a cruel man, and because cruelty was something that he despised, he had convinced himself that perhaps the cruelty was stupidity. Of course not. A person could be cruel and yet be horrendously clever. It was one of the great injustices of the world.

His father was clever.

But Matias was cleverer still, and he would see that he won this game.

His father wanted revenge for the loss of money.

Matias wanted revenge for the loss of his sister.

His motivation would always run deeper. It would always be more intense.

His motivation would always allow him to win.

Surely the monster couldn't win twice.

He stepped toward the dining room, and Augusta followed him. Then she went on through to the kitchen. "My staff has made coffee," he said.

"Excellent," she chirped.

Chirped.

She was far too cheerful about all of this. She returned with two cups of coffee, and set one in front of him, before taking a position down at the opposite end of the table and staring at him through the steam billowing up from her coffee mug.

"This relationship will be purely for show. No wedding. Just an engagement announcement."

"Agreed."

"I'm putting it in writing in the contract. There will be no sexual contact between us."

"*Tesoro*, surely you understand that there must be a level of physical contact between the two of us in public."

"A level. But remember, the fascination here will come from the fact that you're acting as a romantic and not a player."

"Your point?"

She lifted a shoulder. "What would people think if you looked at me differently. If you held onto me differently?"

"Why aren't you a publicist?"

"I don't want to be a wholesale minder of thoughtless billionaires."

"And yet you're so very good at it," he said dryly.

"I'm embroiled. I am at the center of this. Whether I want to be or not. That means I have to take some responsibility for it. I accept that. I intend to do that. I intend to come out of this like a damned Phoenix. I will rise from the ashes of your father. Not from yours."

She picked up her coffee mug, and took a sip.

"You are ruthless," he said.

"I can be. I don't come from anything. I don't come from wealth or status. I come from a small town in Oregon. I never thought that I would see the world. I spent my life working to survive. Navigating complicated government systems and the flawed American medical system. I've been a caregiver. I'm not doing it again. What I do, I do for myself."

If he had been another man he might have asked for details. But he wasn't a man who knew people. He didn't need to know Augusta.

Still, it was impossible to ignore her fierceness here. Her conviction.

"All right. Romantic. I can do that."

He wouldn't sleep with her. Sex was what had gotten him into this situation, and he felt the need to reevaluate some things. That was the problem. He had committed to this one hundred percent. He gave no quarter. He had to become what the media saw in many ways. He didn't pause to reflect. Because the character that he played would never engage in self-reflection. But also because the predator within knew the steps.

He wondered how long it had been since he had engaged in any kind of reckoning.

Perhaps because the last one had been so painful, he had simply decided not to have them anymore.

Because breaking the connection between his heart and the world, his soul and himself, often seemed the most expedient way forward.

"I will require you to be available on demand."

"For a period of time," she said.

"Two months, and we reevaluate at that point."

"All right."

"But if I don't feel that the job is done, then the job is not done," he said.

"You must promise when all of this is done you'll

speak highly of me. You'll make sure that my character is not besmirched, and you will recommend me, and my business to all of your billionaire friends."

He chuckled. "Done." He lifted a shoulder. "I am notorious for keeping things beyond cordial with women that I've associated with in the past. Thus ending our engagement will never reflect poorly on you."

"It can't reflect poorly on you either."

"No," he said. "If it does, then the whole thing will be for nothing."

"We'll evaluate that narrative at the end of the two months as well," she said. "We'll see how the wind is blowing in regard to the headlines."

"How soon can you collect your things from your hotel?"

"I only brought one bag."

"We are going to fly to London."

"London?"

"I think it's the best place for rampant media attention. It's either that, or New York or LA. I have offices in both places, but..."

"No. London."

"Perfect." She looked down at her hands. "I need to stop by Your Girl Friday before we make any public appearances."

"That is acceptable, but you will have to come to my penthouse no later than two o'clock in order to ready yourself for our public debut."

"That's fine. I can do that."

"Perfect. I will simply secure some new flight staff, and then we will be off."

CHAPTER FOUR

AUGGIE HADN'T FULLY thought through what he meant by securing new flight staff until they boarded the plane. Where she found herself being treated as Matias's guest, and not as the flight attendant. She knew a total out-of-body experience when she looked at a woman standing next to the liquor cabinet, wearing the same sort of smart outfit that Auggie normally did.

"Can I get you a drink?" the woman asked.

Auggie blinked. "Sure."

"Champagne," said Matias. "We are celebrating."

The woman, to her credit, did not ask *what* they were celebrating. Because of course people in her position knew that details would be revealed to them as the employers wished to reveal them.

It was the sort of thing that Auggie knew well.

Their champagne flutes were filled near to the top, and she took a seat with him in the position usually occupied by his arm candy.

She grimaced internally. She didn't like to think of the women in reductive terms. Perhaps he was their arm candy. So there. Equality.

She took a sip of the champagne, which was undoubtedly the best quality she had ever had.

She was going to have to try and explain all of this to the work wives. She had a feeling that Irinka would be proud of the resourcefulness. That Lynna would be slightly wary, but overall see the merit of it. It would likely wound Maude's softer soul. For her part, Auggie didn't feel like she could afford to be a romantic. She had never messed around with men. She had too many important things to try and build. Too much to make up for. Too many experiences to reclaim, and relationships hadn't been high on the list, because they would come with an obligation to another person.

It just wasn't what she wanted. So this was… Strange, but it didn't mean anything to her as far as romance went.

As far as attraction went…

She knew exactly what he was. She had watched him engage in all manner of uninhibited behaviors.

She wasn't stupid enough to get herself involved in that.

He might not be quite who the media thought he was, but he was indiscriminate with his body.

And that was fine. His decision.

But she didn't need to go involving herself in it.

Auggie liked to be an expert before she jumped into anything.

And sexual contact with Matias would require expert-level skills.

She didn't even have entry-level skills.

So when they finished their champagne, and he extended his hand, drawing her out of her seat, his hands warm, and much rougher than she would've imagined, her heart leapt up into her throat. "Time for us to retire, I think." His eyes were intent on hers, and she could barely breathe.

It was hammering against her breastbone. But she followed him, into the bedroom. The one that she had just sneaked into so that she could make sure the woman he was with was not taking pictures of him.

He closed the door behind them and lounged on the bed.

"Nothing to do but wait for a while," he said.

She pressed herself against the door, her shoulder blades tight against the hard surface.

"I'm not going to molest you," he said. He rolled over onto his back and looked up at the ceiling. "I don't have any need of that."

"Oh, I'm aware," she said. "But this is slightly uncomfortable for me."

"Why?"

"I've been in here many times after you've finished entertaining yourself with your guests. Like I said, I check their phones. For nudes."

"You cannot tell me this has actually been an issue."

"How are you naïve? It's laughable. There have been many instances. I always come in and make sure that those photos are deleted. And they never realize it."

"You must be joking."

"No."

"I don't think anyone else ever did that."

"Maybe not. But there are pictures of you floating out around on the internet."

"I don't care about that."

"You don't care if your naked body ends up posted on the internet?"

"Do I strike you as someone with insecurities?"

"That doesn't mean you want the entire world to have access to..."

"Does that mean that you see me naked?"

"This is the kind of thing that I was worried about. Lines are being crossed."

"It's a genuine question," he said.

"Yes. Though, I can't say that I… Lingered on it."

"Then you have more restraint than some," he said.

"Nice to know that your ego is very healthy and undented in spite of everything that you've done to create the situation," she said.

"I didn't hire someone to break into my files."

"You also didn't protect them very well."

"Fair. I admit that I was complacent."

"I imagine it's difficult not to buy into your own press."

He frowned. "I don't think that I buy into my own press. I know how much of it's a lie."

"You know what everyone thinks about you. And I suppose it's easy to imagine that is true universally. That you are… This beloved playboy who is so enjoyed by women that of course one of them wouldn't actually be out to get you."

"I don't think that's the case."

"You don't think that's the case, but do you know any of the women that you slept with? Am I the first woman that you've ever conversed with in this room?" She wished that she wasn't like this. She wished that she didn't have to belabor the point. But she found that she did, even as the topic was making her uncomfortable. Even as she felt like she was breathless from talking to him about sex and his body in the enclosed space of this room.

She knew who she was. If she did choose to take a

lover, it wasn't going to be him. Not one with so many strings attached. Not one who… Who created such powerful feelings inside of her. It was attraction, she knew that. And the worst thing was she knew that it was an incredibly basic response to him. It was simply how he made women feel. Because he was Matias Javier Hernandez Balcazar, and he was widely considered to be the most beautiful man in the world. It would be strange if she didn't respond to him in this way.

No. If she ever did decide to take a lover, it would be an English man, perhaps. And they would have a casual arrangement, where they met at a cottage on rainy afternoons, and they would drink tea and make love.

She did not think that Matias made love.

She rather thought that there was a rougher and cruder term for what he did in bed. And she ignored the tightening in her stomach that indicated she was interested in discovering for herself.

"No," he said. "But I don't actually talk to anyone. In fact, you and I have exchanged more honest conversation in the last few hours than I have with anyone in years." He didn't sound surprised by this, but a bit grim. And she felt…

How strange. How strange to know that this man had given more to her than he had to anyone else for a long time.

His connections were physical, theirs wasn't.

It made her feel…she couldn't parse it. She wasn't sure she wanted to.

"Anyone?"

"Anyone who knows me knows me on my own terms. And my terms are that I do not wish to be perceived."

"Why is that?"

"Because who I was doesn't serve me. At least not in any way beyond guiding me toward getting revenge on my father."

"You should tell me why you hate him."

"You've done research on me, I assume?"

"I know about you, yes. I've read your bio."

"Then you know I had a sister."

"Yes," she said slowly, "I know that you had a sister."

"What you don't know is that I'm responsible for her death."

He watched her process that information, her birdlike features knitted together tightly as she tried to take into consideration what he had just said. He didn't know why he wanted to push her like this. She was helping him. But perhaps what he really wanted to see was if she was up for this. Because it wasn't going to be easy. The truth was, Javier had set his sights on him. And that meant there would be more. So there could be no secrets between himself and Augusta, not really. He would have to make sure the same was true with her. Because things would come out. That was the truth of it.

His father would stop at nothing.

"You… You were responsible?"

"Yes. In order to explain, I will have to paint a clearer picture of how my father ran our household. My mother was meek and compliant. There was no other way to survive a life with him. He was cruel. He ruled with an iron fist. Though he never stooped to hitting us with it. He was an emotional manipulator, he would set a bar, and if we would clear it, he would tell us that we hadn't.

He changed the metrics often. I wanted to please him. I bent over backward trying to make myself into the son that he wanted me to be. Seraphina… She kicked against it. She couldn't stand what he made of our mother. She couldn't stand being subjected to his demands. When she began rebelling, he did everything he could to stop it. He cut her off financially, he stopped our mother from speaking to her. I still kept in touch. It wasn't until later that I realized he allowed it for reasons of control. As long as there was a link between himself and Seraphina then he could still get to her. And as long as there was still someone she cared for in the family… There was something to exploit. I was… I was convinced that what he was doing was necessary. That Seraphina was harming herself, and… It wasn't wrong. Some of her behavior was self-destructive. And yet, his methods were not… It was not the way. But I didn't believe that, not at the time. At the time, I was a boy. I was his thing. His robotic soldier. I ordered the staff around the way that he did, I lived my life with ruthless precision. I denied myself all pleasures of the flesh. And when he told me that I had to go and give Seraphina the hard word that I would no longer be able to support her or be in her life unless she came home and complied with all of my father's demands… She overdosed. That same night. Because the one person she had thought cared about her had been acting as surveillance, had betrayed her in exactly the same way."

He had never told the story out loud before, and it sounded strange in his voice. He had said it in his own head many times. Cementing his culpability in what had happened.

He hated himself for it. He didn't hate himself less for hearing it said aloud. If anything, he hated himself slightly more, because it made him feel closer to the twenty-year-old that had done his father's bidding with such vigor. With such conviction.

"The most truly terrifying thing to learn about yourself is that you have the capacity to harm those you love, because you have been brainwashed. Manipulated. To realize that you are not half so clever as you think you are. That was when I decided that it all had to end. That was when… At Seraphina's funeral, when my father stood there without a tear on his cheek, I vowed that I would end him. But not only that, that I would prove the way he saw the world meant nothing. I decided to be all the things he had ever told me not to be, to compete with him, and to win. To destroy him. While smiling. You see, I have no desire to steal secrets from my father, I don't need them. But I do like to keep tabs on him."

"Matias… I'm sorry, I didn't know."

Her words were like a balm, but he refused to let it soothe anything.

"Why would you know? I've never spoken to anyone about it. It is immaterial. What happened then can't be changed. And that is the truly chilling thing about revenge plans, Augusta. They fixed nothing. They're simply more destruction in an already destroyed landscape."

"But if you feel that way, why do it?"

"Because I want scorched earth. I don't want to fix anything, I know it's impossible. I just want to salt the ground so that nothing can grow there ever again."

"Pitbull," she said. "I knew it."

"You said pitbulls weren't that aggressive."

"Mostly, they aren't. Like I said, they're reactionary. But when they're abused… They get mean."

"Apt, then," he said.

She seemed to be sitting with the revelation, though her next question wasn't about Seraphina. "Why let the media think you're… Simple?"

"Because I prefer to be unknowable. All evidence suggests that can't possibly be true, doesn't it? It's amusing, I think, that they see me as being something so utterly unthreatening."

"It allows you to move in the open," she said.

"Yes. Exactly. And in the end, I cannot imagine a more poetic headline. My father's fool of a son putting him out of business. Better that I'm not thought of as ruthless or brilliant or exacting. It makes my father's eventual downfall that much more humiliating for him."

"You thought of everything," she said.

"Absolutely everything," he repeated. "Except what I'll do when it's finished."

"Won't you just… Live?"

"Maybe," he said. But he didn't mean it.

The truth was, he was accomplished at numbing the pain. At blunting his grief with alcohol, with sex. He didn't touch drugs, because they had been the undoing of Seraphina, and he would never line the pockets of any of the people who had sold her illegal substances, he would never contribute to that trade. It had less to do with treating his own body like a temple of any kind and more to do with the festering rot of the industry.

"You can have a life, you know," she said.

"My sister doesn't," he said. "You can see where my dilemma is."

"Do you think that maybe it's not a great tribute to her to not live at all?"

"And what would you know about that?"

"I know about grief. Whether you can compare the two or not."

"Comparison is the thief of joy, I hear."

"My mother died," she said. "When I was eighteen. I never knew my father. She was the only parent that I had."

"I'm sorry. Let me tell you, a bad father is worse than no father."

"I suppose so," she said. "Neither of us would really know."

He nodded slowly. She had been alone in the world at eighteen. And she didn't seem to come from means. He wondered how she had navigated that. What she had done. He didn't ask.

It explained her. The determination, the scrap.

"We should land soon," she said. "Maybe I'll try to do some work."

"Is your computer in here?"

"Yes. I'll just… Sit over here."

And she did, at a desk in the corner of the room, working away, and he watched. Fascinated by her. By the focus that she gave to what she did. There was definitely more fire to her than he had ever seen when she was simply acting as his flight attendant. But she wasn't an entirely different person. She interested him more than he would like to admit. But he supposed that was a good thing. Because over the next couple of months they were going to spend a lot of time together.

CHAPTER FIVE

AUGGIE DIDN'T THINK she breathed properly until they landed in London, and she separated from Matias. She went as quickly as she could to the Your Girl Friday headquarters, in a lovely little office space in London. As soon as she arrived upstairs to their suite, she spread her hands wide and threw her arms up over her head. "I came up with a solution."

"Good," Irinka said. "Because I'm hearing rumblings through my contacts that the brewing storm is going to be a big one."

"I'm going to pretend to be engaged to him."

Everyone stared at her. Mouths open, eyes wide. Irinka did not look overly proud of her like she had predicted.

"You what?" Lynna asked.

"I decided that I would get a bigger boat. A bigger headline. And that headline is that notorious playboy Matias Javier Hernandez Balcazar has traded in a life of debauchery for one of commitment."

"This is…not a good idea," Lynna said.

Auggie was instantly annoyed.

"Oh, are we going to talk about *bad ideas* now, Lynna? And what we all think they might be? Because we all agree that it is a bad idea you continue to go and stay at Athan Akakios' house once a year and *make him meals* when his father is responsible for the ruination of your entire family."

Lynna waved a hand like she was brushing Auggie's words out of the air. "You don't know what my eventual plans are. Perhaps I'm playing a long game. Death by Chocolate doesn't always have to be a metaphor, Auggie."

"If you're plotting murder on company time we do need to know about it, though," Maude said.

Maude could never stand for a creature to be in distress. But apparently beautiful Greek billionaires with dark souls were an exception.

Auggie couldn't argue.

But then, Maude turned her wide, compassionate eyes to Auggie.

"Let's not get derailed with Lynna. Why *you*?" Maude asked.

"Because, actually trying to find somebody who would do this, who could be trusted, fast enough… It is not even reasonable. I was there. I have to do it."

"In exchange for what?"

"Contacts. He is going to help grow our client base beyond our wildest dreams. I really do believe that."

"Do you?" Irinka said. "You really can't see what might go wrong with you pretending to get engaged to a client? It could open you up to all kinds of harassment. I am extra concerned with keeping boundaries in place."

She did know. Because Irinka's job was tricky, and it required total discretion. No one could know, broadly, that she did it, and yet the right people had to know when they needed her. But there could be no confusion among clients that she was an escort, either. Her lines had to be neatly and clearly drawn, while she stayed in the shadows and that was a difficult task.

Auggie never envied it.

"I know. I *know*," she said a second time just to make sure that she emphasized it appropriately. "I know exactly how loaded it is, and how big of a risk it is. Trust me. But either way, it's a sticky situation."

"We could just walk away," Lynna pointed out. "We don't have to be the cleanup crew."

"But if we are," Auggie said, "then imagine what that will do to our reputations. Imagine."

Everyone looked up, and it was clear that nobody wanted to endorse her acting as a sacrificial lamb in this way, but they could all absolutely see the benefit.

"I promise that I'll be safe. I'm drawing up an agreement." She went to the computer and sat down at her white desk. They had chosen to make their office bright, filled with light colors, golds and pastels. Because they were as tough as any man, but they didn't have to demonstrate that by sacrificing femininity. Far from it. Maybe that was her problem now. She was trying to right too many wrongs every time she did a single thing. They all were, honestly. The combination of the four of them, and all of their issues meant that they were a company comprised almost entirely of a desire to prove something. There were worse things. She really believed that. Far worse things.

But it made everything feel weighty. And just a little bit more intense at times.

She opened up a document, their boilerplate for a nondisclosure agreement, and then for terms and conditions of their association.

"You aren't going to sleep with him," Irinka said.

"No," Auggie responded, fighting the urge to laugh out of discomfort and a feeling of being caught. "Of course I'm not."

"Well, I just want to make sure you get that in the agreement."

She felt warm, and very uncomfortable. Like Irinka could see inside her head, inside to where all her secret fantasies were.

"Believe me, I've covered that. I know that you deal with a lot of men who try to push the boundaries of your agreement."

"Not anymore. My reputation precedes me. They know better."

"Good. I hope your reputation insulates me." The first thing she did was add in a clause that said no more physical contact than absolutely necessary, and only in public.

"You should put no contact below the waist. Or… In the front, above your waist."

"Are you telling me to put *Don't grope me in the Ts and Cs*?"

In spite of herself, her breasts felt heavy. He was not going to grope her. She didn't want him to anyway. It was actually laughable to think about Matias doing anything quite so prurient as that. Everything he did was sexual, yes, but there was nothing grasping or adolescent about it. She knew that all too well. She had watched the way his hand skimmed the curves of the women that he was with on the plane. Even while she had done her best to redirect her focus elsewhere. She had been aware.

It was impossible not to be.

She had done her best to try and block out the raw

sexual nature that radiated from him, but of course that was extremely difficult.

She didn't like admitting that she was vulnerable to that part of him. Because it was pointless. She didn't want to be vulnerable to anything or anyone, frankly.

"You're snarling," Maude said.

"I am *not*," Auggie responded. She finished with the papers and sent them directly to his email. Then she slammed the laptop shut and stood up from the desk. "And do not tell me I look like a hedgehog, Maude. I'm good. Honestly, I just came to tell you all because it's going to break and it's going to break big. Tonight."

"That sounds so ominous. Like a prophecy from a fantasy novel," Maude said.

"It's not," she said. "Not even close. Thank you, though."

Their intercom buzzed. "Ms. Fremont, a car has arrived for you."

She frowned. Then she looked at her phone, and saw that she had a text from Matias. I need you to prepare yourself for tonight. Get in the car.

She scowled.

"Why are you scowling?" Maude asked.

"I'm scowling because he's already being annoying. But that's… That is the agreement I've made. To continue to deal with the Pitbull."

"Guard your chastity," Lynna said.

"Thanks, Lynna," said Auggie. "Do you happen to have a belt on hand?"

"No," she said, grinning benignly. "I've never needed one."

"I'll be safe," she said, scurrying back out of the office, and into the elevator.

She looked down at her phone. And then she sent back a text.

I hope this isn't going to be degrading.

When have I ever degraded anyone?

It was a good point.

I don't know. I'm not in your bedroom the entire time we are going on long-haul flights.

Very funny.

I am very funny, Matias.

I didn't know that about you.

You never really bothered to talk to me.

She had watched him be amusing, and witty. She had seen him be filled with a dark rage that made a sense of disquiet expand inside of her. But she had mostly been nothing to him. Nothing at all.

It was on purpose. How could it not be? But still, she realized that actually put her at a slight advantage. He didn't know her.

She pondered that all the way to the ground floor, and then when she exited the building she saw a stark black car parked against the curb.

She opened up the door and slipped inside, and shrieked when she slid down the seat, and against his hard body.

"I didn't know you would be in the car," she said, jumping back like an angry cat.

"Well, that's not going to be very convincing," he said.

"You startled me. There was a whole human in the car I wasn't expecting to see."

"I gather that."

She practically hissed and gathered herself into the corner of the car as it drove away from the curb.

"I have arranged for several stylists to come to my penthouse."

"Oh. Do you need a makeover?"

He treated her to a grin that was a bit more to see than the one he generally showed the public. "I'm fine the way that I am."

"Oh. So only the woman needs to be changed irrevocably to be acceptable. I thought you were supposed to be a progressive playboy."

"If by 'progressive' you mean that I love and respect women, then I suppose I am."

"Many people would argue that a man who is as promiscuous as you are doesn't respect women."

"That would only be true if you find sex inherently disrespectful. I believe that using another person for sex can be disrespectful. I believe that a man who acts as a selfish lover, who sees the woman that he's in bed with as less than him, or as someone worthy of contempt because she has chosen to sleep with him, is a man who ought to be hanged."

"Strong words," she said.

"It contributes to that great, unsolvable problem created in the world by men, does it not?"

"Explain," she said.

"Men want women to be sexually available. Yet judge them when they are. I have always found the standards of men to be unfair in that regard. And I have certainly never sought to perpetuate that sort of behavior."

"An activist."

"You said it, not me."

"Your father was that sort of man," she said, understanding then.

"Yes, he was. An exacting set of standards for others that he did not hold himself to. A hypocrite. I have no patience for hypocrites, Augusta. My sister was cruelly treated by a society that hates a rebellious woman. Who sees a spark of defiance in them is something to be crushed, not cultivated. What was a strength in me that could be reframed, was seen as a portent in her. I am a great many things, I have committed a number of sins in the pursuit of revenge against my father, and I have no doubt that I will commit innumerable sins more. But I don't hurt women. I do not hold myself to different standards than I would anyone else."

"And yet I'm the one getting the makeover," she said, though not quite so sharply as she might have, because the mention of his sister gouged her a bit.

"I already had mine. I think perhaps you don't understand exactly what I was back then. I might well have worn my suit as a military uniform. I was barely able to smile, let alone tell a joke. I could no more have amused a companion with a witty story than I could have pulled a rabbit out of the hat. I can do both, now, incidentally."

"Cheap magic tricks?"

"Sleight-of-hand can be useful for many things."

For some reason that made her face get hot. It should conjure up ridiculous images. Of Las Vegas and cheesy shows. But there was something about how he said it, how he looked at her when he did, that made it very clear he was talking about something else entirely.

Her body couldn't help but respond. She hated herself then a little bit. For being so… Susceptible to him. Even while he was saying exactly what he was. Maybe that was the secret. There was no shame in him, and he was exactly what he appeared to be. Every woman who got involved with him knew exactly what she was getting. It was well-publicized.

"Is that your secret?"

"What exactly?"

"You don't promise women anything. You are actually quite honest in some ways."

"In a sense," he said.

Of course, she also knew that he hid his intensity from everyone. She had seen it. It was a force. The kind that… That was the thing that could trap a woman. That intensity. When he played easy and affable, it was easy to believe that nothing else was there. That there was nothing deeper to him. That he was only the very shallow puddle he pretended to be, and that made it easy to think of him as a jungle gym that a woman could climb on and leave behind.

Not her, necessarily, but a woman. One who had experience of that kind of thing.

She had seen the intensity.

Just then, the car pulled up to his penthouse, delivering her from her thoughts. The building was beautiful, well appointed. She had been here before, but had never gone inside his residence. Just to the lobby. Which was all gold and marble elegance, ostentatious and fitting a jackdaw. A man who put brightly colored feathers over his plumage to disguise what he really was.

"You're the Scarlet Pimpernel," she said.

"Excuse me what?" he asked as he opened up the elevator that led to his floor.

"I was just thinking. You disguise your true nature behind a façade that allows people to underestimate you. It's a book. About a nobleman during the French Revolution who pretended to be an empty-headed fop in order to escape detection as a man who was helping people escape the gallows. It is also a movie, one that my mother liked quite a bit. So, I can pretend that I read the book, but I didn't."

"And you think that's me?"

"Yes. Essentially. It suits you to have people underestimate you, but only on your terms."

"Yes," he said, smiling wryly, "only on my terms."

They arrived at the top floor, and the elevator doors opened, revealing the grand scope of his penthouse. It was filled with people. She was trying to take in the opulent details of the room, but was distracted by the crowd that immediately rushed around her. "Jewel tones, I think," said one of the men. "Matching manicure," said a woman.

"I think perhaps a champagne-colored diamond."

She was being made over.

And she had no choice but to surrender.

CHAPTER SIX

MATIAS TOOK HIMSELF to his study while his team went to work on Augusta. She had looked deeply irritated with the whole thing, and he thought it best to let nature—by which he meant his well-paid team of experts—take its course.

He decided to make a phone call to his father.

"Hola," he said. *"Como estas?"*

"Is that you, Matias?" his father asked in Spanish.

"*Si*. I had wondered when we might connect again. What a shame it has to be under these conditions."

"The conditions that you have been stealing from my company?"

"A neatly fabricated fairy tale," Matias said.

"I do not think the information the whore sent to me is wrong."

Matias bit back a growl of rage. "No Father, don't hire a woman to do a job and insult her because she did it well."

"Don't say I never gave you anything."

"Perhaps I cannot say that. But you took something from me. And I will never forgive it."

"If you are still upset about your sister, you must understand. There are people who are disposable. They will not amount to anything. Your sister might have lived ten more years, but the path she was on, she would've died young. On that you can trust me. Absolutely."

"You can say that about your own daughter?"

"I do not have a daughter."

Rage poured through Matias's veins. "I would never steal from you. Because you have nothing I value. Let us make that one thing exceptionally clear." It cost him then, not to make threats. Not to tell him exactly what he wanted to do to him. How what he really wanted was to wrap his hands around his father's neck and squeeze tight until the life left his eyes. No. Because he would be recording the conversation. Of course he would. He would want evidence that Matias was every bit as dark and damaged as he was accusing him of being. It was true.

"My life is going well," he said. "I'm on the cusp of a personal triumph. You can try to spread lies about me, but they will not prevail. How could they? I am well-liked, well-regarded, and more famous than you will ever be."

"You also behave as if you don't have a brain in your head. And people truly do love to uncover the sins of nepo babies these days, don't they? That is what they call it. What was once a legacy is now seen as an unfair advantage. And if they thought you steal directly from your father…"

"I think you'll find there are more interesting stories for them to read about this week." He paused for a moment. "I only want one thing from you, really, Father."

"And what is that?"

"When you get to hell, give me a call and let me know how hot it is."

Matias hung up the phone, not entirely satisfied with

his discretion, but at least it hadn't been a literal threat. He considered that something of a triumph.

When he made his way back out into the living area, the flurry of activity was gone. It seemed as if they had all melted away now that their jobs were complete.

He stood there for a moment and looked around the ornate space. It was not to his taste at all. It was overly luxurious, overstuffed, over comfortable. It was made to be a haven for someone else. Someone who didn't exist.

He heard a door open, and he turned.

And there she was.

She was extraordinary.

Her glossy brown hair fell past her shoulders in sleek waves, a deep side part held fixed into place by a sparkling diamond flower. She was reminiscent of a Hollywood actress from the golden age. Her dress was strapless, her shoulders bare. The color a sort of electric orange that he would not have thought would be fetching on anyone, but was astonishing on her. Her matching lipstick and nail polish added to the effect. But it was the massive diamond ring on her left finger that truly drew the eye.

That was the point of all this. Not the way the dress shaped lovingly to a body that was curvier than he had realized, not the way her legs looked, elongated by the brightly colored pumps that she wore. No. The ring was the star of the show, and he could see it from across the room. A stunning display. That would call attention to itself instantly.

"Perfection," he said.

Her face shimmered, and while he was certain it had to be makeup, it seemed to come from deeper as well.

"And you say that I'm the Scarlet Pimpernel," he said.

It was like he had forgotten that anyone else was standing there.

"What does that mean?" she asked.

"Surely you must know what it means."

"I wouldn't have asked you if I knew," she said.

"Come," he said. "We will go downstairs and get in the car."

"Thank you," she said, turning around and facing the team. He did not bother to issue a thanks. They were well compensated.

"What happened to your famously good-natured demeanor?" She asked that question as soon as they were in the elevator. He could hardly recall having a good-natured demeanor.

"I just had a phone call with my father."

She blanched. "Oh. That doesn't seem like the best idea."

"Don't worry, I resisted the urge to transform into a mustache-twirling villain."

"Well, while that is good to know, it does seem as if perhaps it was ill-advised timing on your part."

"I will see to my own timing, thank you."

He looked at her profile, at the gentle slope of her nose, the sharp curve of her cheekbone. She was an exceptionally beautiful woman, but beauty was a common thing. It didn't feel common just then.

Her beauty cut through the rage he felt now. The anger at his father. His anger at himself.

He was caught, just then, suspended between the reality of what he was, the role he played in the world, and the truth that was Auggie, and what she made him feel.

That she made him feel at all.

She challenged him. She unearthed parts of him long buried. He hadn't asked for that. He didn't want it.

She was silent for a moment. "But what did you mean by that? That *I* was the Scarlet Pimpernel."

It was her words that sliced through him. Cutting his normally impenetrable façade to ribbons. He wanted to return the favor.

"You have always seemed a perfectly pleasant looking woman, but you have a way of hiding yourself. You are more beautiful than any woman I've brought on the plane in your time there, and yet, you found a way to sort of blend into the background."

Her cheeks went red. "It's my job," she said. "Also, I am not *so* beautiful."

"How do you know that?"

"Because the only time a man has ever put a ring on my finger it has been for a ruse?"

"I've never been engaged either, and yet it is a truth universally acknowledged that I am extremely handsome."

"And very modest," she said, smiling up at him overly sweetly. Her complexion was clear, her brown eyes addictive. He wanted to keep searching for other layers of color in their depths. But that was a foolish thought. One perhaps that more matched a man who would've chosen that particular decor for his penthouse. And not who Matias truly was.

They got into the town car again, and were whisked to the trendiest part of the city where it was an absolute certainty that they would be seen and photographed. And that her ring would be noticed.

"We likely won't be set upon by paparazzi," he said. "Not until after this story breaks. This will be the calm. This will be the moment where we spark the imaginations of those around us."

"What is it like inside your head?" Augusta asked.

"What do you mean?"

"I have never thought that my mere presence would spark the imagination of anyone."

"And why not? You are stunning. Your mere presence could incite whole volumes of sonnets."

She looked away. "You're too good at that."

Was he? Was that what he was doing? His same old sort of display. He didn't think so. But then perhaps it didn't matter.

Perhaps all that mattered was that it had accomplished his goal. She looked happy. And they would look believably a couple. What else could he possibly want?

They arrived at the restaurant and when he opened the door, he reached out toward her. "It is time," he said.

She took his hand, and he pulled her out into the night. Into his world.

She had to remember not to get lost in this. Admittedly, she was kind of entranced by her own appearance. She had never looked like this. She had never looked so… Beautiful before. She had never really thought of herself as beautiful. She had thought of herself as someone who had an adequate canvas, she supposed. She knew how to fix herself up, though nothing like the way she had been fixed up today. She would never have chosen this color for herself, and yet it highlighted her pale complexion to perfection, it made her hair color seem deeper, more exotic—which was not what she would normally refer to the mousy brown as.

Indeed, nothing about her seemed mousy now. She was more than just Auggie from Oregon, who had lived a quiet life, learning to pay bills and manage medical visits before she had learned how to drive.

She felt… Special. She felt like she was sparkling. Nothing had ever been like this before, and it was tempting, so tempting, to let herself get lost in the fantasy.

To let herself get lost in him. Especially when he closed his large, firm hand around hers and pulled her out of the car.

His touch made her flutter. She couldn't deny that.

And then he looked at her and she… She melted. Inside.

She knew that it was a game. They'd just talked about how they both had the ability to hide themselves when they needed to. It should reinforce that this was fake and so were they, but it made her feel closer to him.

This man who was…only a day ago he'd been her boss. She'd watched him touch other women, but never her.

She'd never even let herself fantasize about it, and now here she was.

He was a force. It wasn't a mystery why women flocked to him, but there was something more in this moment. In being next to him and being so aware of the heat of his body, the masculine scent of him.

And how this had never been her before.

She was the one who took care of people. Who arranged things. Organized them. She was like a very accomplished stapler.

She didn't feel like a stapler, or wallpaper, or like a

girl who had been stuck in her house for years taking care of her mother.

Right now, she felt like a woman.

That it was a game didn't change that. If anything, it *heightened* the way she felt.

So far away from the girl she'd been. A woman who was sophisticated enough to play games with the world's most renowned playboy.

She didn't feel like Auggie, not right now.

She was Matias's date.

He reached for her hand, and as his fingers wrapped around hers, her breath left her body in a gust.

She found herself relishing the feel of his touch. Rough hands, strong. His walk was sure and certain as he led her down the sidewalk to the restaurant. She looked to the left, and the right, she could see people taking photos of them with their cell phones. She didn't see any paparazzi, as he had said.

"If there are official photographers it will take them a while to arrive. Though I have deliberately taken us to a high-profile place. Where there are certain to be many celebrities out and about, which means there will be paparazzi."

Of course. It was a game, she knew that. In her sort of jack of all trades type of work, she had managed schedules, images and a great many other things. She didn't know how every sausage was made, but the fact was, she knew that the world was primarily comprised of complex sausage. It didn't just make itself. There were whole teams that were in charge of cultivating images, and making sure people were elevated in the right spaces and places. She just wasn't used to being the sausage.

That metaphor had run itself out. But she was trying to distract herself. Trying to get a handle on her emotions. Because this wasn't real.

Anyway, she had never wanted this. She had never needed this kind of fantasy. It wasn't her. She didn't harbor secret dreams of being Cinderella. She didn't need that sort of thing.

Not even a little bit.

But it was a heady thing, feeling like she was part of this, even for a second. Having a man that looked like him on her arm. Yeah. It was a little bit more intoxicating than she would've imagined. She suddenly understood. Why women did this, even for a night. Nothing could've made her feel more beautiful than standing next to him, and she would've thought that it was quite the opposite. But no. To be seen as someone who was worthy of his attention… It was like a drug.

Powerful.

She hadn't realized that she was susceptible to such things. She truly hadn't.

But here she was, high on it and him. On feeling beautiful and shiny because she was in his orbit.

"You must endeavor to look happy," he said.

It was funny that she didn't look happy, because she was actually enjoying herself. "I *am* happy," she said, looking up at him and smiling.

She knew that she had a very convincing smile, even when she was feeling other things. But she did feel happy now. It was just an enormous sort of happy that came with a weight, and an end point, and it made the happy feel weighted down. Sad at the same time as magical.

"You look very worried."

"I'm not. I'm only just… This is outside my experience."

"It won't be. Not in a couple of months."

Months. Two months of this.

"No." But it would be over then. Of course. That was the truth of it.

Her mouth filled with a metallic tang, and she chose to ignore it.

They walked up into the restaurant, and were ushered into a glorious, well-appointed corner. It was an old-style place, dark inside, rather than bright and modern like so many of the newer restaurants tended to be. It had a classic British menu, and she found herself charmed by it.

She found herself forgetting that they were on display.

What if she just pretended? What if just tonight she pretended that she was on a date with a beautiful man. What harm could it do? Anyway, it would allow her to be all that much more natural.

"I really never dreamed that I would travel the world," she said.

Sometimes it still shocked her to realize that she had. Sometimes she would count through all the countries she had been to—many of them since she had started working for the constantly in motion Matias—and she had to pinch herself.

"You didn't?"

"No. I'm from a small town. People don't really travel. I mean, sometimes they go to Disneyland, because it's not a very long drive. Only twelve hours."

"I forget how intrepid you Americans are with driving."

"The West Coast particularly is big. The states I mean.

They're quite vast. So if you want to go to another state you have to drive."

"Like countries here."

"Yes. True."

"Where you from?"

"Oregon," she said.

She looked around. People were making conversation in the restaurant, and there was music. No one would be able to hear exactly what they were saying. They simply looked like they were engaging in conversation.

"A place I have never been."

"You should go. It's beautiful." She thought maybe it was a little bit of a silly thing to say to a man with a private jet who could fly absolutely anywhere. But she did stand by that. She had been to so many places now, and she still thought her home state was one of the most beautiful places she had ever been to. Someday, she would probably go back and live there. Someday.

It would be different to live there if she wasn't stuck.

"It is cold there, isn't it?"

"Not as cold as some places in the US. And if you're thinking of all the rain, you're thinking of the northern part of the state. It actually gets very hot where I'm from."

"That would work for me," he said. "I'm used to Spain and I did a significant amount of business in London."

"Do you prefer London to Spain?"

"You would have to be a fool not to prefer Spain. In my opinion."

"You don't spend a ton of time there."

"I have memories there that are far too complicated."

She nodded. "I understand that. I mean… I remember feeling trapped. Trapped in a small town. Trapped in my life. I didn't think it would ever change. I didn't think I would ever go anywhere."

"And what changed?"

"My mother died." Unexpectedly her eyes filled with tears. It had been so long. It didn't usually hit her like that. And yet, it was always so complicated. So many layers. Her own trauma, her own pain. Her own sadness. Her own gratitude. She was swamped by all of it then.

"Did your mother not want you to travel?"

"Someone had to take care of her. She was terminally ill for most of my childhood. And… We had to make it seem like we had it all together, otherwise Child Services would've gotten involved, and I didn't want that. But you know, she was a single mother. A little bit older. I had to make sure that she was able to get to her fusion appointments, and she took her medication. I had to help her manage the symptoms of both her illness and her treatment."

"How did you go to school?"

"I finished at home. I… I didn't mind it. I didn't. She was my mother, I loved her very much. There was a time where I couldn't see past it either. And the truth is, when you start to wish away the burden that comes with care like that, you realize that you're wishing the person away too. And that is a horrible feeling. One that I… I never really wanted to contemplate."

"I'm sorry for your loss," he said.

And she thought maybe he even meant it. She had told him already that her mother had died, but not about this.

"I learned to be organized, meticulous. I learned to look like I had everything together even if I didn't. I learned to smile. It actually set me up for my job. Better than school ever did. And when she died I had a bit of money, and I used it. I sold the house, all the things. There was some insurance, and I went to school, met my work wives, and we decided that an adventure in London would be the way to go. Connect us with the world a bit more."

"Work wives?"

"That is what I call them. Irinka, Maude and Lynna. They really are about the only family I have."

She knew that it was a performance, she wasn't foolish. She knew that this was the kind of thing that he did every day of the week, and even though there was some more heft to this performance than usual, it was just a regular Saturday night for him. For her it was something singular. She understood why they did it, in that moment. All these women that had fallen to his charms, she understood it. Because this was intoxicating. He knew exactly how to make you feel like you were the center of attention. Like there was no one else in the world and never had been. She felt beautiful, in a way that she never had. And perhaps, most outrageously, most unfairly, she felt like she was the center of everything.

This beautiful man looked at her as if he had nothing else to look at.

She hadn't even realized that she craved this until this moment. Until she felt the intense magnetic pull of his gaze.

What would it be like to surrender and have one beautiful night with him?

"You really shouldn't look at me that way," he said.

"Like what?" She felt breathless. She knew that she

was tempting something by asking him that question. She knew it.

"Like you're considering violating the terms of the agreement."

"Neither of us have signed anything yet."

"That is true. There is still time to revise."

He was a shameless flirt. It was confusing, though, because she had seen just a little bit of the real him. Because she had seen beneath the façade. So why bother now? Was it simply because he didn't know another way to be? Or maybe… Well, he was a man. She supposed it was possible that his sex drive was simply that healthy. Yes. That was definitely possible.

"I don't know about that," she said.

Irinka had warned her. About how people would see her. About what clients would think. And she understood something brilliantly true in that moment. It didn't matter whether she slept with him or not. People would think that she had.

And so, was it so outrageous to consider the possibility of getting something out of that?

She was a virgin. Not because of any strict morality on her part. Not because she was waiting for somebody. Because she had never been swept off her feet. Because nobody had ever inspired her to do something, to want something, other than what she had.

The idea of a lover felt like an interruption. But Matias Balcazar had crashed into her life like a freight train. They were trapped together. And if they were going to be the toast of the town, the delights of London, New York and every other city, why shouldn't she know what it was to have his hands on her body, his mouth on her neck? She had seen him kiss other women, touch other women.

She had also seen the way that he looked at those women. He thought she was beautiful.

But if he just feels the same about you as he does everyone else, is it really special?

You don't need it to be special.

No. Of course she didn't. Why should she have a need to be special? Special was… It wasn't important. Special didn't signify. Not if this was just a ruse. Something to help them pass the time.

"You've probably never been celibate before," she said.

He chuckled. "You don't think that I was a late bloomer?"

"Somehow no."

"You would be wrong." His dark eyes searched the vicinity of the table, as if he was making sure no one was eavesdropping. "I was my father's minion, remember. My behavior was above reproach. Until it wasn't. I stayed away from the pleasures of the flesh until I was twenty."

That was like a small hand grenade thrown into the center of the table. She had imagined he'd been a libertine his entire life. Yet, she'd known that there were parts of him that didn't match his exterior and this gave her a window into that which almost felt…wrong to have. Illicit in a way.

It made her mouth dry. It shouldn't.

It was just the subject of sex. When she wanted him, no matter how she tried to pretend she didn't.

The subject of virginity when she knew full well the status of her own.

"Wow," she said. "I would never ever have guessed that you were a virgin until you were twenty." She shifted in her seat, being a virgin at the ripe old age of twenty-five and feeling quite rude for calling him out for holding on to his virginity for a mere two decades.

"Twenty-one," he said. "I didn't immediately jump into bed with a woman in the throes of my grief."

"And you spent all the years after making up for lost time?"

"I don't know that I would put it that way. What I did, I suppose, is decide to be different. In every way. From what I had been before. From what my father had tried to make me."

His eyes were dark and sharp, and they collided with hers. She felt something grow taut in her stomach, at the same time her limbs began to loosen.

She wanted him. It was outrageous. They were sitting here talking about their lives. Having a fake date that felt more real by the moment.

She shouldn't be thinking about sex. It was a performance. But she wanted this man. This man whose father had wounded him so deeply it had scarred him forever. This man who had fashioned himself into a libertine as a form of revenge, not because it was who he was.

This man who, she had known from the beginning wasn't what he seemed, because she had just…known.

Because she knew what it was like to have the potential for who you could have been stolen from you by life, by tragedy. Even when it wasn't something another person did to you on purpose, she knew.

She could never know who she would have been if she hadn't had a sick mother.

She could never know what she might have done if she'd been born into a happy, carefree life. Maybe she wouldn't be here. Maybe she wouldn't be a virgin at twenty-five.

But she was. And she was here.

She'd said she wouldn't sleep with him. She'd promised her friends.

She wanted to break her promises. Because for a moment she just wanted to be Auggie. Stripped down to her deepest, most basic needs. And she wanted to have those needs satisfied.

She had stopped being careful around him that day in Barcelona. She wasn't going to be careful now.

She was going to ask for what she wanted.

"Do you want me?" She had to know the answer to that question.

His dark eyes flickered over her. "You're very beautiful."

"You've been with a lot of beautiful women. Beautiful women that I've seen. More beautiful than me. So if that's the only thing that matters…"

"You fascinate me," he said. "And that is the very reason that I should tell you I don't want you. I cannot afford fascination. Nor do I want it. I don't need a woman to be special. I treat her like she's special, and in that moment she becomes my world. But when I decide that she is no longer my world, I walk away. I create the intrigue. I do not succumb to it. You intrigue me. Without my permission. And I'm not quite sure what to do with that."

She loved that. That she was destroying his shields in the same way he did hers. That she wasn't alone in this.

A heady rush of need filled Auggie. She wanted to be the focus of that. For just an evening.

She looked down. "I've never been with anyone. I spent all those years taking care of my mother, and then… Then I just tried to get away. I tried to put as much space between myself and the old world as I could. I tried to be somebody different. I… I never stopped. I never wanted to take care of anyone ever again. Just myself. And so I have. But it's a very lonely sort of existence. Sometimes I… Okay, that's a lie. I was going to say sometimes I want to connect with someone. I don't. I never have. I have my friends, and that's been enough. Right now I'm wondering. I'm wondering if I want more. If I need more."

"Are you propositioning me?"

"They're going to call me a slut. I might as well be one. If I can't control the way that people are going to see me when all of this is over, then perhaps I should get something for my trouble."

"You've never been with anyone?" His dark eyes were alight with a terrible fire that excited her, that thrilled her down to the soles of her feet.

"No one."

"You realize that's a rare and precious thing to offer to a man like me. I don't traffic in the rare and precious. I am very good at what I do."

"What is it you do?" She leaned in, tenting her fingers, resting her chin on top of them.

"Little girl, don't push me."

"Tell me," she said, the tension inside of her rising up to unbearable levels. The temptation to throw everything away, everything but this, everything but her need.

"This seems very out of character for you," he said.

"It is. But all of this is. It's an incredibly foolish thing. But I've never played with fire before, and I'm sort of enjoying the idea of it."

"What I do, is I give women pleasure. But then I forget about them. And you must never lose sight of that. At the end of this time together, I will never think of you again. I can't anymore."

"I know that you're not a silly playboy who doesn't feel anything."

He took a breath. "I'm worse than that. I'm a monster who puts on a playboy smile, and charms everyone around him. But I feel very little."

She didn't think that was true. She'd seen him shimmering with dark emotion on more than one occasion. She thought he felt too much.

He would never admit it, though. But she knew it all the same.

She didn't know where her boldness came from. She got up from her seat, and moved to the one next to him, her heart pounding heavily. "Do you feel pleasure?" she asked, her mouth inching ever closer to his.

"Auggie," he said. The first time that he had ever said her name out loud like that. August, that was what he normally called her. And she didn't mind it, but hearing him say her nickname did things to her.

"What?"

"I'm attempting to warn you off. I've never carried on a two-month affair with anyone in my life."

"It doesn't need to be two months."

"We are going to be in each other's vicinity, and you honestly think that if we sleep together, once will be enough?"

"Maybe it will be. I don't care about the future. And all I have ever cared about is the future. But I want… What I want is this fantasy. This one. Where we are both beautiful, and nothing else matters."

There was a look in his eye in that moment that she couldn't quite define. A desperation. Like he wanted to claim that for himself as well. Like he wanted to believe in the façade too.

"Why can't we?"

"All right," he said. "My beautiful fiancée."

It sent a shiver down her spine. This wasn't her. It was a character she was playing. But it was glorious all the same. She loved it. This was the sort of dangerous game she would never allow herself to play under any other circumstances. This was the luxury of touch, of being desired, being wanted that she had always denied herself, because she never wanted to be needed, not ever again. Not emotionally. She could be needed at her job, but it was different.

But this was only a game. He couldn't feel anything, couldn't want anything from her.

And all she could want from him was this.

Her friends would be appalled. But they would understand. They all worked so hard. They all had their own issues, their own demons. Their own hang-ups when it came to men. Surely they wouldn't resent her trying to reclaim some of what had been lost to her.

"Take me," she said.

"I will. Don't you worry."

CHAPTER SEVEN

THIS WAS A very bad idea, and he knew it. But he was gripped with need. He didn't want her to know what a terribly rare thing this was. Yes, he enjoyed sex, he enjoyed women. He was not the sort of man to allow himself to be taken in like this. He did the seducing, not the other way around. And having a woman, a virgin, affect him in this way was…

It was…

He knew he shouldn't want it. He knew he shouldn't want her purity. That he shouldn't want to be the first person to ever touch her, to ever take her, to ever show her what pleasure meant.

She had captivated him from the first moment he'd seen her. And then again at his house, and again when she'd had this makeover. And it was something other than beauty.

He just… He just wanted her. After the conversation with his father today, he wanted something to distract him, but not in the same sort of way he often craved mindless desire.

It was something new. Something different. And for a man like him novelty was an art.

A rare gift, and he intended to seize it. Intended to have this moment out of time.

As if you deserve it.

Everything felt raw and close to the surface, but that made him want this even more. He had a feeling that she saw him. More the real him than most women did. Than most anybody did.

And yet she still wanted him. Perhaps, she even wanted him because of it, and there was something about that that drove him now.

They left the restaurant, hand in hand, they didn't stay out as long as they should have. The entire point of this was to put on a show. But he found himself growing impatient. He took her hand and led her to the car. And once they were inside, he gripped her face, forcing her to stare into his eyes. "What is it you want from me?"

"Nothing," she said breathless. "Nothing more than you."

"And what do you see when you look at me?"

She searched his gaze.

"A beautiful man. But a troubled one."

"Not wrong. And you want me anyway?"

"I find you fascinating."

"Why?"

"I don't know," she said. She was being honest, he could tell.

"Maybe you just waited to have sex too long, and you think that I'll make it good."

"Yes. But that's not… No offense, but there are many good-looking men. I went to college with quite a few."

"As good-looking as I am?"

"Maybe not," she said, shaking her head. "But if all I was after was a handsome man, I wouldn't be a twenty-five-year-old virgin."

"So tell me that. You're a virgin. You steadfastly refused to have sex with me just earlier today. Why now?"

"Because you made me feel special. And I don't care if it's real or not. I don't care if it's true. That's why I need it to be tonight, in fact. Because I want to stay in this dream. I want to be the person that's seen. Do you understand? That has never been me. That's never been my life. I am the wallpaper, Matias. Always and ever. I am the woman who blends in, the woman that serves drinks, the woman who assists. The child that brings medication, and makes doctor appointments, but I am never wholly myself. Or special. Or wanted. And you make me feel like I could be. I just want that. For a while."

He wanted the same, he realized. Because she looked at him and saw someone who might treat her right. Might give her something real, something good, and he wanted to be that fantasy for a while. More than just a fantasy of good sex, more than just seduction. He wanted to have the same fantasy she was having. Because maybe, just maybe, they were both special in that world. Maybe she mattered and he wasn't beyond redemption. Just maybe.

Then, he could hold back no longer. He closed the distance between them, bringing his mouth down hard on hers. She whimpered. And froze. He could feel that she wasn't an expert, but she was soft, and she tasted like magic.

Sex had long ago lost any sort of magic. He enjoyed it. But it didn't feel like this. It never had. He could remember his first time, which he had gone about grimly. Because it was time. Because he was trying to strip off the last vestiges of what he had been. Of who he had been.

Because he was trying to learn to be the playboy. Sex for him had been a series of scourings. Of stripping back layer after layer of who he had once been, to make something new beneath it.

But this didn't feel that way. This felt like something singular. Something real.

He could not quite fathom it.

So he kissed her. He poured everything into that kiss. All the need, all the darkness that he suspected she saw. She gasped, and he took the opportunity to take the kiss deeper, to slide his tongue against hers, and make her his.

He kissed her. Again and again.

He wanted her. He wanted this.

"I am going to take you," he said. "Just as you demanded. But you must be very certain that it's what you want. Because you're right, I don't degrade women. Unless they ask."

Her cheeks were bright and flushed, her eyes glittering. "I don't even know what to ask for."

"Then I shouldn't have you. I shouldn't have anyone so innocent that she doesn't even know what she wants."

"Everyone has to start somewhere, don't they?"

Maybe that was the magic. That she was asking him to help be the one to reform her. To shape her sexuality. To make her his. Maybe that was it.

Because for all the experience his jaded palate had tasted, this was unique.

He had never experienced this.

Not ever.

Maybe it was the novelty.

And it would wear off. But not tonight.

"Will your friends be consumed with worry if you don't contact them?"

"I'm a grown woman. I can take care of myself."

"Some would say that you're perhaps doing a very bad job of it right now."

"Maybe," she said. "But some would say that I'm doing a very good job."

He chuckled. "A good point."

"After all, you have to think that sex was inherently dangerous to think that I was putting myself at risk." He rubbed his thumb over her cheekbone. "The way that I do it can be quite dangerous."

"I need you to show me. Otherwise I'm going to be convinced that you're all talk." She was so bold. She always had been. But then, he imagined that she would have to be. To build this business out of nothing. To take the sorts of chances that she and her friends had when they were so young. When she had come from nothing. It was easy to believe that it wasn't a skill to stand in the background. Easy to convince oneself that it was the wealthy who had succeeded through their cunning and prowess, but this woman came from nothing, and had created from that so much.

Of course she was brilliant. Singular. And very, very brave.

"You don't fear much, do you?" he asked, his voice hoarse.

"No, not much," she said.

But she was afraid of things. Of course she was, everyone was.

But there was no room for that now. And thank God.

Because he just wanted her.

So he kissed her again, until the car came up against the curb. Until it was time for them to get out, and headed to the building. But he did not take his hands off of her. He found he didn't want to. Dimly he was aware that they had been followed. The photographs were taken. All the better. Because people might cry PR relationship, no matter what they did, but if they saw them together like this, clearly about to go upstairs and engage in intimacy, then it would be much harder for them to convince the world of it.

There would be headlines tomorrow. A cascade of them. He knew that. But tonight there was just them.

That was all.

They were in a cocoon of passion, and he allowed that to propel them to the elevator, up to the top floor. And into that lavish penthouse. Where he was suddenly grateful that it was a playboy's haven, because every surface was soft for a reason.

He took her into his arms and he kissed her. "I will show you," he said. "Everything you like." He kissed her neck, and he began to unzip her dress as he traveled down her body, kissing the curve of her breast as he separated the fabric away from her curves. As he stripped her down to brief, lacy underwear, and her red high heels.

"Beautiful," he growled.

Her eyes were round, and he could see a hint of nerves, but she was doing her best to hide them, and he thought that he would honor that.

A virgin.

Of all the things.

There were gifts that no man could ever possibly deserve. This was one of them. To be the first man to touch her beautiful body? Outrageous.

He was worth very little. He had failed the one person that had ever loved him. That had ever needed him. Surely that meant he shouldn't have nice moments like this one.

You are outside of time and space. Let her take you away.

That was a first. Sex, to him, was an opportunity to remove himself from everything he had been raised to be, one encounter at a time. He took pride in pleasuring women, and honoring them with the act, but he did not feel as if he was escaping. Did not feel as if he was getting something out of it.

But tonight, he did. Tonight he was claiming it for himself just as much as he was claiming it for her, whether he deserved it or not.

He licked the plump curve of her breast, and then undid her bra, exposing her generous breasts to his gaze. He was starving for her. So he fastened his lips to one raspberry nipple, sucking it in deep. She arched her back and gasped, forking her fingers through his hair. He loved her boldness. That she wasn't bothering with protests, and virginal proclamations of embarrassment. But then, how was he to know if virgins actually did those things. He had never been with one before.

Plus, he couldn't speak to the nature of her fantasy life. Or to the amount of other experience she had with men. She arched against him, and he pressed her firmly against the wall, before kissing down her body and tugging her underwear down her thighs. He parted her legs and began to lick her deeply. She gasped, moving in time with the rhythm of his mouth, his lips, his tongue.

She tasted like the dessert that they had left before they could have.

She tasted like a dream.

And he was getting as much as he was giving in this moment, if not more, he was on edge. Fulfilled and undone by the taste of her.

He licked her, deeper and deeper and she cried out, on the verge of a climax. So he decided to push her there. He pushed one finger inside of her as he continued to lick her, and he felt her unravel, felt her internal muscles clenched around him. Then he moved back up to her mouth and kissed her deep. "Let's go into the bedroom."

She nodded wordlessly. And then, naked except for the high heels, she began to walk toward his room.

She didn't know herself. But she didn't want to.

She didn't want him to say her name, not again, even though it had thrilled her slightly to hear it earlier. Because she didn't want to think of herself as Auggie Fremont right now. She wanted to be out of space and out of time. She wanted to be someone different than she had ever been before.

She wanted to be somebody new.

She wanted to weep because she didn't feel like her. She felt like something more special. Brighter, better.

She felt exquisite. And it was because of him.

The orgasm that he had just given her had rocked her, shaking her. It was so much different than pleasuring herself. She had no control over it. He had called it from her body like he was the master of her pleasure.

And she wanted to surrender. So when he ordered her to go into his room, she obeyed.

"Wait for me on the bed," he said.

She did, her heart hammering.

He stripped off his suit jacket, his tie, his shirt. She had seen him half-naked a hundred times. But nothing prepared her for being on the receiving end of the intense look in his eye as he removed his clothing. Realizing that body was for her. That his touch was for her.

She was overcome with it.

She watched as his muscles rippled, his golden-brown skin making her mouth water. The dark hair that covered his muscles made her fingertips itch. She wanted to touch him. She wanted to lick him. It was like a dam had burst inside of her, and every desire that she had held back for all this time was ready to burst forth.

She had tried so hard to be good. Maybe she wasn't good. She was okay with that.

Tonight, she was okay with it.

He moved his hands to his belt buckle, to the closure on his slacks, and he stripped off the rest of his suit, and right then, she understood something dark and terrible. Looking at the full power of his rampant masculinity, she knew something, a deep, real truth that had always been hidden from her before.

This was an addiction. This was why countries fell to ruin. It was why good women craved very bad men. It was why good men broke apart families. This was something more powerful than she had fully given it credit for. And she wondered if she was horrendously naïve to believe that it was something that she could shut off after tonight.

It doesn't matter. Because tomorrow is going to take care of itself.

Yes. It was.

So she surrendered to his beauty. To her need. To his touch, when he made his way to the bed and moved himself over the top of her. She kissed his neck. Kissed her way down his chest, his ridged abdomen. She moved to that sick, glorious masculine part of him, and took him into her mouth. She wasn't nervous. She wasn't anything except filled with the most alarming, terrible, painful need.

She took him in deep, pushing her own limits. She reveled in the fact that she could make him groan. That she could affect him at all.

And maybe it was because he was a man. And men were that simple. But maybe it was because she was a woman, and she was that powerful. She was going to remember that.

From this moment onward.

She licked him, because she couldn't help it. Luxuriated in the taste of him, in the feel of him beneath her tongue.

Until he gripped her hair and pulled her back up his body and claimed her mouth in a furious kiss. "Now," he growled, opening up the nightstand next to the bed and taking out a box of condoms. He took out one plastic packet, tore it open and rolled it over his thick length. She gave thanks for his speed and efficiency. He moved between her legs, but before he penetrated her, he pushed one finger inside of her, then another. "So wet," he ground out, and his appreciation sent a spark of need shimmering through her, threatening to set off an explosion. "This may hurt," he said.

"That's okay," she said.

He withdrew his fingers, and moved back to her, kissing her mouth. Then he tested the entrance to her body with the head of his manhood, pushing in inch by glorious inch. It did hurt. But she didn't mind.

It was wonderful. To be filled by him, possessed by him. Claimed by him.

She arched her back, and cried out as he filled her to the hilt. As he took her. Just as she had demanded.

This was everything. And so was he.

He began to move, the spell he was casting over her finding her in its dark magic. Binding her to him. The pleasure that built inside of her was deeper than the pleasure from before. The climax coming from somewhere at her very center.

And as she cried out his name, she lost herself completely. But the real triumph was when he let go. When he shivered with need, pulsing deep within her, his own control lost at the threshold of desire.

She clung to him.

Matias.

Perhaps she whispered his name. Perhaps it was only an echo in her soul. She didn't know.

But for tonight, it was perfect. Tonight, everything was wonderful.

Tomorrow would take care of itself.

CHAPTER EIGHT

IT WAS FIVE THIRTY when his phone buzzed.

"You will regret trying me."

His father's voice, angry and acrid, came down the line, but before Matias could respond, he was gone.

Matias sat up. Auggie was lying in bed beside him, the sheets pushed down to her waist, her arm thrown up over her head. She looked like a marble statue in motion, her breasts on display, her beauty arresting. But he could not focus on her beauty. Not just now.

He got out of bed and pulled on his pants.

"Where are you going?" Auggie asked, her voice sleepy.

"I just have to..."

The next phone call was from his publicist. "About time you got in the game," he snarled.

"We have a much bigger problem than we anticipated."

"What is the problem?" He asked the other woman.

"Your father has decided to drag everything out into the open."

Well. Not everything. Matias knew that without even checking. Because the truth would only paint him in a bad light. But what he had decided to reveal...

His phone buzzed, and he looked at his text from his publicist. At the headline there.

Matias Balcazar Accused of Corporate Espionage Against His Father, Causing his Sister's Death!

"Bastard," he said.

"What statement would you like me to make?"

"Isn't my job to figure out what statement you should make. It is yours. Do it." He hung the phone up.

He turned around and saw Auggie standing there with her sheet pulled up around her body, her hair in disarray. "What's wrong?"

"This is… This has escalated."

Auggie moved across the room and ran for her purse. It was obvious that she already had a raft of texts. "Oh, no," she said.

"Yes," he said, his voice hard. "Oh, no, indeed."

"You're not responsible for her death."

"I am," he said. "I am. I delivered the exact message that my father told me to give her. And I told her that with the shame she was bringing on the family would be better off without her."

"Matias…"

"What was she to assume except that she would be better off dead?"

"A lot of people have issues with their family and they don't overdose."

"But she did. She did, because she was fragile. Because she needed me to be her ally, and I was not."

"You can't take responsibility for all of it."

He turned, fury in his veins like fire. "Yes. I can.

And my father is demanding that I do. This is what he's doing. To eclipse our attempts at controlling this. Come with me."

"Where are we going?"

"We need to get out of the city. We need to rethink things."

His heart was pounding harder than it should. He felt like he was perhaps about to have a heart attack.

"What happened?"

"He's putting out everything about my sister. Everything. And my involvement in her death."

She shook her head. "But you didn't kill her. You weren't responsible for her death."

"I was," he said. "Believe me, I was. And it is all being put out there in black and white, and anyone who reads it would think the same."

"If you are responsible, then so is your father."

"But it doesn't matter to him. It doesn't matter. It matters to me. That he would… This is sacred ground to me."

"I'm sorry," she said.

She looked small, hurt. He imagined that what she was hoping for was better treatment the morning after she had her first sexual experience, but he couldn't afford to think about that right now. He couldn't afford to let it matter.

She had seen him make a mistake with Charmaine. And now this.

He growled, moving into his bedroom and beginning to dress as quickly as possible. She blinked, and he noticed that her eyes were full of tears.

"I don't have anything to change into."

"It doesn't matter. If you're seen leaving my house in the same thing that you wore inside, it only lends itself to the illusion."

"Do you honestly think that it matters now?"

"I'm sure that it's in the news somewhere. Buried beneath this."

"Then I will make a show of standing beside you. Whatever you need." She would make a show of it. Because of course it was a show. For a moment, last night, it had felt like perhaps she knew him. Much in the same way it felt like he might know her. It had felt like something different. Something real. Something that he had never experienced before. But it had been a game. All of this was a game. Every moment of every day that he had breathed since Seraphina had died had been a game, and forgetting that had been his first mistake. You could not escape your past. You couldn't escape the darkness there.

She left, her clothes in her arms, and returned moments later, dressed in the same clothing from the night before. The color that had seemed so suitable to her last night seemed somewhat garish today. In the bright light of the morning, clearly announcing that he had debauched her, that he was using her.

That's what he was doing. That's what he had been doing to every woman that he had ever met since he had embarked on this.

How he had thought that he had escaped bad behavior simply because he was a good lover, because he considered himself respectful, he didn't know.

It was all a game.

He might not have chosen to play it. He was.

And in the end, when the headlines were released, the truth was he was no different than his father.

He was a man who had his own way of doing things and did it regardless of the impact on others. A man who behaved in supremely selfish ways, and treated those around him as if they were pawns in a game, rather than human beings.

But this was not even the time for self-pity. Because this was a mess of his own making, and he would do what needed doing to clean it up. Because it wasn't only what had been written about him, but what was being written about Seraphina. The way that it seemed to indicate that he didn't care about her. "We need to get down to my office."

"All right," she said.

"I suppose you want to call your friends."

"It can wait."

They headed down the street, and this time, when he called for a car, he did not ask for a driver. But as his car was brought into place for him by the valet, he noticed that there were paparazzi. Everywhere. Lining the streets, their black SUVs a telltale sign.

"Quickly," he said.

They got behind the wheel and he began to drive, maneuvering out of the city.

"Where are you taking us?" she asked as they crossed the first bridge.

"I have a house. In the country. If we make it there, then the paparazzi will not follow us. I'm certain that once we leave the urban sprawl, they'll give up."

"I thought that you had to get back to your company."

"It would be a good idea, but do you not see…" He

looked in the rearview mirror. "There's an entire cavalcade."

She looked, worried. And then she began to text.

"Your work wives?"

"Yes. I'm asking them for some help."

"See if they can create a diversion."

"I will."

But the car was gaining on them, and there was a photographer hanging out the window, taking his picture.

It sent panic through him. He couldn't quite say why. Because Seraphina was dead, so what did any of this matter? Except it was him. He disliked seeing all of this in black and white so intensely because it highlighted his culpability in all of it. And if he was going to take his father down, perhaps he should take himself down with him. Perhaps… Perhaps there was nothing about him that was worth much of anything at all.

Perhaps he deserved to be gone as well.

But it was better, yes, it was better, and perhaps it was for him, to go through life as an avenging angel. To act as if his mission to destroy Javier would atone for something. How could it?

A few of the cars abandoned them as they continued on down the winding roads, as he began to drive faster.

"Be careful," she said, hanging onto the door handle.

"I'm being careful," he said.

But then, they came to a crossroads, and a dark SUV pulled out quickly in front of them. He swerved, and the car went off the road, and when he realized that the passenger side was about to connect with the tree, he corrected sharply, hitting the front end, the airbags failing to deploy, his head making a cracking impact against the steering wheel. His face was throbbing, and he felt warm blood running down his cheekbones.

"Matias..." Her voice was distant.

"I'm fine," he said, seeing if the engine would start. It did. He threw his car into reverse, and drove even faster down the road, blood spilling into his eyes. His vision blurred, but he kept on driving. At least the paparazzi were no longer in pursuit. He pulled off quickly to a hidden road, and then the other, which would take him to his gated estate here in the country. He entered the code, and started to drive up the road and toward the house. It was several kilometers off of the main road, and they would not be disturbed there. It was nearly impossible to get inside.

"Matias."

For the first time, he glanced over at Auggie. She looked terrified, pale. There was a large bruise forming on her cheek.

"Are you hurt?"

"I'm not great. Why didn't the airbags deploy?"

"I don't know. And I will buy the manufacturer and put them out of business."

"I don't know that that's necessary."

"You're hurt," she said.

"I'm fine."

"You're not fine. Your head has been split open."

"It will heal."

"You probably have a concussion."

"I'm fine. I'm thinking clearly. I was able to drive us here."

Admittedly, his vision was growing blurry.

"It's just… It's just the media. We didn't have to run from them."

Her words scraped him raw. "I am protecting you. And myself."

"They're going to print whatever they want anyway. Whether they have a picture of you or not."

But he couldn't bear their questions. He couldn't. He didn't know why he felt that with such certainty, only that he did.

"Here," he said, the edges of his vision darker now. "There's the house."

"Do you have staff here?"

He shook his head. "No. There will be no one here. We can… Bring people out. Get food."

His speech was beginning to slur, his mind beginning to turn slower. He couldn't remember quite why they had been running. Only that he had felt like a hunted animal. Only that it had reminded him so starkly of the unending, unforgiving grief that he had experienced when Seraphina had died that he felt overrun with it.

Because that had been the darkest day of his life. Because it had been when he had discovered that his father was wrong about everything. Everything.

He suddenly felt gripped with nausea.

He got out of the car, and wiped blood away from his face. He looked down at his hands, the edges of his vision growing ever darker. And then he vomited onto the grass.

"Matias," she said, moving over to him, throwing her arms around his back. "You have a head injury."

"I just hit my head, that's all. Let's go inside."

"I have to get back to London. I can't be out here. In

the middle of nowhere. And you need to go to a hospital."

"I am not going anywhere. Not as long as that pack of hyenas is after us."

"I agree, it's terrible. But surely we can get another vehicle. We can go back to my apartment. We can—"

"We will stay here."

He went to the front door, and entered his code, the doors giving for him as he ushered her inside.

"What is this?"

"One of my places. A place where I can go for privacy. I don't like everyone to know everything about me. I like them to think that they do."

"Oh. Of course."

It was austere inside. Like him. It was the truth of him, unlike the apartment she had stayed in last night.

"We have got to stop the bleeding on your face. Sit down."

He obeyed her, mostly because he was dizzy. This was an infuriating time to discover his own mortality.

"I'm sitting," he said.

"Yes, you are. Do you have a doctor?"

"What kind of question is that?"

"I assume that rich men like you have doctors who will drop everything and come see to them, is that correct?"

He waved a hand. "Of course it is."

"Then we need to call your doctor. And get him out here immediately, because I might be able to stop the bleeding but I'm not going to be able to stitch you back together."

"Soon," he said.

He heard her retreat. And when she returned, she had a large white towel. She pressed it over his eyes, his forehead, and he leaned back against the chair, trying to relax.

She held it there, counting, whispering.

"It'll be all right," she said.

He remembered, with a start, what she had said about caring for her mother. He could definitely feel that energy now. That familiarity that she had with the medical.

He didn't know how he felt about it. If he needed medical care, then there was a professional to do it. This wasn't her job. And she had been hurt…

"You're sure you're all right?" he asked.

"Yes," she said softly. "I'm fine."

"I feel like we don't know that for sure."

"I know it well enough," she said. And when she removed the towel from his forehead, and when he opened his eyes he found that he could see nothing at all.

CHAPTER NINE

AUGGIE WAS COMPLETELY SHAKEN. Everything that happened this morning felt jarring and shocking. From them fleeing London, to ending up at this manor house. In the accident…

She had hit her head, but not as badly as he had. The impact had ended up on his side, because he had cranked the wheel sharply and taken her out of harm's way. The gash on his forehead was severe, but she was more worried about the trauma that the impact might've caused.

And now he was looking at her, his dark eyes fixed at a spot just beyond her.

"What?"

"I can't see," he said.

"What do you mean you can't see?" She was so aware that she was stupidly repeating his words like a Muppet, and she couldn't stop herself.

"Just what I said," he ground out. "I cannot see anything."

"We need to call your doctor."

Panic shot through her. This had to be very bad. And it was entirely possible that there was an injury to his brain.

"You can get into my phone. The doctor's name is Carlos Valdes."

She grabbed hold of his phone, which had his blood on it. She grimaced. Then she turned it toward his face and unlocked it, the way that she had done before with his girlfriends. Had that been only a week ago? Had that been the same life even? He didn't seem like the same man. She didn't feel like the same woman. She hadn't even had a moment to try and fully comprehend what had passed between them last night, and now she had to… She just had to save his life.

She called the doctor. "Hello. I am with Matias Balcazar. We are at his country estate in England. I assume you have the address on file." The receptionist on the other end of the phone confirmed. "He's been in an accident, and we need a trauma team to come out right away. Fly if you can. He cannot go to a hospital. He needs to be treated here if you can." He was a billionaire. She knew that he could be treated here. They would bring equipment. "He has a head injury. He cannot see. Please."

"A team including Dr. Valdes is being dispatched immediately," the woman said. "Not to worry."

"How long will they be?"

"Fifteen minutes. They will go by helicopter."

"Thank you," she said.

She hung up, looking around the room, trying to avoid looking at him. Because it made her stomach cramp painfully. Then she sat down, looking straight ahead, in the chair next to his. "I'm right here," she said.

At least the bleeding had stopped on his forehead gash. Though the wound was angry and deep. "They'll be here soon."

"I'm being punished," he said.

"For what?"

"Because I'm not any different than him. And perhaps God is making things right. I blamed my father. I set out to destroy him. Perhaps true justice is understanding that if I am to destroy him for what was done, then I have to destroy myself."

"Stop. Don't get nihilistic. You just have to live through this."

"If I can't see, I don't know that I want to live."

"Stop it. Many people live without their sight. Or various other senses. Do you think that they shouldn't live?"

"I didn't say that."

"You didn't. Because you don't mean that. Which means on some level you must understand that whatever happens, you will learn to live. You will."

"Perhaps I'm tired. Tired of learning to live in new realities."

"Don't get self-pitying. It's only going to make it worse."

"You have a bruise on your cheek. Don't speak to me about self-pity."

"Matias. You didn't deserve for this to happen to you. And you will… You will be all right."

"You don't know that."

She didn't. She was actually just afraid that he was going to suddenly die on her. If something was wrong enough in his brain to take his sight away, who knew what else could suddenly happen. He could have a stroke. Or something. Old anxiety churned through her, along with new.

That she had watched her mother die in spite of all the advancements in modern medicine, grabbed hold of her now. As she looked at the one man she had ever been intimate with, and watched as he seemed mortal for the first time since she had ever met him. Then she heard the sound of rotor blades outside.

"Thank God."

The next piece of time was a flurry of activity. A stretcher was brought in, and Matias was moved upstairs. There was equipment that came in behind them. And a medical team assembled.

She wanted to follow them, but they kept her sitting downstairs, as they began to examine her.

"You were also in the accident?" the nurse asked, touching Auggie's cheek. "It looks like you were injured."

"Yes. But I'm fine."

She was checked over nonetheless. And given a clean bill of health. Nothing but the contusion on her face.

At that point, Dr. Valdes came back down the stairs.

"Augusta Fremont. You are the one who called for me?"

"Yes. I'm… I'm his fiancée."

She was. For all intents and purposes. And she was going to use that here.

"We will keep a team here overnight. The concern of course is that the swelling will get worse, and we will have to fly him back to the city to do brain surgery."

"He doesn't want to go back. He was… He was bound and determined to leave the city."

It occurred to her that he probably didn't want brain surgery either. And she was arguing about medical emergencies that nobody in the room had any control over.

"We will do our best to treat him here. A scan shows

that he has swelling in the brain, centered on the optic nerves. Once pressure is relieved, it is highly likely his sight will return."

"Do you see this often?"

"No. But… It is not unheard of. The concern would be that there's a possibility for a bleed, or a stroke."

"Oh."

"He is very alert. But… His vision."

"And what if it doesn't return?"

"That I would assume that the damage done through the compression of the optic nerve isn't readily repairable. But we would do surgery to see."

"I see."

"If he makes it through the night, then he is undoubtedly stable."

"If he makes it through the night?"

"Without coding. I will not let him die. Don't worry. We'll just see if he needs assistance to continue to live."

"It's not fair," she said. "He hasn't done anything. He didn't…he didn't cause this—the paparazzi were after him. It isn't fair."

"Unfortunately, in my line of work, what I have learned is that often the good die and the bad live. Pickled by bitterness and deceit. I do my best to try and even the playing field."

She didn't know quite what to do, she wanted to go to him, but there was a team up there. She was his fiancée, publicly, and yet she wasn't. But she was his lover. She was his lover and… That night didn't even feel real. Because the fantasy had been shattered in such a cruel way.

Finally, when she was entirely alone downstairs, she called the work wives.

They were still in the office, and each picked up at their desks. "Auggie?" Lynna asked. "Where have you been?"

"In an accident."

Everyone made loud exclamations, and began asking questions all at once.

"I'm with Matias. He's been injured."

"You see the headlines. It's awful. Stories about his sister's overdose, and apparently there's a recording of his final conversation with her. And he told her that if she continued on being an addict that everyone would be better off without her."

Auggie's heart clenched. "He feels… He feels responsible," she said. "And now I know why. But I know that there were other circumstances leading up to her death."

"His father is playing the victim, painting him as a Machiavellian madman who always planned to put a rift in the family, who was part of his own sister's destruction, and who then actively worked against his father. Basically, they're saying that everything he has pretended to be all this time is a lie."

"Well, it is," Auggie said. "He's hurt."

"Oh, no," Maude said.

She noticed the other two didn't react. "He isn't everything they're saying," Auggie said. "I know he's not. You just have to trust me. His father is a terrible man. And no, Matias isn't everything that he appears to be. And he does feel like he has some responsibility to take for his sister's death. But it isn't like that. His father is the one who manipulated his children. He treated his daughter like trash. And he treated Matias… He made him feel like he didn't have another choice but to do all of his bidding all the time."

"Everybody has a choice," Irinka said.

"But some choices are harder to make depending on where you're from."

Irinka looked at her sharply, but didn't say anything.

"I'll keep you all posted," she said.

They all got off the phone, and she breathed out heavily. Then her phone rang again. Just Irinka.

Not on a video call. Auggie picked it up. "Yes?"

"You slept with him, didn't you?"

"What makes you ask me that?"

"Because you're so sure of him. And because you're clearly staying wherever he is."

And not giving details on his injuries. Because she felt protective. She trusted her friends completely, and yet she found she couldn't talk about what had happened today.

"I didn't see why I shouldn't. Since he was going to be part of my reputation either way."

"This is a disaster for us, Auggie. You realize that, don't you?"

"Not if we stick it out," Auggie said. "Because I don't believe that he's a bad person. And I do believe that it will all come together in the end. I do."

"Why do you believe that?"

"Because I have to. Because…" Because she had already watched her mother die. Because she had built this up from nothing, and she wasn't foolish enough, or naïve enough, or even traditional enough to buy into the idea that she could have a happy ending here with him just because the idea was nice. But she did believe that she was a better judge of character than all that. She did believe that the man that she had gone to bed with was a decent one. She believed that he was the good guy, and she just wanted to believe that things were going to be okay. But she knew from experience that they might not be.

That his father was the bad guy. And she wanted to be part of making sure the world knew it too. She didn't know how to explain all of that to Irinka.

"It isn't just that I'm attracted to him," she said softly.

"I hope not."

"He's hurt, I can't leave him now. And if I do, it will be even worse for us."

"Undoubtedly."

"Trust me. Trust me please. That I can fix this."

"I will. Because you're my friend. Because you haven't been wrong about moves with the business before. But it does kind of seem like every wrong thing has included him."

"I know. So just let me… Let me see it through."

"Where will it end? Are you going to marry him? Have his babies?"

The idea made her feel warm.

"No. But let me help him rebuild."

"Okay, Auggie."

She hung up the phone, and stood there, staring out the window at the back garden for a very long time. She didn't want to believe that she had ruined everything with this. But it was possible that she had.

But for now, she was going to do what she could for Matias. Because the truth was, she had thrown her lot in with him, and she had to see it through.

And more than that… She cared about him. Because she knew what it was like to be alone in the world. And she had her friends. He had his money. It wasn't enough. She knew that it wasn't.

She took a deep breath and her chest ached.

Then she sat down in that same chair she had been in beside him earlier. And she drifted off to sleep.

CHAPTER TEN

WHEN HE WOKE up the medical staff was ready to leave.

"It's been forty-eight hours of observation," the doctor said. "You are well, but there is still an issue with the optic nerve."

"That's why I can't see?"

"Yes. I would rather not rush into brain surgery. Because the recovery can be punishing. I would rather see if it will resolve on its own."

"How long will you give it?"

"A couple of weeks at least. At that point, we will take you in for further testing."

"And in the meantime?"

"You are a billionaire. I assume you have the resources."

He knew the doctor was being practical, and not dismissive, but Matias still found himself in rage.

"I am in the middle of a crisis of image."

"You have bigger issues. You will have to physically recover."

There were flashes of light in his vision at times, but he wasn't entirely sure if he was hallucinating them or not. There was the occasional blurred edge. And again, he wasn't certain if that was real or not. "Stay here," the doctor said. "Your fiancée will take care of you."

His fiancée…

"Auggie is here?"

"Yes. She has been pacing the halls and barely sleeping. She clearly cares about you a great deal."

Well. Auggie had managed to convince the doctor that her feelings for him were real. If only he knew the truth. Auggie was here because it benefited her. Because the truth was, she couldn't abandon him now. It was too late. Her reputation was already twined together with his. It was a self-sustaining problem at this point.

"You know I can be here in under twenty minutes if you have need."

And with that, he was left to his own devices. Without the constant beeping of monitors. And without his vision.

He heard footsteps, though he could not figure out where they were coming from. He didn't know this place well enough. That was the problem. If they were in his apartment in London, he would have a better sense of the direction of everything. Of course, if he was in London he would have to listen for the sounds of the city, and out here it was distressingly quiet.

"I overheard."

Auggie. He thought of her sitting in the passenger seat, that bruise on her cheek. But then again, in his arms, naked. Beautiful. He held onto that image. He held onto it tightly.

"Then you know he thinks that I'll be fine."

"That isn't quite what he said. But, yes."

"You will have to take care of me," he said. What a lowering realization.

"I will," she said.

"I need you to tell me what the press is writing about me."

"I don't see how that's going to help you."

"Because I want to know."

He was suddenly consumed with helplessness. He knew that there were many ways that people without sight navigated the world, but he didn't know any of them. He knew that there were ways to use technology when you are visually impaired, but he had not learned how to do that. He had no skills for navigating this, and he had no idea what he was supposed to do.

He suddenly felt replete with rage and helplessness. If she chose not to show him, he wouldn't be able to find it for himself.

"I need to be able to trust you," he said.

"Can you trust me to tell you that you maybe don't want to know?"

"No," he said.

"Okay," she said, cautious. "Well, you're just going to have to deal with it."

"Do not play with me," he said.

"I'm not playing with you," she responded. She sounded exasperated. He couldn't know for sure. He couldn't see her.

"I will not heal," he said.

"You just thought that it wasn't an option for you to remain like this."

"But I will. Because this is what it was like for my sister. I'm certain. She slipped into darkness. Alone.

And here I am, doomed to a life of darkness, and I will not even be granted the release of death to soften this."

"Is that what you think? You think that death would be a release?"

"From this? What is the point of any of it. Perhaps this is what I have been avoiding all this time. To defeat my father is to defeat myself. Everything that I have done, everything is to try and avenge the death of my sister. But the truth is, in order to fully avenge her, I must take myself down as well. And now the world has done it for me."

"Stop it," she said. He could not see what she did, but he heard a clattering. "You are… You are offensive. Do you think that you're being punished? You think that this accident was some sort of light brought upon you. You didn't die when your brain swelled up, maybe you could be grateful for that."

"I find it difficult to be grateful," he said.

"Clearly," she said. "Clearly you find it difficult to be grateful. But I find myself sorely lacking in sympathy for you. Let me ask you this question. Do you think that my mother deserved cancer?"

He frowned. "No. What does your mother have to do with this?"

"Your logic indicates that you think that people are struck down because they deserve it. You were spared. Perhaps you can focus on the fact that you didn't die. Maybe you can figure out all the ways in which you deserve to live."

"You don't understand," he said. "I have dedicated my life to avenging my sister's death."

"So you've said." He heard her voice soften slightly.

She sat down. At least, he was fairly certain he recognized the sound of her sitting. "Tell me. From the beginning. Tell me how all of this was supposed to avenge her."

He stared at nothing. He had no other choice. He was enveloped in darkness. He felt the wall that he had built up inside of himself erode, crumble. And all of the acrid, toxic emotions that he had been holding at bay for all these years poured out. Poured forth.

"I needed to do everything in my power to be different from him. Not simply to make myself a better person, I'm beyond redemption, and I am aware of that. I decided to prove to him that everything he had done was pointless. That allowing his daughter to die, alienating his son, and turning his wife into a ghost of a human being, all of those things were unnecessary to his success. I set out to do that by being the antithesis of everything that he was."

"And that's why your reputation for treating women well, for being good, that's why that reputation matters. Not because you have an investment in being good."

"I am not good. Have you not paid attention to anything that I've said? I am beyond help."

"All right. What else then? What else have you done to try and avenge your sister."

"All of this. Everything that I am. I intended to destroy his empire. Eclipse it with my own. I intended to… To be something he never could be. Which was loved by the public. Not because I… Not because I deserved it, not because I even wanted it. Because he said it couldn't be done, and what better way to win, than by beating him while not playing his game at all?"

"Right. So, with this headline, you understand that everything you are is called into question."

"I am aware," he snarled.

"I'm not sure that it's fixable."

She might as well have dropped a boulder on his chest. He felt as if it had caved in. "And what is the point of anything?"

"You're going to have to figure that out. I can't tell you what the point of your life is. But you're going to have to ask yourself a very serious question. What if you can't win?"

"That isn't an option," he said, rejecting it instantly.

"I'm sorry, you can sit here and tell me that you deserve to be blinded for the rest of your life, deserve this accident, but you cannot take on board the fact that you might fail at your mission."

"No," he said. "It is my purpose."

"It's not your purpose. It is somebody else's purpose. You don't have a purpose. The only thing that you do is react. To the death of your sister, to the bastard behavior of your father. That's it. To the headlines the paparazzi print about you, to all of these things. You shape your life around them."

"You know nothing," he said, wanting to turn and face her, not entirely certain where she was. "You know nothing. You are a child. You lost someone, and for that I am sorry. But it is nothing compared to what I went through."

"Oh, are we doing that? Are we measuring trauma? The reason my trauma seems smaller than yours is because I've done something to deal with it rather than sitting in self-pity for the past several years."

"Self-pity. Is that what you think this is? It is not self-pity that I have remade myself into an instrument of my father's destruction. It is not self-pity. It is the only way that I can find a shred of sense in the fact that I draw breath still. And now… I know there is no sense to it whatsoever."

He bent down and picked up something, he didn't know what, and threw it as hard as he could. He heard the sound of cracking glass, and Auggie gasped.

"You are a child," she shouted. "Sit in here by yourself then. I'll come bring you food when I think you're hungry."

More of her making decisions for him.

"You cannot leave me," he raged.

"I can and I will. Because you are a self-pitying fool. I put myself on the line trying to help you. And you might be unfixable, Matias Balcazar. Not because you're blind, but because you can't see a life that extends beyond playing this game with your father. This is where it got you. You are here because of you. Not because of fate, not because of God, not even because of your dad. You are here because you couldn't handle sitting in your own discomfort without doing something. You had to react. And that's what you've been doing all along."

"You don't know me. You can't tell me what I've been doing for all these years when you weren't even around until a couple of months ago."

"I could leave you up here," she said. "I could leave you up here to rot. And frankly, at this point, I wouldn't even be sorry."

Then he heard something clattered to the ground. Her

ring, he realized. It was followed by angry footsteps and a slamming door. She had genuinely left him there.

He growled, to the empty space. And he wished she was there for him to growl at.

The anger came from somewhere deep inside of him, and he had not given voice to such darkness in more years than he could count. But he was the darkness now. Surrounded by it. It was outside of him, and within. It was… It was untenable.

He stood motionless, uncertain of which way to go. And then he began to slowly walk with his hands outstretched, trying to get a gauge for everything in the room. He ran into a side table, and he cursed. He felt for furniture, the smooth surface, down the sides. Then he moved and found the bed, his hands moving over the blankets. He decided that was good enough for now. He sat down on the edge of the mattress. He wanted alcohol, but he would need her to get it for him. He didn't have his phone, and even if he did, he didn't know how to use it in his present state.

It really did remind him of the day that Seraphina had died. Because even then he had felt helpless. Useless. Frozen.

And responsible all at the same time.

If he had said something different to her. If he had not said anything to her at all.

He had broken the one person that loved him.

The one person he had loved.

And now there was nothing. Nothing at all. Nothing but this void. But this black hole of need. He had tried to cover it all up. He had managed to find a façade that had… Let him live.

He might not have ever truly taken the joy in life that he pretended to, but it had been better than this.

There had been noise. Distraction. And it might not have ever penetrated down to his soul, but it kept him moving.

The stillness… He despised it.

And right now, he despised Augusta Fremont. A convenient target for his rage. For refusing to do his bidding.

The personification of how the world had turned against him, rather than bending to his will.

He sat there in the darkness, and he understood. Profoundly, the urge to take a substance that might remove you from your reality. Remove you from everything.

If it had been in his hands, he might've done so.

It was a rock bottom he had never faced down before. Because he had always had something to do. He'd always had a mission.

And now that mission was gone.

CHAPTER ELEVEN

SHE WAS BEGINNING to feel guilty. It wasn't fair to be so mean to him. Maybe. But he was… Maybe she needed to feel sorry for him. Maybe. She had known that the playboy thing was a façade, but it was a horrible thing to lift the lid on and find nothing more than despair underneath it. Darkness. That was what he was. He was a black hole. And she had just left him up there.

She was beginning to calm down now. The truth was, she didn't care about what this did to the business's reputation. It would actually be pretty easy to get out of it. What had been revealed about him was a big family secret, and since nobody had known about him, she would have plausible deniability also.

She sighed, and she put in a group call to the work wives.

"I have to stay here," she said.

"Of course you do," Irinka said.

"You seem alarmingly okay with it."

"Is he still… Is he still blind?" Irinka asked.

"Yes."

"And it's completely understandable that you can't leave."

She pinched the bridge of her nose. "The thing is, I

either need to completely cut bait with him, and say that I was taken in, I didn't realize that he had such a dark past, or… Or I'm all in."

"What do you think about him?" Lynna asked.

"I think that the situation is a lot more complicated than the media is making it out to be. I think that he's a mess. He's certainly not the world's favorite boyfriend. And he's not a golden retriever. But we already knew that." She paused. "I don't think I realized how much of it was a conscious façade."

"You have our support," Maude said. "Of course you can't abandon him in his hour of need. He's a real person, and so are you. You aren't just a business, or reputation."

"Well, I'm not very happy to end up caregiving for somebody again. I didn't ask for this."

"Of course you didn't," Lynna said. "But since when does the world care if you asked for something or not?"

"I keep thinking that maybe I'd earned an easy stretch, Lynna."

Lynna laughed. "Oh, Auggie. None of us can earn that."

"Well then what's the point?" Auggie asked, feeling flat and exceptionally angry at whoever had made the rules of life, because they really weren't working for her right now.

Why was she attached to him?

Maude was right, it wasn't just about business.

And she felt slightly feral with that realization. Because she hadn't asked for this. Any more than she had asked to love a mother who was slowly dying for years.

Any more than she had asked to be the one who had to bear the burden of that love, of that care.

She curled her hands into fists and tried to calm herself down. She didn't like this part of herself. The one that would get so awash in her own tragedy. She wasn't the one who had been sick, just like she wasn't the one who was experiencing temporary blindness now.

But it hurt her. And there was no place for it to go, and maybe that was the problem.

She had not asked to care about this man. He was a registered disaster. She knew better than to like him, even the slightest bit, and yet she did.

Worse, she had gone and made him her first lover.

"I need to go," she said, shaking her head.

"Are you okay?"

"No," she said. "I am very deeply not okay. This has been the weirdest week of my life. And… I am enmeshed. In a way that I really wish I wasn't, but I am. And… I'm woman enough to take responsibility for it. But that doesn't mean I don't feel horrendously sorry for myself."

"I like a little bit of self-pity, personally," Irinka said. "Take care of yourself. And you know if you need anything we'll be right there for you."

"Just hold down the fort. I don't know what kind of storm is awaiting you all in terms of media."

"We'll handle it. Our official stance, of course, is that we support you, and your judgment. So anything to do with him is likely a gross exaggeration. Also, if you want me to dig up dirt on his father…"

"You don't need to go that far," said Auggie. "However, if dirt presents itself…"

"Mudslinging typically just gets everyone dirty," Maude said.

"But it's sometimes necessary," Lynna said. "Because life is unpredictable that way."

"Indeed." She said goodbye to her friends, and then returned to staring out the window. Shc closed her eyes, imagining the press of his mouth against hers. Imagining the way that he had touched her just a couple of nights ago. How she had felt him moving inside of her.

How had they gone from that to this?

It was supposed to be a fantasy. She had accepted that it would be a temporary fantasy, but she really hadn't had any clue that it would be… That it would be so temporary. They were supposed to have their two months to act as an engaged couple. They were supposed to…

There was no supposed to. She just had to get over it. That was life.

Her father had been a genetic material donor and nothing more. Her mother was dead. There was nobody left in the world that really loved her. She had her friends, and she was grateful for that, but there was no real… Family. And it wasn't supposed to be that way, but it was. She had given her virginity to the first gorgeous man that she had found herself in proximity with who wanted her, and now he was injured. It wasn't supposed to be that way. But it was.

She knew better than to be fanciful, she knew better than to be a whiny brat about it.

But it was going to start with him not being a whiny brat.

She closed her eyes and willed herself to move. She made some sandwiches and packed them away into a basket. She looked outside at the sun. It was a beautiful day. A beautiful day in England, for God's sake.

They were going to take advantage of it. She was going to keep him from sinking into despair, partly because she needed to keep herself from doing it. She didn't have the time to be self-pitying. So she wouldn't allow him to be either.

She stamped up the stairs, and flung the door open to his room. He was sitting on the end of the bed, and the expression of desolation on his face caught hard in her throat.

"You aren't doing this," she said.

"Excuse me?"

"You aren't sinking into the abyss, Matias. Not while I'm here."

He had the audacity to lounge back on the bed, looking in her direction like he was a particularly uninterested cat. And she knew that he couldn't see her, and yet, his dark gaze felt penetrating.

She was a bit annoyed for thinking the word *penetrating.*

She gritted her teeth. "Did you have commentary?" she asked.

"I have nothing to say. But I do not know what you think is happening here. Are you a schoolmarm? Do you seek to whip me in shape? Or perhaps you haven't realized that it's too late for that. I am beyond redemption."

"Well, unhappily for you, I don't believe in that. I don't believe that people are garbage. I don't believe that people are to be disposed of just because they have made some mistakes."

"Mistakes. You say that as if I have gotten a poor

grade on a math test, not said the very wrong thing that sent my sister to her grave."

"You didn't inject her with the drugs."

His face turned sharply, as if she had slapped him.

"I'm sorry, but it's true. You're taking away her agency in all of this. Yes, your father was horrible, and he clearly made her feel bad about herself, but he obviously manipulated you too. He is still doing it. You're doing it back, but so is he. You're engaged in this ridiculous, unwinnable game with a man who just sounds… Frankly awful. Even now, he's exploiting his daughter's death to hurt you. To hurt your perception in the public eye, I don't even think it's about your feelings. He probably isn't even aware that you have them. He probably doesn't consider feelings at all. That is a horrible thing. An utterly horrifying proposition."

The growing realization inside of her felt so big that she couldn't stop. She was trying to read his face to see if this surprised him as much as it did her. She was… Undone.

"So what if you let him win. What if you let him have this. Because what is there to say? Do you continue to rake over the ground of your sister's death so that the public can be satisfied that what happened was just a horrible mistake. Anybody reading the article is going to understand that. Is going to understand that she was a woman who was troubled because of… Because of her upbringing. But if she was troubled because of her upbringing then so were you."

"No," he said. "That isn't true. I… I should've been stronger."

"Why? Why should you have been stronger, Matias? It doesn't make any sense."

"Because I was stronger. Inherently."

"Why? Because the way that you lived, and the things that you did were closer to what your father found acceptable? It seems to me like you were a child who could simply do the things laid out before him, and because of that you avoided the worst of what your father was, until you fully realized just how monstrous of a man he was. Your sister couldn't fall in line, so she didn't have those years of being able to fool herself. But what you did was not easier, and it doesn't mean that he was any kinder to you. It just didn't manifest itself in the same way."

"I am stronger, and I should've been stronger for her. I should've realized. I should have had insight."

"You didn't. You were just a child. Even if you were twenty years old, you were a child. Under your father's thumb, with no real sense of the world and how it was. So I'm going to ask you again. What if you let him win? Because what do you gain by continuing to fight this? At least right now. At least now… You're free. Because here we are, out in the middle of nowhere, and we aren't going to let anyone know what's happening."

"It will look as if I'm hiding."

"That's fine. I've asked the work wives to handle it. They will. The thing is, your grief has just been dredged up to the surface, and it's actually completely all right if you don't engage in playing games with the media to get back at your father."

He was silent for a moment. "They will think that my silence is an admission of guilt."

"Some people will. But when we actually do speak,

perhaps people will see this for what it is. You're the one that actually cares. You're the one that can't bear to use your sister's memory like this."

"Everything I do is for my sister's memory."

"I know that. But that's different. It's different than this. Different than the way that he is trying to destroy you over the top of her story. Her reputation."

"Perhaps you're right."

"I have made us a picnic. And I think that we should have it."

His expression contorted into one of horror. "I do not want to go on a picnic. I don't want to go on a picnic even when I can see, much less so now. Are you going to lead me around like a stumbling fool in the daisies? With a basket?"

"There are no daisies."

His lip curled in disgust. "What is the purpose of this?"

"I think that the purpose of it, perhaps, is to get you out of your own head. You are not going to heal as long as you're sitting here in distress."

"I am not in distress."

"You could've fooled me. You were, only moments ago threatening to drink yourself to death. I think maybe some perspective is in order."

"I think you might need to be able to see in order to have perspective."

"And I think that you are being a cantankerous fool."

"Enough," he said sharply. "I will have a picnic with you. But you must endeavor to be less ridiculous."

"Oh, well I'll try."

She walked over to the bed and rested her hand

against his. Instantly, the contact between them sent an arrow of desire through her. She wanted him. Still. In the stillness, the silence, the space of this moment, she might even want him more than she had that night when it was a fantasy. Pure and perfect and lovely.

This was sharp, awful and weighted.

And yet…

She felt lonely, standing there touching his hand, looking at him, wishing that they could be closer, wishing that she could be further away. She saw something like desolation in his dark eyes and she wondered if he felt it too.

"Come on," she said, tugging his hand gently.

He stood, and she laced her fingers through his. "I'll make sure that you get there okay."

"And I have to trust that you're not leading me into a field of daisies."

"Most people would be more worried about a hornet's nest."

"Not me. I'm much more concerned about softness."

"Well, that is an interesting thing to hear you say. Especially considering your apartment is one of the softest places I've ever been."

"You know that's for the women who come to visit."

"Maybe the daisies are for me," she said. She did her best not to dwell on the reality of other women visiting him. She had seen those other women. She had seen them in bed together. Of course, it felt different now. Sharp.

She held on to him more firmly, and began to lead him out of the room. "Two more steps and then we're at the stairs," she said.

"Thank you."

There was a hardness to his tone, and she could tell that he wasn't happy that he had to be led.

"It is temporary," she said. "You'll be just fine."

"You don't know that."

"No. I don't. But I used to say it to my mother all the same. I told her that she would be fine, and then I told her that I would be fine. Because what else are you supposed to say? That I don't know?" Her heart started to beat faster. He kept in step with her, as if the familiarity that he had with stairs helped. But of course he had one hand on her, one on the railing, and she did her level best to keep him steady. He must hate this. But she hated it too. Hated being put in this position again. Hated that he wouldn't even let her give him the lip service that would at least make her feel better.

"What are you supposed to say to someone? That you might not be fine? That it might be like this for you forever. It might be. Maybe you won't be okay. None of us will be." She let out a heavy sigh, and her foot reached the bottom of the stairs. "It's just floor now. You stand here, I'm going to go into the kitchen and get food."

"What if I don't wish to wait?"

"That's too bad. There are going to be concessions that you have to make. That I have to make."

She went and she picked up the basket of food, and stood there for a moment. She took a deep breath. And she tried to make some sense out of her feelings. Her utterly selfish, uncharitable, mixed-up feelings. Because she wanted to kiss him, and she wanted to shake him, and she wanted to go and find a doctor and rail at them for not fixing him immediately, because she also hated seeing him helpless. As much as she hated seeing him hopeless.

She took a deep breath, and went back out to where he was. "I'm here," she said.

He didn't reach his hand out for her, she went and grabbed it. "Come on," she said, propelling him toward the door.

"You have too much power over me," he said.

She paused for a moment. "Well, that's unusual."

"I am aware that I generally enjoy an outsized amount of power. I do not enjoy the loss of it."

"You never really had it," she said, tugging him out the door. "I mean, if it makes you feel better. That's one thing you learn when you have a parent who gets ill. Or, if you ever get hurt. Or sick. We live under the illusion of having control. That if we do certain things our lives will turn out a certain way. But it isn't true. Even I have fallen back into that belief system. I guess it's just been too long since life coldcocked me. Not so much right now."

"Does my injury inconvenience you?"

"I already said that it did," she said. "I'm not trying to be mean. I'm not. It's only… Whatever power you thought you had, it was never real."

He let out a hard, short laugh. "I suppose not."

"It doesn't mean that your father is in control over you. Also, you're a billionaire, so technically, you don't even need the public to like you. You could just step away from everything, never work again."

"But don't you understand how that feels… Wrong."

The sun was shining through the trees, and it really was a beautiful day outside. There were no daisies, but there were other wildflowers, and she was tempted to drag him through them. No one would ever know, least of all him. She didn't, though. Instead, she walked with him to the shade of a large, expansive willow. She spread a blanket out on the ground, and then guided him down to sit beside her. It was beautiful. But, much like everything in her life, it was the simile of something tranquil. Because this wasn't the truth of it. He was here under sufferance, they were hiding from a rabid media. She was his keeper more than anything else, and the fact that she had been his lover probably meant nothing to him.

It meant everything to her.

It had been a singular experience as far as she was concerned.

And of course for him… It had basically just been a Tuesday.

He might've even forgotten that they'd slept together. He had hit his head, after all, and it might have been any woman.

Really, it might have been any woman.

"It is not because of work ethic," he said. "Not because of a need to succeed. It is simply that my sister is no longer alive. And if I don't do something, if I don't make something of myself, of my life, or destroy what remains of my father, what was the purpose of anything?"

"I don't know." She felt immeasurably sad, a sense of dread hollowing out her chest. "I don't know. It's something I certainly haven't figured out. All I know to do is to keep going."

She looked down at the kingdom blanket, at her hand,

so close to his. But not touching. Not now that they didn't have to.

"Maybe we don't have to solve any of life's mysteries right now. Maybe you just need to heal."

He snorted. "I have never sat idle."

"You don't really have a choice. Your body is sort of commanding that you do it. So maybe you need to listen. Maybe you need to heed the lesson."

"Maybe you are too."

She snapped her head around to look at him. "I'm sorry what?"

"Maybe you are meant to rest."

"I'm taking care of you."

"I suppose it is in your best interest to make sure I don't fall and hit my head. Again."

"Who knows, maybe another knock on the head would cure you."

"I very much doubt it."

She stared at the side of his face. "Are you really suggesting that I take a rest?"

"Well, you asked me, what is my life if I'm not trying to defeat my father? I don't know the answer to that question. But what is your life. If not putting a great distance between yourself and who you once were?"

Auggie didn't know what to say to that. "I'm not doing that consciously."

But here, sitting in the space that was so reminiscent of being a caregiver all those years ago, she felt uncomfortable. More than uncomfortable. She felt trapped, in many ways. She felt afraid. Like she was never actually going to find her way out of this. Like she was regressed. So maybe he was right. Maybe that was her life. Putting as much distance between herself and the scared girl she had been.

Except… No. He was right. It was why she had never slowed down to take a lover, or sightsee when she was doing business travels, or any of the other very normal things that most people her age did, and had done.

She had her friends. She loved them dearly. But she had gathered them up on her way forward, and they had helped propel her. She didn't only love them for what they did for her, but the fact remained, they had been part of her goals. And when was the last time she had done anything that wasn't about… Those goals. Getting somewhere new, somewhere further away. Somewhere exciting. It had been him. The night that she had spent with him had been the one nod to herself as a whole woman, to just feeling good, to just enjoying life.

It had been the only time.

"Well, I guess there were worse things than taking a break here in a beautiful home."

"Is it beautiful?"

"You've been here before. You could see when we arrived."

"Still. Where are we sitting now?"

She began to unpack their sandwiches. "We are sitting beneath a sweeping, green willow tree. The leaves are light green. We are sitting on a blue kingdom blanket. The grass is darker than the willow tree. I steered us around the clutch of white flowers that we might have sat in. But they're there. Off in the distance. Not so close that they'll get their softness all over you. The sky is uncharacteristically blue. The clouds are round and fat and white. It is a glorious day. Perfect."

"I smell the flowers."

"They're sweet," she said.

"I don't think I can remember ever pausing to smell flowers before in my life."

"You know, I don't think I have either." She blinked, her eyes stinging. "Actually, I can remember spending a great deal of time trying to get the scent of too many flowers out of my nose. When my mother went into hospice. And old, well-meaning friends sent bouquets. Mostly, those flowers that you get sent from online florists just don't smell very good. It is the same as this. But it is nice to have some of the glorious outside brought in I suppose. When it's the only way you're ever going to experience it again."

"They sent flowers, but did anybody come and help you?"

The question hit her with the unerring quality of an arrow getting to the heart of its target.

There was a difference. One she had never even pulled apart before.

Roses were lovely, but they did not hold you. They didn't help clean or deal with paperwork. They didn't tell you what to do next. They were not company.

She shook her head. "No. Nobody was close enough to her to do that. Not anymore. After she had me, I think she sort of receded from her life. I don't know if she was embarrassed because of my father or… I don't know. And I can't ask her now. This is the worst part about losing somebody. You get older, and you gain perspective, and there are so many questions that you wish you would've asked. So many ways that you wish you could have known them. I feel devastated by the fact that I will never truly know her. It's the grief that keeps on giving."

"I can understand that. I will never understand what drove my sister to her addiction. Not really. Not the way that I want to. I will never be able to share my experiences of my father with her. She was the only other person to have him as a father. To understand. And I wish… I wish she was here now. Because I would be different with her. Because I know myself, and my father in a way that might allow me to know her."

"I'm sorry," she said. "I think it's cruel. To be robbed of a relationship like that."

"I took it for myself."

"You didn't."

"I did. It was my words. My actions. I just wish that there was another chance. A chance to atone and have it really mean something, rather than just being… A dark, futile thing, that feels like a necessity. It feels like the only way that I deserve to go on breathing."

"Maybe she would want more for you than that. More for you than breathing. Because the really sad thing is… Your sister can't know you better either. If she were here, you can't simply think about how you would be different. But about how she would be different, too. So maybe the version of her that you knew… Who was perhaps very poorly, maybe she couldn't have wanted more or better. But you don't know the woman that she would've become. If she would've been more patient with herself. If she would have given all of it just a little bit more time."

"I thought that I was here to rest. Not engage with all my old ghosts."

"Well. I guess so. But you and I just have so many."

He shifted, and along with his body's movements, she felt something change in the air. "What are you wearing?"

He was done with ghosts, then.

Immediately, heat flooded her cheeks. "What do you mean? What am I wearing?"

"I'm curious. The last time I saw you, you were wearing that orange dress. The one I had taken off of you the night before."

"Are you back to playing a role?"

"No, but does that surprise you that I would rather think about you, and the encounter that we shared, rather than the death of my sister?"

"Just tell me. Really. Are you doing this because it makes you comfortable, or are you asking because you… Because you want me?"

"I want you."

She swallowed hard. Her heart was thundering. And she considered. Considered what this meant for her. Considered if this meant that she should indulge him or not. Because they were here alone. For all this time. He couldn't see. But that didn't mean that he couldn't…

"I'm wearing a white dress. And I will say that it is somewhat see-through. It comes up above my knees. And it has a scooped neckline. It is not modest. You can see the… The curves of my breasts." The words came out in a hushed whisper.

"Good," he said.

"You should eat your sandwich."

"What are you wearing underneath it."

She bit the inside of her cheek, and rather than question the wisdom of any of this, she indulged him. She indulged herself.

"A white lace bra. You can see through it. You can see my nipples. And… The panties match. You know… What that probably looks like."

He growled. "I do."

"And now you should eat."

"What if I find it's not food that I'm hungry for."

"Well, you should…"

He found her mouth. Unerringly. Like it was no trouble at all. His lips pressed to hers, and her heart stopped. They were out in the open, but no one else was here. Need was coursing through her body, and she found that she wanted…

She wanted this. She wanted to give him this. There was no one, not for miles. No one would know if they did this out here in the open.

Suddenly, she was gripped by the bitter regret that he wouldn't be able to see this. Them. Beneath a wide, expansive sky.

"I don't need to be able to see to know my way around your body."

She shivered. And at the same time, she felt a pulse of jealousy, because of course she was going to benefit from all the women who had come before her. Of course she was.

"I want you," she whispered. "I want this. Every time you took a woman into that bedroom I wondered. I wondered what you did with her. I wondered how good it felt."

"It felt nothing like being with you," he said. "I have been with more women than I can count. I won't pretend. I won't pretend that I have not… Indulged myself in this way. But it wasn't the same."

"Why?"

"You see me. And right now, in the darkness of my own mind, it is the most… The most bitter thing to say. But you saw something in me that nobody else ever did. And I felt like… When I touched you, was closer to seeing myself. And now, I can see nothing. But there's you. You, and you make me feel like perhaps… I'm not floating and nothing. Like I'm not alone."

"Matias," she whispered, putting her hands on his lips. And then she leaned in and kissed him, consuming him, pushing her tongue deep inside of his mouth like she was a woman who knew full well what she was doing, rather than a woman who was being led by the desire that was clawing at her chest.

"Matias," she whispered.

He wrapped his arms around her waist and lifted her up, bringing her to straddle his body. Her dress pushed up to the tops of her thighs, and the hard ridge of his arousal pressed firmly against that aching place there. Oh, how she wanted him. Deep inside of her.

She told him so. Whispered against his mouth in the crudest possible way. Felt him surge with pleasure beneath her.

She didn't feel any shame. With him, she never had. With him, it was like she was a new version of herself. Like she was the woman she might have been. If she hadn't always been running. Running and running with no hope of ever stopping. With no reward at the end. No goal but distance. Between herself and the sad girl she'd once been. He was right. But here and now in the bright warmth of the sun, with his hands on her body, she was something else entirely. A new creature, remade beneath the insistence of his touch. It was glorious.

She had felt that urge earlier. To close the distance between them. To really touch him. To not be so alone.

He must feel alone. With everything so dark around him. So she touched him. Everywhere. Moved her hands over his shoulders, down his back. She kissed him, his face, his neck. Until she found herself lying on her back on the blanket with him stripping his clothes off quickly. She moved her hands down that sculpted chest, his ridged stomach. To his proud, glorious masculinity. "You're so beautiful," she said.

"You are too." He moved his hands over her curves. "It doesn't matter that I cannot see. I know it. I feel it. You taste beautiful. The feel of your skin beneath my hands, is beautiful. And I would… I would trade heaven and earth to be able to see. The glory of your skin. The color of your nipples. That beautiful, slick pinkness between your legs. I would give my very soul. But the trouble is I no longer have my soul. But thankfully, I have you."

He said it ragged, his voice rough. She believed every word.

At least, she believed that he did. That he felt soulless. Shrouded in darkness.

So she tried to make her kiss the light. As they came together, as he moved inside of her with quick, decisive strokes that carried her right to heaven, she tried to give him all that sunlight. To pour it into her touch, her kiss.

In every fractured word of pleasure.

She tried.

"Matias," she whispered. "Matias please."

He put his hand between her legs and slid his thumb over her most sensitive place. And she shattered. Screaming out his name all the way up to the sun, the sky, the clouds.

And when she came back down to earth, he was there with her, his forehead pressed to hers as he spilled himself inside of her.

"Dammit," he said, his voice rough. "I forgot to use a condom."

"It's okay," she said. "I'm on the pill. Just as a precaution. I know it's not… Safe, necessarily. But…"

"I would never hurt you," he said.

"I know."

But right then, she knew that wasn't true. He would hurt her. Because in the end they would go their separate ways, and it would tear her into pieces.

But he wouldn't do it on purpose. He just would. Because of who they were.

This wasn't real. And neither were they. How could they be? She was taken out of her life, and he was removed from his. He had even lost some of his senses. Maybe that was part of why they were out here, naked in a field. They had lost their senses.

"Why haven't you been with anyone?" he asked.

"Well, I have now."

"Before. Us… This. It got swallowed up by the accident. By everything."

She lifted a shoulder, but then realized he couldn't see the gesture. "I would've thought that us sleeping together was just a mundane thing to you."

"It wasn't. It meant something. I know you, Auggie, and I can't say the same for any of the other women that

I have ever taken as lovers. I respected them, I even liked them in a casual sense, but I didn't know even half about them that I know about you. And I find myself curious."

"I just didn't have the time. And mainly… I don't think I wanted to let anyone in. I had great practice at being a fortress, and it's difficult to be something else. In the last seven years my life has changed relentlessly. Every month, every year has felt different to me."

She plucked at a piece of grass. "When my mother's health declined even more than it already had, I had to be as strong as I possibly could be to get through that. To finish high school while I was taking care of her. I had to grieve her while she sat in front of me. I had to keep going, because you can't stop, because when someone is dying it doesn't stop. It changes by the day. And so do you. I wanted it to stop. There would be a moment when it all felt manageable. Where she wasn't in too much pain, and she was still there, and I would wish that everything could just… Stop. For a moment. And then when it was hard, sometimes I would just wish…"

She swallowed hard, the truth, the honesty, cutting her throat on its way out. "That it was over. But there was no one that I could say that to. Nobody that I could share with. I got used to processing all of that inside myself. While I tried to look okay, tried to be brave. Then my mother died, and I had to learn how to grieve while I kept on walking. Because I had the opportunity to go to school, so I had to keep moving. And I did. Farther away from home with every step. Farther away from who I was, but I was the same, really."

She swallowed hard, her throat feeling tight. "Some days I feel like I've never actually sat down and sorted through all of it, but really, what's the point?" She looked at him, beseeching, even though she knew that he couldn't look back. "When you go through something that painful, isn't it better to just keep going?"

"That's the only way that I know," he said. "But I managed to find the time to have sex."

She laughed. "I dunno. I don't know why it was different for me. Maybe it was just not knowing how to connect with another person."

"Again, I managed to have sex without doing that at all."

"Do you really think so?" she asked. "Do you really think you don't know how to connect with another person?"

"I know I don't. I don't even know how to connect with myself." He smiled. He stared on, unseeing at the flowers that she had told him about but that he hadn't witnessed himself. "Sometimes I wonder if I am hollow. If I became the character that I fashioned for myself. If there's nothing left anymore. Of who I really am. I would almost hope so. Because the man that I was… He was also nothing." She watched as he swallowed hard, his Adam's apple bobbing up and down, a muscle in his jaw jumping. "I was my father's creation then. But what you said earlier haunts me. I am little more than his creation now. Because everything I do is in response to him."

"I didn't say that to be mean," she said. Though she was conscious of the fact that it had been quite mean, and she had been frustrated. "I think it's true of all of us, isn't it? Our bodies are temples that house our greatest successes and failures, that build altars to our trauma and our tribulations. It's what keeps us going. I think we're all objects forged in the fires of the good and bad things we've been through. We are all just doing things in response to what happened before."

"Let's say I think you're right," he said. "I think I have not lived for myself. And now that I can see nothing… I see that."

"Oh, I'm right now, am I?"

"Yes, and I am sorry I threw the glass. I was not thinking. I could have hurt you and I didn't—"

"You didn't hurt me," she said. "But you can say I'm right again."

"Don't push me."

"Why not? You wouldn't see me coming."

He looked annoyed, and she loved it. She liked sitting with him, talking to him. Teasing him even when they were talking about deadly serious things.

"How do you stop? How do you…get ahead of the action? I think that's what I've been trying to do, and yet, then my father came in and showed that he still has the ability to pull the pin on the grenade sitting dormant inside me."

"I think in this case, your father proved that being a sociopath makes that easy." She looked at her hands. "You're a lot of things, Matias Javier Hernandez Balcazar. But a sociopath isn't one of them."

The ghost of a smile touched the corners of his mouth. "You know I wish that felt like an accomplishment."

She touched his hand. "Maybe someday it will."

"Maybe. You have very neatly turned this around. I wanted to know why you were a virgin."

"All I have is speculation." But she knew that was a lie. It was a knot in her brain that she hadn't yet unspooled, not even for herself. But she decided that she would try. For him. For her. Because they were both different here. There was no one to perform for. They just got to be. They got to breathe. "Maybe the truth is in what you just said. I didn't know how to want anything for myself. And then I met you. And there was something so… Compelling about you. And it isn't the way that the media talks about you. I found you to be so wholly different than what they said."

"The Pitbull."

"Yes. Anyone who thinks otherwise is an idiot, in my opinion. Or they just haven't looked into your eyes."

"There's nothing there now."

"That's a lie. Whether you see it or not, I see so much there. And I wanted you. In a way that I never… I never wanted anyone like that before. I told myself it was because I wanted the fantasy of what we had that night. Because I felt beautiful. Because I felt… Special. Because I felt like the one being taken care of, instead of the other way around."

"And here you are being my seeing-eye dog."

"I don't see myself that way. It isn't that. It's not. I'm sorry. If I made you feel that way."

"Don't apologize to me. I'm not so easily wounded. I'm not even entirely certain that I have feelings."

"I think the problem is that you do. We both do. It doesn't mean we especially know what to do with them, but we both have them."

"It's a nice thing to think." She wondered which thing he meant.

That they both had a lot of feelings, or maybe that she

connected with him in a way that she never had with anyone else. In a way that no one else had.

"I didn't even know what wanting someone felt like," she said. "I understand what attraction feels like. Not the need to act on it. Not until you."

"Why me?"

"Maybe we are the same," she said.

"How?" He sounded completely uncertain, but not angry, not derisive.

"The way that we've built walls around ourselves in order to survive. The way that we became other people. I don't know that I was conscious of becoming another person. I don't think it was a decision in quite the same way yours was."

"You're like me before," he said slowly. "A creation of my surroundings. There was no decision made. It was only after, when I decided to become an entirely new thing."

She nodded. "I didn't do that. I stayed the same. I just move myself. But nothing else changed. This was different. You were different. Reaching outside of myself, rather than wandering around trying to be self-contained."

"I'm not certain that I'm worthy of any of this."

"It's not about you," she said. "Well, it is. It's about you creating a response in me, I suppose. But acting on it… That was for me. In the very best way."

"Well, I am pleased for you then."

"We are naked in a field," she said. "I think maybe we're both the same kind of fool."

"Is it foolish to want someone, do you think?"

"You should know. You're the playboy. Many more women have wanted you than men have wanted me, and certainly you wanted more women than I've ever wanted men."

"No. That is true. I have wanted sex in the same way a person wants a piece of cake. Wanting you is different."

"Oh."

"It is like the moment where the air is caught between winter and spring. The last week before school lets out for the holidays. The longing for something, so specific and sharp it takes your breath away. I cannot say it better than that."

"Well," she breathed. "I don't think I can say anything better than that."

She moved closer to him, her bare skin touching his. And she let the sun warm them both. It was a long time before they went back inside.

And when she led him back upstairs, and to his bed, she went with him.

Because for the first time in a very long time, she wasn't simply moving forward. She was still.

She intended to feel everything in this stillness. Because it was probably the only time this was ever going to happen.

CHAPTER TWELVE

THE NEXT DAY she became a taskmaster. All night she had been pliant and beautiful in his arms. And now that night and day were all the same to him, the hours bled into one another seamlessly. Time had stopped meaning anything. There was only the darkness, and Auggie. He could not say that he minded it. But then she became a little taskmaster. Forcing him to memorize the layouts of the different rooms.

"This is not permanent," he said as he stood at the threshold of what she had informed him was the living room, trying to make him navigate his way into the kitchen. "Neither my lack of sight, nor staying here."

"But it is now," Auggie pointed out. "It is the reality we're both living in. And I don't want you to break your neck."

"You are much happier when I'm breaking your back."

He heard her sputtering, blustering, and he really did wish that he could see her expression.

"That is a crude thing to say."

"I rather thought it was clever."

"You are an enigma. Because sometimes you are still that…shameless, charming playboy, and then other times you are…"

"A black hole of impenetrable darkness?"

"Yes," she said. "That."

"Maybe both things are true. Maybe both men are me. Though, I don't know if I can figure out how to join the two together. I don't know if I would want to."

"I don't know. I like both."

She liked him. She liked him. He turned that over within himself. He couldn't recall a woman ever *liking* him before, not the real him. What a strange thing.

He was used to the world having a favorable opinion of him. To being regarded as a highly likable person, but he knew that it was fake. Because he knew that he was fake. She knew something else about him, and she seemed fond of him anyway. She was still here.

"Why are you here with me?"

"Where else would I go, Matias?"

"Back to your real life?"

"This is my real life right now. You are my real life."

"Because you are an endless martyr to your need to care for other people?" That was possibly taking it too far. But she had cared for her mother as a teenager, and it was entirely possible that it was what drove her now. She had said herself. They were all walking altars to their own trauma, after all.

"No," she said. "It's about me. It's about… The sex, frankly. I feel more in touch with myself than I have in a very long time, and actually, I would've told you that were I faced with another situation where I had to take care of somebody having a medical issue, I would run fifty miles. To get away from it. To get away from them. But it doesn't feel the same. I want to be here. With you. Don't let it go to your head."

"My ego is as big as it can possibly get."

"That isn't true at all. You are the most self-loathing person wrapped in a cloak of false ego that I have ever met."

Her words struck him. And he decided that he was done talking. So he went on navigating through the kitchen. And he managed to do it without running into too many things. Though part of him resisted the exercise, because he was not going to become accustomed to blindness. It was not a permanent state.

In that he was determined.

She continued to work him like that for the week. But at night, she went to bed with him, and the intimacy that they built there was like a glimmering kingdom. He might not be able to see anything, but that had become more real to him than anything else ever had. It was the only reality he cared to lose himself in.

They could have called in staff, but he was resistant to it, and she didn't seem to mind. She was the one who had to do all of the work in the absence of anyone there to cook for them. Because he was at such a disadvantage. But he found himself growing in his trust for her.

He couldn't recall ever having trusted another person before. Growing up with a father like his, he had only ever been able to trust himself. Especially with the way he had pitted him and his sister against each other.

He was good. She was bad.

It had only made him want to protect her, to be better to keep the focus off of her. It had made him feel like… like he had to be hard on her sometimes so his father wouldn't be. Like he could protect her with his correction because he actually did care.

It had ended badly anyway.

He navigated his way into the kitchen, listening to the

sounds of her moving around. Something was cooking, and it smelled good.

"Nothing fancy," she said. "Just some soup and bread."

"That sounds sufficient."

As he stood there, surrounded by a hominess that was completely unfamiliar to him, he felt as if he might be willing to make this trade. His sight for this life. This normalcy that was so beyond anything he had ever known.

Of course, she was having to take care of him, and she might feel different. He was potentially a burden to her, no matter what she said.

The girl who had been running away from this for so many years.

"Sufficient," she said. "Don't hurt yourself with compliments."

"Of course I was being dry."

"I know," she said. He could hear the warmth in her voice.

"I made a fire in the parlor; I thought we might sit in there and enjoy the warmth and the soup."

"You put a lot of thought into it." It was a bland thing to say, and yet there was nothing bland about it. The realization that she had done this for him. That she seemed to put effort and thought into this care.

"It feels like… Like reliving another life here."

"Agreed."

"I'm going to dish everything and bring it into the parlor. Do you think you can find your way?"

He paused, and oriented himself in the room. He found his touchpoints, and then he figured out which way he needed to go to make it into the next room, locating his path and making his way there slowly.

There would be a time when he wasn't entirely dependent on her to take care of him. He was getting better.

Do you want to get better at this?

This was the strangest thing of all. He wasn't living his life. The life he had been living for all these years. One of endless revenge.

No. He was… Living life. In a way that he never had before. In a way he had never thought he might want to.

But this wasn't him. It wasn't anything he had earned. He had to stay wounded in order to stay with her. It was a strange dichotomy.

He moved carefully to his chair, feeling the warmth of the fire. He took a seat, and heard her walk into the room.

"I have a tray with two bowls on it, soup and bread."

She was telling him so that he knew what to picture. But he didn't care about the food. Instead, he thought of Auggie herself.

Tried to picture her face as it might be right now. The strongest image of her was of how she had looked the last night he had seen her. When they had been together as lovers for the first time. He had touched her countless times since, and had tried to memorize each dip and hollow of her body with his fingertips.

But he missed her face.

"What are you wearing today, Auggie?"

She chuckled. "You used to actively avoid calling me by my nickname."

"It's a silly name."

He heard her set the tray down on the table. "Hold your hands out," she said.

She placed the bowl of soup in his hands.

"I agree," she said. He heard her settle down, heard

the clanking of her spoon on her bowl. "It is a silly name. I wanted very badly to be called Gus. That, I thought at least was a bit edgy. Sort of a nice, boyish name. Auggie sounds like somebody's pet dog."

"That isn't quite what I thought. But a valid concern."

She laughed. "I got used to it. It's just what stuck. There's not much you can do about that. I always wonder what my mother was thinking, though."

He took a cautious bite of soup. It was sweet and spicy. There was a hint of curry to it.

"Curried sweet potato," she said. Which made him aware that he must've made a face, and she had responded to it.

"Very good," he said.

"Thank you."

"Your mother was always single?"

"Yes," said Auggie. "She never married. She didn't give me any details about my father, not really. I mean I know I could do a DNA test or something, and find out more about him, but part of me is hesitant to do that. Once you open Pandora's box you can't close it again. What if he's married, I mean, what if he was married when they got together? Or what if he's a bad person? Or what if he's dead. And then it's just more grief that I didn't have to sign on for."

"I don't blame you for that," he said. "Life has proven to me that it is more often cruel than not."

"I'm not sure that's my takeaway. But I'm also not sure that I want to take on any more family members."

"You had a lonely childhood."

He felt her stillness. The way that it shifted the air around her when he said that.

"Yes," she said slowly. "I did. I knew other kids who had very strict parents. Who had to be mature because there was some expectation being put on them. Because their mother or father didn't really like them being children. But that wasn't what happened with my mother. She needed me to be there for her. She didn't want that, but at the same time, I think she was very grateful that she had a daughter who could help take care of her. Her own mother lived far away and wasn't able to help care for her. She died before my mother did. There was just no one else in her life."

She paused, and he heard her shift in her chair. "It's funny I… I feel like talking to you about your past, it's making me think of mine differently. I always had the feeling that she had made a lot of decisions that put her in a very lonely place, and that she regretted it, but I didn't know how to talk to her about it. I was caught in a place where I still saw her as my mother, and therefore not only human, not fully frail. But she was. I did my best to be there for her, but it meant not being there for myself. But I had limited time with her, so… It isn't like I could have deferred caring for her until I was older. And if not me… It would've been just home care nurses, and a rotating group of them at that. It wouldn't have been the same. And how much better would my life be if I was off at homecoming or prom instead of at home watching movies with her. They're memories I don't have the chance to make up for again."

She sighed heavily. "And she really was a wonderful mother. She did everything she could. She tried. We went for walks in the evening when the weather was nice, even when she didn't have a lot of energy. She told me that I was smart, and that I was brave. I was lonely, but I often don't think that I really have the right to be. Because she was there for me. It's just not the same as having friends and toys and a social life. It's not the same as having easy. I think you can have a life filled with all kinds of different love. And when you're a child often that love is free of responsibility. It's easy. I never really got to experience that love. For me, it always held responsibility."

Something tore at him. This image of a child who didn't know what it was to have a love that didn't have cost. He was not often moved by other people's stories, his own was so difficult, it was often difficult for him to find empathy.

But not now. She got beneath his skin. She touched him.

He knew exactly what that was like. To never have love or care feel like something you could take for granted. He knew what that was like. All too well.

He felt undone by this. By the heavy feeling in his chest. She hadn't chosen that life, and she had emerged from it strong.

So many children were born into loving, easy families. But not her. Not him.

If she hadn't chosen this, then perhaps he…

He pushed that aside.

"What about your mother?" she asked.

He paused. "I… I don't even know how to talk about my mother. She is still living. I never hear from her. I guess you could say she was never a major influence in my life. My father took control of everything, my mother sat back quietly. She spent his money…she gave him his heirs. I'm not angry at her. I'm not. She can't even grieve her own daughter properly because he won't allow it, because he says she can't cry for a person who caused their own death. He owns even her thoughts, and I can only pity her. I am not angry with her."

He sat there for a moment, and wondered if that was true.

But their father had not abused them with fists. He had ruled over them, had manipulated them. But their lives hadn't been in danger. In truth, they had all been like frogs slowly boiling in water.

"Were you ever happy?"

"I never thought about it. I just… Lived. As any child does." He was silent for a moment. "Were you?"

"I suppose it was the same for me. I didn't think much about whether or not it was all difficult until it was over. No. That isn't true. Toward the end it all got very hard. And knowing, I think that it would end I started just wishing that it would. It made me feel… Terrible. Once she was gone. Like I had made it happen faster. Like I had been impatient, selfish."

"No one wants to watch someone they love die. I understand. I…" It was very hard for him to get out the words that he needed to speak now. "My sister was lost in her addiction for a long time. I worried about that phone call. The one that we eventually got. There was a time when I did treat her as if she was fragile. And then I got angry. And my father's anger fueled me. I forgot my fear. Because part of me just thought… If it happened, then I would be able to move on. That I would be able to live. Without thinking of her all the time. Without worrying all the time. The first thought that I had when I found out she had overdosed was that at least I didn't have to worry about her anymore."

That tore at him. It made his stomach ache. It made him feel like he was falling. And surely she would tell him what a monster he was. Because it was a monstrous thing to think. It was. Truly.

"I understand," she said. "I do. When my mother died… The night that she was the most poorly, I gave her pain medication, and I went to bed. I woke up at four in the morning. She was gone. And I felt… Relief. It was like all the breath left my body, and like everything that was tying me to that town, to that house, was suddenly just released. The worry. I didn't realize how much worry I carried. Because every time we would think she was getting better, I would just find out later that she wasn't. Waiting for test results. Waiting for everything. And I hadn't realized how much it was weighing me down. And of course if I had a choice I would choose to keep her. Of course I would. But nobody gave me that choice. So in the end… In the end, there was something easier about just being free."

"Do you still feel free?" he asked, his voice rough.

"I don't know. Not every day. I feel like I don't recognize myself sometimes. Like the life that I live now is so different from the life I had then it's like I'm someone new."

"I don't feel free," he said. "Because in that one moment when I realized that I was happy, I didn't have to worry about my sister anymore, I also realized that I was the one that had pushed her. I was the one that had done it. I was the difference between her staying and going. And I could've changed the entire time, but I didn't. Because I didn't know how. Because… My entire foundation is rotten, but that is not an excuse. It just isn't."

"Why isn't it? You didn't choose to have the parents that you had. Neither did she."

"No. But it… I don't want to think about it anymore."

It was too painful. All of this. Just too damned painful.

"We don't have to. Tell me one good memory from your childhood."

He laughed. "That's the problem. There are no good memories. Not anymore. It's just… Everything that was good is now sustained by grief."

"No. It's like this. Like this moment, completely taken out of time. Remove it from time. Nothing came before, nothing came after. Tell me."

He took a deep breath. He didn't have to close his eyes to block anything out. And he could see in his mind, a clear view of the olive groves, of the cypress trees that he and his sister used to ride horses through. The only time that they were free. "I remember being young with my sister. Pretending we were vagabonds. That we were running away. We would pack up green apples and bread, and put them in a pillowcase, and ride our horses until we reached the edge of the family estate." He could see it so clearly. The horizon stretching out before them. There had never been a wall there. But they had acted like there was. Like that boundary was impassable. "I don't know why we didn't just keep going. We should have."

They had built a fence with their own minds. But it had been as real as it needed to be. It had kept them in line. Their father had created it with his cruelty. With the control that he exerted on all of them. He had waged a battle with their minds when they had been only children, and he had won.

Does he still wage that same battle?

But then, she was there, putting her hand over his, and he could feel the warmth of her body, could taste her breath. It was sweet, and lovely just like she was. And when she pressed her soft mouth to his, he allowed that warmth, that need, that desire to spread through his entire body. This was real. Everything else… It could wait. Everything else… It didn't matter. No. How could it? This time out from his real life felt like the most consequential thing he had ever experienced. He could not explain it. He would not try.

Instead, he just let her kiss him. Instead he just pulled her onto his lap, and saw his way into her beauty with his fingertips. Moving them over her soft face, down her back. He pulled her shirt up over her head, and then unhooked her bra with deft skill. He stripped her bare and learned her every curve. He moved his hands down her hips, and then pushed one between her legs, feeling how wet with need she was. That she could see him like this and still want him, that she could hear those pathetic stories from his childhood and still be like this…

He was grateful, and even that made him feel like less, but when her mouth rained kisses down upon his face, his neck, when she pulled his shirt up over his head, and continued down to kiss his chest, down his abs, he did not feel anything like pathetic. And yet at the same time this did not feel like a return to the man he had been. It did not feel like the real wakening of a playboy. It felt like something entirely new. Something he had not yet experienced before.

She slid off of his lap, and he could feel that she came to rest on the floor between his legs. Her hands moved to his belt, where she undid that, and the closure on his slacks. She pulled his pants down just slightly, freeing him. And then she leaned in, her mouth soft now on his shaft, her tongue making dark magic as she tasted him, as she took him into her mouth, sucked him deep.

He felt like pushing through the darkness inside him, and he wished… He wished that he could see her. Wished that he could see her with her head bent over his lap like this. Because he hadn't seen Auggie enough time since he had truly begun to see her, in ways that his eyes could never have comprehended. And now that was lost to him.

They had that night. That night when he had really understood, how beautiful she was, how singular she was. And all the times before that, he had been bringing women on his private jet, women who weren't her. He had been satiating himself on bread and water when there was a feast on the other side of the door. Because as lovely as those women were, they had not fit him in this way. It wasn't the same. There was something singular at work between himself and Auggie. He would've said that he was not capable of a singular connection. He would've said that he wasn't capable of connection at all.

That it was lost on him, wasted on him.

He had learned to feel one thing. The driving desire for revenge, and it blotted out everything else, but with her he had found something more. It was not the loss of his sight that had heightened his senses. It was her.

Knowing her, talking to her, feeling for her. Wanting to know her, rather than simply wanting satisfaction for the death of his sister. And he wanted to resist it, but here and now he simply couldn't. In the same way he couldn't resist her.

He had decided that he would no longer feel helpless. That was the thing. He had decided that there would be no more invisible fences. He had taken his life and fashioned it into whatever he wished it to be. He had fashioned himself into an instrument of revenge. He was not at the mercy of anything anymore. Not of his feelings, not of the way he wanted another person, but right now he was.

And he wanted to believe that it was all right, that he could have it because they were here, and he couldn't see. Because he was being forced to take a break from everything he was.

But it felt like something deeper than that. Felt like something more powerful.

And as she drove him to the brink with that clever mouth, he gave himself over to her.

In the same way he had given himself over to revenge all those years ago. Right now, in this moment, his only loyalty was to Auggie.

He was drowning. In her, in the sensation.

And just as he was about to be pushed over the edge entirely he lifted her up and brought her down onto his lap. He found that she had nothing on beneath the skirt that she wore, and he found the glorious entrance to her body, and thrust home.

She gasped with need, and he drove up into her, pushing them both toward the ultimate end. Toward their glorious satisfaction. And when they both found their release, they clung to one another. And he knew something in the stillness that was almost like peace. He didn't want to move for fear he might shatter it. He didn't want to breathe for fear that it would prove to be only an illusion.

He held onto her. He was afraid to breathe.

She rested her head in the crook of his neck, and he put his hand on the back of her head, holding her there.

How long had it been since he had the chance to comfort another person. To be there for them. How long had it been since someone had done so for him, and in this moment they were doing it for one another.

He felt whole in a way he had not in so many years. Perhaps ever.

He wanted to sit there in that.

"We can do the dishes tomorrow," she whispered. "Let's just go to bed."

He nodded in agreement. And he let her take his hand. Allowed her to lead him up the stairs, because it felt good to let someone care for him. Because it felt good to be cared for. Because for some reason he had the deep and certain sensation that this was a very fragile thing. And that when it broke there would be nothing that could be done to stop it. And so when he went to bed with her that night, it was with the knowledge that the dawn wasn't guaranteed. Nor anything afterward.

And the last thought he had before he drifted off to sleep was that losing her would never be a relief.

Because this was something he had never known before. A weight and responsibility that felt like joy. And he had no idea what to call it.

No idea what to do with any of it.

He was satisfied.

Without his sight, without his revenge, in this out-of-the-way manor, hiding away from the world, Matias Balcazar finally understood what it was like to have everything.

CHAPTER THIRTEEN

LAST NIGHT HAD been transformative. Truly. Auggie was still pondering it the next day. She had been pondering it the entire time. Not only her changing feelings toward him, but the situation they found themselves in here. She knew that she needed to talk to him about… About potentially making a statement. But she hated the idea of bringing the outside in at all. It had been two weeks, and he wasn't better. He was going to have to go see the neurologist, and even though there was still a lot of hope as far as restoring his sight, it was all… It was all converging. The need to handle the headlines, the need to make intervention with his health… All of it.

Your feelings.

True. But her feelings could wait.

She stared down at her hands, where she had them pressed to the top of the kitchen counter. Her feelings. Did she love him. What even was love? She had never been certain. Maybe that was why she had never really wanted it. Maybe it was why it was easy to avoid men and desire and all of those things because she couldn't imagine love in a way that didn't feel heavy.

And this did feel heavy, but it was different.

He made her feel supported. He made her feel like she mattered.

He listened to her. He was like a different person than the one that she had met initially. Not just because she had gotten to the bottom of that dark wound that existed beneath the playboy veneer. But she had also found parts of him that were less intense. Parts of him that were giving, rather than selfish. He was in fact a very deep thinker, which she had always known. But she realized it was why he committed so hard to the other version of himself.

Because his own deep thinking often hurt him.

His memories of his sister were still so vivid. His grief at losing her complex. It mirrored her own. She had never imagined that she would have something in common with him. She had more than something in common with him, in fact. She had a spirit that recognized his. A deep wound that saw his and recognized it. Deeper than empathy.

Or maybe this was just… Her wanting to keep on living in a fantasy. Maybe she was dangerously deluded. Maybe this was what everyone thought. That they had a unique connection with him. That he was most especially their brilliant and perfect lover. That while he might've touched other women it could never have been this.

Maybe that was an easy lie to tell herself.

She couldn't be certain.

But when he came downstairs, maneuvering slowly on his own, she felt it burst inside of her like a firework. That certainty.

She wanted to spend the rest of her life with him. It

was now a clearer goal than anything else ever had been. It didn't erase the other things that she wanted. It didn't mean she no longer cared about her business, she did. It didn't mean she no longer carried baggage from her childhood, or felt a strange amount of anxiety regarding any proximity to her childhood. She did.

But there was room for this. Room for him.

To want something more than success, to want something more than distance from her past. To want something more than to simply succeed on her own. That was what she had been chasing all this time, a sense that she would be okay on her own because the crushing feeling of being left to her own devices seemed inevitable. She had always known that her mother would die young. Ever since she could understand the implications of the kind of cancer she had, Auggie had understood that.

That isolation. She had seen that the potential for that existed. They had had an accident. He was mortal. He had been injured. There were complications from that injury and they might continue.

But that reality didn't seem bigger than the hope that they could have something together.

She loved him.

She couldn't say anything right now. She had to sit with it. Because Auggie was the sort of girl that needed a plan.

"I was thinking," she said. "That since we have to go into the hospital to see the neurologist, it is probably time for you to put out a statement about your sister."

He paused. "I thought you said it was better to not engage in PR."

"What I think is better is maybe you saying something real about it. I don't think you should go through your publicist. I think you should just tell the truth. No spin."

"No spin?"

"Yes. What if you told the world the story of your sister. The way you told me. And maybe it's messy and you're not universally loved in the end."

"I never cared about being universally loved."

"Didn't you?"

She wondered if maybe he had, in a way. If part of him had craved that because he had never gotten it anywhere else.

"I suppose it was better than being a disappointment. But that was never the goal."

"No. It was to show your father that he was wrong in every way. But… Maybe the truth does that more effectively. You loved Seraphina. Flaws and all. You loved her even though it was difficult. You're a better man than your father. It's evident just in that."

He tented his fingers beneath his chin. "I don't know how to talk about my feelings."

"We've been doing a lot of it since we've been here."

"But this doesn't count." He waved his hand in a sweeping gesture, and she felt like he had taken all her chess pieces off the table in one fell swoop. Because he had just dismissed this entire experience. This experience that had been so profound to her.

He doesn't mean it that way.

She bit her bottom lip. "Well, maybe it'll count for something."

"Once we leave here, Auggie, you're not obligated to me. You never were."

"Yes. I could've just left you blind and stumbling around."

"You could have."

She could have. It was a strange thing, actually, to really sit with that reality. There hadn't been anything stopping her. She could have done that. She could have.

She could have.

That was actually true of her caring for her mother too. She felt like she had had no other choice. But she had.

But when things had gotten hard, that was how she had chosen to love her mother.

She felt like realization had just exploded within her.

She had chosen to do the hard thing because her love was strong.

She had seen herself as sort of a victim of it. Of her circumstances.

But he was right. She had chosen this.

"You're right," she said. "I could've walked away. But I didn't. Because I… I care about you."

He looked at her, even though he could not see her. Those dark eyes landed on her unerringly. "You shouldn't."

He said it so final. Heavy. Like he'd set a stone on her chest.

He didn't want her to care.

This was how it was going to be. He was going to resist this. All the way.

No matter the conversations they'd had, no matter the way that she knew him. No matter that she had been trying to show him that he could have a life apart from pursuing revenge against his father, he was going to make this impossible.

"Let's go," she said.

"To?"

"The doctor. And the paparazzi might come after us. But I believe that my work wives have planted a story about us jetting off to St. Tropez. It is also entirely possible that your private jet is making a decoy flight there."

"Genius," he said.

"If nothing else it should get us out of here and to the hospital without being inundated. And then perhaps we can sneak back to your town house."

"I had just learned how to live here."

She felt that. All the way down to her bones.

She packed up anything important, the clothing that had been sent for her, and any remaining food, and put it in the back of the new car that had been delivered for them a few days earlier.

She was tasked with driving them back to the city. She wasn't entirely comfortable with driving on the other side of the road, but she managed, and navigated them to the doctor.

They did a scan of his brain, and the neurologist explained that he still had fluid pushing against his optic nerves.

"The best thing to do would be to go in and drain it."

"That sounds hideous," she said.

"Whatever will work," he said.

"We can do surgery tomorrow morning. Do you wish to stay here tonight?"

"No," he said.

She tried not to put too much stock in that. That he had made the choice that would allow them to be together. That would allow them to be together this last night.

Last night? Nothing is going to happen to him.

Maybe not. But if this fixed his vision, he wouldn't need her around anymore. It would be revenge, as usual. And his reputation… Well. It was going to take more than an engagement for her to fix it. It was going to take the truth. And he was going to have to find it in himself to be somewhat… Real. She knew he could do it. The question was, would he?

When they returned to his London home, he made love with her like the clock was ticking. It was. She understood that.

And then she couldn't hold it any longer. She looked at him, watching her fingertips drift over his face. What a familiar sight he was to her. But she wouldn't be to him.

"I love you, Matias."

And then everything broke apart.

CHAPTER FOURTEEN

He didn't know what to say to that. There was no joy in it. There was... Nothing but pain. She was offering him something that felt like treasure, but he could not reach out and grab it.

It was darkness. All of it was darkness.

Because he didn't deserve this. He didn't want it. How could he?

How could he when he was... He was responsible for all of this. For the loss of his sister. He didn't deserve to absolve himself of it. He didn't deserve to have that surgery tomorrow to have everything fixed.

They were going to cut his brain open. Perhaps he would bleed out on the table. Perhaps that would be the ultimate justification. What had not finished him during the accident would finish him then.

She couldn't love him.

"Auggie... If I have given you the impression that this was something that it wasn't..."

"Don't. Don't be the charming playboy. Don't lie to me. Don't deflect."

That made him angry. "I'm trying to be kind to you."

"You cannot break someone's heart kindly, Matias. Do it with honesty. Do one damn thing with honesty. Do you even know what that is anymore?"

"I… I damn well do. I know that the honest truth is my life is a mess of my own making. And if I never managed to clean it up it will be my just desserts."

"That's a lie. It just is. And I don't know if you're telling it just to me, or to yourself as well, but it is a lie. You loved your sister. Do you know how I know? Because you feel that great and terrible grief. The one that is nothing simple. Loving her hurts as much as losing her, and that is love. Hard and sharp and nothing simple. You would never have chosen to lose her. You would do anything to fix it. Look at you. You have sacrificed your entire life in the name of trying to fix it in some fashion. You are heartbroken, and that tells me everything I need to know about you. About whether or not you're actually worthy of anything."

"No, I… It doesn't matter. There is one thing. One thing that I'm here for. One thing that I was put on this earth to do in the wake of losing her."

He was scrambling to find new reasons. To find a new way to push her back.

Because what she was offering was… It was too painful. Too bright. A light pushing through the darkness, and he was far too accustomed to the darkness.

Far too accustomed to the mess that he had made of himself. The facsimile of a human being he had created. His body was one he simply existed in. His soul was long since gone.

He had never been his own person. He had been a creation of his father…

He still was.

All of this was his father's doing. Every last bit of it. From him going to shame his sister for drug use, to this. All of it. The blindness. The accident. He was his father's creation. And that was worse than being at fault for the death of his sister. A mindless drone who walked the earth for no other reason than that that man had created him. Physically, and emotionally.

He was nothing more. And Auggie was… She was everything. She knew herself. Truly. She lived a life that helped make things better for other people. She had loved her mother in a real intentional way. That she had created a life that outshone his own in every way.

He had never felt like less. And he could not respond to this thing that she was giving to him.

"Auggie, I am not the man you should give that to. I have never proven that I could be more than my father's pawn."

"So what? You'll die that way because you started that way?"

"Maybe. Maybe that's the generational curse. Maybe it's the best thing that can happen. My father's line will end with him. Whether I live long or short, perhaps that is the best way for it to be."

"No. I'm not having this. I'm not listening."

"I have surgery tomorrow and I cannot see, and I am not myself and…"

"You are yourself. You were the most yourself that you had ever been. This last week, that was a taste of it. Of living. Why can't you choose that?"

"Because it is not that simple."

"No. This is you riding to the edge of the property and stopping, because you feel that there is a fence there even though there isn't."

Her words were like a shotgun blast.

Fences that were never really there.

Was he destined always to live that way.

"Maybe you're right," he said. "But I will always see them."

"You can't see anything. You had a chance. To have it all wiped away. That was what we were just living. Your clean slate. Even your vision was taken away, and you still choose to see the fences. I can't fix that for you."

He heard her get out of bed. Heard her dressing.

"I will send someone for you in the morning, but it isn't going to be me. I need to take care of myself. I need… I need to breathe."

He didn't argue. But he wanted to. He wanted her to stay with him. Desperately. Because he had never felt alone in this darkness until she walked out of the room. Until he heard her walk out of the house. And then he felt hopeless. Then he truly felt the loss of control. Then it really felt like he would die of this.

Without her. Without his vision. Without everything.

He had known on some level that he would have to stay wounded to stay with her.

Or maybe you have to heal. Maybe you have to push through this. Push past it.

But what was on the other side? Those fences might be made up, but he still couldn't see beyond them.

Make a statement that's real. Make one that's from your heart.

She had told him to do that. To make a statement about his sister that was the honest truth.

But right now… He had never been more aware that he could not see. And it was not a lack of sight that made that true.

CHAPTER FIFTEEN

AUGGIE WAS IN misery and regretting every decision that she had made. From telling him that she was in love with him to leaving him.

And when she dragged herself into the Your Girl Friday headquarters she didn't bother to hide any of her regret.

"Auggie," Lynna said, looking shocked. "You're back."

"I am."

"No one else is here. They all have jobs."

"Right. Well. I'm here. And everything is terrible."

The story of what happened with Matias poured out of her, and she wasn't quite sure what to expect of Lynna as far as reactions went.

But there was no judgment.

"So what are you going to do?"

"What can I do? He made his position on all of this really clear."

"It's true. But you don't have to listen to him."

"It makes you kind of pathetic to keep going after a guy who said he didn't want you."

"He didn't say he didn't want you. And anyway, I don't know. I think people should be willing to be a little bit pathetic for love. Isn't that the point of it? I mean, I certainly wouldn't bother with it if it wasn't. So maybe I never will. But..."

"No. Everyone is supposed to be balanced and healthy and not ask too much of each other, and not need each other too much."

"What a boring reality."

Auggie found she couldn't disagree. She didn't want quiet or reserved. She didn't even mind this breaking her open, because it had helped her find new parts of herself.

She didn't want to end up without him, however. But at the same time... She just wanted him.

And she wanted to be this version of herself that had blossomed with him.

So maybe there was something in all this.

"He's going into surgery soon. I won't be able to make it to the hospital in time to see him beforehand."

"You should probably go anyway. Because the way you feel about him isn't really contingent on how he feels about you, is it?"

With that truth, Auggie took her bruised heart down to the hospital. She was informed that he was in surgery. But told that she would be updated when he was finished.

Her phone buzzed in her pocket, and she pulled it out, seeing that she had a text from Irinka.

Was this your doing?

She frowned, and opened up the link that Irinka had sent.

It was a statement. From Matias.

He must've dictated it to someone last night after she left. Before he went into surgery.

She sat there, holding the phone, her mouth agape as she read.

Augusta Fremont encouraged me to make this statement before she left me in the early hours of the morning. She is another person that I have failed. But that is not the point of this statement.

By now rumors, planted by my father have run rampant that I am responsible for the death of my sister.

I have spent my life feeling that I was responsible. It is why I live the way that I do. But always, always I wanted to destroy my father with my success. I blamed us both for her death. My own harsh words that I spoke to her the last time I saw her, but also him, because he raised me to be that harsh, and because he raised her to feel so much shame.

It was the perfect counterpoint. I was the match, and she was gasoline. I have walked in guilt all these years, because it was more comfortable than grief. And it was not until I had an accident two weeks ago that forced me to sit and recover...it was not until I spent that time with a woman who showed me what life could be...that I began to see things for what they were. There were fences in my mind. Roadblocks that I was convinced were the real truth. She made me see that they weren't.

But I was not able to change my opinion on that truth until it was too late. I'm writing this ahead of brain surgery. I don't know how I will come out of it. The doctor made it sound as if it would be easy, but if I have learned one thing about life it's that things are rarely easy. Perhaps I did cause my sister to overdose. Perhaps she would've done it anyway. All I know is I live with the grief either way. And blame and revenge felt active in a way that the loss of her doesn't. Living in anger and regret has felt much more manageable than living in hope. Than wanting to find a joy and love that I never truly had in my life.

I manufactured fake joy and kept it all around myself. I cultivated a persona in the media that allowed me to bask in the warmth of fake flames, so that I could know at least a fraction of what it was like to be cared for. After having someone give me love for real, I recognize that it isn't enough. She told me to be real. And I am. I have no answers. Only pain. I cannot bring my sister back. I can only grieve her. If I destroy my father, nothing will be rebuilt. And that too is pointless. The only thing that has not felt pointless is the hope that it gave me to have someone love me.

To begin to fall in love with her. I'm clinging to that hope now, because now that I've got a taste for it, I fear it might be the one thing I have ever been well and truly addicted to.

And that is all thanks to her.

Whatever this means for my future, for my company, for my place in the tabloids, I don't care. I care about Auggie and the truth, in that order. The truth is that I love her. The truth is that I'm still figuring out what love is.

And so, however I come out of my surgery tomorrow, with my sight or without, having lost motor skills or not, it is the one thing that will be true about me. I am not a creation of my father's. I am not a man who has everything. I am not the best beloved playboy in the world. I am not a golden retriever. All of those things are fake.

But loving Auggie is real.

A tear splashed down on her phone screen. It was a statement that wasn't going to do anything for him. It was a personal revelation, and nothing more. There were no neat bows. And the public didn't like that.

But it mattered to her. It echoed inside of her. As real as anything had ever been.

Irinka sent another text.

What exactly is happening?

He loves me.

He loved her, and she had to wait for him to wake up.

She needed him to wake up. But she didn't need him to be physically perfect. She would care for him. She would stay with him.

You are going to marry a billionaire and abandon our business, are you?

No. I mean, I might marry a billionaire. But I'll always be your work wife.

Work Wives Forever.

A man in scrubs entered the room. "He did well. He woke up talking."

"And his vision?"

"Come and see him. And let him see you."

On shaking legs she walked into the recovery room.

And there he was, his head leaned back against the pillow. Looking alarmingly handsome in spite of everything.

His eyes fluttered open and came to rest on her. He could see her. She knew that he could.

"Auggie," he said. "I hope that I can see and that this isn't a dream. I hope that you're here."

"I'm here."

"You came for me. You saw what I wrote."

"I did. But not until I was already here. Because… Just because you sent me away didn't mean I didn't love you. And I needed to be here for this. I had to."

"That is more than I deserve."

"It's how I love. Fierce and tough and forever."

"I don't know how I love," he said. "I haven't even been certain of what it is until… Until you. I am afraid that it is hard and complicated. But it will take a long time for me to figure out how to get it just right. But I want to try, Auggie. I want a life. Not a mission. I want picnics. And smell the flowers. And to live. I want to be my own, but most of all I want to be yours."

"You're just saying that because you're so happy you can see."

"To be honest, I cared about that less than I could've imagined except… I wanted to see your face. I wanted to see your face since I fell in love with you. And you are even more beautiful than I remembered."

She closed the distance between them and went to his bedside. She reached out and took his hand and pressed her cheek against it. "Now you really are delirious. I haven't slept and I look like garbage."

"No. You are the most beautiful thing that I have ever

seen. And I am seeing you really. For the first time. Because I really do see it now. I was running from pain, but you can't run from that. Guilt and anger were preferable to missing her. To mourning a childhood I did not choose. But if you didn't choose it then neither did I. These hard things… They just are. You are a living testament to the fact that it is what you do after that matters. You did so much more with your hand than I did with mine. I want to be like you. And maybe I will not be a simple character for the world anymore. But I will be a real person. And that is infinitely better, I think."

"I love you."

"I love you too."

EPILOGUE

The Pitbull puppies are on board.

MATIAS SENT THAT text to his wife's group chat, even though the women were just outside in the waiting room. He smiled to himself as he looked down at his beautiful bride and the two babies she held in her arms.

Twins. He had never imagined so much joy.

A boy and a girl.

He had thought that he was destined to live a life alone. To live without love. And ever since he and Auggie had gotten married it had been nothing but the most pure influx of love he could've imagined.

He had been given his sight back. In more ways than he had realized he needed to have it restored.

"What are you on about?" she asked, looking at him.

"I was just letting everyone know that the babies are here."

"Thank you," she said, smiling up at him. "For everything."

He laughed. "What do you mean? You have given me my entire life."

"Well, that's kind of our whole thing. White glove service."

"This is definitely above and beyond."

"We aim to please."

"And that, my love, you have done."

* * * * *

If you couldn't put down Billionaire's Bride Bargain *then be sure to look out for the next instalment in the Work Wives to Billionaires' Wives miniseries, coming soon!*

And why not try these other stories by Millie Adams?

The Christmas the Greek Claimed Her
The Forbidden Bride He Stole
Greek's Forbidden Temptation
Her Impossible Boss's Baby
Italian's Christmas Acquisition

Available now!

Read on for a sneak preview of Millie Adams's
His Highness's Diamond Decree,
for Mills & Boon Modern.

PRINCE ADONIS ANDREADIS HAD ALWAYS known that his wedding would be a magnificent spectacle. A man of his wealth and stature could have nothing other than a glorious and singular occasion to mark his nuptials. Even if those nuptials existed only to secure the bloodline, and therefore access to the throne of his country.

It was just he hadn't expected to feel anything about it.

His father was dying. There was no denying the reality.

His father had told him that he had done enough damage to the crown and the family reputation that he owed him a marriage minted in perfection.

Adonis couldn't disagree.

What Adonis knew was that he had done a fair job of exorcising his demons in the form of debauchery, all around the globe.

And while he had not intended to besmirch the crown, it was likely he had.

Well. Besmirch in the eyes of citizens his father's age. The younger generation was…decidedly fond of his exploits. He was a meme.

Knowing his time as king was on the horizon, he'd agreed to his father's demand. That he marry a suitable woman. His father had provided him with a folio of acceptable women.

He had spent years being a terrible playboy but even he had never chosen women off of a menu.

He couldn't say he felt like he owed his father, so much as he owed his country. His years of debauchery had never been intended to cause strife for the citizens of Olympus. No, his target had been much more personal.

The end result, however, was his infamy.

Adored by the youths, decried by the elder generation.

He had to find a way to unite the two schools of thought, however. And marrying seemed the way to do that.

He'd chosen Drusilla Stalworth not because of any blinding attraction to her, or her profile in the folio provided by his father, but because she was American royalty. The granddaughter of a former president, the daughter of a billionaire business mogul.

He had decided to reform, to forge an appropriate alliance and to marry as quickly as possible. His decisions had been clear, concise and quick.

He couldn't recall deciding to get married in a cathedral by the sea, however. But it seemed as if that's what he was doing.

The building was glass, glorious light shone through the windows.

It was warm. Odd. He'd expected it to be cold.

He looked out into the pews of the church. There was no audience. And for a moment he felt outside of himself. But he continued walking up to the front. And there he stood, waiting for his bride. The doors opened, and there she was. A halo of glorious gold. White.

Her hair was piled on top of her head, and a veil concealed her face.

She was like a floating confection. An angel.

Spun sugar and sweetness. So strange that he should have a visceral reaction to her, because he could not recall ever having a reaction like this to Drusilla in the past.

No. He had always been decidedly neutral on his intended, which had been fine with him.

She was beneficial. She didn't need to be anything else.

But now, the sight of her held him suspended.

It was like being reborn.

And then, he was certain he felt something bite his leg. He looked around the room, and was struck yet again by the fact that it was empty, except for himself and Drusilla.

He reached down and gripped his thigh. And there was warmth there.

He was confused.

Groggy.

Why?

Suddenly, the doors to the church blew open, and the wind was an icy blast. All the warmth from before faded away. And Drusilla kept on walking toward him. But then her veil blew off. And he looked into the eyes of a stranger.

As snow began to fall inside the chapel.

The chapel?

No. There was no chapel.

He wasn't in Cape Cod having a wedding. He wasn't…

Suddenly, everything around him fell away. And the

wedding dress transformed itself to a parka. While the chapel became the vast wilderness.

And then, his vision went black.

And he tried to cast his mind back, to figure out exactly how he had gotten here…

Don't miss the new Millie Adams romance available wherever Mills & Boon Modern books and ebooks are sold.

MILLS & BOON®

Coming next month

ACCIDENTAL ONE-NIGHT BABY
Julia James

Siena took a breath, short, sharp, and summoning up her courage, stepped into the lift that would take her to the one man in the world she did not want to see again.

Vincenzo Giansante.

'He'll think you're chasing him – and he's made it clear he's done with you.'

Siena's mouth tightened. Vincenzo Giansante had, indeed, made it crystal clear he was done with her – had walked out in the briefest way possible in the bleak light of the morning after the night before.

Well, now she was walking back into his life – to tell him what she still could scarcely believe herself, ever since seeing that thin blue line form on the test stick.

He has a right to know – any man does – whether I want him to or not.

The lift jerked to a stop, the metal doors sliding open. For a moment she just wanted to be a coward, and jab the down button again. Then, steeling herself, she walked forward.

Continue reading

ACCIDENTAL ONE-NIGHT BABY
Julia James

Available next month
millsandboon.co.uk

Afterglow Books is a trend-led, trope-filled list of books with diverse, authentic and relatable characters, a wide array of voices and representations, plus real world trials and tribulations. Featuring all the tropes you could possibly want (think small-town settings, fake relationships, grumpy vs sunshine, enemies to lovers) and all with a generous dose of spice in every story.

@millsandboonuk
@millsandboonuk
afterglowbooks.co.uk
#AfterglowBooks

For all the latest book news, exclusive content and giveaways scan the QR code below to sign up to the Afterglow newsletter: